ASSASSIN'S BANE

JAMIE SCHULTZ

Library of Congress Control Number: 2025907889
ISBN (paperback): 979-8-9928935-0-2
ISBN (eBook): 979-8-9928935-1-9

Cover and Interior Design by Ashton M. Smith
Illustrations and Hand Lettering by Christian Alejandro Vera
First edition 2025

Jamieschultzauthor.com

This one is for my mom, dad, and sister
I would die of a broken heart for you people
But that seems a tad dramatic, so please accept this instead

TABLE OF CONTENTS

1

ELLIE'S 72ND

THIS JOB COULD NOT HAVE COME AT A BETTER TIME. THE CONCRETE is hard and unforgiving beneath me as I lie on my stomach, peering through my scope at the bustling citizens of New York City. A dark beanie over my carefully braided hair and a kerchief around my face protect me from the worst of the ferocious mid-November weather. My gloves, I am realizing however, have seen too much action and the worn fingerpads are nearly enough to compromise my mission.

Icy rain weeps relentlessly from the dark clouds, preemptively mourning the loss of life. The wind picks up, whipping through the litter-covered streets and over my rooftop, trying to shove me off.

My older brother pops into my head then. Mark would surely be on the wind's side, given the conversation we had just yesterday. I was glad to have the job to take my mind off of what happened, but somehow even the wind is enough to bring it all rushing to the forefront. So much for a distraction.

"All this time," he said, and I could hear the tears clogging his throat even over the phone, "you've been his assassin?"

What was I supposed to say? That when Mom and Dad split, leaving me with him and my brothers with her, I refused to be a part of Dad's business and decided to strike out on my own? I was four! Of course I did whatever he told me to do. Growing up, it didn't seem so bad. I practically idolized my father and wanted to do everything like him. For a while, it was only training, and my dad's pride in my progress was more than enough to make me forget what it was all for.

It's a long-kept secret that I'm the infamous Enforcer, Emily Richards. Mom knew. But she never told my brothers, and neither did I. They know about Emily Richards, for sure, just as they know of the Enforcers; they just don't know she's *me*. Until now, that is.

Black clouds gradually turn to gray as the sun rises behind them, letting the world know it's too early to be awake. NYC, however, hasn't received the message. People flood the sidewalks on their way to who knows where in various degrees of haste. It's all the better for my work. The boss likes it when we make a spectacle.

Everything would have been fine if Mark hadn't dared to call Dad. If Dad hadn't bothered to pick up the phone.

I know the agreement upon my parents' divorce was shared custody; my cousin helped me find the documentation. And I have a pretty good idea as to why it didn't happen, and why Mom never fought for it. I remember the devastation on her face when I begged to go with him that last Christmas we all spent together. So I don't blame *her* for that being the last I saw of my family. It was my fault.

It was eleven years before I reached out to my brothers again, and by then, Mom was already gone. They've lived in that cozy apartment in the unmapped coastal town along the Chetco River for five years now. At first, keeping my secret was easy. Cancer had just taken Mom, and at only sixteen, I was still reasonably without a path in life, though I had already completed my first two missions.

Now at twenty-one, I tell my brothers that "work is work" and it's too mundane to talk about while I'm trying to enjoy my time with them. Jake, my twin, has been fine with that. Mark, apparently, was not.

Dad happily bragged to my older brother of his Enforcers, an elite organization of assassins, and one frequently featured on the news for our *heroic* dominance. He also bragged that I was the best of those assassins.

"Why do you *still* work for him, Ellie?" Mark had asked. "We can get you out. You can live here with us. Get away from him."

Get away from him. It's just not that simple.

The bottom half of a giant, twinkling Christmas tree can be seen in the lobby of the skyscraper apartment complex from my perch. Thanksgiving is still a few days off, but that doesn't matter to most people, I've found. It doesn't matter to Mark. He will have had a gaudy tree up and decorated since approximately 12:01 a.m. on November first.

I used to love the holidays. Christmas, Thanksgiving, New Year's. Now it's a beautiful backdrop to the ugly scenes I paint.

It's not that I think Mark has no right to be upset with me. It's my life, but this path I'm on is one that any person with moral standing would seek to correct. I respect him for it, but it doesn't change anything. Mom's responsibility passed to me when she died, and I won't let her down.

I peer through my scope, ready to wrap up my next masterpiece.

Finally, he emerges. A middle-aged businessman with short, aggressively slicked-back brown hair and a sharp jawline, wearing a contented half-smile on his face. Burying the guilt is second nature, like breathing. Focus on the details and forget the picture. Forty-six, five-foot-nine, pale, fit but not muscular. Maybe a family man. Maybe a loner. I learned a long time ago never to learn that particular detail.

I let myself slip into the routine of it all, casting my troubles far away.

I take aim, pull the trigger, and hear the familiar sound of the bullet leaving the chamber and money entering my bank account as my uninterrupted streak of successes reaches seventy-two. He drops to the pavement with the rain. A few screams erupt from the street as people walking by notice the blood pooling beneath him and realize what's happened.

Witnesses have never been a problem in this industry. They're the goal. In fact, in just a few moments, the live footage of this assassination will be on many of these billboards with a reporter filling North America in on the man's crimes. Dad has gotten faster with releasing the footage. It used to come out the next day, but now he has a team of analysts following each target until they're taken out so it can be fed directly and immediately into the prepared script. Reporters jump on the story with only a moment's notice.

The biggest problem with the justice system, Dad always said, *is that the punishment isn't sufficiently advertised.* A problem he solves by having his Enforcers strike in the daylight hours and reporters there to tell the public exactly what crime earned it.

I try to avoid mingling, but I know there are several people in my apartment complex who stay obsessively tuned in to the news, so they aren't ambushed if one day, it's their loved ones taken out. Because that's the other thing that happens. The families of the victims get dragged out of their houses and regularly told on live TV that their loved ones have been assassinated. It's all very *Hunger Games*, but far be it from me to question my father when I cannot possibly understand the world as he does.

I pack up my rifle, concealing it in the guitar case, and hasten off the roof. There's a reason I don't look into my targets' family lives, and I don't care to stick around for the broadcast. Whatever crime the man committed doesn't matter.

All that matters is that my father knows I did my job because as long as that stays true, I am the only one who has to pay for it.

»»»»»»

EVERY TIME I ENTER THESE HALLS, I HAVE TO REMIND MYSELF I NO longer live here. Why Dad built his business underground, I will never understand. He claims that we cannot be targeted easily this way, but I always thought this does half the job for whoever would try such a thing. It's already underground; the entire structure just has to collapse in on itself, and the problem is taken care of.

A lot of the assassins still live here, the cost of living taken out of their earnings. I found an apartment as soon as I turned sixteen and spend as little time here as possible.

Unfortunately, with Dad's obsessive need for secrecy, communication is done the old-fashioned way, which means that when we finish an assignment, we have to turn in the physical report in person. It's one of the measures his business partner, Hartley, implemented early on.

If not for these measures, I would never step foot down here again. Not only that, but I would live closer to my brothers. The only saving grace there is that it means our father's business is the hell away from them in DC, while Mark and Jake live peaceful college lives with their roommate in Oregon.

Piles of paper are littered over every available surface when I finally reach the office I'm looking for, and columns of file boxes rise from the gray carpet to the asylum-white ceiling. Hartley is in his mid- to late-fifties, and the best way to describe him is *Santa Claus*. Round belly, thick cheeks, more than one chin, and for some reason he always wears black boots. His bald head shines under the florescent lights, and he has a frosty beard that tries to cover the chins, but they demand recognition and present themselves anyway.

"Do you have a report for me, Emily?" His deep voice greets me— decidedly less than jolly. It's the most menacing thing about him. Any physical intimidation is entirely too well protected under layers of donuts and butter.

Instead of responding, I toss the completed file onto his desk. The yellow folder includes my full report of the mission and the tiny one-sheet rundown of the target I received when he assigned it to me.

He takes a moment to flip the folder open and make a show of checking my work, and I use that time the same way I always do. There's a small stack of files in the corner of his desk, and I run my eyes over the names. I've never recognized any, but it's another reason I have to keep coming here. If I'm not here to inspect the names, my brothers will pay the price.

My gaze trips on one of the folders. I read the name twice.

Three times.

Five times.

Shit.

"Well!" Hartley slams the folder closed, kickstarting my heart again. I jerk my gaze from that name and find him begrudgingly nodding at me. "Seems your luck has yet to run out."

"Not luck, sir," I say with a grin I know he can't stand. "Just good at my job."

He blinks slowly. "Sign." He slides a sheet across the desk which outlines my payment and the punishment for disclosing anything about the target beyond what the company releases. The number is always the same, but after each mission every assassin must sign the same document, so our signature will be filed with each of our assignments. Insurance. If the company goes down, so do we.

I don't take the pen he hands me, instead plucking up the one he was using before I came in and sign the form.

Hartley tucks the form in with my file. "Your payment will be in your account by the end of the day." He holds his hand out for his pen back, but I study the gold metal. It's heavier than your average pen. Writes smoothly too. Like butter.

"Can I keep this?" I ask him.

"No, you may not." He glares. His eyes latch onto the pen, a child he's negotiating back from a kidnapper. Briefly, it makes me smile, then I frown at the pen. With a shrug I hand it back. He snatches it out of my hand and doesn't even notice when I leave his office with a file tucked under my shirt.

2

BRANDON'S ANXIETY

tidy room, not obsessive, but orderly. Everything has a place.

You wouldn't know it from looking at it now. Flashcards and notebooks litter the whole of the floor and my desk. My bed lies half-made because I didn't have the energy after staying up until two in the morning studying and then getting up again three hours later because anxiety told me I'd fail if I didn't get back to studying for a test that I'm not even taking for three days. There's a pile of laundry by my dresser that I've been meaning to get to for a few days now. And I don't even know where my desk chair's gone off to. Medical school has really thrown a wrench into my once moderately healthy lifestyle.

Why I thought it a good idea to endure this torture of an education, I will never know. Some days I regret it and think there's something else I should be doing with my life. Then I remember that I don't suck at this, I'm just tired. No one ever accused the medical profession of being simple. If someone did, doctors know exactly where to hurt you without killing you, so one would learn quickly why they are wrong.

My roommate, Mark, knocks and enters my room, his short, stocky build filling the doorway. He's not big, but he's not fit either. I've taken him to the gym with me a few times—the best way I found to work out the stress—but he hates it. He prefers to keep his slight paunch—protection, he says.

"Woah." He surveys the mess and nods, lower lip jutting out. "You cleaned up."

I eye the stack of notebooks I just gathered up and placed aside on my desk. "I'm consolidating what I need to study."

"Where there is no peril in the fight, there is no glory in the triumph." His tone is admirably righteous, though I've lived with him long enough to know he's not that wise, especially in the morning. I raise a brow. "I read that somewhere. Thought it was fitting."

"Well," I sigh heavily, "there's been a lot of peril."

He puts a hand over his heart, sympathizing. I'm two years behind him in this journey to doctor, so I know it's at least genuine. "Are you almost ready to go?"

I frown. "Where?"

His brows scrunch together. "Ellie."

There's a distant bell ringing its heart out, but my brain is still working its way out of the flashcard fog. "What?"

"She's coming today," he reminds me, eyes wide. "You said you'd pick her up."

The bell smacks me in the face. "Oh!" His sister. Jake's twin. The woman too gorgeous to be related to either of my roommates yet somehow still is. She's staying with us for Thanksgiving. I cringe, looking down at my sweatpants and second-day green t-shirt. "I need to change."

"Why?"

Because your sister is hot, and I won't be caught dead wearing this in front of her. "I'm all sweaty." I don't think that's much better, but it's true. I fail the sniff test. "Do I have time for a shower?"

"I mean…" He checks his watch. "I guess. Her plane doesn't land for another hour."

I do the math in my head. Half an hour to get to the airport, another five or ten minutes to park and get from the parking garage to baggage claim. I flip around, dig out a pair of jeans and a clean t-shirt from my dresser, and hurtle past Mark to the bathroom.

Five minutes later, I'm grabbing my keys. Mark is sitting at the I-can't-believe-it's-not-granite counter which bubbles up in a few places. He's separating a bag of chips into another smaller bag, picking through them very meticulously, like a proper surgeon.

I stop. "What are you doing?"

His head pops up, blinking a few times as if he was in some sort of trance. "I'm…sorting the chips for Ellie."

I give myself a second to try and piece this puzzle together to no avail. My brows click together. "I'm going to need a little more."

He goes back to sorting. "She usually doesn't eat chips, but she likes the folded ones. We had some chips in the cabinet, so I'm putting all the folded ones in a bag for her."

"She only eats the folded ones?"

"Yeah."

"What makes them different from the others?"

He shrugs.

I nod as he continues the intricate work. I get siblings knowing obscure things about each other—I have a sister too, but… "How do you even learn something like that about someone?"

Another shrug. "I don't know."

Something warms in my chest, and I smile, but he's oblivious to my amusement. It's actually comforting to know this about her. It makes her only slightly less intimidating. It won't stop me from clamming up in her presence, but still.

"You're going to be late," he says, not looking up from his task.

"Don't you have a hospital to get to?" I grumble, pulling on my jacket.

"Thank you," is all he says.

"I hate you."

My stomach is in knots the entire drive, and deep breathing does nothing to ease the nerves. I'm usually visiting my own family when Ellie comes out as it's generally some holiday or another, but when I first moved in with her brothers, she came for a few days, and I met her. It was awkward, to understate it. We—or maybe it was mostly me—avoided being alone together like the plague. I told Mark that, and he still decided to send me to the airport for her alone. If he weren't my best friend, I'd hate him.

I just want this ride to be over quickly. Like ripping off a Band-Aid. Quick and painful and leaves you with a little regret that you did it, but it's done now, so what are you gonna do? There's no other way to beat nerves. It's that pesky visitor that refuses to take a hint. Never wanted, always there. Reliably intrusive.

My leg bounces up and down as I wait in baggage claim, earning concerned glances from passersby. I didn't want to pay for parking—I wanted to just drive through and pick her up outside—but I don't have Ellie's number to be able to ask her where she is, and I don't trust my ability to recognize her through a window. Mark is pretty confident in her ability to recognize me, however, so he told her to meet me here. Besides that, I can exercise gentlemanliness and carry her bags for her. Maybe that will take some of the heat off what is sure to be an awkward car ride.

Her plane landed just before I got here, so she should have gotten off by now. I stand and push through the steadily growing crowds by the luggage carousels. My height lends me a slight advantage as I peer out over the sea of bobbing heads, but nothing familiar stands out. To be fair, it's been almost two years since I last saw her.

Brilliant green eyes belonging to someone too beautiful swivel in my direction, and she smiles. Her long, blond hair is braided over her shoulder, and she wears a gray beanie to combat the late autumn chill. A loose, light gray t-shirt peeks out of a dark blue winter coat. My stomach flips over itself as she cuts through the crowd toward me. Startlingly beautiful.

And I'm stuck in a car with her for the next thirty minutes.

"Brandon, hey." Her chin barely reaches my shoulder when she's finally standing in front of me, and that observation helps nothing. "It's been a while."

I rub my nose for something to do and nod. "Hey. Hi, yeah, um… Ellie." Her smile brightens, and I might just keel over. "Do you have any more bags?" Logical. Good. She's only got one slung over her shoulder.

"Yeah. One more."

Once upon a time, I might have been good at human interactions. I honestly can't remember because my brain is busy noting the different lilts in her voice as she talks. It's a little deeper than I remembered but soft as butter. No, that's not right…but now I've been staring at her too long while she waits patiently for me to do something.

I reach for her duffle, and she hands it over with a grateful, slightly amused grin. It takes forever for the carousel to start releasing the luggage, and I stare off at random anythings until it does. Finally, she points out her bag, and I grab it. We make our way through the doors toward the parking garage, and it finally occurs to me to ask, "Did you have a good flight?"

She nods once, unenthusiastically. "About as good as could be expected."

I huff a laugh. "Can't be great when you're in a giant metal tube, suspended thousands of feet in the air, cramped in with a bunch of people." I bite my tongue to keep from babbling. *She does not care about your plane rant. Nobody cares about the plane rant.*

She grins, and it hits me like a bullet. I look away from her under the pretense of following the signs back to the parking lot. "Not a fan of flying, huh?"

I wince. "Not at all." Even being at an airport puts me on edge. Can I blame this weirdness on that?

We find my car solely because of the picture I took of my parking space. She laughs when I wield my phone like a hero wields a sword. Pride swells in my chest that quickly dies on the drive home, faint Christmas music filling the otherwise dead silence.

After the slow death of thirty minutes, I haul her bags into Mark's room—which he's certainly cleaned up. He shares a room with their brother, Jake, when Ellie visits and then transforms his own room into something like a BNB. The bed is neatly made, and it even smells of

Febreze in here. Although, I wouldn't be surprised if I were to open his closet and have his laundry spill out onto the floor. It's her brother, though, so she probably knows to stay away from the closet catastrophe.

I turn to her, tenting my fingers like a supervillain. I change my mind and clench them into fists instead. Then I decide to put them on my hips. *Hands are pointless, can I just say?* "Um, are you hungry?" I end up expressing with them. *I never talk with my hands.* Apparently now I do. "I can order something."

"That's okay." She starts digging in her bag, and I take that as my cue to leave, but she halts me just before I make the threshold. "I have something for you."

How am I supposed to react right now? "Really?"

"Don't worry, you don't have to get me anything," she jokes, laughing at my presumably befuddled expression. "I was going through some things at my place. Anyway, I thought you could use it more than me." She pulls out a small black case and hands it to me.

The nerves have made a frightening reappearance, or maybe they never really left. Hard to tell now that they're my new best friends. I flick open the case. I don't know what I expect, but a gun isn't it. "Woah." It's a small, concealable handgun. Admittedly, one of the coolest things she could have given me, but it begs the question… "Why?"

"You live with my brothers." She shrugs like that's all the explanation required. "I'd feel better knowing that someone here has a gun in case anything happens. You know how to shoot?"

My dad started me off with a Nerf gun. I was supposed to pretend it was real. I got whooped whenever I pointed it at someone whether it was on purpose or an accident. Learning to be completely alert when holding one was drilled into me before he ever put a real gun in my hands. He eventually gifted me the hunting rifle passed down from my grandfather. I still have it in the safe in my closet back at my parents' house.

I try to remember the last time Ellie was here if we discussed my past with guns. It's possible I mentioned hunting with my father, but my memory has blanked on any conversations we may or may not have had. Maybe she heard from her brothers. Does Mark talk to her about me? *Why are you thinking about this now?*

Oh, right, *because she gave you a gun.*

There must be more to this than she's telling me. Am I even allowed to ask?

"Yeah." I open my mouth to question her but then switch course like a coward. Or a wise man. Time will tell. "How did you get this on the plane?"

"I checked it." Another shrug. No big deal. I nod once. "Look, don't worry too much over it. This is more to make me feel better than anything."

"Okay." And then I finally remember my manners. "Thank you."

She gives me a thin-lipped smile.

I blow out a long breath, closing the case back up. "Well, I'm hungry, so I'm going to order a pizza. You sure I can't tempt you with your choice of toppings?"

She grins. "My choice, you say?" And even after the weird moment we just shared, her smile still ignites the butterflies in my gut. This will be a torturously long visit.

3

ELLIE'S SIBLINGS

SOMEONE FUMBLES WITH KEYS ON THE OTHER SIDE OF THE DOOR, but I ignore it, focusing on the argument at hand. Jake got home not too long after the pizza arrived and stole more than his fair share.

I remember their apartment from my past visits. It's small: the kitchen and living room share the same space, and there's only room for a shower and a toilet in the bathroom. They have three bedrooms, at least. And there is indeed a five-year-old fake Christmas tree in the corner covered in colorful lights and mismatched ornaments.

A red and Dalmatian-spotted blanket twists around my waist as I face my twin. More blankets cover the already lacking surface area of their apartment. Apparently, Brandon's mom likes to sew.

"It's more romantic that way," Jake is saying.

"It's completely illogical!" I spot Mark in the doorway then, my braid slipping over my shoulder. "Ah, would you please tell your brother you can't actually die of a broken heart?"

Mark's gaze flits to the TV where we are clearly *not* watching *Revenge of the Sith* as the course of our debate would imply. Brandon turned on *Iron Man*, but it's taken a backseat in my brain.

Jake tenses when Mark turns back to us, but Mark ignores my question. "Hey!" He smiles instead. "Good to see you!"

It's late, but of course we waited up for him to get off his rotation. His hair is still damp from the shower he took at the hospital, and water flicks onto my brow when he bends over the couch to put an arm around me and plant a kiss on top of my head.

"You too." At his clear joy, I feel a prickle of guilt. I blink it away and turn back to Jake, determination settling in my gut. "Anakin had just finished choking her, and she was giving birth. Not to mention she gave birth to twins! She died because of all the stress her body was put through. She was weak."

"You wouldn't die of that." Jake scowls.

"Well, it's more plausible than your 'broken heart' nonsense." I put air quotes around the words, and Jake rolls his eyes.

"All I'm saying is we don't know the rules of that universe. The Force connects things, right? So, isn't it possible that in a marriage, there becomes a bond there? It could be that the Force inside her depleted because of her misery over everything her husband had done."

I blink at him. He should consider becoming a lawyer, despite how wrong he is. Or *because* of how wrong he is. "You are such a nerd."

Jake squints and swirls a finger at me. "Is that…a white flag I see?"

I cross my arms, raise a brow. "Okay. Fine, with that logic, her death would have been due to Force depletion."

Jake gestures dramatically, nearly smacking Mark who bails for the seat next to Brandon, collapsing into it with a heavy sigh. "Because of her broken heart!"

Brandon nods, humoring the validity of our arguments, and Mark asks him, "How long have they been at this?"

Brandon consults his watch. "I'd say it's been about twenty minutes now."

At this point, I know the argument is stupid. It was stupid from the beginning, but the second Jake and I realize we have differing opinions, we must prove the other wrong. It's been that way all our lives. Our parents' divorce and the eleven-year separation weren't quite enough to change that.

Mark leans forward and hits my knee. "How was your flight?"

I blink. "Fine." An ugly feeling swirls in my stomach. I know he's exhausted, but I flick my nose with my thumb and stand. "Listen, we should talk."

I catch the hitch in Mark's breathing. I don't blame him for the reaction. The others sink into the movie, not picking up the tension between the two of us at all. The oblivion of men is not always a bad thing.

Mark follows me into his room, closing the door behind him. I stop in the middle and turn, keeping my expression blank. "Are we going to be okay?"

His eyes widen slightly, and he looks around the room. Anywhere but directly at me. "Of course. I just…needed time to process. You're an assassin." His whisper is raspy, appalled even days after finding out.

It's not a question, so I don't answer. When he called to confront me last week, he was devastated, but there was also a hint of anger under his tone. It's only been five days, and I would have given him longer if circumstances hadn't arisen.

He takes a couple breaths and wrings his hands before asking quietly, "Why?"

"Why am I an assassin?"

Mark's gaze jerks to the door, worried the others can hear me even though I'm speaking as quietly as he is. He nods.

I can't lie to him anymore. I want him to trust me, but I can't tell him I do it for him. To keep him and Jake safe for Mom. "It's my job." Before he can tell me that's not a good enough reason, I continue. "Why did you talk to Dad?"

"What?"

I don't repeat myself. The whole reason our parents' marriage didn't work was because of the Enforcers, which our father started. Mom kept it a secret from the boys to protect them. Dad initiated me into the program. I was happy to follow Mom's lead and let them live in blissful ignorance until Mark took it into his own hands to speak with the man who singlehandedly destroyed our family.

Mark's an open book, something I noticed immediately when we reconnected after I turned sixteen. There's not much he won't tell me, so he spills it all after a few moments of silence. "I was worried about you. You never tell me anything. You were so closed off, and I was afraid something was wrong. He was the only person I thought I could call."

I frown. "I've always been closed off. Why does it bother you now?"

"It's always bothered me!" He glances at the door and quiets back down, finding an itch to pick at on the outside of his wrist. "Lately, Jake and I... I guess, if I couldn't fix that relationship, I wanted to focus on one that I could. I want to be there for you."

My heart clenches. He and Jake have their differences. The main one is that Jake acts like any idiot his age, and Mark is trying to fill the hole Mom left. Mark only goes three places: the hospital, church, and home. Jake goes to parties with friends. He goes to bars and gets wasted. He used to call Mark for rides home when he couldn't drive himself. Then he started calling an Uber. Less judgmental, he claimed. Mark pushes him to be more responsible; Jake pushes back. Mark tells me these things; Jake keeps it light when we talk. Jake and I fight all the time but never about real stuff. Not like him and Mark.

I study the faded stains on the otherwise gray carpet. Of course Mark would reach out to Dad. And Dad has no qualms about spilling my secrets. Any effort to distance me from them. Personal connections don't end well for assassins.

After a moment, wiping his hands on his jeans, Mark steps toward me. "Is there something else?"

A deep breath, and I lift my eyes, stuffing my thumbs in my pockets. "I gave Brandon one of my guns."

His thick dark brows shoot up into his mass of curly blond hair. "You gave him your gun?"

"One of them, yes." If he wants to strengthen our relationship, this will be the first major test. I can't stop the churning in my stomach, desperate for his trust. Desperate for his ignorance.

My jaw clenches involuntarily. Part of me is relieved he knows. Some small part of me sees justice in it. I've had to live all these years training, killing, essentially raising myself while he and Jake grew up with Mom in a loving normal family dynamic with holidays and birthdays and joy.

For the past five days, I have tried to quell that voice inside that tells me his knowing is a fitting punishment for the life he was given—while I was stuck with *this*.

"What?" He puts his hands up. "You're the one who gave it to him. Don't blame me."

I want to be able to joke with him, but my words come out harsh. "Ask me why I did it, Mark."

He straightens but doesn't back away. A flicker of pride awakens in the dark pit. "What are you so mad at me for? I didn't make you give up your gun."

I pull the file from my bag and slap it down hard on the bed near where he's standing. He reaches for it and freezes when he sees the name on the side. *Brandon Harwood.* The paper inside could be a résumé if I led a normal life.

He swallows thickly and sways on his feet, spotting the small picture of his friend in the corner. "What is this?"

"An assignment."

His face goes white. He sits down hard on the bed, upsetting the red and green decorative pillows he added for me. "You're supposed to—" he chokes on the word—"*kill* him?"

I shake my head. "Not me."

His eyes manage to widen further, and he stares at the papers in front of him. I wish more than anything that burning these papers was all it took to solve this problem. That Brandon's damn name never showed up in the first place.

"I swiped it from Hartley's desk, but it's just a matter of him typing up a new one."

"Hartley?"

"Dad's business partner." A long time ago Mark knew Hartley. He used to babysit us. Now he pushes paper for our father. "What the hell put him on that desk, Mark?"

"I don't know." His words are muffled by his hand. "You didn't tell him about this, did you?" His head shoots up, his eyes bulge, and his hand slams over his mouth as he swallows deeply.

"He's still here, isn't he?" I snap. I can't stop the anger from taking over. It's completely irrational to be angry with Mark. This is all new to him. But the gravity of the situation doesn't lessen just because he doesn't know what to expect.

My temper doesn't bother him too much. "Can… What can we do? Can you stop this?"

"You think I have the influence?"

"Maybe you can talk to Dad?"

I take a moment to force down a breath. He can't be that naive. "Dad allowed this to happen. The file wouldn't have been on that desk if he was going to stop it." My lips curl back until my words are forced through bared teeth. "He. Doesn't. Care."

"We can't just let this happen!" His breath shudders, then the rest of his body is trembling. He whispers, "I'm not going to let him die. He's my best friend."

"And just what the hell do you think I'm doing here?" I hiss.

I know I should regret the words as soon as that hurt flashes in his eyes. He thought I'd come just to spend Thanksgiving with them. I wish I had. I wish that argument with Jake could have been the main attraction of my visit. I wish Brandon had picked me up at the airport and not immediately received a gun for his efforts with the flimsy excuse that it would make me feel better. I wish I didn't know I could pull on that string all day and not scare him off because of his obvious attraction to me and love for my brothers.

But reality is rarely so pleasant.

"Alright." Mark rubs his hands together, some calm settling with a plan forming in his head. "How do we play this? Can you, like, hack into the system and figure out who has him as their target, and then take them out first?"

A terrible plan. "There's no electronic trace I can follow. They're typed up on a Word document, Mark. They're handed to the person, and there's no record of who takes it until the job is done and a report's handed in."

"So, we keep him locked up here," he offers. "How do we do that without raising suspicion? What?"

I'm shaking my head. "If he's locked up here, they'll just target him through the windows." I won't be letting any assassins near this place. Any *other* assassins.

"Wha…" he splutters, muscles locking up, fists clenching as he tugs at the sleeves of his sweatshirt. "What do we do, Ellie? You're not really helping me figure this out."

"Telling you your ideas won't work *is* helping," I object.

"Well, why don't you come up with something for a change?"

"Fine, I think we should let him go about his routine. I'll tail him."

He nods, then snaps his fingers. "Or you can just go with him everywhere. Like the buddy system."

I close my eyes, take a deep breath. "First, we're not that close. Second, if you don't want him knowing what I do, I think my carrying around a rifle might give it away."

"Okay, good point. Good point." He nods and keeps nodding. "How long can you keep that up?"

"Until a move is made or my next assignment."

"I really wish you would stop this." I knew once he found out, he would try his best to make me quit. Mark's a sympathetic person. He won't force me to do anything, but he will try his damnedest to change my mind. It will be a lot of heartache for him when I shut him down every single time.

"I know." I level a hard glare on him, but he matches it. "I have to, Mark."

"You kill people."

It's been so long, even hearing the accusation from my brother's mouth doesn't make me flinch. "Not innocent people."

He raises Brandon's folder between us, and my jaw clenches. "How do you know that?"

4

ELLIE'S SHOT

BRANDON IS SET FIRMLY IN MY SIGHTS, HIS CHEST RISING AND FALL-ing behind the crosshairs. He's been fitting people with shoes in his black and white striped uniform for almost five hours now. Tomorrow is Thanksgiving, and I'm perched on the rooftop across the courtyard from the entrance to the small department store, essentially my home for the past three days.

The outdoor mall makes for convenient surveillance. And the small proportions of the shop means that I haven't gone without seeing Brandon for more than a few minutes at a time.

The color-changing Christmas lights around the windows of Brandon's place of employment have me ready to snap. The blinking has made spotting a laser difficult. Most of my father's assassins don't use lasers, but some like to spook their targets with the light before ending them. Those are the same ones who savor jobs during "the most wonderful time of the year."

I will not let Brandon fall victim to one of them, but I won't lie and say part of me isn't tempted. There's a reason his profile landed on that desk. I've been studying the guy my brothers live with from the moment he moved in. Nothing stood out or has stood out in my tab keeping until this assignment. He genuinely smiles at all his customers. His supervisor appears to be on friendly terms with him. And he's busy with school when he's not working. Clearly, I'm missing something.

My phone buzzes for the twelfth time in my pocket. Jake thinks I'm out shopping for the meal I'll make tomorrow. He keeps texting me things to pick up while I'm out. I fully intend to get all of it after I make sure Brandon is secure back at his apartment. My cover has been blown apart with Mark, but Jake is still safely in the dark. Plus, I can afford to buy their groceries.

It would make things a lot easier if we could go back to no one knowing anything. But even then, Brandon would still be a target, and I would have no way to find out why. Not that Mark was helpful on that front. His saint of a friend is holding up to all of Mark's praise when I desperately need him to misstep.

Mark didn't want Brandon to go to work that first day despite what I told him about being targeted in their apartment. He tried to get Brandon to stay back and take the day to get to know me. I pushed Brandon to go, much to the annoyance of my brother. Under no circumstances do I want the setting for any type of showdown to be their apartment. It helped that Mark and I saw how stiff Brandon went at the suggestion. Mark, wisely, hasn't made another fuss.

Today is the optimal time to eliminate the target. It's overcast—so no sun or rain interference—and Brandon is dependably out in public a day before a major holiday when it will be a spectacle.

The setting reminds me of my first assignment. Some girls get a car for their sixteenth birthday; I got handed my first target, and it meant more to me than any gift. It was a symbol of my father's trust, his faith in me to do what he'd trained me to do. I didn't know any better back then. I studiously researched Edward Comb and found that he had a family—a wife and a daughter, but it hadn't mattered then. He was my job.

My execution was flawless. One shot right to the temple. The patience drilled into me kept me from making any sloppy mistakes, even that first time. I expected my father to be proud, but he just handed me my earnings. I told myself not to care. I did my job, and as my boss, he gave me my pay. But I knew deep down, as my father, he was proud.

That night, the story of Edward Comb's crimes was on the news. I watched it eagerly on the floor of my mentor's bedroom. *Emily Richards Eliminates DC Businessman*, read the headline. I was so proud to see my alias attached to the accomplishment. For years, I watched the other Enforcers be feared and respected by the media, and now it was finally my turn. It was the first the world was hearing of Emily Richards, and it would be far from the last.

His wife denied all the heinous accusations of fraud against her husband. Allegedly, he stole so much money from the business that it was barely staying afloat, and many of the employees faced bankruptcy, home foreclosures, and worse. All of which could have easily been avoided. I'd seen it a thousand times. No one ever wants to believe those they love are capable of evil. I rolled my eyes then.

My cynicism died abruptly when his daughter came on screen. I've never forgotten her face. Her hair was up in pigtails, her pale cheeks puffy and tear stained. She couldn't have been more than six, but she held her head high as she said in a high-pitched voice, "My daddy wasn't the person you say. You lie. You always lie."

She didn't scream, or throw a tantrum, or sob into her mother's leg. She stood in front of the cameras and calmly told them they were liars.

That more than anything scared the hell out of me. I spent the night on my bathroom floor, quivering from head to toe. I tried to ignore it, to shove it from my mind. But that was the moment I realized my father's business might not be doing as much good as he wants to portray. I stopped caring about making him proud, but I continued to fulfill my role as his assassin because it was only days after that first broadcast that I knew I had no choice.

It's all I've done since. Until now.

My father thinks I'm in my apartment back in DC right now. My cousin, Jaythan, helped me with that one. I tracked him down to his isolated cabin in the woods just before I reconnected with my brothers, and he already knew everything about the Enforcers and my part in it—being the tech-wizard, he is, he'd been following my father's business for a while. He's done anything he can to help me since. Including confusing the tracker issued to every assassin via neck implant. Most recently, my cousin hacked into the security feed for the mall and erased me from the scene. I'm a ghost on this rooftop.

Brandon disappears into the back of the department store and reappears moments later with his jacket, walking out the front door, having just clocked out. I do a quick scan of the rooftops before he steps out from under the overhang, presenting himself as a prime target. There's the barest glint of light on the roof across from me, and I've had enough time to notice where the Christmas lights are and what they reflect off of to know that's not what this is. *Gun.*

I can't be sure I won't shoot right over the assassin's head, not being able to see him. Quickly, I angle my gun down instead and fire.

The bullet punches through Brandon's shoulder, ripping a hole in the glass behind him. Brandon stumbles back under the awning not a moment too soon: dust flies up from another shot right at his feet.

I allow myself one breath of relief.

I peer through the sight at the roof across from me, but I still don't see the other assassin. Protocol would have him turn back. When there's another player on the field, it means something is unsatisfactory with your performance. He'll return to base, and he won't say a word, expecting my father—but more likely, desk-jockey Hartley—to want a word with him. He'll assume the other player has taken Brandon out instead. That will buy me time, but not a lot.

I wait a minute more to make sure he's gone, then hook a line to the roof. I hastily break down my rifle, stuff it into the guitar case, and set the lock before vaulting off the roof. Clenching the line, I slow my descent, detach the wire from my belt, stash the case behind a plant, and take off toward Brandon.

Most of the people in the mall have already run off screaming. Brandon's boss dragged him back inside the store. I slam open the front door, and the man swivels wide eyes toward my intrusion as he applies pressure to the wound. Brandon's seated on a bench, his bronzed skin now a sickly pale.

"Ellie?" Brandon winces when his boss readjusts. The man's shoulders loosen slightly at Brandon's recognition of me.

I push him aside, yanking the bandanna from my pocket. "Has anyone called nine-one-one?"

"I don't know." The man looks from me to Brandon frantically. Unhelpfully. I glare at him, and he winces, taking a step away.

"Do it." My voice is pitched low, pure command. I pull Brandon's jacket off and tie the bandanna around his upper arm, pulling tight to cut off the blood flow. He snaps forward, his head ramming into my stomach.

"Sorry," he grunts.

I push him back up, applying pressure to both sides of his arm. The bullet went straight through. The worst I did was cut through muscle; I didn't even nick the bone. He's going to be fine.

"What the hell are you apologizing for?" I mutter.

He huffs a laugh, then groans.

I frown, forcing down the butterflies that have taken flight in my gut. I didn't maim him permanently. He'll have a scar, yes, but he will also have a heartbeat. He's going to be fine. "How are you doing?"

"I'm…seeing spots." He attempts to meet my gaze, but his dark eyes are already half-glazed. He blinks heavily.

"You're going into shock."

"*You're* going into shock." He laughs again, then his smile slips into a frown. "Sorry. I think I'm going into shock."

"I think you're *in* shock," I amend. He hums. "What's your blood type, Brandon?"

He mumbles something too low for me to hear. I lean down in time to catch his whispered "…so pretty."

"Your blood type," I snap. "Brandon." *He's in shock, cut him some slack.* Of course, I learned his blood type approximately four minutes after

Mark told me he was moving in, but Brandon needs to stay conscious and present.

His mouth is moving, but no words are coming out. Then suddenly, his breath is hot on my neck. "I like the way you say my name. You're a good person, you know? Helping me…live." I freeze. "When you smiled at me at the airport, I thought it was like being shot." He groans again. "I was way off."

For a moment, I forget what I'm supposed to be doing. I notice the haze of panic around the edges of my vision and fight it back. *He's in shock.* Nothing he says now should be taken as anything more than delirium.

Then he turns his head, and his lips brush the shell my ear. I suck in a breath and jerk back. Whether he did that on purpose or by accident, I can't tell. His eyes are squeezed shut in agony. "Keep talking, Brandon. The paramedics will be here soon." I look back at his boss who's still on the phone. I raise a brow, and the man nods. I say quietly, more to myself, "You'll be fine."

5

JAKE'S FRIEND

I MEAN TO GO STRAIGHT TO MY CAR AFTER CLASS. I REALLY DO. HOWever, I find something to distract myself from doing just that. In my defense, she's just sitting on the bench, protected from the slight drizzle only by an overhang.

She's focused on the small book resting in her lap. Her auburn hair is flipped over to one side and held back by the hand she's using to prop up her head. The flaming cascade calls to me.

A flirty grin slips across my lips. "Care for some new entertainment?" She looks up, and I'm blessed with the sight of freckles sprinkled over her nose and cheeks and a faint blush rising beneath them.

She grimaces. "That's never worked, has it?"

"It only takes once."

She wrinkles her freckled nose, shaking her head. The flame of her hair sparks. "I'd suggest you keep trying if I didn't think you actually would."

I shrug. "Persistence is key."

She shakes her head again, bright green eyes flashing as she pats my arm. "Not always." Her attention floats back down to her book.

I can't hide my confusion. This doesn't usually happen to me. Not to sound conceited, but I'm usually able to get a little more out of women before being shut down. It shouldn't matter, but something about her is intriguing to me. I'm hooked, and I'm no quitter…this time.

"Did you just start here? I haven't seen you around before."

She sighs, flipping her book closed. Point: Jake Spencer. "Well, it appears you're not going to let me get back to reading."

I purse my lips and ignite the smolder. "Not if I can help it."

A smile with pristine teeth. She wants to laugh; I can see it in the way the light dances in her eyes. We're back on track. "I've been here all semester, actually. I just don't usually hang around after class, but I drove my roommate today." She eyes me. "And it's clear you get around. What's your story?"

"Ah, well, it's an interesting one. See, it all started when I graduated high school. I got accepted here as a business major, and now I share an apartment with my brother and his friend."

Her head tilts, and I catch the slight twitch of her nose. "Not *your* friend?"

I shrug. I do like Brandon. He's a great guy. But that's also what I hate about him. That and the fact that my brother only invited him to live with us because he thought he would rub off on me. Two years later, and he hasn't. "He's a good guy, I guess. So, you like the story, right?"

"Sure, yeah. Except that—" she folds her hands together, holds up a finger and points at me—"it sucks." It's possible I'm already in love.

My hand goes to my heart, and I flinch for show. "That hurts." Her chin tips up with her grin. I've won. I take a seat next to her, and she scoots to make room. Not too much though. I leave just enough space between us that we're not touching. "Alright, let's see how you do."

She sits up straight and clears her throat. "Okay. I, too, graduated high school, and I did two years online at home while I saved up enough money to move out here. I had to deal with a bunch of financial aid stuff to be able to come which was *really* fun." She rolls her eyes as if reliving it, and honestly, the mention gives *me* chills. "But I made it work, and I'll graduate next year right on schedule."

"Alright, your story was only slightly better than mine." I laugh. "What's your major?"

"English."

"Oh," I say on an expelled breath, leaning forward and resting my elbows on my knees. "So, you cheated. That makes sense."

She shakes her head, red hair swishing back and forth over her shoulders. My hands squeeze together in front of me to keep from reaching out. "That's not cheating; it's winning."

It hurts not to argue that point, but I hold back. "What are you reading?"

She flips the book around. "It's actually a re-read." She turns it for my inspection, but my eyes dip immediately to her aqua painted nails. "*Fellowship of the Ring.*"

My brow lifts of its own accord. "Yeah?" How is it more intimidating and yet also more intriguing that she's a nerd?

The woman shrugs, looking back down at her book, suddenly sheepish. She can't see the wicked grin on my face now. "I like to read the series every couple years. It's a masterpiece, you know." A warm smile spreads on her face, then she meets my eyes. "Have you read them?"

"No, I haven't," I lie. It was actually one of the first books that I really enjoyed. But it's been years, and I hardly remember them. I slide a handful of centimeters closer, and my arm brushes against hers. She barely covers her shiver. "But I have watched the movies, and they're fantastic."

She groans, turning more toward me. "No, you have to read the books! I promise, they're worth it."

"See, the thing about me is, I'm not big on the reading so much." That's mostly true. I used to love reading and took whatever I could get my hands on. Since Mom died, though…I haven't.

"I'll bet I could change that." She leans in, eyes sparkling like the forest after rainfall. Playful.

My grin turns wicked again, and she returns a shyer version. "You really think so?" She only gives me the one-shoulder shrug, bright pink lips scrunched.

I'm about to ask for her name when Mark comes careening out of a still moving vehicle.

That's not his car. *He called an Uber?*

He must have spotted me as soon as they turned the corner, and he nearly collides with me as I stand. Annoyance at his interruption quickly melts as I take in his manic and obvious terror. His face is white as a sheet, and he's breathing way too fast. If I were a betting man, I'd say my brother's heart is ready to pound right out of his chest.

"What's wrong?" A sick feeling weaves through my gut, and my first thought is that something terrible has happened to Ellie. *Please not Ellie.*

Mark gulps down air, not acknowledging my companion who is now standing behind me. "Hospital," he gasps. "We need…to go. Ellie…" He stops to suck in more air, but now my pulse is racing. I can feel each individual bead of sweat forming on my skin.

I grip his shoulder hard, and snap, "Damn it, Mark! Tell me what the hell is going on! What happened to Ellie?"

My brother shakes his head vigorously, trying to tug me after him. "Not Ellie. She's at the hospital." My heart trips, but Mark goes on. "With Brandon. He's hurt."

"What?" It takes me a moment to register that he said Brandon is hurt, not Ellie. I try not to be too relieved. Brandon's a great guy. Just because my brother has been using him as a pawn doesn't mean I wanted anything to happen to him. With shaking hands, I sling my backpack over my shoulder. "What happened? I thought he was at work."

"He got shot outside."

"*What?*"

"Ellie's already there. We need to go."

The woman I was just hitting on twirls her keys around her finger. "I can drive you."

I shake my head. I don't even know her name, and she's offering to take us to the hospital? "You don't have to do that. I've got my car here." I desperately hope she can't hear the wobble in my voice that's still trying to work off the adrenaline.

"No, please. I don't think either of you should be driving right now, and I've got time before my roommate's class lets out. You need to get to the emergency room, right?" Mark's head bobs in what might be considered a nod, clearly going into shock. She gathers up her things. "It's the least I can do."

I blink a few times. "Thank you."

It becomes immediately clear that my companion made the right choice not letting either of us drive. I can't clench my hands into submission, and I'm starting to wonder if it's more than just coming off the adrenaline of thinking Ellie was the one in trouble. Brandon and I aren't close. Our only connections are Mark and the fact that we live together. But he was just shot. *Shot.*

Brandon. Breaks no rules, loves his family, goes to church, Brandon. How does that even happen?

Mark sits in the back seat, running his hands through his hair so intensely that it's going to start coming out in chunks. Every inch of him trembles, and the traffic isn't helping calm him down. He casts furtive glances out the windows and keeps groaning and digging his fingers into his temples.

"Hey." I reach back and smack his knee, lightly. "He'll be fine. Brandon's a tough guy." He still taps his hand incessantly against the door. "You could be too if you went to the gym with him once in a while."

At that, he cracks a fraction of a smile. But the second we pull under the hospital overhang, Mark bails with a quick, "Thanks, Jake's friend."

I start to follow but turn to the girl first. "I'm Jake." She got as much from Mark, but she nods appreciatively at the gesture.

And with a worried smile, she responds, "Chelsea."

My lips quirk. "I'll see you around?"

I know in my haggard, anxious state, I've lost all my swagger. But she nods and hands me a slip of paper. "I hope so."

6

ELLIE'S AFTERMATH

MARK BURSTS THROUGH THE EMERGENCY ROOM DOORS, EYES WIDE and lips parted, Jake close at his heels.

"What happened?" Mark is out of breath when he reaches me even though the waiting room is right off the main entrance.

"He was shot leaving work." I take my brother's shoulders and steer him into a chair. He nods, gesturing in a circle for me to go on as he catches his breath. I hand him my unopened water bottle. "The bullet went straight through his arm. He doesn't need surgery."

Jake lets out a heavy sigh. "Good." I glance back at him, and he's clenching and unclenching his fists. His eyes shift around the small room, taking in the stark white walls and vinyl tiles offset by the dark blue furniture and small plant in the corner. "How does this even happen? Who would shoot Brandon?"

"What?" Mark snaps, lowering the bottle, now with only about a sip left. I frown. "Suddenly you care what happens to him? My 'pawn'? Isn't that what you called him the other day?"

"You came and got *me*, Mark." Jake throws his hands out in exasperation. "You didn't have to, but *you* came to *me*."

"Maybe I shouldn't have!" Mark explodes out of the chair.

"Alright!" I shove him back down and push Jake away. Some curious looks turn our way which I shut down with a sharp glare. "Shut up! We all care, alright? Leave it at that."

Jake blows out a breath, still glaring, but wisely turning his attention away from Mark. "When can we go see him?"

"The doctor is coming out any minute with an update."

Truth is, it's another twenty minutes before we're told anything. I stand, recognizing the thin dark-haired man as soon as he steps out of the long hallway. He doesn't look worn down—that's good. There's some spring in that step. Mark and Jake crowd in close behind me, pinning their gazes on the approaching doctor.

He glances over the three of us, and recognition lights his eyes when he sees my brother. "Hi, Mark. You here for Brandon Harwood?"

Mark merely nods.

The doctor smiles sympathetically. "Well, he's all patched up. Per regulation, we'll keep him overnight for observation, but if all goes well, he can go back home in the morning."

The regulation to which he's referring is a result of some wannabe assassins poisoning their bullets so that any shot was lethal. I was never clear on where they got their poisons from, but rumors speculated some used mucus off the back of a certain rainforest treefrog. Anyway, states then regulated that any patient coming in with a gunshot wound is to be kept and monitored closely overnight.

Hartley had his hand in implementing that regulation. It doesn't reflect well on the Enforcers when people are killed by these impostor assassins. Some of them come up as targets. Truth be told, hunting those people down is easier to swallow than any other assignment.

The doctor continues. "Your friend was very lucky, though."

"Luck, I'm sure, had nothing to do with it." Jake takes two fingers, kisses them, and raises them up. Mark's jaw clenches, but he says nothing. I cuff Jake in the arm with the back of my hand, meeting his glare with my own. He reads the warning there and rolls his eyes but doesn't say another word.

"Can we see him, Dr. Bingham?" Mark totters on his feet, peering down the hallway and nearly losing his balance. I pull him back.

"Nurse Hayes can take you back," the doctor offers.

Brandon's sitting up in one of those awful hospital gowns, his arm in a sling. The rich bronze has returned to his skin, noticeable even under the florescent hospital lights. He smiles at us as we walk in, but upon closer examination—left hand fisted in the sheets, closed curtains though it's still light out, and back not resting fully against the headboard—he's not okay. It's to be expected, but he'd be a lot worse off if he knew what really happened.

More like Mark, watching Brandon like he might die if he was to turn away. His whole body is angled toward his friend, ready to help with anything and everything, and his breath is coming up short again. Mark looks at me, needing confirmation. I don't give him any. That's not my job.

Jake is more reserved in his worry, but there's a hardness around his eyes and his mouth. This isn't something that should have happened.

Brandon is Mark's friend; Jake is generally indifferent toward him, but even he can't pretend away the agitation. This hit too close to home. I mimic these reactions, letting my eyes stay wide, and crossing my arms tightly over my chest. It's not that I haven't felt real concern for Brandon in the last couple hours. I just don't quite trust myself to automatically express the correct emotion right now. I still have no idea why he's a target.

I stay near the door while Mark and Jake rush to Brandon's side.

"How are you feeling?" Mark asks.

Brandon gently pushes away Mark's extended hand, tension straining his smile. "I'm fine. My shoulder's sore, but the doctor said it could have been worse. I was lucky." I watch him closely as he says it. His voice is surprisingly light, but I catch the slight cringe in his eyes. He doesn't mean that. *Of course he doesn't.*

Jake has the same thought, apparently. "Lucky? Brandon, you were shot. That's not exactly winning the lottery." His hands tremble slightly at his sides which he tries to quell, his knuckles turning white.

Brandon takes a deep breath—unnerved—but shakes his head. He finds me then with so much emotion in his eyes that I don't want to decode. "Thank you for what you did. Jake will agree with this, at least; I *was* lucky you were there."

More than you know.

I shrug and turn my gaze down to my feet. My arms tighten across my chest as I try not to think too much about the weird fluttering in my stomach. "It was nothing." *Deep breath. Focus on the present.* But what he said before the ambulance showed up refuses to leave me alone. *You're a good person, you know? Helping me...live.*

A prickle of sweat tickles the back of my neck, and I fight back a shiver. I plaster a smirk on my face and look back up, but only at the end of his bed. "Who knew shopping could be so exciting?" For a second, my eyes flick up to his, and he smiles, relaxing just a little. I wish I could do that.

7

ELLIE'S ACCESSORY

JAKE MAKES DINNER FOR THE THREE OF US THAT NIGHT. SHEDDING his bulky winter coat at the door, he immediately pulls out some chicken and a can of sauce to prepare. But Mark drags me into his room. I expected it. Carefully, to hide it from Jake—who definitely already knows we're having a private conversation—Mark shuts the door.

"So." He turns, rolling his wrists, picking at his sleeves, moving constantly so the polyester shifts and swishes too loudly. I pull my own coat off and toss it on the bed, drawing my braid over my shoulder and waiting patiently for him to continue. "Did you handle it? Was the situation handled? Taken care of? Is it over?"

I raise a brow. Part of me finds his innocence amusing. He's taken off guard by all of this, and watching his brain process it is a new experience for me. A small, distant part of my brain, though, hates him for it. He's had no need to desensitize to things like this. He's caught off guard because he didn't believe his family to be a part of any of this two weeks ago. I grind my teeth, my jaw starting to ache from the repetitive action.

When Mark clamps his lips tight, I finally respond. "Yes, Mark. I took care of the assassin."

His breath is shaky, head bobbing on his neck. "Okay." He wipes his sweaty palms on his jeans. They start trembling, and he jolts. "Wait. Does this make me complicit? An enabler? What qualifies as an *accessory*? I asked you to handle it. Does that mean I'm an instigator? Conspiracy to commit murder? But it was for Brandon's safety. Does it still count? Am I a murderer now?" He groans, hands pulling at his hair.

I shake my head. "What are you so worked up about?"

"I practically just gave you an assignment. I told you to go after this guy, and now he's dead. Did I do that? I'm as bad as Dad."

I watch him, at a momentary loss for words. I learned a long time ago never to ask such questions. Sometimes living in the dark is better than living with the burden. My mouth tightens. "I didn't kill him."

His eyes flick up to mine, crinkled at the edges in disbelief, and I wonder if I should be offended. "What?"

"I didn't kill him," I repeat. "So, relax."

He trades all his fidgeting for becoming a statue. "Why doesn't that make me feel better?"

Is there no pleasing him? I take a long, deep breath. "He's not dead, and he's not coming back."

"I don't understand. Did you, like, sit down and talk with him?"

I let him sit in the knowledge that he just said that for a few moments. He waves his hand frantically at me, urging me to go on. I fight the instinct to snap. *He doesn't know how this works. Calm down.*

"Protocol states that if there's another Enforcer in your field, you must retreat. He's well on his way back to DC by now."

"What…so…he took the shot, realized you were there, and left?"

"I took the shot."

"You took the shot?"

"Yes."

It doesn't hit him at first, but then his entire expression opens like a damn flower. His jaw drops, his eyes widen, his brows shoot up into his scruffy hairline. "*You* shot Brandon!"

My lip curls. "You thought the assassin missed?" He really should have seen that one coming.

"Why would you do that?"

"If I hadn't, he'd be dead."

"But…"

"Mark," I snarl. I try to mellow out my tone, but it only sounds sarcastic now. "He's okay. I did the job you asked me to do. Can you trust *that,* at least?" *Can you trust me?* I refuse to acknowledge the sick anticipation of his answer.

He hesitates, looking me in the eyes. My gaze remains hard because I don't know what else to do. This is who I am. This is who he needs to trust. If I soften even a little bit, he will be trusting a lie again. I did what he asked. Whether he agrees with my methods or not, this is how I handle things.

Finally, he nods.

»»»»»

THE FLUORESCENT LIGHTS ARE STILL TOO BRIGHT, AND BLEACH BURNS through my nose, but at least Brandon's sitting up. His phone is pressed to his ear, but he shoots us a strained smile. "No, Mom, you don't have to come down." A pause. "Yes, I promise." Another. "I will."

I stop in the doorway to exchange a few words with the nurse, who tells me Brandon's free to go home. They did another scan and found no traces of poison, obviously. He'll come back in a few days for a quick checkup and hopefully to get the sling off. Until then, he's good to go.

I step fully into the room now. "Good news." I point at Brandon, who's off the phone now, then my focus shifts to the tray hovering by him. "Is that pudding?" Jake's gotten himself a cup which he's dipping his fingers into. Brandon grabs one of the many cups at his little table and tosses it to me. I, like my twin, use two fingers in lieu of a spoon. I ignore the disgusted glare Mark throws our way. "Anyway, you're free to go home now."

"Hey!" Brandon exclaims, spreading his good arm. "That's something to be thankful for today." He takes another pudding cup—why the nurse supplied him with so many, I have no idea—and tosses it at Mark, who fumbles with it. "Celebrate with a pudding cup."

I had forgotten Thanksgiving was soon. *Today.*

Mark scrunches his nose, picking at the lid without actually opening it. "Are you really okay?"

"No, I'm freaking out," Brandon confesses bluntly. I freeze, my pudding-covered fingers halfway to my mouth. My eyes flick to Brandon, but I keep my expression carefully blank. He's swirling his little plastic spoon in his cup, staring deeply into it. "There's nothing I can really do, though, right? The nurses keep telling me I was lucky, but I'm pretty sure that's…" He cuts himself off from what I *know* was about to be a curse. "I mean, sure, it could have been worse, but with the Enforcers, *worse* just means *dead.*"

Mark instinctively turns to me, but I refuse to look away from Brandon who's still playing with his spoon.

"Why do you say that?" I ask, wiping the pudding off my fingers back into the cup. Given he's alive right now, the Enforcers should be above suspicion.

Brandon glances at me and quickly away, cheeks going red. He shakes his head but doesn't answer.

"They have the bullet, though, right?" Jake tries to be encouraging. "They can examine it and see what gun it came from, at least."

"It went right through me." Brandon shrugs. "It's somewhere in the shop, but even if they find it, what good would it be? If it really was the Enforcers, we'll probably never find out since I'm still here. And if it wasn't…" Another shake of his head.

He's right. Law enforcement has already done a thorough search of the place, but knowing which gun it comes from won't help them. I retrieved my weapon last night, and my father doesn't let anyone graduate training until they know how to properly dispose of a weapon. That gun is long gone. The law will be chasing a ghost until they slap a cold case label on it.

Brandon picks at the horrible baby-blue knit blanket, then cringes. "Sorry, guys." He withers with a self-deprecating smile. "That's a bit of a downer."

I slam my pudding cup down on the tray, nearly cracking the thing in an inexplicable surge of anger. They all jump, round eyes turning on me as I snap, "Stop apologizing for everything." I close my eyes, turn, stalk toward the door. We need to get out of this hospital. "The nurse said you're free to go whenever. I'll get the car."

I throw my back into the wall in the bright hallway and force myself to breathe. Brandon is fine, and soon he'll be back to his normal life and normal job and normal schooling. This will all be in the rearview mirror soon enough. He doesn't know it was the Enforcers. He'll forget his suspicions, and I'll find out exactly what made them notice him.

Once the boys step through the sliding doors, I climb out of the driver's seat and into the back. Mark takes the wheel, and Jake claims shotgun, leaving Brandon in the back with me. I need time and space to breathe.

It's a silent car ride, so Mark plays with the radio, scanning until he deems a station acceptable. I don't pay much attention to whatever he's chosen. Then Brandon clears his throat.

"Hey." He draws my attention from the window, speaking softly. Not low enough that Mark and Jake can't hear, but clearly not intending for them to be a part of the conversation. I don't smile, unable to conjure the mask. "I just wanted to thank you again. It could have been a lot worse for me if you hadn't been there." He takes my hand that's been resting between us, squeezes once, and releases it. I swallow against the flutter that the contact sends through me. "Thank you."

I watch him a second longer then finally give him a small smile. As genuine as I can make it. But I can't give him anything more, so I turn back to the window without a word, fist against my mouth, a grimace slipping through the cracks that I'm hoping is mistakable as the ghost of a smile while I sit here feeling like an ass.

》》》》》

I HEAD RIGHT FOR THE KITCHEN AS SOON AS WE WALK THROUGH THE front door. It's Thanksgiving. These guys deserve to celebrate it, but the only turkey in the fridge is lunchmeat. I pull it out and toss it on the counter.

Brandon says something about washing the hospital off him as his steps retreat, and Jake grumbles about a paper he needs to finish. Mark, though, stays and takes a seat at the counter, watching as I continue to look in every drawer and corner of the fridge.

He leans over on his elbows to whisper even though we're alone, "You know you're always welcome here."

I pull eight slices of bread from the round sourdough loaf. "What are you talking about?"

"I don't want you to feel like you have nowhere to go." When I just stare at him in return, he continues, "You always have the option of staying with us while you get back on your feet."

The lid on the butter wannabe cracks open. "Why would I need to get back on my feet?"

"In case…" He wrings his hands, and it's not hard to follow where this is going. "In case you ever decide on a new path. Professionally. We'd be happy to take you in."

My face hardens, and I rip a hole in one of the slices with the butter knife. I sigh and toss it to Mark, pulling a new one from the bag. "That's not necessary."

His shoulders sag, and he picks up the torn bread but merely plays with the edges. "Why do you insist on staying with them?" It comes out harsher than he usually is with anyone. "You don't have to keep doing this. There are better things you can be doing with your life. Other, more fulfilling, careers."

"I'm well aware of the other things I could be doing." I turn on a burner and slap one slice of bread on the skillet and lay a couple slices of cheese and meat on top. Two sandwiches fit in the pan, so I get the other one going too before I continue. "I choose not to do them."

"Why do you insist on not letting this go?"

"Why do you insist that I do?" I keep my back turned to avoid throwing him a nasty glare, hoping beyond reason that he'll drop this.

"It's dangerous." The sizzle of heating butter is the only sound, but I swear I can hear him mentally admonishing himself for that comment.

"I can handle it."

"You kill people, Ellie."

"And yesterday, it worked in your favor."

He pauses, long enough that I flip a sandwich and believe he finally gave up for the night. But he only switches tactics. "I saw your face when he told us how terrified he was."

The second sandwich falls off the spatula and hits the pan with the top slice crooked and cheese melting onto the cast iron. I scowl at it, fixing it with a fork. "I didn't make a face."

"You didn't have to." He's much calmer now. He thinks this will work. "You've never interfered with the Enforcers' business before. You've never had to face someone who survived and now has to live with that fear."

I scoop the finished sandwiches onto a plate and prepare the last two. What am I supposed to do? What can I possibly say that will make him understand? I say nothing.

Mark takes a shaky breath. "Please, Ellie."

But at that moment, Brandon walks in, taking the seat next to Mark, his hair damp. I grin at him and comment, "You certainly look better."

"I feel *much* better," he says, and Mark smiles at that too. "And I didn't realize how hard it would be to wash my hair one-handed." He says it with a laugh, but I note the way he rolls his damaged shoulder just a bit.

Wordlessly stepping away from the sandwiches, I retrieve an icepack from the freezer and toss it to him. He catches it with his good arm, surprised, but he smiles gratefully. He nods to the food, "What's this?"

"Thanksgiving dinner." I drop the last two sandwiches onto the plate and gesture to the miniature feast. "You only had deli slices in your fridge, so I did what I could."

"Would it be too much if I said this Thanksgiving, I'm thankful for you?"

"After you try this amazing grilled cheese, I'll expect it." I wink and turn away, but not before I catch the still tortured look in Mark's eye.

It would have been better if I'd remained a stranger to them. There was one Christmas after our parents' divorce that we got together as a family. One Christmas where they tried to make the shared custody agreement work for our sake. I was only five then, but I remember how terrified Mom was of Dad. She refused to let him near us the entire day, but she couldn't stop him from taking me home with him that night. She couldn't stop me from begging until I sobbed to go with him. It came down to me or the boys, and I don't blame her for the choice she was forced to make.

That was the last time I'd seen my brothers until five years ago. I wasn't there when Mom died. That didn't stop me from taking on her responsibility of protecting them when she no longer could. It's the least of what I owe her.

It was a misstep to reconnect with them, though. An error in judgment when I was most vulnerable. I tried to keep them in the dark, but I should have stayed the hell out of their lives. They were better off without me.

After dinner, when we're all spread out on the couches in front of a movie, I break the news that I'm leaving in the morning. Jake and Brandon give the standard reaction of "that's too bad" and "we'll miss you," but it's Mark who I watch. His face crumples. He can't win, and I won't even let him fight.

"Fine," he grumbles, getting up off the couch. He retreats into the kitchen.

I allow myself one glance back at him. He'll get over this. Eventually.

8

ELLIE'S CONFRONTATION

FOUR DAYS AFTER I'M BACK IN DC, I'M CALLED INTO HARTLEY'S OF-
fice. What Mark didn't know couldn't hurt him, but mere days after
he learned what I do, his best friend became a target. Am I supposed to
believe that's a coincidence? Because everything I've seen of Brandon
says he's perfect, a completely upstanding citizen.

Jaythan handed me a tiny device that looks like a beetle when I
asked him for help. If we want to find why this happened, we need
the company files, which are only available on two computers—Dad's
and Hartley's. And with my father's private—read: locked—office that
he rarely leaves—read: I never even saw him out of it when I *lived*
here—Hartley's computer became the clear winner. The man aided in
the birth of the corporation and even did most of the recruiting. The
selection of the recruits, that is—no one would have joined if he'd been
the one to approach them.

Forcing my facial muscles to relax so I don't cringe as I step into the ever-cluttered office, I squeeze past a stack of file boxes.

"Please, have a seat," Hartley tells me.

I walk around to the chair he's gesturing toward but stand in front of it instead. It requires Hartley to look up at me as I look down on him, which never fails to bring me pleasure—it's the little things.

The old man sighs but tilts his head back to meet my eyes. "We had a complication with one of our last missions." Despite the words coming out of his mouth, he watches me calmly. No accusation in his tone, and no loathing in his eyes. He's become skilled in hiding his hatred for me.

"Not mine, sir." I stand, back straight and hands clasped behind me. A proper soldier in his militia. "I've completed each one devoid of complications, sir."

"Not yours," he agrees, ignoring my theatrics. "But perhaps you know something. The target resided in Oregon. He was young. According to the Enforcer assigned to him, another Enforcer was present. He followed protocol; however, I authorized no such action to be taken." He's careful not to say Brandon's name. If it wasn't me, there's no need to alert me to the target's identity, and he's also hoping I'll slip up and say it. Which means he can suspect all he wants, but he has no way to confirm it was me.

"The proper action seems obvious, sir. If you wish it, I will fire him on my way out and get back to you with a list of suitable replacements."

His head tilts, beady eyes studying me. "There's no need for that." He frowns now. "Did you know about this?"

"How could I know, sir?"

"You have…personal interests in Oregon." He quirks a brow in challenge. "Perhaps you recognized the target and decided to do something to protect him."

I frown, teasing demeanor wobbling. "Was it someone I know, sir?"

Hartley hesitates, realizing his error…if I didn't already know exactly who he's talking about. "Did you interfere with the mission in Oregon?"

"Why would I do that, sir?"

He leans forward, resting his arms on his desk and peering at me over his thin-rimmed reading glasses. "Someone threw off the shot, and I *will* find out who."

"Once you do, sir, will you be sure to alert me? I'm dying of anticipation." I grin at my own pun. He does not share my amusement.

"If I find out you had any part in this, don't think your father can protect you. You will endure the same punishment as any other."

As if my father would care to protect me. But I say, "I wouldn't dream of it, sir."

I'm not worried. There's really no way for him to prove it. I didn't write it down. The only people who know are Mark because I told him face-to-face and Jaythan because he helped me cover it up, all our communication either in person or over phones he secured ages ago. Yes, I have connections in Oregon, but why should I care about a random target there? It's a big state.

Hartley knows about my family situation, of course. He was there when my parents separated. He's been the one keeping tabs on my brothers at my father's request—Dad's never done it himself. Hartley definitely knows Brandon has been living with my brothers for two years now. It's perfectly reasonable to believe I might interfere with something like that. But my past behavior only tells him I'll do anything and everything to get on Hartley's nerves, not that I would risk my father's wrath protecting someone else. The only way he can prove I interfered is if I tell him myself.

"You remember Lucile McKay."

It starts in my shoulders, then moves down to my torso and my legs until the icy chill has run the entire length of my body. Hartley says it as a fact. He knows I remember. Still, he waits. Long enough that I feel the ghost of my old wound in my thigh. Smell the faint odor of wood rot, mold, and dust.

"I thought you learned your lesson after her."

I don't let even a twitch of my face betray the tremors coursing through me at the mention of my second mission. My voice drops low. "Is that all, sir?"

He glares a second longer, then lowers his gaze, refocusing on the papers before him and waving me off.

Back in the hall, I breathe and pull out my phone. The signal in the corner is reading strong which means the bug is working. One of Jaythan's many inventions. Magnetized to the underside of Hartley's monitor, it should be the foot in the door that Jaythan needs to steal the files. And when we're done, I'll simply make sure to get called back into Hartley's office and reclaim it. For now, the bug only needs to stay hidden.

Jaythan lives as far away from society as he can get, so I'm driving deep into the woods before I reach his house. It's a miracle he gets any internet out here, but with all his tech, he gets better service than I do in the city.

I pull my car to a stop before the decrepit gate and lean out the window to press the intercom button. Before I can get a word out, a recording of Shrek yelling, "*What are you doing in my swamp?*" crackles over the speaker—he thinks he's funny. I press the button again. "Jaythan, it's me. Open up."

"*Are you at least going to make me waffles?*" He pronounces it "wha-ffles." It's classy, he tells me.

"You can't make them yourself?"

There's an audible sigh, then the gate buzzes and creaks open on its rusty hinges. Over the squealing, I hear Jaythan mutter, "*You could at least try to be a nice guest.*"

I ignore him, drive the remaining quarter mile, and park next to the rust bucket he calls a truck—if nothing else, the old red Dodge adds a pop of color to the droll browns of the estate. I'll never understand how that thing is able to start and reliably get him to the store and back once a month without breaking down six times in the process. He keeps telling me that's the point, but I can't say I understand how that's a proper response to my confusion.

Smoke leaks from under the door before I even step onto the porch. I let myself in, and the hum of the fog machine is all that greets me. He's covered all the windows in the main entry, so the only light comes from the open door behind me. With the added distortion of the smoke, his appearance in the hall off to my right is admirably villain-esque.

"Hello there." His voice is pitched low, and I can hear the smirk on his lips.

"Hey."

The silhouette of his shoulders slump, and his head rolls back. "That's not…" he sputters. "We've talked about this. Why do you make it so difficult?"

"It's the only thing that brings me joy," I deadpan. "Did it work?"

"Well, you totally ruined a perfectly cool greeting, and you seem ecstatic, so yeah, I'd say…"

I've learned to interrupt before he gets too far into his rants. "The bug, Jaythan."

"Oh." He flicks on the floor lamp beside him. Jaythan's a tall, burly man in his late twenties. He pays the bare minimum for electricity, enough that his computers work, but he heats the house with fires he builds from the wood he chops himself. He's embraced the lumberjack aesthetic, and even has a beard which he keeps close-shaved. He's quite fond of his facial hair and jokes about letting it grow out so he can be like Gandalf. My bet is he'll do it when he's old and the beard's white instead of dusty brown. He's wearing jeans and a flannel—you know, the typical "I live alone in the woods" garb. And he shares the bright blue eyes from my father's side of the family—though, unlike my father's, Jaythan's eyes have some life left in them.

"Yes." He puffs out his chest with pride. "Of course it works. I made it."

"Great. Have you started digging yet?"

"No, there's a whole bunch of security piled onto the system that I have to blow a hole in first."

"How long will that take?"

He inhales deeply. "This computer has all the information your dad's ever wanted to cover up. It has the names of everyone who's worked for him on anything, every assassin, every target, even every plumber. Getting access to the contents could ruin the entire operation. My stuff is built to avoid detection and provide a door for me, but it can't do everything. Basically, what I have now is equivalent to if I was sitting in front of the computer. I still need to unlock it and pull the documents myself, and they've got firewalls on firewalls on firewalls. Not to mention fail-safes and self-destruct buttons."

I raise a brow. "Self-destruct buttons?"

He nods, crossing his arms over his chest. "Every villain knows to put a self-destruct button somewhere in case they're caught."

"They're not villains." His shoulders drop again, and his expression blinks from playful to sympathetic, those eyes losing a bit of that life. My own expression hardens. I straighten. "Are you saying this will take you *months*?"

He steps back, hand going over his heart, playful attitude returning. "I'm…offended. I thought we were friends."

"How long, Jaythan?"

He sighs. "Okay, if I forgo sleep, I should be able to crack it in a little under a week." His lip curls, and he holds his hand out, tipping it back and forth. "Eh. Depending."

I nod. "Then do it."

"What's got you so stressed out?"

"I'm not stressed." I understand that even as I say it, my fists are clenched, my voice is tight, and my heart feels as if it's going to explode. I take a few deep breaths. Jaythan quirks a brow. "This guy is living with my brothers. If he turns out to be some delinquent, I'd like to know sooner rather than later." Though he seemed the farthest thing from a delinquent during my time with him.

"But we did that background check on him when he first moved in, right?"

"And look how well that turned out."

He bobs his chin, the brown curls on his head bouncing along. "Point taken. You know, I can do this myself. You can go back to Oregon and watch over things from there in case the Enforcers decide to move again."

I shake my head. "They won't." The Enforcers can't be tied to the shot in any way now. If they take Brandon out, it will be harder to see him as a bad guy no matter what story they release, especially with him being so young. He would have been shot not long before, so he'll be a victim and someone to point to as evidence that the Enforcers are slipping. My father has way too much pride to let that happen.

For now, there's always the fallback copycats. This incident will be tied to them, and the Enforcers will deny any knowledge of it. Brandon is safe. My brothers should be too. For now.

>>>>>>>

THAT NIGHT I DREAM OF LUCILE MCKAY.

Years ago, I mouthed off to Hartley in front of the rest of the assassins, and this was my punishment. At first, she looked like any other assignment, but Lucile McKay didn't exist. She was really Sierra Donovan but under witness protection which made her virtually impossible to target since guards watched her like hawks. Guards trained to sniff out Enforcers.

I rented a room on the top floor of the hotel. One of those dingy, rundown establishments that smells of mold and shouldn't be open anymore. So much dust, I was worried about choking to death before I could take the shot. But I set up at the window and waited.

Someone found me first. The butt of the rifle slammed hard into my skull, followed by a warm tingle of blood sliding down my face. I dropped my rifle but pulled free a knife.

A woman stood before me, swinging her rifle around to aim at my chest. I kicked it aside, sending the bullet into the floorboards. A flick of the wrist sent my blade into the meat of her shoulder. She didn't even scream.

She became just sloppy enough for me to grab the rifle and slam it into her gut. I cracked it against her skull next, sending her to her knees, but she came back with a pistol.

It was only a distraction.

I shoot up in a cold sweat and find myself alone in my empty room under the puffy blankets. My heart pounds against my ribcage, and I focus on breathing. In and out.

I make fun of Hartley, but he can still hurt me in ways I won't see coming if I go too far. Playing dumb doesn't get me suicidal missions, but publicly humiliating him had.

Jaythan covered my tracks. My tracker says I was home during Brandon's botched assassination. None of the security cameras from the mall will have caught me. I was trained to leave no tracks. There's no way for Hartley to know about my involvement.

Except for the bug I planted on his computer.

9

BRANDON'S LUCK

Mark is slumped on the couch in his sweats, a bright green and blue blanket wrapped loosely around his shoulders, and he's staring off into the corner, eating the rest of Ellie's folded chips. The TV sits dark before him, and there's no music playing. Just silence. He's been acting strange ever since Ellie left a couple days ago, and I barely get the chance to talk to him about it because my mom has been calling nonstop to make sure I haven't been shot again.

I can't blame her, really, but every phone call adds an extra weight to my chest. I didn't expect to have to force myself to go about my life as I normally did before, but I can't afford to skip classes for fear of getting shot again. Eventually, life will have to go back to normal. Sleep has been dreadful, and school is the only reprieve I have since my boss won't even let me come back into work for at least a week.

Mark doesn't even look up at me when he answers with a noncommittal "Mmhmm."

The dreary state of the room does not concur. I need something to do, so I take some blankets and fold them as best I can with one human arm and one T-rex arm, then set them back on the couches—our closets have long been overrun. Mark pays me no mind.

He's been down since the last night of Ellie's visit. After she told us she'd be leaving, Mark got up and went to the kitchen for a few minutes, looking a little annoyed. When he came back, though, he wrapped his arm around her, and she rested her head on his shoulder throughout the rest of the night. It was sweet and confusing. But I guess that's siblings for you.

My sister and I have never been very close. We love each other and get together on holidays, but she's nine years older than me. We didn't spend much time together growing up. By the time I was old enough to want to spend all day outside, she was old enough to want to spend all day with her friends or in her room. I started first grade; she got her license. I got my learner's permit; she got a job at a law firm. I went to college; she got married.

The thing that gets me is that Mark's parents had such a bad split that Mark hadn't seen Ellie for eleven years before she showed up again out of the blue, and they're much closer than I've ever been with my sister who I *did* grow up with mostly.

I take a seat next to him, and he finally looks at me. "Don't you have a doctor's appointment?" he asks.

"Eventually." I shrug my good shoulder. "Tell me what's bothering you. You've been all gloomy since Ellie left. You know she'll visit again."

He nods, glancing away. "I know."

"What's wrong, Mark?"

He shakes his head, pulls at the loose neckline of his t-shirt. "Just…" He takes a breath. "I don't think there's any way I can win a really important argument with her."

I nod, trying to understand what kind of argument it could be. From the state of melancholy, I'm guessing not the sort that has to do with *Star Wars*. I come up empty, so I try to think of something to say that vaguely applies.

"I'm sorry." It's lame, but it's at least something. I'm at a complete loss for anything that won't make me sound like an idiot feeling around for the right words. Instead, I shut my mouth and put my hand on his shoulder. It seems like something I should do in the moment, but it just feels awkward.

He smirks at the gesture, though. "Thanks. Hey, so was this visit better? You seemed more comfortable with her."

I cringe. This is the other thing that's been haunting my thoughts. "Um." He gives me a wary side-eye, and my stomach roils. "I might have done something stupid."

Mark blinks. "Wait, you didn't…" He turns himself fully to me. "Did you kiss her?"

I nearly choke on my next breath. "What?"

He smiles, then it morphs into a frown. "*Did* you kiss her?" He glances at the window where the rain knocks. "I'm not sure how to feel about that. Just give it to me straight. Are you two together now?"

"What? Mark, stop. No, that's not it."

"Oh." He blinks. "Okay. Good. I mean, no offense, but she'd ruin you. On the other hand, you might be really good for her." His fingers come up to his chin to stroke an invisible beard as if he was the flamboyant villain in a cheesy action movie. "Hmm. Now I'm wishing you *had* kissed her."

"Okay, Mark, stop. You're so weird. I didn't kiss your sister, and I don't want to." Not true. I catch myself thinking about it much too often, but he does not need to know that because I will never act on it. I squint at his slight deflation. "I meant I might have *said* something really stupid." Mark nods, scrunching his nose and adjusting to the new situation. "So, you remember when I was shot?"

"Vaguely. Shoulder, right?"

"Well, she was there right when it happened. The thing is, I was in shock. I don't know; it had a really weird effect on me where I was half-conscious. It was like I knew what was happening, but I didn't. Or, like I couldn't keep my thoughts inside my head. They just all came spilling out."

"That's weird. I don't think that's what's supposed to happen."

"Excuse me, were *you* shot?"

He nods again. "Fair point. Continue. What were your thoughts about?"

"Um…" *Rip off the Band-Aid. It's going to cause you anxiety either way, might as well take away the stress of him finding out himself.* "I might have told her that I really like her and think she's a really good person."

He blinks once. "You told her you think she's a really good person?"

"Y—yeah." I shake my head. Not what I expected him to get stuck on, but I'm not done yet. "I also might have told her that when I saw her at the airport, I had thought it was like being shot."

"Seeing her made you feel like you were shot?" He frowns.

"Well, she grinned at me."

"Is that supposed to make *more* sense?"

"Wha—I don't know! I was half out of my mind. I'd just been shot!" He's laughing at me now, which is somewhat unhelpful. "I don't know what to do. Should I talk to her about it? Apologize?"

"What did she say?"

I blow out a breath. Maybe that bullet should have killed me. I keep the flinch off my face. "She didn't say anything." For a second, I wish she had. But then I'm glad I avoided that conversation. But then I also know I have to talk to her about it. It was way too awkward to leave alone.

Mark's head tilts slightly. "She just ignored it?" I pause then nod once. Mark shrugs. "Then I think you're off the hook. I doubt it bothered her at all."

"You're saying I just forget it? I think it'll still be really awkward."

"Then call her."

That flinch is harder to hide. "That would make it so much worse."

"Ah." He pats my arm. "You're overthinking this. You *do* really like her."

That felt like being shot. I jump way too fast into denial. "No! No. I don't. I mean, she's nice and all, but—"

"Take a breath, man." Mark grins, snorting. "I'm messing with you. You've got your checkup today, right?"

I should be relieved by the subject change, but this shift just puts a nasty gray cloud over me to match the ones sobbing outside.

〉〉〉〉〉〉

MARK DRIVES ME TO MY APPOINTMENT AND IS ALLOWED IN THE TINY room with me. I'm seated on the exam table while the nurse prods at my shoulder where she's taken off the bandaging. After only a few days, the skin around the wound is practically as white as Mark.

"Everything is looking great, Brandon," the nurse tells me. "No infection. Closing up nicely. We can take the sling off, but you still need to rest your shoulder. Give it time to heal itself. It should be good as new in a few weeks. You were lucky."

I huff. "Right." It comes out more bitter than I mean it to, but I'm so tired of hearing that. There's a buzz in my pocket. I don't have to look to know it's my mom again. My gut twists. I'll have to call her back in a few minutes so she doesn't think I'm dead. "Except that I was shot." I know it could have been worse, and I *am* lucky it was just flesh and muscle that got hit. But what about the fact that someone shot me? People seem to forget someone actually did this to me.

I suppose in a way she's right. When I talked to the receptionist about the bill, worrying if my insurance covers assassination attempts, she informed me that someone had already taken care of it. In cash. They didn't leave a name. I haven't been able to decide whether this was an act of kindness or something possibly very twisted. After all, I have many admirers in the media now after one reporter tracked me down at the airport when we dropped Ellie off.

My mom keeps telling me to go to the police. Even if they can't help, it might settle my nerves a bit to do so. I haven't. They already asked me their questions and examined the scene. There's nothing more they can do.

I called my brother-in-law instead, Wyatt. He's like the big brother I always wanted. Lately, though, it's been strained between us. I try not to blame him, but it's hard knowing what caused that bullet to tear through my shoulder and being unable to tell anyone. I refuse to bring the police into this. I couldn't do that to him, and I definitely couldn't do that to my mom.

"Well, at least you can rule out Enforcers." The nurse tapes new gauze down.

Mark's head snaps up. "What? Why would you say that?"

"Well." The nurse squints suspiciously at Mark, but then her shoulders curve in. "An Enforcer wouldn't have missed. Sorry. That sounded more encouraging in my head."

Mark absentmindedly nods and looks back at his phone, tapping away at it furiously.

"Who are you texting?" I ask. He's rarely ever zeroed so far into his phone. He's like an old man, happy to go through life with an old phone that he only uses for calling and texting. Only two games: solitaire and sudoku. No social media. It's respectable. But this level of focus is unheard of.

"Hmm?" He looks up at me. "Oh, no one. It's nothing." He runs a hand through his hair, skewing the golden curls. "Um, is he good to go then, Lacey?"

"Yes." The nurse smiles, finishing wrapping my shoulder tight and patting her work. "Good as new. Well…almost. As per our governor's orders, after an injury like this being at your place of work, you can't go back for at least a couple more days. More if you feel it necessary."

I pull my shirt back on. "It didn't happen at work. It was outside of work."

"Four steps outside, right?"

I scowl. It's no use arguing. My boss won't let me go back for at least the next four days anyway. If anyone were to report it to the authorities, both he and I could be fined a handsome amount that I wouldn't be able to pay off for years.

I need the money, but what does that matter to the government? What does anybody care? A week when I'm not able to work on top of the days I already can't work because of school takes that much off my ability to pay rent. Mark and Jake were kind enough that they told me not to worry about it this month, but I don't want to be *that* roommate.

Nevertheless, hours later they find me on the couch, the TV playing quietly in the background as I pore over the textbooks in front of me.

10

JAKE'S MEETING

I FEEL BAD FOR BRANDON. I REALLY DO. HE'S A NICE GUY, SO I HAVE no problem covering his rent with Mark this month. If it means Mark is too busy doting over him and being his mother rather than mine, I'd gladly pay the man's rent every month. Even so, being stuck in the apartment with the two of them—Mark *still* sulking because of Ellie leaving a week ago and Brandon trying to hide the fact that he's still dealing with the psychological repercussions of getting shot—is stifling to even think about. Instead, I'm at the bar with all my textbooks. Something about the numerous distractions tends to sharpen my focus.

I'm hunched at a table in the corner, going over statistics. I'd prefer to sit alone, but one girl has been persistent about forcing me into a one-sided conversation. She sat down maybe thirty minutes ago and has yet to take a breath. She hasn't even noticed I've not been participating.

"My sister's sweet and all, but she just doesn't understand relation-ships. I mean, you should see the guy she's with now. He's all wrong for her. He doesn't even pay attention to her." *Ironic.* She speaks over my concentration on conditional probability, so I close my book too dramatically, rest my elbow on the table, and *really* look at her. The act completely shocks her into silence.

She's not unattractive. Blond highlights in dark hair that flows wavily past her collarbone. Brown eyes, thin lips, straight teeth. I'm about to just tell her I'm not interested when something catches my eye over her shoulder. A flash of red.

It's that girl again. Chelsea. Her auburn hair is bound in a high ponytail that still manages to cascade over her shoulder. She saunters up to the bar confidently and oblivious to my presence. I stand up, ignoring the talker and making my way to Chelsea. With any luck, Miss Cathy will take the hint.

Chelsea spots me just as I lean beside her and offer her my most dashing smirk. She smiles very little, then bites her lip and turns away. A shy one. I grin wider. In the light of the bar, her freckles are more visible across her nose and cheeks. I'm tempted to lean closer.

"Well, well, if it isn't Chelsea."

"If it isn't the man with the lines." She smirks at me, forest-green eyes glinting with a hint of mischief.

I thump my chest. "Don't remember me as I was. Get to know who I am."

That slender red brow rises in a graceful arc. "Another line. I shouldn't be surprised."

"Now, now, I chose that cheesy bastard just for you." I wink. "I've got more if you stick around to hear them."

She shakes her head, pursing her lips to hide her smile. Her hair slips off her shoulder with the movement, drawing my gaze. "You're the one who never called."

I cringe. "You're right. Can I use the excuse that my friend just got shot and my sister left town in that time?"

She turns, mirroring my posture in leaning against the bar—am I imagining that she's moved closer? —and tactfully juts out her chin. "Oh, see the last time we spoke, you claimed he wasn't your friend. You're changing your story on me now." I would think she was mad if not for the little smile playing on the corner of her lips that keeps twitching to life.

I hum. "I need more practice. Teach me?"

She tilts her head. "Oh, I can't. It's an inherent skill." She glances back at the bartender who's on his way with her drink. "Unattainable."

"I seem to be out of luck." Her grin is almost ferocious when she turns back to me, a tall glass of some red drink in her hand now. "I have a table in the back." I nod to the table strewn with my textbooks and am relieved to see that Chatty Cathy has left. "Would you care to join me?"

Chelsea sighs dramatically. "I suppose if you won't leave me alone." I grin and follow her back to the table where she pulls one of my history texts close. I watch her face as she scans the text. Her smile grows as her eyes glide across the page. "This looks fascinating."

Now I laugh. "Yeah, right." The chair groans when I lean back, and I wonder if I might have the bad luck of it collapsing on me right in front of Chelsea. "So, English major. Do you want to teach or something?"

She throws her head back. "Everyone always asks that. You know, there's more to do with an English degree than just teaching."

I squint. "So…not teaching?"

"No, I plan on teaching." A new grin spreads across her face. "I just wanted to see your reaction. See if you had any other ideas for the degree." She quirks a brow and sips her drink. Oh, how I envy that glass. "But you were pretty useless."

I shrug. "It's what I'm best at."

She smiles, then runs her finger along the glass's rim before asking, "What do you plan to do with a business degree?" She nudges me playfully with her shoulder. "Either of your parents have a business you can take over?"

"No, actually my mom…" *Nope. Abort.* Not gonna throw that wrench into this conversation. I swallow down the lump. "I've actually not talked to my dad in sixteen years, so I don't know what he's got going on." Why did I mention how long it's been? *Idiot.*

"Oh?"

She clearly wants more, but that's definitely not going to help the situation. "He left when I was young, and we didn't stay in touch. Pretty sure he has some sort of business, but I've got no idea what it is—and he probably wouldn't be giving it over to me anyway." There, that's enough for her to be satisfied and move on.

She pouts her lip. What would she do if I leaned closer and nipped at it? "That's a shame. I think you'd be pretty great at it."

I decide to ignore the knowing look behind that statement and shrug instead. "Sure, why not?"

"Do you ever want to get back in touch with him, though? Do you even remember anything about him?" I open my mouth to say it doesn't matter, but she keeps going. "Wouldn't you like to?"

I blow out a breath, glance back down at her mouth, come to a decision, and shake my head. *Not worth it.* "I actually should get back to studying. Finals coming up."

"Oh." She frowns, then scoots her chair closer. I try not to interpret anything from it. But then she rests her hand on my arm, and my eyebrow shoots up. "Really?"

"Well." I shrug, turn away from her, take a drink. That decision was stupid anyway. "I guess that could wait a little bit." When I turn back, I yank her chair right up against mine and plant my lips on hers. She squeals happily and meets me stroke for stroke. Her mouth is soft under mine, and her fingers tug greedily at my hair. But a couple minutes into kissing her, her phone buzzes in her back pocket.

She answers with an apologetic look that extends until after she hangs up. "I'm sorry, I have to go."

"What?" I frown.

"Sorry." She rubs my arm, stands. "What if we meet up for dinner sometime?"

"Y—yeah." I nod. "Um, I guess I'll text you?"

She smiles one last time and leaves me alone in the bar.

I attempt to go back to studying, but my mind keeps wandering back to our conversation, of all things. Specifically, my father. I might be going insane. I was just sitting with a beautiful woman—correction: *making out* with a beautiful new woman—and I'm thinking about my father?

Why *did* I decide to be a business major? It's not what I wanted to do with my life, but it was an easy choice. I barely paid a thought to my decision. It seemed smart after high school. I was trying to prove my own capacity for intelligent decision making to Mark, I think, after our mom died. To myself also, probably.

What I wanted wasn't stable. It was too risky, and ultimately, I decided against it. Instead, I went for a much safer option: business. But I never thought about taking over my parents'. Mom didn't have a business. She was a teacher up until…

But my father has one. I meant what I said to Chelsea. I've got no idea what he does. I never much cared, but perhaps that could lead to a career after college.

I sit back, forgetting my studies. Mark never speaks of our father. I get the impression he's not fond of the man, but he's never told me why. I never bothered to ask.

Maybe I should.

11

ELLIE'S MISSION

IT'S BEEN SIX DAYS, AND HARTLEY HASN'T FOUND THE BUG YET. BUT even Jaythan's tech can't stay hidden forever. Especially not from the Enforcers who quite literally run on secrets. A twenty-nine-year-old nerd cannot outsmart a whole team of men who built the system to withstand even the government's interference.

I'm retrieving the bug today. Jaythan's been downloading as much as he can, and we'll file through it all once he decrypts it. However, from what we've seen so far, there's nothing on Brandon that could make him a target. He's like any other student—fighting debt and sleeping in his free time. Damning stuff.

Seriously, this guy is so squeaky clean, he doesn't even have a speeding ticket. It's so confusingly frustrating, yet also comforting since he's living with my brothers. But he was still a target. There must be something we're missing. There has to be. I can only hope Jaythan got enough because Hartley summoned me again, and there's no way I'm waiting for the *next* time to cover my tracks.

I enter the tiny, cluttered space on high alert. Hartley's behind his desk, scribbling away at the papers in front of him. He doesn't even look up at me. I stop in front of his desk without taking a seat. He doesn't offer this time. Silence stretches while I wait for him to address me. He doesn't.

"You wanted to see me, sir?"

"Not me." He still doesn't bother to look up, making it clear he wants me here even less than I want to be here. "I'm supposed to bring you to your father."

My gut clenches, and it takes more effort than it should to keep my expression neutral. It feels like I was just clubbed over the head and told to walk straight. I notice my more labored breaths, so Hartley must too. He doesn't mention it.

"My father?" It's stupid to ask, but it's been a long time since I actually saw him. As the Enforcers grew, he faded further and further into the shadows. As *I* grew, I distanced myself further and further from him. I hear from him sometimes. He'll write letters to me as if we live states away, and that's only to update me on important things going on with the Enforcers, things he wants me to keep an eye on and report back to him. I keep my responses brief.

The last time I was face-to-face with my father was just after Mom died. The fact that he wants to see me now makes me want to hurl, cackle, cry, jump off a *cliff*. So I ask, "Why?"

"You think he tells me that?" Hartley finishes whatever he's working on and stands. He's about to take me out of the room. I need the bug. I reach for its hiding place...

It's not there.

I feel around some more, but…nothing. Finally, Hartley looks at me, so I'm forced to pull my hand back, heart beating a tad too fast in my chest.

"Let's go." He sounds bored, leading me out down a hallway I've avoided for five years. But obediently, I follow.

It can really only mean one thing, right? Dad wants to see me, and there's no bug to retrieve. They must have found it. *Of course they found it.* They're not stupid! Jaythan's plan didn't work. They would have cut off the bug's connection immediately upon discovery. When did they find it? We didn't get what we needed.

All too soon, we're standing before a door that I used to see a lot. It's unnaturally taller than any other door in the building and the only one that isn't glass. There's nothing else special about it; no design, no color. Just a giant, intimidating slab of wood.

When Dad was still making an effort, he summoned me here to tell me how great I was doing and also how I could improve. Naive child that I was, I thought it was a good thing. It's a big reason why I never quit. That all stopped after my second assignment.

Hartley hovers behind me, so I step up to the door and land a tentative knock on the solid surface. It sounds too loud to my ears. The answering "come in" is immediate.

Dad's gotten old over the past five years. His once dark hair with flecks of gray has gone entirely gray now. He let his beard grow out; the tight curls hug his chin. The wrinkles in his forehead are more defined, but he looks as fit as ever. He's avoided the saggy muscles for now, but his pasty skin makes his overall appearance like that of a ghost. He silently makes the same assessments of me. I wait for him to speak first.

"You look well."

I nod. "So do you." We stare at each other for a few moments. I can't tell if he's at a loss for words or just wants me to speak now. I've pushed him a few times before to speak first. Now, I know I can't handle the anticipation because whatever this is…I need to know…now. "You wanted to see me?"

His eyes flick lazily to Hartley. "Leave us." His order is low and rattles the walls—no, that's the nerves talking.

I only know Hartley obeys by the click of the door closing behind me. I don't dare take my eyes off my father. His office is much larger than Hartley's, able to fit multiple filing cabinets, a few safes, two full bookshelves, and his large desk where he taps his fingers in a steady rhythm that sets my pulse pounding.

He pulls something from a drawer and sets it atop the desk. I need only a second seeing the tiny black bead to know. *That's the bug.* I hold my breath and school my expression. "This was found on Hartley's computer. Why did you put it there?"

I blink. "I…I don't know what you're talking about."

"Don't waste my time, Emily."

My jaw clenches. When Mark used my birth name upon our reconnection, it was the first time I'd heard it in eleven years. It threw me. I wasn't used to people knowing that name, let alone using it. I'd been *Emily Richards* for years. Even to my father. Nothing's changed.

"The last target survived." He looks down at the bug in disappointment before training all that on me. I hate how it stings. "Hartley suspects you, but I know. The target was Brandon Harwood. The boy living with your brothers."

Your brothers. Not his sons.

"Tell me," he orders.

I straighten, swallowing. There's no point in denying it. He knows I reconnected with them. Despite my precautions, he probably knows I'm in Oregon most the time too. I won't confirm anything, but denying it won't help me either. "Pretty sure you already know what you need."

"Why did you bug Hartley's computer?" I stare back into his lifeless blue eyes, wondering how a man who once had a loving wife and three kids turned into this. He sighs. "Emily, I am being very patient with you right now. Do you know how many other Enforcers would have bugged Hartley's computer and not immediately been fired?" *Fired*, as if this really is a normal business. "But I know for you this one was a bit too close for comfort."

Understatement. He still sees me as a child who has yet to learn how the world works. "Why was Brandon a target?" I blurt.

"We're Enforcers, Emily." Because I needed to be reminded. "Our job is to enforce the will of our superiors."

"Who are…?"

"You ask too many questions." He places the bug in my palm, his hands damn soft despite claiming to be one of us. "Take this and remember if I find another one anywhere near this building, the consequences will not only fall on you but that cousin of yours as well."

I swallow again. I just need to walk back out that door and then everything will be fine. We'll figure something else out. "Of course, sir. It won't happen again." I turn to leave, but he stands.

"One more thing, Emily." My stomach drops. He holds out a folder. "Your next target."

My hands shake as I take it from him. I hold my breath to keep from screaming when I see the name on the side. It's hopeless to try and hide my panic now, but I do anyway. I clear my throat to jolt my breathing into submission.

"Problem?" His brow is raised, and there's almost the ghost of a smile on his lips. I could have gone the rest of my life without seeing that expression on his face.

Deep breath. I make my voice as steady as possible, replying coldly, "Not at all."

He nods, pleased, and not at all the father who just handed his daughter the job of killing her brother.

12

JAKE'S CONVERSATION

Brandon's gone back to work which means I no longer have to hear about the people whose plane crashed on a weird island anymore. To be fair to him, the show was really the only interesting thing he had going on for almost two weeks besides all his tests coming up. Just last night, he was upset because his favorite character died. Getting back to work was the best thing for him, and the best thing for me because wow, that man needs something to do besides sit around and study all day.

With him gone, it's just Mark and I in the apartment as my brother doesn't have a shift at the hospital until tonight. It's a situation that historically only has two outcomes: fighting or silence. Today's certainly won't be silence. Mark is standing at the counter, hovering over a bowl of Cocoa Krispies—for context, it's noon. But that sounds pretty good, so I pour myself a bowl too.

"Got any plans for tomorrow?" Mark slides the milk across the counter to me. I nod my thanks. "Brandon and I would love for you to join us."

I catch his cringe when I huff a laugh. "Church again?" Mark is annoying, but at least he's predictable. "When are you going to give that up?"

"You don't have to sing or anything," he bargains. I mix the cereal around a bit, waiting for the milk to get chocolatey. "You don't even have to pay attention. Just come with us. Sit with us. We'll do lunch after."

Another laugh as I bring the spoon to my mouth. Cereal for lunch is criminally underrated. "You know what you need?" He grips the countertop a little tighter, and I force myself not to bite his head off. "You need to loosen up. Get a girlfriend or something."

He blinks. I've told him before to get his own life. It's always been out of anger, but now I don't want to fight. I'm tired of the tension between us whenever one of us opens our mouth. Besides, if he were to have something to keep him in his own lane, he might stop pushing over into mine.

He takes the olive branch and shrugs. "Girls can't handle me."

My brow quirks. "You mean, *you* can't handle *girls*." Mark frowns, but then I grin at him. "Come on, you haven't even tried dating. You might like it."

That's not entirely accurate. He dated a little before Mom passed. It never went well. He came home from each one a nervous wreck, and it would take hours for him to calm down. Then after Mom, he decided it was his job to raise me. He hasn't been on a date in well over five years, and his only real friend is Brandon. He cut out his social life for me, and I still resent him for it.

He chuckles halfheartedly. "Yeah maybe." His phone beeps then.

"Oh, could that be a girl now?" I lean forward, careful not to slosh the too-full liquid contents out of my bowl.

"No." He shakes his head, reading the text. "Just Ellie." I only have time to squint. "She's coming back."

Something tightens in my gut. "Why?" I love her, but it's only been a week and a half. Could something be wrong? It's not like she'd tell us. I know her life can't be perfect, and she's definitely had her fair share of difficulties, but I like to believe she's been lucky. That she's made a life for herself, and it's going well.

"She didn't say." He turns his phone over in his hand as if the answer is on his four-year-old R2-D2 case that's chipped in the top corner. "Maybe she misses us already."

I shake off the worry. It's probably nothing, anyway. Then I snap my fingers and point at him, trying to hold onto the ease between us. "Maybe she's taken a liking to Brandon."

His eyebrows come together like a released bungee cord. "What?"

"She spent a lot more time with him than usual. She was with him when he was shot. You know, trauma bonding and all that. And you can't have missed their interaction in the back of your car when we brought Brandon back from the hospital." A wicked grin slashes across my face. I like to think I'm pretty good at picking up those kinds of signals. "There's something there, I'm sure of it."

He shakes his head with a scoff but smiles. "You're ridiculous."

"Ellie works for Dad, doesn't she?"

Mark's gaze snaps up from his phone. I lift a brow and try not to let it irritate me. "What?"

"Well, look," *Keep it light.* "I just want to get some options out there. I'll need to do something with this degree after graduation."

"And you want to work for Dad?" His face drains of color.

"It would be nice to know what he does first," I say slowly, "but it could be an interesting area to explore, right? I know he and Mom didn't have a clean split, but he's still our dad. It could be good to reconnect."

Mark shakes his head. "That's not a good idea."

I set down my bowl harder than I mean to, and some of the chocolate milk splashes out. "Why not?"

"It's just…not." His hands start trembling—*trembling.* He grips his spoon like a lifeline, and that infuriates me. "Please, Jake, stay away from him. He's bad news. Trust me."

I roll my eyes with a humorless laugh. My willingness to keep it light vanishes the moment those words leave his mouth. *Trust* him. "You're not going to tell me anything about him?"

Mark's eyes widen, and his chest concaves. "Why do you want to know so bad? It doesn't matter."

"Maybe it does," I snap. "He's my dad too. I have a right to know things about him."

"Just trust—"

I cut him off before he can finish that sentence, slamming my spoon down into my bowl. More milk splashes over the sides, but I ignore it. "Trust goes both ways, Mark. Let me know when you've figured that out." With that, I take my cereal and lock myself in my room. If he won't tell me, I'll have to find out some other way.

13

ELLIE'S TRIP

PLANNED ON CUTTING MY BROTHERS OUT OF MY LIFE AGAIN. I planned on never seeing them again—except at a distance where I could watch out for them. I planned on Dad never sinking this low. I planned on a lot, apparently, and it got me here, hastily packing up my apartment to go back to Oregon.

More guns, more ammo, more knives. My apartment is practically gutted. The closet I stored all my weapons in now only has a few of the larger firearms and some knives. Anything that can help me stop this is coming with me. I haven't given myself even a second to think through what happens next. All I can think is that this absolutely cannot happen.

When I went last for Brandon's sake, I knew I couldn't stay. I was ready to run if I got an assignment to keep my father's suspicions at bay. This time, I leave the phone he'd try to contact me with in pieces on the kitchen floor. He knows I'll never go through with this, and maybe it's only a test.

Or maybe he really does want his son dead and will send another assassin to finish the job. Either way, I have nothing keeping me in DC now.

I also found the lump where the tracker has been buried in my neck since I was four. With only a small incision, I pulled it free. For good measure, it bursts under the heel of my boot next to the phone.

For forty-eight hours I've been tearing my brain apart to figure out my father's angle. Why the hell would he do this? It doesn't make any sense. Is it punishment for my bugging Hartley's computer? Would he have his son killed over that? He also determined that I'm the one who interfered with Brandon's assassination. *That's still so excessive!*

Whatever the reason, it's not going to happen. He's clearly unstable, and I can't work for him anymore. It's not much of a decision. I guess Mark gets his wish after all.

The snow has gotten worse the further we creep into December, but I still brave the mountain to see Jaythan. He, as usual, is tapping away at his keyboard in the big empty house.

"Have you found anything yet?" I dread the answer but need to know. If no, then we're still at square one when it comes to finding anything on Brandon. If yes, that means my brothers are living with someone who's going to get them killed. If yes, it might tell me why my father is doing this.

"I've dug down into the deepest trenches of this guy's life." My heart sinks. There's only one way for that sentence to end.

I slam my fist down on his desk, and he jumps. "Keep looking. There must be *something*, Jaythan."

He's shaking his head, though. "Well, if there is, it's extremely well hidden."

"If my father wants him dead, there's a reason for it. They would have released it in a statement after anyway, so find it."

"Hey, calm down." He reaches out a hand but wisely rethinks that move. "What's got you so worked up? What happened? Did you get the bug back?"

I chuck it on his desk where it bounces off the bottom corner of his screen. Jaythan winces but—again, wisely—says nothing. "Widen your search to include Mark."

He blinks. "Mark? *Your* Mark? Your brother, Mark?" With every question, his eyes grow wider until I can see the whites all the way around them.

"Yes." It comes out as more of a growl, but I'm trying so hard not to snap at him again.

"What happened, E?"

I release a harsh breath and turn my back on him. "Do it. I have a plane to catch." I slam the door behind me, knowing it's childish. My hands are shaking. I can't get them to stop.

»»»»»

THE FLIGHT IS HORRIBLE. I SAVED SOME MONEY BY FLYING COACH SINCE I'll be cut off soon, and the seats press so close together that I can't keep from brushing the thigh of the girl next to me. Stewardesses go up and down the aisle, passing out tasteless cookies and drinks. I tuck the cookies into my pocket—Jake will like them.

Fighting back nausea in an aisle seat next to two passengers who won't stop yammering on about nothing is not how I wanted to spend my day. The tiny one by the window practically glows in the light reflecting off the clouds while her friend next to me is heavier, reminding me of Mark and the paunch he owns with pride. I'm going to throw up. I force myself to focus on her hat—cowgirl style and purple. *Who wears a hat on a plane?*

"You know," Cowgirl says to her vampire friend, "it could have been one of those situations where a woman was ordered to fire on her lover. Of course she missed! She loves him!"

"But why would she shoot in the first place?"

"Because it's her duty."

I nearly scoff. What is duty but orders we're too afraid to ignore? I used to think that if I did my job, my brothers would be safe. My father would ignore them because I did what he wanted of me. Oh, how naive that was.

These women have been throwing out ideas about the circumstances of Brandon's injury for an hour now. I knew getting on a plane to the very region in which it happened meant everyone and their mom would be talking about it since his "story" found popularity on gossip sites.

One in particular, *Buzz 'Em.* The reporter, Sarah Michaels, actually ran down Brandon in the airport when he and my brothers dropped me off after Thanksgiving. She bombarded him with questions before he even had a chance to acknowledge her, claiming her article was on "public safety and how to better prepare for unusual situations." All that meant was she could ask questions like, "*Did you suspect anything like this would ever happen to you? Did anything tip you off? Do you have any enemies?*" and it would be appropriate.

I stepped in when it was clear Brandon was uncomfortable. She took my referring to her site as *Bosom* as only a minor blow to her confidence.

She left as soon as I threatened to call it harassment, but not before she handed me her business card if we ever felt like talking.

Sarah Michaels published her version of the story, and it spiraled from there. In just two weeks, theories have sprung up everywhere. Jaythan keeps tabs on them all, but no one else bothered Brandon about any of it. The press is perfectly content to make up their own version of events.

I had just hoped life would be kind enough to put me next to people who sleep on long flights. Perhaps this is to be my penance.

The two passengers sitting next to me consistently assume that it was the Enforcers. They've been tossing out romantic theories like schoolgirls, even though they're probably a few years older than me. At their next theory about a lovers' spat, I've had enough.

"It wasn't the Enforcers," I mumble.

The vampire hears me and leans around the cowgirl. "What was that?"

"It wasn't the Enforcers." I rub my temple.

"Why do you say that?" This, from Cowgirl.

I cast a scathing look at the hat before answering. "Assassins don't miss."

She scrunches her face, irritated at my raining on her parade. "But you don't know the circumstances."

"Do you know how far an assassin gets if they have personal attachments?" All the muscles in my body are tense. "They can't have anyone they care about because it makes the job so much harder. They have to give all that up."

Her thick dark brows furrow. "I think you're wrong. I think some people could have been forced into the job to protect the people they love."

I clench my fists, nails carving half-moons into my sore palms. "That's a very romantic way of looking at it."

Cowgirl shrugs. "Well, I don't think many people would actually choose that life. At least, I like to think so."

I breathe heavily, my head going light. I don't know what makes me continue to cover for my father. The cowgirl's talk of *duty* floats through my mind as I say, "Then let me ask you this. The man who was shot. If it was the Enforcers, what's kept him alive since?"

She doesn't have a response for that. Their conversation continues, but now in a whisper that I can barely hear over the roar of the plane. I shut my eyes and try to sleep for the few hours I have left on this flight.

14

JAKE'S DISCOVERY

MARK RUSHED US ALL OUT OF THE APARTMENT A GOOD HOUR BE-fore we really had to leave. I can't figure out if we all planned on coming to pick Ellie up together or if we kind of just…let it happen. None of us had other plans. I'm sure we could all be studying, but the three of us are at the airport anyway.

I'm anxious to see Ellie again. Having had time to think about my approach, the only way I might get information on Dad is through her. It will always inevitably end in a fight with Mark, and he's stubborn when he wants to be. But Ellie's grown up with the man; she's bound to have some stories she can tell. My plan is to tug at her sentimentality. I feel terrible about it, but I'm quickly running out of options. It's not fair that they get to know our father, and I don't.

"Are you okay?" I nod to Mark's raw hands strangling each other in his lap.

He looks down to find them indeed much paler than normal. "No, I'm fine." He nods, but even Brandon doesn't buy that. "I'm fine! Just… airports make me nervous."

"Well, she just landed, so we'll be out of here soon." Brandon slaps Mark's shoulder.

We've been sitting across from baggage claim for an hour already, and it's another half hour before she makes an appearance. Flocks of people crowd around the carousel, waiting for their luggage to be released. I stand and take the lead through the sea of humans because Mark and Brandon are too polite to shove their way through.

Finally, I spot her coming around the corner. Her hair is frizzy in its braid, her pace rushed, and her expression is tight. When she spots us, she gives a thin-lipped smile before her lips part like she'll say something even though she's too far away for us to hear. There's an oily feeling in my gut as I realize something *is* wrong.

She speeds up, reaching us and immediately throwing her arms around Mark's neck. He rocks back a step, then his arms come around her, and he rubs her back. "Hey, are you okay?"

I step up beside her and grab her shoulder. "Everything okay, Ellie?"

She lets go of Mark, smiles, and turns a hug on me. "Yeah, of course. Just happy to see you guys." The lying in this family today is subpar. She smirks at Brandon—nonchalance making an appearance. To my surprise, she gives him a side hug. "How's your shoulder?"

"Practically good as new. I'm slowly working it back up."

She smiles, and it's not so forced this time. I can feel the tiny sting of sparks from here. "Glad to hear it."

At the carousel, we pick up two large suitcases. Brandon gets one while I take the other. Hauling it off the moving surface is a feat. Thankfully, it has wheels, but I do note that she's brought two suitcases instead of her usual one. Should that make me more concerned for her?

Brandon had the good sense to take a picture of where we parked, and he and Ellie share a knowing look. I toss a raised brow Mark's way, and some of the tension leaves my brother as he rolls his eyes.

A split second after Mark pulls the keys from his pocket, Ellie snatches them. "I'll drive. Mark, you can sit in the back with Jake."

"Why do you assume I'm riding in the back?" I put on an offended front even as I reach for the handle to the back door.

She gives me a playful smile. "You're too young to sit up front."

I gape at her and scoff. *Offense taken.* "I'm two minutes older than you."

She smirks, pats my cheek, reaches into her pocket, and tosses something at me. "Take these and shut up."

Airplane cookies. *Don't mind if I do.*

"Ellie, I can drive." But even as Mark says it, she's folding herself into the driver's seat. "You should relax. It was a long plane ride. Give me the keys." He holds out his hand. Her only argument is a long, hard stare. No expression on her face, and I know this has something to do with why she's really here. Whatever it is, she would clearly feel better driving herself. Mark comes to the same conclusion and takes a shaky breath, climbing into the back with me without further discussion.

No time like the present. Chelsea suggested I get it over with quickly, lest I lose my nerve. I snorted then like I didn't even understand the meaning of cowardice, but I know she's right.

I lean forward in my seat as Ellie's pulling out of the parking garage. "I need to ask you something." Ellie glances up in the rearview mirror at me, and I hear Mark's deep breath. It only makes me more curious. "Why don't you ever talk about Dad?"

Ellie's hands turn white-knuckled on the wheel. Another big reaction to a simple question…but her version of a big reaction. Ellie's calm and collected. I mess with her and engage in pointless arguments because it's fun, but I've never argued with her for real. I've never made her react in anything other than jest. My mind spins in this uncharted territory.

Her voice is cold when she says, "There's nothing to talk about."

My face hardens until I'm glaring at my twin, my tone dropping to match hers. "He's my dad, and I know nothing about him. You guys both know him. Or *knew* him." I glare at Mark too who looks like I've hit him. Maybe I have. But I was too young to know Dad as Mark did.

"Leave it alone," Ellie snaps, then she takes a deep breath. "He's not worth it."

Silence. She stares out at the road, and Mark says nothing. Brandon tosses a cautious glance her way, but then focuses his attention out the window. The tension in the small vehicle grows, and no one does anything to dissolve it. I have a feeling Ellie will be just as stubborn as Mark about this. She might well let the tension linger forever if given the opportunity and not feel the slightest impulse to budge.

I lean back in my seat again and puff out a breath. "I'd really like to be the judge of that."

Her eyes soften then, but it still stings when she says, "No."

》》》》》》

LATER THAT NIGHT, ELLIE'S CURLED UP ON THE COUCH NEXT TO ME, half asleep before we make it an hour into the movie. Her phone sits on the coffee table in front of her. The sight of the pale pink case is making me strangely nervous.

I got nothing from her in the car. She's never snapped at me before, and while I'm mad, I'm more curious than ever. Did something happen between her and our father to draw that kind of reaction? I wish I could ask. I wish I knew our father well enough to venture a guess.

I told Chelsea about it when we got home. We've talked on the phone a few times since our run-in at the bar. It started as trying to set a time to get together. Then she brought up my father again—or maybe it was me.

This whole thing has me thinking way too much. I never cared before that I didn't know the man. I knew there was a business tied into the reason for the divorce, but it was never a goal of mine to take it over or even know what it was. That wasn't a consideration when I picked my major. I said as much to Chelsea, and I have no idea why.

She listened, though. Told me lots of people don't speak to their fathers. People fall out of contact. It happens.

It never bothered me before, so why does it now? Chelsea's suggestion was to learn about him on my own. There are plenty of ways I can find out who he is without Mark and Ellie. The main one being I could talk to him directly. The problem there is I'm not sure the phone number I have for him is accurate.

Mark is spread out over the love seat, focused on the movie. And Brandon is slouched so far down on the single, I can't even see his face. I look back at my sister. Her eyes are shut now, her breathing deep and even. This is a great movie, but she's *gone*. I blow out a breath.

Here goes nothing.

I lean forward and snatch her phone up before I can think better of it. I follow through with the movement, standing and walking out of the room. The bathroom is the least likely place anyone will bother me. Too bad I didn't take time to set the precedent of taking forever in there.

I flick the light on, but as soon as the switch is up, the light blinks out again. I sigh and attempt to balance the switch in the middle. It's a process, but the light stays on then. I hold my hands out toward it as if that'll do anything. The last thing I need is for this moment to be me huddled down in the dark bathroom with my sister's phone like some kind of lunatic. I take a tentative step back and sit myself on the toilet seat.

For a moment, I don't even turn her phone on; I just stare at it. She's always had this pink case. Same phone, I'd bet, too. This feels so wrong. Like an invasion of privacy. I've been less than honest with Mark in the years since we lost Mom, but never with Ellie. *But it's not dishonest. The only reason you have her phone is for Dad's number.* I only need her contacts. It's not like I'm going through her messages.

I still take a deep breath before clicking the thing on. Second surprise of the day, there's no password. She's such a private person, I naturally assumed it would be locked. That would have killed this whole Dad thing right there. Problem solved! Somehow, it's not comforting that it didn't.

I blink when I see the home screen wallpaper. It's from almost eight years ago. Mom used to get herself, Mark, and me matching Christmas pajamas each year, and in this picture, she's standing in front of the tree with Mark and me on either side of her, all in our bright green Grinch onesies—ugly as hell, but I still have mine. There's a sudden deep ache in my chest. I hate it. I take another deep breath.

Ellie doesn't have many contacts. Actually, it's only me, Mark, some guy named *Jaythan*, Dad…and Mom. Tears automatically burn up my throat. Sometimes it's hard not to think things wouldn't have gotten this bad if she were still around.

Move past it, Jake. I click Dad's contact and immediately realize the ten digits that flash onto the screen are different from the ones in my phone. Disappointment settles in my gut even though I tell myself it's not a big deal.

Mom never once changed her phone number. She had a lot of run-ins with sketchy messages meant for the number matching hers in all but the last digit, but she refused to change it. She didn't want to lose contact with Ellie. I'm not sure how much they talked. Obviously, Mom sent her the Christmas photo, probably every year. But did Ellie ever respond?

It takes a massive amount of willpower not to go into her messages. She's probably deleted them by now anyway.

Instead, I enter the correct number into my phone. Now I have it. I stare at it. Just because I have it doesn't mean I have to use it. Dad has never once reached out to me. The last time I heard from him was Christmas when I was five, and that was a disaster. He'd wanted full custody of all of us, but Mom wanted us away from him. She never said she regretted marrying him because, as she pointed out on more than one occasion, she wouldn't have had us without him. But I always got the sense that nevertheless, some part of her did regret him. It wasn't hatred she held for our father; most the time it looked more like fear. She had tried to get Ellie back from him, but it failed every time. I don't think she ever forgave herself for that.

I don't have to talk to him. Mark and Ellie say I shouldn't. Maybe I should listen for once. But now I have the option, assuming he doesn't change his number again. I shake my head. I don't have to use it; that's the bottom line.

In my attempts to cover my tracks by clearing the history, I see that the last open app was the messaging app. And my treacherous thumb clicks into it automatically. I'm ready to click back out when I see them.

There are only two threads. One is Mark's, and the other is Mom's for which the previewed last message is an image. And, though it's tiny, I can still make it out. It's the last Christmas picture Mom, Mark, and I took together.

Mom was in the hospital again. Mark and I brought her gifts there and spent the whole day with her. We ate cheap sandwiches from the hospital vending machines since the cafeteria was closed for the holiday. The staff didn't confine us to visiting hours. Not that day. We stayed well past them until Mom made us go home and rest. But not before we took a picture together. Despite the wires and tubes and the fluorescent hospital lights, we all have great big smiles on our faces. Mom's was the biggest of all.

I hate myself for doing it, but I click into the messages and start scrolling. The only ones are from Mom. Ellie never once responded. There are lots of pictures, and even more encouragements, and nearly every other message simply says, "I love you, my Ellie."

It's like falling into a black hole. I desperately want to pull out, but I keep getting sucked deeper and deeper, unable to outrun the unconquerable force of nature. My chest feels too heavy, and my fingers go cold and start shaking. The more I read, the more I tell myself this is wrong.

I shouldn't be doing this. It's not my business, and it's an invasion of Ellie's privacy.

I force myself to click her phone off and fist my hands around it, knocking it against my forehead. A boulder has just dropped down on my chest, and a few tears slip unhindered down my cheeks.

I'm forced to relive that moment when she died. It was the worst I've ever felt. I honestly didn't think there was a way out. It felt like the end. This feeling can almost rival that one.

Ellie didn't have anyone. At least I had Mark. We fought constantly, but he was there. Most nights after it happened, when one or both of us couldn't sleep, we'd stay up watching TV together until we passed out or morning came. Ellie didn't have that. She started visiting after Mom died, but she never talked about Mom. She wouldn't let us either, always changing the subject. I figured they weren't very close anyway, not having seen each other for eleven years. But she was still Ellie's mom. Ellie lost her too.

And even five years later, she hasn't deleted any of the texts.

The pressure in my chest is almost unbearable, and I don't know what else to do. She picks up the phone almost immediately. *"Hey there,"* Chelsea drawls.

It hurts so much that I can't speak, but the sound of her voice…

"Jake?" she asks, confused now. *"Are you there?"*

I open my mouth, but all that comes out is a broken sob. Immediately, my hand slaps over my mouth. *What are you doing calling her at a time like this?* I like this girl. I'm not trying to drive her away with my whimpering neediness.

"Jake," her tone softens, and the gentle sway of it eases a little bit of the pressure. *"What happened?"* She doesn't sound disgusted, only

empathetic. Maybe it wasn't a mistake to call her.

"She…" I start, but a bubble in my throat prevents me from saying the rest. I swallow and take a deep breath. "She kept all the texts."

"*What?*"

"The texts," I say again, rubbing my forehead, willing my eyes to dry up. This is pathetic. *You're fine.* "My mother's texts. She kept them all."

"*That must be hard,*" Chelsea says calmly, not asking for more information even though I know I haven't given her enough to understand. "*Do you want me to come over?*"

"No," I say too quickly, but the thought of her meeting everyone is enough to shock my system back into check. "No, I just wanted to hear your voice."

"*You're sweet.*"

"You're gorgeous," I respond, and she giggles. She stays on the line silently as I compose myself. I can't go back out there looking like a wreck or they'll know something's up.

Finally, I whisper, "Thank you."

"*It's going to be alright, Jake.*"

I nod, aware she can't see me. I mean to lighten the mood with some flirting, but I hear Brandon's room door shutting beside the bathroom followed by a mix of murmurs and pauses. I can't hear individual words, but Brandon's tone becomes aggravated and angry. I've never heard him like that before.

"I have to go," I tell Chelsea before hanging up.

I don't hate myself as much as I should for pressing my ear to the wall separating his room and the bathroom. Our apartment is the cheapest we could find with space for all of us and pretty rundown, but if there's one thing they got right, it's the walls. Even pressed close and holding my breath, I can't decipher words.

Eventually I give up, and once I'm satisfied it doesn't look like I've been crying, I step into the hallway. It's at the same moment Brandon leaves his room, and we stare at each other, both looking like we have something to hide.

Then he smiles. That genuine friendly smile that he gives out to everyone. I try not to glance toward his room as I start to think it all might be a facade.

I quirk a brow. "Everything okay?"

"Yep," he answers, too cheerily. "You?"

"Yep," I return. And because we're both being suspicious, neither of us questions any further.

We exchange nods and file back into the living room. Ellie is still fast asleep on the couch, her face relaxed and peaceful in sleep. The sight of her brings all those messages back to the forefront of my brain.

Ellie's never been one for hugs or physical contact beyond the initial greeting phase. But at the moment, I really don't care. She's unconscious anyway. I wrap my arm around her and bring her close. She shifts a bit but settles into me, her head resting on my chest. My arms lock tight around her, and I rest my cheek atop her head.

We couldn't be there for her when Mom died. But I can be there for her now. Even if she won't admit she needs it.

Mark glances over, a concerned wrinkle in his brow. "You okay?"

My answering nod is a lie.

15

BRANDON'S PARANOIA

This visit is noticeably different from Ellie's last. It's been three days, and all I can think is *paranoid*. For the first two days she drove anywhere we went and wouldn't let Mark or Jake sit up front. She's been adamantly against going out to eat. And more than once when we were watching TV, she dragged a chair over by the window and spent more time staring out that than at the TV.

Her behavior has put Mark on edge. When Ellie finally seemed to be calming down, Mark only became more anxious. He too has shot down every attempt to go out, something Jake has been pushing hard, and I'm not convinced it's not just to get under Mark's skin.

The argument in the car a few days ago was quick but brutal. The peacemaker in me wants to sit them all down and referee a healthy discussion, but I know better than to involve myself in their problems. Besides, Ellie and Jake seem to be on fine terms now, and Mark and Jake are maybe just a little more strained than usual. They'll be fine, though. They're brothers. That's the wishful thinker in me.

This morning, Ellie declared she was going out for groceries, to which Mark had issues. So, she tagged me in to appease him. I'm not sure how it helped, but Mark let her leave after that. It calms me down too, being out in public with her around. She was right there with me when I got shot, and my brain filed that away as meaning she's base. Like when I played tag as a kid. As long as I'm with her, no one can hurt me.

So, now I'm pushing the cart one step behind her. She doesn't consult a list but keeps tossing things in. She grabs a toilet plunger, inspects it, and throws it in the cart.

I squint. "I think we have a plunger."

She raises a brow, glancing back at me. "You mean that shredded rubber bowl on a stick beside the toilet?"

I should probably be embarrassed, but it's not our fault it's like that. We were dog-sitting for a friend once, and the Cattle Dog took it as an appetizer. I just nod. "That's the one." She snorts, shaking her head. "Is this everything then?" The cart is nearly filled.

She shakes her head. "Not quite." She eyes the stacks of toilet paper. "Do you guys have enough toilet paper?"

I bite back my smile. It's like she thinks we can't get by on our own. She might be right, but it's adorable to watch her slip into this caretaker role. "I think so."

She peers at me, then grabs the paper anyway. "You can never have too much." I can't argue with that logic.

"You know, you don't have to shop for us. We can get our own groceries."

She throws her head back with a laugh that knows better. "I know my brothers. Frankly, before you came along, I visited a lot more just to make sure they were eating regularly and somewhat properly. So long as I'm here, you guys will not be living like you're homeless." She pats my arm and continues down the aisle.

I laugh and push the cart after her.

I wish her being back meant I was getting to know her better, but she's a very private person. The only thing I know about her is her family situation, but that's because it's Mark and Jake's too. While I'm wishing for things, it would also be great if I could work up the courage to talk to her about what I said when I was shot. She hasn't mentioned it, but I still feel like it needs to be addressed. Maybe one day.

"So, you live in DC. What's that like?" I ask instead. She's been deflecting my prying questions with simple answers, but it hasn't stopped me yet.

She shrugs. "It's just like living in any city. Lots of people. Lots of dumb problems. I wish I could move. Very beautiful."

A jolt goes through me at the flippantly honest response. "Wait, what?"

"It's gorgeous there." Lavender and lemon compete for dominance in my nostrils as we enter the cleaning aisle where Ellie stops in front of the carpet cleaners. "Sunsets are otherworldly."

"No. You want to move?"

"Oh, that." She shakes her head, pulling a cleaner off the shelf to examine closer. "I don't know. I travel a lot, so it's not like I spend much time in the city anyway."

"You travel? Like, for work?" I try to imagine what type of work that would put her in. Journalism, maybe? Given how she cut down the reporter at the airport, I kind of doubt that. Maybe she's CIA. I smirk to myself. *That would be cool.*

"Sometimes."

"That sounds exciting."

"I guess." That answer doesn't breed hope that she will divulge any more of her life with me. I'm surprised I was able to get that much out of her. I mean, it's really not that much, but it *is* two more things that I didn't know before. I can't make sense of any of it and piece together what her life must be like, but I would still call that a win.

In the condiments aisle, perhaps a bit unwisely next to the cleaning products, we cross paths with an older lady from my church with a large man who looks like he was pulled straight from a bodybuilding gym.

Ellie takes a small step between me and him. I give her an affirming pat on the shoulder and smile. "Hey, Mrs. Bishop."

The little old woman looks up from the ketchups and returns my smile. "Hello, Brandon. You remember my grandson, don't you?"

I offer the man a nod and gesture for Ellie's sake. "This is Mrs. Bishop and her grandson, Jackson. She goes to church with Mark and I." She brought Jackson to church once last year. He's in his mid-thirties and not much of a talker. When I tried to ask him about what he does for a living, he only said it was guard duty at some company. Not which company. Our conversation was short to say the least. I'm not sure whether I like him or can't stand him—it's a strange line.

Mrs. Bishop notices Ellie then, and her smile widens. "Who's your friend?"

Ellie gives her name and smiles at the woman, but Mrs. Bishop isn't satisfied with that and goes in for a hug. Poor El tenses immediately, clearly not sure what to do about it. She glances at me as if I might be able to help, but I don't know my role here. I bite my lip to keep from smiling, and she throws me a glare. Jackson stands to the side, watching everything closely.

"Mark's sister," I add.

"It's so nice to meet you, Ellie." Mrs. Bishop tries to hold eye contact with her, but Ellie's eyes shift between her and Jackson.

"You too." She pulls away and moves behind the cart with me, keeping her eyes on Jackson now. I grin at her uncharacteristic squeamishness. This is more adorable than her being a mother hen. I strangle the thought.

Mrs. Bishop pats her grandson's shoulder. "Jackson just came to visit me for a few days."

The giant studies Ellie the same way she studies him, almost as if they're gauging each other. *Are they squaring up for a fight in front of the mustard?*

I interject before this gets too awkward. "That's really nice." Jackson, thankfully, tightens his lips in my direction which I take as his version of a smile.

"I won't keep you two." Mrs. Bishop turns back to me, unaware of whatever it is that just occurred, and pats my arm. "It was lovely running into you. I do hope you bring her to church sometime, dear. Everyone would be so happy to meet her. You two look very sweet together."

My brain short-circuits, and I can't come up with comprehensible words to respond with. Ellie just bobs her head, finally breaking her intense focus on Jackson, says, "Okay," and walks away with the cart.

"We're not…" But Mrs. Bishop has already turned away, Jackson slinging an arm around her shoulders. I stop my stuttering, shake my head, and jog the little way to catch up to Ellie. "Sorry about that."

"About what?"

"Well…" *Do I honestly need to explain?* "Now she thinks we're together. I'm pretty sure that's what she'll be telling people." And then I'll be bombarded with questions, and—oh no, so will Mark. I think about turning back and setting the record straight.

But then Ellie asks, "So?"

And the way she asks it makes it sound like it really isn't that big a deal. Okay, she's right. It's fine. Mark knows I would never do that to him. It's a misunderstanding. The fact that I'm freaking out over it can't be good for me. "I guess it doesn't matter."

In the ensuing silence, I decide now is as good a time as any to bite the bullet. I almost laugh at my pun, but this is serious. "Hey, I want to apologize for what I said when I was shot."

"Why?" Again, the question is so simple. Does she not have this problem of overthinking literally everything? I envy this superhuman ability.

"I just…it made you uncomfortable, and I didn't mean to do that."

She shrugs. "It's fine. Nothing to apologize for." It really looks like she means it too. There's no residual awkwardness, just like Mark said. Does nothing faze her? I'm starting to wonder if she really is somehow superhuman. She glances up at me, then at the cart. "Well, good news: we're done here, sweetie." She flashes me a wicked grin, and I roll my eyes even as my cheeks heat.

Ellie's not a very typical human case. My brain automatically likens her to a cat, something that has adapted to the domestic setting but was never meant to. I read what the reporter from the airport wrote about Ellie: "*aggressive but protective.*" Protective in a way that would have her watching our backs in all aspects. That's certainly how I'd classify the last few days. Given how she was conveniently around when I was shot, and how Mark seems to be treating her the same way he treated me in the days leading up to my wound, I'm beginning to think it might not be too crazy a thought after all. She might know more than she's letting on.

I stop her from leaving the aisle, which has emptied out so it's just the two of us. Before I can talk myself out of it, "Can I ask you…why were you at the mall that day?" She shakes her head, confused. "You said you were shopping nearby when I got shot."

She frowns. "And?"

"You didn't have any bags."

"I hadn't bought anything yet." Her frown deepens when my lips tighten. "Is something bothering you?"

I take a breath. "I think you know something about…" I gesture to my still bandaged and sore shoulder, "that you aren't telling me."

She laughs a touch darkly. The sound comes without any levity reaching her eyes, and she licks the back of her teeth before meeting my eyes with her signature hard green ones. "What am I supposed to know? Why someone decided to shoot you? You think I can back up your Enforcers theory?"

I flinch at her jab but hold firm. *I'm not wrong.* She knows something. "I don't think you know why. I think you know who did it."

She raises one slick brow, gaze darkening, and my stomach swirls with unease. "Oh?"

"You gave me a gun a few days before it happened. You were right there when it did, and now you're back, and you're acting super weird." I'd like to soften the blow, but what if I'm right? Then she's been lying to me this whole time about something that nearly cost me my life. "What else am I supposed to think? I don't know that much about you."

"Brandon." She pauses, breathing once. "I wish I could tell you I knew who did it or why they did. But I can't. I have nothing to give you. I'm sorry."

Shame has trickled through me slowly throughout this confrontation, but now it's a crashing wave. It was a weak theory anyway. No matter what people say, sometimes a coincidence is just a coincidence. Maybe she really did give me the gun to feel like her brothers had some extra protection. It would fit with the aggressive but protective view of her actions. And she may well have been shopping nearby, bags or no. It's not unheard of to go to a store and not end up buying anything. I was lucky. That's what everyone keeps telling me. Lucky she was there. Maybe I'm the paranoid one.

But before I can apologize, she pushes, "Why are you so sure it was the Enforcers?"

My eyes widen involuntarily, and I take a step away from her, fear replacing guilt in an instant. This was a terrible idea. We don't need to get into this discussion. "It's just a possibility."

"Why would they go after you?"

"I…" I gape about for words. Her tone borders on accusatory. She definitely knows more than she's letting on, but not why it happened. That much is certain. She waits patiently. "I don't know."

Then she's nodding, scanning me up and down. She doesn't believe me but nods toward the registers. Clearly, neither of us will be divulging any of our secrets right now. "Come on."

Her distrust would hurt if not for the fact that I don't believe her either.

We silently wait in line behind a mother and her three small children. They keep grabbing items off the belt before the cashier can scan them, and the mother is becoming increasingly exasperated. She sends Ellie and I apologetic looks every few seconds, but I shake my head and hold out a hand to tell her it's fine. Ellie simply watches, and I honestly can't tell if she's annoyed or not.

Finally, everything is scanned, and the woman inserts her card into the machine. The clerk shakes his head after a few seconds, and the woman frowns at the screen that beeps at her.

"I'm sorry…" She gives a self-deprecating laugh. "Can I try it again?"

But it declines even after the third try. A flush rises in her cheeks, and her shoulders curl inward as she digs in her wallet for another card. "I'm so sorry. I'll just…put it on my credit card. Where is…" she mumbles to herself, then pauses, "*Shoot*. I gave it to my husband. Um…" She looks at her groceries.

I'm reaching for my wallet when Ellie steps up next to the mother, extending her own card. "Use this."

"Oh, no." The mother holds out a hand, her blush deepening. "I'm sorry. I'll get out of your way."

"It's not to rush you," Ellie says calmly. "Just to help."

When the woman still doesn't take the card, Ellie hands it to the cashier who turns the machine around to complete the transaction.

"Are you sure? I'll repay you as soon as I can. Just let me know how I can reach you."

Ellie shakes her head. "Don't worry about it."

The mother of three is blinking rapidly now, swiping at her eyes to keep the tears from falling. "Th-thank you."

"It's the least I could do." Ellie looks to the children who have all stopped their antics to watch the odd exchange between their mother and this stranger. "You seem to have your hands full."

From most people that would sound like an insult, but on Ellie's lips is such a longing smile that my heart aches for her. It mixes with the guilt and mistrust in a sickening cocktail.

The woman gives her children loving pats on the head as the smallest girl attaches to her leg while the two older boys climb on the cart. "They're certainly worth it." Then her smile drops, and she points at them. "But none of you heard me say that. You're all a bunch of headaches. I'm going to have to get rid of one. Choose amongst yourselves."

At once, the children start pointing fingers at each other and laughing. The clerk finishes bagging all her groceries, so the woman turns one last time to Ellie. "I have to give you something. Would you mind if I hugged you?"

She doesn't hesitate to accept it. With many more thanks, the woman herds her children out of the store.

Ellie turns back to get her own groceries paid for as if my entire view of her isn't being pulled in two completely different directions. As if, even though we just got into a fight in the middle of the store where we seem to have reached a mutual distrust, I am not simultaneously realizing I'm falling for this woman.

16

ELLIE'S DINNER

It's not that I'm itching to get away from Brandon, but when the elevator in his building stalls on our last trip up with the rest of the groceries, I bite back a curse. Brandon reaches over to hit the button for his floor again, but nothing happens. Sending me an uncomfortable but apologetic smile, he presses the call button and lets the man on the other end know we're stuck. And then it becomes a waiting game.

It feels as awkward as the first time we met. Not at all fit for how comfortable we've gotten with each other. It hits me then that we still haven't known each other very long. I'm carving into the recesses of his life with a damn scalpel, but we're still virtual strangers. So why doesn't it feel like it?

That he doesn't trust me does not hurt so much as fill me with an oily sickness in my gut. He shouldn't trust me; I *have* been lying to him.

But things between us have started to feel more relaxed. Friendly. It's been too long since I had a friend I could trust.

Brandon shakes his head, immediately anxious in the silence. I've noticed his avid avoidance of silence, especially when we're alone. He tends to babble. I'll admit…it's cute. "Ellie, I'm so sorry. Again." I sigh. I hate his apologies. "I shouldn't be jumping to those kinds of conclusions."

"Well, I haven't given you much reason to trust me. I'm used to my brothers, and they don't really need reinforcement. Family code and all."

He laughs a little at that. "You have, though. You were there for me after I got shot, you helped me out with the reporter, and today at the store, paying for that woman's groceries…" He stops, looking down at his feet.

I frown. The woman needed help. I'm not sure why Brandon is making such a big deal about it until I remember he doesn't know what I do for a living and how much I make doing it. He doesn't know it was much more an act of penance than generosity.

And seeing that mother with her three children—two boys and a girl…

Shit, it was like looking into an alternate reality.

"I…" Brandon says, drawing me back. He steels himself and meets my eyes. "I really like you. I've loved spending time with you, and I don't want anything I said to ruin that. I think we could be really great friends."

I take a deep breath, fighting the warmth that filters into my chest. I've enjoyed it too. It's different than spending time with my brothers. Somehow, easier. No expectations. Being around him is fresh air. I find myself wanting to be his friend. Wanting to trust him.

"I do too," I tell him softly. Then I force myself to admit, "I've also had fun with you. It'll take a lot more than that to get rid of me."

He lets out a relieved breath. Another smile. Then there's silence, and we just watch each other. His gaze keeps attempting to shift away, but it always bounces back. It doesn't take a psychic to know what thoughts are running through his mind. They creep into the edges of mine too.

My father wants this man dead. Why? The same bullshit reason he wants Mark dead? Brandon is harmless. He's a solid student. He's racing against an empty bank account, yet still making rent on time—with the exception of the month he couldn't work because I shot him. He's thoughtful, kind to my brothers even when Jake is being an ass. Tagging along on boring errands with me simply because I ask, and he knows it makes Mark feel better even if he doesn't know why.

Suddenly I don't want to stand here talking until the elevator starts working again. He's absolutely messing with my head the way he's so thoughtful. That he would worry about keeping up his friendship with *me*, of all people. He cares so much. So genuinely.

Dad wants him killed. What if I kissed him instead?

I take a step closer, testing. He takes one toward me, eyes so dark that the copper of his irises is nearly drowned out. It brings us nearly chest to chest. Tentatively, his hand comes up, and he brushes his knuckle along the length of my braid which slips down my shoulder before his fingertips slide up my neck.

I've never kissed anyone before. Never had time for a relationship, and kissing wasn't a pastime I cared to make room for. I didn't think it would ever interest me as much as it does right this moment. My eyes drop to Brandon's full lips, and I wonder how they'll feel against my own.

My hands fist in the collar of his shirt, pulling him down to me. His hand slips around the back of my neck. And then his fingers drift over the healing scar where my tracker implant had been.

With his breath mingling with mine and his mouth a hair's breadth away, I suck in a breath, several thoughts assaulting me at once. He's my brother's best friend. I shot him. He doesn't know me. If he did, he certainly wouldn't want this. He wouldn't want our friendship either.

Brandon *is* a good guy. He doesn't deserve to be a pawn in this power struggle with my father.

I step away from him just as the elevator hums back to life. Closing my eyes, I thank whoever is out there that we don't have to wait around in close quarters after that.

He watches me for a second as we start going up again. "I'm sorry—"

But I shake my head, cutting him off. "You've done enough apologizing for one day, Brandon. This one's on me." He's going to need more than that or things will get very uncomfortable again. "I'm more suited to…friends." He swallows and nods, even though that's not true either.

>>>>>>>>

BY NIGHT FIVE, I'VE HAD ENOUGH OF THE ANTICIPATION AND SUGGEST we eat out. Brandon and Jake jump all over it, but Mark casually suggests he'll make pizza instead. He plays it off, but no one's fooled. I see the strain in his smile, the tension around his shoulders. I've tried to calm him down, but he's certain that my being here means something bad is coming for Brandon. There's no way in hell I'm telling him Brandon's not the one in danger anymore.

I heard from Jaythan this morning. Still nothing. On the bright side, my father hasn't sent any other assassins after either of them. There have been no whisperings about them at all. Most likely it means my father is waiting for me to push the boundaries, see what I do next.

So, I'm testing the waters. Not far from the guys' apartment is a small Mexican restaurant that I've already scoped out. Every exit is visible from the table I reserved, and I'll be armed to the teeth under my clothes. Brandon and Jake are starting to ask too many questions. Policing them to stay inside like this isn't helping anything.

I take a deep breath. If everything goes well tonight, maybe I'll be able to relax a little bit.

The reservation is for six-thirty. I told the boys it was for six.

The thing is, Brandon—unsurprisingly—is very punctual, so the fact that my brothers are making us late for the "six o'clock" reservation is stressing him out. He's lived with them two years now, but he hasn't yet learned my tricks.

He's pacing by the door, ready to go in his nice jeans, plain t-shirt, and thick winter coat. The rain comes down aggressively and drums against the window on the other side of the living room—the only sound to accompany the rattle and clack of Brandon's keys as he beats them against his reddening hand. I'm leaning against the wall by the door, smirking as Brandon loses his mind.

He looks at his watch for the fourth time in as many minutes and makes a guttural noise in his throat like a growl. "Guys, we're already late!"

"You can relax." I decide to put him out of his misery. Shame, it was entertaining—and adorable, if I'm being honest. I shut down that thought. "The reservation's for six-thirty."

He stops, turns to me, stares, letting the knowledge settle over him. I raise a brow. "That's genius."

"I know." I expected some weirdness after our almost-kiss two days ago, but there hasn't been any. Silences are still poisonous to him and maybe a bit more than before, but it's not all that bad. I really shouldn't have done it. Even having him as a friend is dangerous, but I'm falling fast and hard into that trap.

He has no idea how close he was to the truth during our fight in the grocery store. The only choice I had was to make him feel horrible for thinking such a thing, but he has every right to *because he's right*. But I can't tell him that, or I risk not only him but my brothers as well.

In a perfect world, Brandon should know why and by whom he was targeted, but the very existence of the Enforcers is evidence to this being a far from perfect world.

Brandon still nags my brothers to get out the door, albeit less aggravatedly, and we make it to the restaurant a whole five minutes early. The waitress shows us to our table, and we order our drinks.

Mark thanks her as she leaves. "I'm glad we didn't lose the table."

"Yeah, sorry, guys." Jake passes out the waters. The dumbasses believe me every time.

"For what?" I ask, casually reaching for my glass.

"For…" Mark frowns, one brow creeping up under his flop of golden hair. "For making us late."

"You didn't." I take a sip—not the best. Somehow the quality of water could be better. Or it's the nerves.

Mark sighs heavily. "Did you move back the threshold again?"

"Yup."

He shakes his head, and Brandon squints, the question in the furrow of his brow before he voices it. "What does that mean?"

"My thirty-minute threshold." Brandon nods at my explanation, but I continue anyway. "It started out as ten minutes, and I lengthen it on occasion to keep them on their toes. I've done it for the past five years."

He turns to my brothers, confused again. "If you guys know what she's doing, why does it still work?"

"We kind of just have this terrible procrastination problem." Jake holds his water out like he's toasting with it. "You've probably noticed."

"If there's one thing you guys are pro at, it's *crastinating*." To his credit, his delivery is on point. I shake my head, Mark drops his head to the table, and Jake pats Brandon's shoulder sympathetically.

"What?" Brandon looks around at us in turn. "Come on. That was a good one." I will never admit I'm struggling against a smile right now. Brandon scrunches his face, leaning back in his chair. He grumbles, "I need friends with better taste."

"Yeah." I nod, playing with the edge of my cloth napkin. "*That's* the problem."

It's pure luck that has the waitress coming by with chips and salsa for the table then. Brandon takes a chip when she leaves and hurls it at me. His luck runs out when I—maintaining eye-contact—catch it and crunch down on it. I stop myself from wondering if he chose one of the folded chips on purpose and chalk it up to coincidence. Brandon resorts to glaring. I grin. So entertaining.

Then my grin disappears. This isn't right. I shouldn't be having this much fun with a target. Something put Brandon on that desk, and I shouldn't be able to sit here and laugh with him. This isn't right. *But it's so damn easy.*

The drinks are next to come, and I take a good look at the pink one placed in front of Jake. I heard him order it, but it's all the more ridiculous to see it sitting in front of him now. "Why a Shirley Temple?"

"Don't judge, sis. It's delicious." He plugs the end of his straw, lifts it out of the drink, and drops the miniscule amount of trapped pink liquid into his mouth.

He hasn't mentioned our father again since that first day, but I know better than to think he's dropped it. I'm not surprised he's suddenly curious. Why wouldn't he be? I just don't know how to get him off the scent. Mark has been understanding, all things considered, but Jake is a wholly different person. I don't want to think what it would be like if he knew.

Logic says I should tease him while I still can. "It's a girly drink, Jake. Do you order this stuff on dates?"

He spreads his arms. "Since when is Sprite *girly*?"

I shake my head slowly, sipping my Coke. "You wonder why you don't have a girlfriend."

"What? No. You make me sound desperate. Is it a girly drink? Guys?" He looks to the other two.

Brandon does the one-shoulder shrug—his good shoulder, I note. "Kinda."

Mark nods to the beverage. "It's got a cherry in it."

Jake scoffs. "Your Coke came with a cherry!"

Mark looks down at his drink, takes the cherry out, and throws it in mine. He then gives Jake a challenging look while Jake's mouth hangs open in personal offense. My twin glares, takes his own cherry, and tosses it over to my drink.

I slouch back in my seat and use the straw to drown them. "Thank you," I singsong.

Jake gapes at me. "You could have just asked; I would have given it to you."

"Where's the fun in that?"

Mark laughs at us, but then he stands. "I'll be right back."

I catch his eye. If he leaves the table, he's on his own. I haven't shared anything with him no matter how often he's asked—that would be a lot, by the way—but he knows I'm here out of necessity, and I can't watch two different places.

Just once, I'd like to do something because I want to. Come see my brothers just because I feel like saying *hi*. Kiss Brandon just because I want to know what it feels like. Go out to dinner just because I'm hungry and not playing a game of chicken with my psychopathic father. We all have dreams. This being *mine* feels like I've never had any real control over my life. Which is fun.

Mark takes the hint and nods, sitting back down. I feel terrible for the tremor in his voice as he says, "Actually, I just remembered, I found this movie I think you guys might like."

I sigh, leaning back in my chair as he explains that it's a thriller with a murder mystery. I can't keep Brandon and Jake at the table all night without raising even more suspicion, but I can at least keep Mark. I take a big gulp of my water, wishing it was something stronger. This may have been a bad idea.

»»»»»

THAT DOESN'T PROVE TRUE UNTIL WE'RE NEARING THE END OF OUR meal. The heavy scent of enchiladas and tacos wafts around us. Jake sucks at the straw of his drink which has been empty for five minutes now. I toss another chip at him, and he stops…again. Brandon chuckles around a large bite of his quesadilla.

Mark's plate lies scraped clean in front of him while he wraps up a story about what happened during clinicals. A guy's thumb was all screwed up or something—I don't know. Honestly, I haven't been paying as much attention to the happenings at this table as I should. I've made myself busy watching the door and studying the other patrons. Waiting. Anxiously waiting.

Jake and Brandon are enjoying themselves. They've told their fair share of stories tonight and have thrived in the time outside their apartment. The two of them don't get along great—for the most part Jake just avoids Brandon—but tonight, you'd never know it.

Brandon's default is friendly, but Jake hasn't been responding to it. I noticed that at Thanksgiving. Jake isn't cruel, but he clearly would rather not deal with Brandon. And for the life of me, I can't figure out why he hasn't broken down yet. He's lived with the guy for two years. Even I'm having a hard time maintaining that distance.

I turn to Mark. He started out the night anxious. When I didn't let him leave to use the restroom, it dropped him into a silent panic. But he's slowly grown more comfortable at the table as the evening progresses.

I wish that could be me. Every time someone passes by us, I watch them until they're out of sight. My attention has shot from one thing to another all night while trying to keep up the appearance that everything is fine.

It's not, though. Of course it's not fine. Nothing has happened. That should be a good thing, but that alone has caused more of my agitation than anything else. *Why hasn't anything happened?*

I was sure the man at the store the other day was going to make a move. That old woman's grandson had that look about him, and I'm certain I've seen his face around the Enforcers headquarters. He's not an assassin, for sure. But he could easily be one of the guards my father insisted on hiring. Jackson didn't appear to recognize me, though. Or else, he did but didn't want to create a scene with his grandmother around. Feeling the same with Brandon there, I respected it. But will he come back when his grandmother is *not* with him? Will he—

Someone shoves my chair into the table from behind.

I jump up immediately, throwing my chair back into the person and spinning around to assess the situation. The woman reaches for something at her side, but I catch her wrist. She whimpers at the tight grip. I freeze.

She's probably mid-forties, wearing a sleek red dress with a sparkly belt tied around her waist, high heels, hair done up in a braided coil. Her date—not husband, I note from the lack of a ring on the hand I've captured—stands behind her, ready to help and even take me on if the firm set of his mouth says anything.

"Sorry." She settles her feet under her, her date putting his hands on her shoulders and eyeing me suspiciously. "It's these heels. Can't walk in these things." She chuckles.

I realize I still have a hold on her wrist when she gives a little tug. A flush of embarrassment heats my face, and I let go.

"I didn't mean to frighten you. So sorry to disturb your evening." She glances at the guys apologetically.

"It's fine." It comes out weaker than I'd like. I'm still trying to stop my heart from beating out of my chest. The adrenaline pumps through my system mercilessly, waiting for the fight. I'm almost dizzy with the anticipation. I convince myself I won't be able to breathe unless I put my fist through a wall. "Sorry," I whisper.

She taps my wrist once and pulls her hand back. "Have a great rest of your evening." And then she's gone.

Jake stands, coming close and taking my arm. "Hey, are you okay?"

I stare at him, blink. All night I've been waiting for my father to make his move. I brought them out here—the people I care about most in the world—as bait. I tried to force my father to act by creating the perfect situation that I could still be in control of. And nothing happened. Nothing except me.

I'm the only thing that's gone wrong this entire evening. They were all sitting around telling stories, relaxing. Everyone was safe. Then some woman trips into my chair, and all hell breaks loose. I was half a second from pulling my gun, my left hand still hovering near the waistband of my pants. What would have happened if I had?

I force myself to take three deep breaths before I ignore Jake's question and grip the sleeve of the first waiter that comes by. "We need our check. *Now.*"

"Certainly, miss." He nods and hurries away. I ignore the concerned glances I get from Brandon and Mark and chug the rest of my water.

17

JAKE'S SHOES

ELLIE JOINS ME IN BUYING SHOES A COUPLE DAYS LATER. WE'RE AT Shoetopia, the little store in the mall Brandon works at, though he has today off. There are only four aisles of options, but they're tall and will allow me to waste plenty of time. She's been accompanying us whenever we want to leave the apartment, so I've been making every excuse I can to get her alone. And one of these times I'll say what I really need to.

After her scene at dinner the other night, we brought her back to the apartment and watched a movie to calm her down, though she refused to admit anything was wrong. Maybe it's twin telepathy, but I knew it was a lie.

I've heard of trauma victims being set off by random stimuli, and I'm coming to realize I don't know anything about my sister's life. I don't know if she's been through anything traumatic to set her off like that.

Her visit was an abrupt turnaround from the last, and given the way it started, does that mean the trauma happened after she left us? Would she keep something like that from us?

She never told you about the texts from Mom, you had to steal her phone.

She absolutely wouldn't tell us if something was wrong. We just need to help her from the other side of one-way glass. It's one area Mark and I are in total agreement.

"Jake!" Ellie's an aisle over, and I walk around to find her crouched on the floor, holding up a pair of black and white sneakers with bright yellow soles. "What do you think of these?"

I take one of the shoes to examine. It's a very nice shoe, actually almost exactly what I'm looking for. Briefly, I wonder what Chelsea will think of them—she's the one that told me my current pair is out of commission. In my defense, though, I don't enjoy shoe shopping, and I don't care to get Brandon's expertise. Ellie, however, presented a two-for-one opportunity. Shoes and information.

But I do like this pair, and I've put off asking her any questions, so my plan becomes *dilly dally through a bunch of other shoes and end up right back here later.*

"These are good. I think we should keep looking, though."

She shrugs and puts them back in the box. I mark the place she found them. I'll be back. But for now...

"So, you still work with Dad? How is that?" *Careful.*

Another shrug, studying a box with shoes that are too small for me. "It's a job."

Not really an answer, but she isn't white-knuckling anything or losing her temper. "So, you don't like working for him?" I think that much can be guessed from her response. Plus, the fact that she never talks about it anyway. It occurs to me that maybe the reason she hates talking about our dad is because he's tied in with whatever caused her episode at the restaurant. As long as she doesn't start panicking again, I'm not going to stop asking my questions. He's still my father, and trauma or no, I deserve to know.

Her lips pull to the side noncommittally.

"Why don't you just tell him that you don't want to work with him? Wouldn't he understand?" I hate the way my throat constricts on the last sentence. That's something I should know about my father. *Ignore it, Jake. He didn't want you, remember? He only wanted* her.

"I don't want to stop working for him."

I frown. "But you don't enjoy it."

"No." She pulls out another pair of shoes. I shake my head, and she puts them back. I try to tell myself it's good that I'm getting this much out of her. I still don't know what she does for work or anything about Dad, but she hasn't shut me down. It's good. But it's not enough.

"Then you should find something you *do* love. Don't waste your time doing something you hate." My mind drifts to the moment I chose my major three years ago. *I'm* one to talk.

She stares at me like I should get it. "I don't hate every aspect."

I can't tell if she's being purposefully difficult. She looks genuine, so it's hard not to believe her. Even if it makes absolutely no sense.

I clamp my mouth shut. This is going nowhere. And thankfully, I know her better than I do Dad, so I know she's notoriously stubborn and simply won't budge. I shift gears. "How *is* Dad?"

She's silent for a moment as if weighing her options about what to tell me. "I don't really know." She looks down again, then rises from her crouch and looks me in the eye. "I haven't talked to him much in the last few years."

"Oh." I blink, surprised. Her eyes don't reveal any pain, and the way she says it is like she wants to know *my* reaction. I'm careful to hide just how curious I am. "I'm sorry. Do you want to talk about it?"

She shakes her head, and I can't help the disappointed exhale. She notices, some strange emotion crossing her features. Again, not pain. "He's just…changed." I nod, not at all understanding what she means by that. She shakes her head. "How are *you*? How is school going?"

I let her change the subject, afraid any more pushing will end in a fight. "It's just as stressful as ever." I pick up a sneaker to "inspect."

"Then why do you stick with it?"

For a moment I worry she's serious, and she's mad about what I said. But she's grinning. "Oh, pfft." I wave her off. "I see how it is."

She laughs. "Breaking any hearts these days, Jakey?"

I pause, tilt my head, reach for sarcasm. "I think Mom asked me that exact question once."

I regret saying it when I finally see the flash of pain cross her face. She never got to know Mom. She'd never be able to pick out all the little things she does that are just like her. But a second later, the expression's gone, and she raises a single, slender brow. "Noted. So? Just because I phrased it like an old woman doesn't mean I don't want an answer. Anyone?"

I laugh, already feeling the back of my neck going red. "No, no." I wonder why I ever thought she'd open up. I don't particularly enjoy it either. This is uncomfortable.

I'm pretty sure she can see right through me. "Anyone you got your eye on?"

Does she *know* somehow? Is it that twin telepathy again? "Since when do you want to gossip?"

She tips her head from side to side, considering. "If it doesn't involve you guys, I don't care."

"Right." She's so much better at deflecting questions than I am, but somehow, I find myself wanting to tell her. "Well, I've actually been talking to this one girl quite a bit."

"Oh?"

"I don't know." My cheeks catch fire. I can't tell if I like this feeling or hate it. I turn away from my sister. "We've been trying to set up a date, I guess."

"Yeah?" I hear her smile in the word, still too chicken to face her.

"It's just weird, though." My nose scrunches, and I force myself to stop. "I've never actually cared to pursue a relationship like this." It hurts with every word I drag out of myself, but maybe if I start the ball rolling, Ellie will feel like she can talk to me as well. Plus, I'm starting to really like Chelsea. Eventually, Ellie will have to know. "She's really great, though. I can't stop thinking about her."

Ellie's smile is soft. "I think that's great. Set a date. See where it goes." She shrugs. "I'm happy for you."

I smirk, then give her a look out of the corner of my eye. "What about you?"

She snorts. "Yeah, right. I don't have time for that."

"You can't use that." I point at her. "I'm a full-time student, and I've got two part-time jobs."

She glares, but there's a pinch in her lips that looks like she's fighting back a smile. "Well, I've got one full-time job and no desire for socializing. I work, and I visit you guys. That's pretty much it."

"No one at work then?" She shakes her head. "No one you've met here?" Another shake. I waggle my eyebrows and whisper conspiratorially, "What about Brandon?" What kind of brother would I be if I didn't tease her about this a little?

Her gaze flutters over to the shoes, and it takes her just a second too long to deny it. I gasp, my mouth falling open. "You *do* like him!"

"Alright, shut up." She holds out her hands to quiet me down. "I will slap you, Jake. I swear."

I pout. "But that would hurt."

"There's really no other reason to do it."

Good point. "Okay, fine. But you like him. Admit it. You're practically smitten."

Nothing about her actually looks smitten in the typical sense of the word, but somehow the way she's scowling reads *heart-eyes*. "Look, he's a great guy, okay?"

"I know." It's annoying.

"He's great, and I love that he's who you chose as a roommate." Not who I chose. "But it would never work. It can't happen."

"Why not?" I ask, genuinely curious now. "Is it because you don't live here? I think if anyone could do the long-distance thing, it'd be you guys." I *did* start down this road to annoy her, but the more I talk, the more it starts to piece itself together. They would do well with a long-distance relationship. She's not a clingy person, and Brandon obviously likes her. If her scowl is heart-eyes, his entire being is heart-eyes. That man wears his heart on his sleeve.

"He deserves better."

"What?" I can't say I'm surprised at her reaction. It's very typical of her to run away from relationships. Mark and I have introduced her to plenty of our friends over the years. The only reason she knows Brandon so well is because he lives with us. He's not exactly avoidable. "Tell me why."

She glares, but there's no fire behind it. Then with a completely straight face, she says, "*Ain't nothing but a heartache.*"

I sigh, wanting to talk to her but not wanting to push her away. It's a very fine line, and I don't know how much room she'll give me. Instead, I grumble, "Damn you, Backstreet Boys."

She grins and brings up another pair of shoes. "What about these?"

I shake my head, half annoyed and half amused by her deflection. "You know what? I think I will go with those ones you showed me before."

18

BRANDON'S DISCOMFORT

Mark is prepping dinner when I get home. The savory aroma of tomato sauce hangs tantalizingly in the air as I walk in. "Hey. What are we having?"

"Spaghetti and meatballs!" he announces, gesturing widely to the pots in front of him. I chuckle. He's always so proud when he cooks, but I happen to know that spaghetti and meatballs is one of the only dinners he knows how to make. It was either that or toast. He does really good toast.

"Are Jake and Ellie around?"

"No. Jake took her on another errand. Turns out, we were out of Parmesan." I smile at that. "They should be back pretty soon, though."

I've been wanting to ask Mark something for a few days, but I don't know how to phrase it so that he doesn't get the wrong idea. I've also wanted to wait until it was just the two of us to avoid being overheard or interrupted. Minimize all chances for catastrophe. Since that seems to be right now, I have no excuse to put it off anymore. I blurt it out in a most inelegant fashion. "How long is she staying?"

He looks up, eyes wide. "Why?" He laughs a little. That's a good sign. "You want her gone now?"

"No!" *Too strong.* "I love having her here. But it's a little weird, right? She's been here eight days and hasn't made any plans to go back home. You know, to her life, her job." Mark's smile disappears, and my stomach turns sour. Is there a better way to ask this question? "I promise I love having her here. She's great. But…is something wrong? Should we be concerned?"

I'm really trying not to make it seem like I'm fishing for any information about her, but I certainly wouldn't say no if he felt like sharing. I'm in so much trouble here. The longer she stays living with us, the more that becomes a deafening screech in my head. All. The. Time.

"She's…her work…" Mark wrinkles his nose, stumbling over an explanation he can't give and shakes his head. "It's…really complicated. I'm sorry. I can't be the one to tell you."

I nod. "I understand."

"I get your concern, Brandon. I'm sorry I haven't been more accommodating there." My stomach twists relentlessly, but this is a conversation that needs to be had. "I don't know how long she's planning on staying, and honestly, the longer she's here, the better. But I can set her up in a hotel if you'd be more comfortable."

I shake my head. "No, don't do that. I love her, really. I just want to make sure everything's okay."

He eyes me with an evil grin now. "You *love* her?"

My face heats in less than a second, my heart jumps into my throat, and my eyes widen to saucers. I don't need to look in a mirror to know that a cartoon has possessed me and taken control of my facial expressions. "No! I mean…not like…that. I just mean…"

"I know." He laughs, finally deciding to let me off. Kind of. *Deep breaths.* Wow, I need to calm down. "Well, if you ever do get uncomfortable with her here, we can get her a hotel room. It's not like it would hurt her feelings. She'd understand."

"Okay, well, thanks. I appreciate it, but it's not necessary. I really do love having her here." *Stop saying that, you idiot.* "I just wanted to know what was going on."

He scrunches his nose. "Sorry."

I hold my breath and try to force my heartbeat to steady. The front door flies open at that moment, and Jake stumbles in with arms full of groceries. He makes it to the counter just in time to dump the bags. Ellie saunters in behind him with no bags at all. She flings her keys on the table by the door, and I'm praying my face is back to its regularly scheduled coloring.

"Hey!" Mark raises his hands above his head. "I literally just asked for Parmesan."

"Oh no." Ellie casts him a wide-eyed look, lips parted, and I'm sixty-three percent sure she's messing with him.

Mark falls for it. "What?" He scans the bags. "All this but not the one thing I asked for? You guys, spaghetti isn't right without—" Ellie comes to a stop beside me just as Mark finds the cheese. When he decides to look back up at her, she's smirking. "You're such an ass," he mutters.

"Please, you know I'm a master shopper." She winks at me, and I swear my stupid heart skips a beat. One day, I will get this under control, but I can guarantee it won't be before I embarrass myself a good forty to fifty-eight hundred times.

"Hey." She bites her lip and drums a short beat on the counter. "I actually need to talk to you guys about something. Good news, I hope. I found an apartment out here."

"What?" Mark asks at the same time Jake says, "Really?"

Jake doesn't wait for an answer before throwing his arms around her neck. I didn't expect when she let slip a few days ago that she wanted to move, it meant she wanted to move *now*. But I am stupidly glad that she won't be leaving again. I smile and pull her in for a side hug.

Mark gives Ellie a strange look that she returns with a small nod. Then he releases his breath and hugs her tight like he might never let go.

19

ELLIE'S APARTMENT

I'VE HAD THE APARTMENT FOR FIVE YEARS, BUT I NEED TO GIVE IT A bit before inviting them over to maintain the illusion that I'm just moving in. It gives me the perfect opportunity to tail them and hopefully find out if Dad will make his move while I'm *not there*.

I hate to expose them again like this, but I don't know what else to do. I keep eyes on their apartment the whole time. Jaythan even hacked into the security feed for their building, so he could report anything suspicious in the hallways.

And the radio silence should be comforting. Perhaps this assignment was just my father's way of firing me. Different from his typical method of *firing* people, but I *am* his daughter. He won't give me more assignments, and my brothers will be in the clear. But I can't afford wishful thinking.

Mark pulled me into his room after I made the announcement, determined to get me to talk. He knows something's wrong. He knows

I wouldn't *move* out here otherwise. I was forced to lie. I've gotten so good at hiding my tells that he didn't even notice. "*Brandon was a target. It hit too close for comfort.*"

I hated using Dad's own words, but it was at least true. Even if I wasn't assigned to kill Mark, I would still be on edge from that. A half-truth—or more of a quarter-truth—and less than he deserves.

Day after day passes, and Dad doesn't show his cards. I'm starting to think this is a losing battle.

>>>>>>>

I LET THREE DAYS PASS BEFORE I'M BACK AT THE GUYS' DOOR. I INVITED them to my "new" place for dinner tonight but didn't tell them I will essentially be escorting them. The monster in my gut hasn't relented one bit.

Brandon answers the door with a polite smile, but as soon as he sees it's me, it turns genuine and brilliant. I couldn't keep a matching smile from my own lips if I tried. The monster settles a bit. "Hey, what are you doing here? We were just getting ready to head out."

I shrug. "I wanted to see you, and my place isn't far, so I thought I'd walk with you guys."

He doesn't say anything, but that bright smile is still plastered to his face. Finally, he simply says, "You're getting a hug."

He waits for me to laugh before spreading his arms and ushering me closer. His arms wrap me in a tight hug, and I have to fight the urge to bury my face in his chest and cry. I haven't needed to cry for so long. I didn't realize how much I'd miss just talking with them every day. It's been three days, and I *long* for their company. Their companionship. *Damn it, that's dangerous.*

"We missed you." Brandon releases me and gestures me inside, calling down the hall. "Guys, Ellie's here!"

"Yeah, I'm coming!" Jake. His door opens at the end of the hall, and he's busy tucking his wallet and phone into his pocket. But then he looks up. And stops. "Wait. She's *here*?" he asks Brandon first, then seems to realize and repeats the question to me directly. "You're *here*?"

"That's what I said."

But Jake ignores Brandon, rushes over to me, and lifts my feet off the ground with his bear hug. I laugh, the urge to cry lessening. "What are you doing here? We were just about to come over!"

My feet touch the floor again. "I wanted to walk you over. I missed you."

Then Mark is there. "Hey!" he exclaims as I'm pulled into a third hug. He squeezes tight enough that for a single second, I can't breathe. "Love you. Missed you. Let's go!"

I glance at the time on my phone. I told them to be at my place by six; it's five forty-five. "You're ready?"

"Yeah, well—" Jake pokes my nose, and I bat his hand away— "it's you." He waits one breath before adding, "We weren't going to be late for your cooking."

I bark a genuine laugh and smack him in the arm.

It's an aesthetically cute walk from their apartment to mine. A few of the buildings have that older look to them with the bricks and paneled windows. It's much better than the newer, uniform buildings in DC for sure. Still, places like this are prime settings for the Enforcers.

People shuffle past intermittently as it's the end of the workday. Mark and Brandon pull ahead and fall deep into conversation about their schooling. They make an effort to include Jake and I, and Jake has some input on how his own tests went, but I mostly listen.

Until my attention snags on a pair of guys walking toward us. Alarm bells start going off in my head. Oversized jackets, ragged hair tucked under dark hats. Maybe I'm being paranoid again. It's been eleven days, and my father hasn't done a thing. I know the stress is getting to me. I can't let it blind me again.

I watch them closely enough that even with only the streetlights to illuminate the sidewalk, I see as he passes Brandon, one guy's hand briefly leaves his pocket only to tuck quickly back in a moment later. *Probably nothing. Probably nothing.*

But as he's walking past me, I grab his wrist and turn it up. He grunts in surprise, and the shock on his face when he sees me is something to treasure. I'm sure in my white knit sweater, jeans, and red beanie I look quite intimidating. And then I think about this turning out to be nothing. But I can't just let it go.

My brothers and Brandon have stopped. They get stuck in a state between making a move to help and complete and utter confusion that leaves them immobile.

The man tries to pull his wrist free, but my grip only tightens. He's probably a good five to ten years older than me; it's hard to tell under the grime and bushy eyebrows. I reach into his jacket pocket and find a wallet. *Please be Brandon's.* Is that a terrible thing to think? But the license is Brandon's—it's not a bad picture, either. Same one that showed up on his file. I try not to show my relief. "I believe this belongs to my friend."

"No." He taps my side with something in his other pocket. I hear Mark inhale an audible gasp beside me. It's just the moron's fingers, but he's clearly trying to make me believe it's a very tiny gun. That's how I know this isn't my father's plan. Just a common street thief. I should be relieved. "I don't believe it is."

Adrenaline races through me at the possibility of a fight, and I actually chuckle. That tension release is a killer. "That's cute." I let him wrench his wrist out of my grip. I've been spoiling for a fight for weeks now, and I know he's ready to provide one. Just to provoke him further, I turn around and start going on my merry way.

He grabs my wrist and flips me back around, holding so tight it will leave a bruise. My grin is positively wicked. He can't have this mark on his record. Not in front of his friend, who merely observes.

Mark grips my shoulder as Brandon yells a warning and slips his arm around my waist, stepping partially in front of me. Jake shoves the guy hard. I'm able to pull free of the thief's grip before he takes me down with him. He stumbles off the sidewalk onto the highway, and I lurch forward to pull him out of the way of oncoming headlights. The driver blasts their horn at the disturbance. If the thief died, Jake would never forgive himself.

It's a good reminder of why I can't have this fight. Not with them here.

My merciful rescue only incenses the man further. He takes a step toward me, aggression rolling off him in waves. "Got your boyfriends protecting you now?" He sounds only slightly less sure of himself. And he should be, since *I* just *saved him*.

I raise my brow.

"Just leave." Brandon attempts to push him away without touching him, but the guy is so power-hungry, he reels back his fist like he'll attack Brandon in lieu of me. I don't think. I push past my brothers, keeping them behind me, grip Brandon's arm, and throw him behind me too, easily dodging the sloppy blow.

"Trust me, they're not the threat you should be worrying about right now." My words come quick and furious. "Back the hell off."

The man might have been willing to back down from Brandon, but there's no way he'll let his reputation take the hit of backing down from me. I know that. He knows that. The three men behind me probably know that.

The foiled thief smiles, baring his teeth, and tilts his head. "Aw, she's a feisty kitty. You gonna call the cops?"

"Cops would be a mercy," I purr. "Last chance. Leave."

A fiery rage enters his eyes, and he brings up his hand. A clear threat.

My self-control disappears on the icy wind. I step close, leaving barely a foot between us. Though I stand about a foot shorter, I still meet his eyes. "Do it." My voice is low, practically a growl.

He does. Or he tries to. I nail the joint at his shoulder with the heel of my palm before he makes contact and kick his legs out from under him, shoving him down hard onto his back. The breath whooshes from his lungs. I'm kneeling beside him now, whispering so only he can hear, "Next time, pick a fight you can win."

I walk away in the next instant, leaving him gasping on the ground. His friend backs off with just a look from me. This was too much excitement. Amateur level, but still it will be hard to convincingly lie about why I taunted the guy. A part of me, however, settles a bit. What if this is all there is to deal with? Common street thieves. Lowlifes that aren't under my father's employ. It's a pleasant fiction.

When Brandon reaches my side, I hand his wallet back.

"Uh, thanks." He frowns; and after our argument at the store, I know he's even *more* suspicious. "How did you do that?"

"I lived in DC." I speed up before he can ask any more questions.

20

BRANDON'S SUSPICION

ELLIE'S APARTMENT LOOKS LIKE SOMETHING YOU'D FIND IN A MAGA-zine. I almost can't believe we live in the same town. Whereas ours is packed full of the belongings of three guys and as clean as we can make it, hers is pristine and spotless. It's cozy with soft sage walls offset by dark wood accents in the coffee table and cabinets. Her light gray couch is one of those with fabric buttons sunk into it and bronze ones along the edges.

Jake plops down there and takes a deep breath. Without even trying, though, I get whiffs of tomato sauce and cheese. A familiar, lovely scent. I will never complain about too much pasta.

When Ellie comes in, Mark is beside the oven. He pulls the door open just enough to see inside. "Is that lasagna?"

Ellie throws her keys toward a hook by the door, and it catches smoothly like she's done it a thousand times. "How did you know?" she drawls. Mark glares at her, still holding the oven door open. He takes another whiff.

"It smells amazing." I plant myself on the loveseat, throwing my arm across the back. It's a different style from the couch—fluffy cushions—but it matches in color pleasantly.

She consults her phone. "Should be about ten more minutes."

"Ah, man." I shake my head with a grin as Ellie makes her way over. I wonder if she notices the hitch in my chest when she takes the seat right next to me. "We came too early."

Batting her lashes and peering up at me, she says, "I can't blame you for being eager to see me."

I laugh, turning away. Attraction mixes heavily with my growing distrust. I try to push the episode on the street out of my mind. Lots of people take classes for self-defense. It's nothing to be suspicious about. And yet, I can't help but feel that she's lying about it.

Ellie scoffs in outrage suddenly, and I find her glaring at Mark who yet again is pulling the oven door open. She grabs a marble from the bowl in the middle of her coffee table and nails him right in the shoulder with it. He turns, face slack with shock, rubbing the spot. Puzzle pieces start falling into place.

"Mark!" Ellie scolds. "Ten minutes. Longer if you keep opening the oven."

Jake's chuckle is muffled by the roaring in my ears. I stare at the woman next to me. Her long hair is loosely braided as always, draped over her shoulder and slightly frizzy from the beanie she left by the door. The scowl doesn't go beyond mild irritation. I must be wrong.

Mark sighs and finally comes over to sit with us, claiming the recliner.

For someone who lives by herself, she sure has a lot of places to sit, and I don't think entertaining guests is a big part of her life. In the back of my mind, I start to think she has all of this just so she can entertain *us*.

I must be wrong, right? It's not possible.

"So," Jake says, rubbing his palms together and leaning forward. "About what happened on the street." My gaze jerks to him, but he's struggling with his own stuff internally, shoulders pulled up to his ears as he addresses his sister. "Are you alright?"

She blinks at him, tilts her head. "Are *you*?"

He nearly killed one of those guys—would have if Ellie hadn't pulled the guy back. The genuine concern in her eyes makes me wish I was wrong.

Jake takes a breath. "Yeah. Thanks."

A single nod from Ellie.

Then because I need her to prove me wrong, I ask, "How did you do that?"

She shrugs, knowing what I mean. "I can show you if you'd like."

I hesitate. This could be a mistake. If I *am* correct, it would be stupid to let her touch me, right? But I follow when she stands and gestures for me to do the same.

"What?" Mark jolts to the edge of his seat. "No fighting before dinner."

Ellie flashes him a grin—mischievous but not wicked. "Better than after."

She positions me to face Mark and Jake and stands at my side. "It's just two movements. Here." She places her palm firmly on my collarbone. "And here." She nudges my heel with her foot. "Same time. Do it fast." She executes the move, and I start going down. My stomach jumps, but

Ellie grips my upper arm and slows my descent. There's barely a thud as I hit the ground.

I breathe fast, but she didn't let the breath get knocked from me. That's a good sign too, right? I blink. She's strong for her size.

"And it doesn't matter how much bigger he is than you," she continues, staring straight into my wide eyes. "He'll be on the ground, gasping, long enough for you to get away." She helps me back to my feet. "Alright, your turn."

I laugh nervously. If her touching me was a bad idea, this one's worse. "I don't want to hurt you."

A breathy laugh, and she shakes her head. "You won't." When I still hesitate, she steps aside and gestures to her brothers. "But if you'd be more comfortable, you could try it on Mark instead."

A part of me knows I should put an end to this. But while it's a strange situation, the practice she's offering could be valuable. After all, I've already had the Enforcers come after me. Self-defense isn't obsolete in my life. I turn to my friend with a raised brow.

"No, you can't volunteer me for your games." Mark scoffs. "I will not enable this rambunctious behavior."

Ellie's grin turns wicked then. Still, I see no truly dark intent glinting in her eyes. "Don't make me drag you off that couch."

While I'd love to see that, Mark seems to want to keep his dignity in check, glaring at her as he stands. He lets Ellie position him, and she shows me again what to do. She only kicks out one of Mark's legs which he swings up for effect. Then she steps aside, catches the cushion she demanded from Jake, and tosses it on the floor behind Mark.

"Please don't hurt me," Mark pleads, and I bark out a laugh.

"No promises, my friend." My palm thuds against Mark's chest, and I cross one leg in front of the other, sweeping out and catching one of Mark's. He flails a bit and starts to fall, but I grab hold of his arms to soften the landing even with the cushion.

"Good." Ellie nods, standing off to the side like an instructor watching her student. "A little faster, and going for both legs would have had him gasping for breath for a good thirty seconds. Maybe more."

"Care to try, Mark?" I ask as he grips the hand I offer.

"No, I think I'm okay." He retreats back to the safety of the couch.

I turn my attention on Jake and quirk a brow. "Jake?"

He hops up immediately. "Yeah, sure, why not?" He squeezes past the coffee table, and Ellie steps back to let him at me. But that's not his intention. He takes Ellie before she can suspect it, sweeping both her legs out from under her. Jake throws his arm around her shoulders to keep her from falling, but she whips hers around his head, pulling him down slightly. She releases instantly, instead throwing her hands behind her to brace.

She laughs, and the three of us join in, but mine is too obviously fake. I can't hide my confusion. That was too quick to have been panic. Almost as if it were a reflex she had to remind herself not to follow through with. Like training she forced herself to forget.

Ellie notes the furrow of my brows and the frown. "What?"

I think quickly. "Do you have to use this *that* often?"

And just like that, the general lightheartedness is sucked out of the room. She fixes her sweater which twisted around her waist as she fell and gives us all a meaningful look. "Not as much as you're thinking," she says slowly. "And definitely not for *what* you're thinking."

I know what I should be thinking; she lives in a city—*lived* in a city. Self-defense is useful for young women everywhere and no less in a place like DC. But now she's making a veiled reference to what I suspect I know is the truth. Is she trying to tell us without actually saying it, or is she just less careful than she should be? I have a hard time believing the latter.

She sighs. "Anyway, I moved, remember? I don't live there anymore."

Dodging the conversation. Sweeping it under the rug. She's so good at that. Finally, I nod. Ellie turns to Mark and a look passes between them. He knows then, too. Their reaction to Jake asking after their father makes sense with this theory, and I hate that.

She says, "Lasagna should be done."

))))))))

MY SILENCE THROUGHOUT DINNER DOES NOT GO UNNOTICED, AND I KNOW I need to talk to her. Even shoving the delicious food into my face isn't enough excuse for it. I can't confront her in front of her brothers, so I give her the courtesy of letting her finish eating before I can't take it anymore.

"Ellie, can we talk?"

Mark throws a concerned look my way, but I drop my gaze to the table. "We can clean up," he volunteers.

She leads me into her room, shutting the door behind us. Her walls are blank, which would make me think she hadn't gotten around to hanging pictures if there were any boxes in sight. No personal effects of any kind, like she has no sentiment.

"What is it?" she asks lightly, but I'm sure she knows something's wrong. She stumbles back half a step when I turn too sharply.

"You shot me, didn't you?" That could have been more delicate, but now that it's out there, I'm almost relieved. There are two options from here: I'm either a terrible friend, or I'm right. I don't know which one I'm rooting for.

She shakes her head slowly, barely fazed. "What are you talking about?"

"You're an assassin, one of those Enforcers. You tried to kill me. It was you!" I need to calm down, but the idea has my entire body vibrating.

"Why are you so obsessed with this Enforcer theory?" She raises her voice to level with mine. "Why would they go after you? What makes you so special?" She steps up to me, getting so close, but I don't let myself back up.

I shake my head. "Does it matter? I know it was you."

"Yes, Brandon. It does matter. If you want to accuse me of this, I should at least know why."

Not a chance. "No, *I'm* the one entitled to answers. Why did you try to kill me?" And here I was falling for her like a *complete* idiot.

"I didn't try to kill you."

"Yes, you did, and I can prove it." At my pause, she crosses her arms. I pull out the first thing that didn't make sense about her. "After I picked you up from the airport, you gave me a gun."

She scoffs. "And I would have armed you just before trying to kill you?"

I cringe. "You were there right after I was shot."

"Saving you!" She flings her arms out, increasingly exasperated. "A decision I'm coming to regret. Is that all you got? Because it's pretty flimsy if you really want to argue this."

I steel my jaw. She's right. "What about how nothing about you has ever added up? You're so private, and those fighting techniques you showed us before dinner aren't just things people know."

"It's called self-defense."

I shake my head. "What about the thief? You could have let him take my wallet, or confronted him calmly, but you attacked him. You *provoked* him into attacking *you*. People don't just do that and pull that kind of move out of thin air. You had training. And what about when you flipped out at the restaurant? You were ready to hurt that woman; I saw it. You've been suppressing your instincts this whole time."

"Alright, fine," she snaps. "Maybe certain things about me don't make sense. I don't particularly enjoy letting people in. That doesn't mean I'm an assassin."

"You hit Mark in the exact same spot I was shot, Ellie. That's pretty impressive aim." Even to my ears, my arguments sound weak, but I'm sure I'm right. Everything about her falls into place with this one piece of the puzzle. She wouldn't invite closeness in relationships if she was afraid of losing them, she has an uncanny ability to shut off her emotions completely, and perhaps this is why she and Mark are so touchy about their father. And Jake doesn't know.

"Okay, Brandon." She takes another step closer, and I do back up this time. The green fire of her eyes can still burn. "Everything you say I did that points to me being an assassin? All of it seems to have benefited you. I gave you that gun so you could protect yourself. I helped you at the mall, and I got your wallet back. Why is that?"

I'm losing this argument even though I know I must be right. Why would she be more angry than hurt over this accusation? If she really were innocent, would she be arguing with me or running away from me?

But I have one thread left to pull. "You've been tamping down your reflexes. I saw it when Jake came after you. You weren't expecting it, and you almost did something to counter the move, but you *stopped* yourself."

Something flashes across her eyes then, and I know I'm reading it wrong because it looks like she's impressed. "Did I?" she asks, her voice like shadows. "How about you prove it, then?"

"What?"

She angles her head in challenge. "Show me you learned something. Come at me and prove I'm hiding something."

The tension in my chest spirals out. "I wouldn't have to if you'd just admit it."

"Make me," she challenges again, glancing down at my hands which fist at my sides.

Is this really the only way I'll get answers from her? I clench my jaw, grab a fistful of her sweater, and kick her legs out. As she's falling, her arm wraps around the back of my neck, bringing me down on top of her. I fling out my other arm to take the impact, but before it can fully register, she throws a leg behind mine and flips us until I'm on my back and she's straddling my lap.

Her chest heaves a few times before she gets it under control again, but I'm completely out of breath, especially as her eyes pierce me with their harsh gaze. She doesn't deny anything now. She says nothing, in fact.

"That goes beyond self-defense, Ellie," I breathe, then pause to suck down a few more breaths. My body buzzes with adrenaline. Reaching up with my free hand, I find the tiny scar on the side of her neck. "When we almost kissed on the elevator, I noticed this. It was new then, and you were acting super weird but had finally started to calm down." I didn't think anything of it then, but it's more than a simple scratch if it's scarring like this. "I think something happened, and you broke from the Enforcers, right? This was a tracker or something?" I was told how the Enforcers are fitted with trackers under their skin. It makes it easier to follow them and quickly broadcast their assassinations.

She's silent, watching me with an intensity that would make me squirm if we weren't so close together.

I drop my hand from her neck. "I don't think you want to kill me now, but that doesn't mean you didn't take the shot. We didn't know each other very well. I don't know how you felt about me before. Maybe you hated me. Maybe I did something to upset you the first time we met." And then just because I'm hurt, I throw out there, "Maybe the gossip sites were right when they said it was a lovers' quarrel. How am I supposed to know?"

"We're not lovers," she spits. *That's all she has to say?*

"Yeah, you can't kiss the person you tried to kill."

She blinks and leans back, putting a little more space between our faces. Instantly, I wish I could take it back. I know she doesn't want to hurt me now, but she shot me *then*. I just want to know why. This person that I've barely gotten to know—started to *like*—is the reason my mother has been worried sick for weeks. The reason I've been treated like glass at work. Why I can't talk to my brother-in-law, who used to be like my own brother, anymore without screaming. And now I've made an enemy of an assassin. Can a person ruin a friendship that never really was?

"Of course not," she whispers. Then, "Damn it, Brandon."

I'm too shocked to move as her mouth comes down over mine. Her lips move against mine harshly, continuing the fight in a completely different manner, but it's really hard to decipher her point when her hands wrap around the back of my neck. My fist tightens, and I realize I still have ahold of her sweater. I release it and plunge my fingers into her hair, drawing her closer as I meet her intensity.

She makes a sound in the back of her throat like a groan, or maybe a growl. I forget why we came in here in the first place. I forget what I just accused her of. All I know is her mouth on mine, her silky hair ripping free of its braid around my fingers.

And then, just as quickly as it began, it ends. She pulls back, her eyes flick to mine, and I don't know what to make of what I see there. Our breaths curl around each other a few extra seconds before she finally climbs off me and back to her feet. My hands remain suspended, cupping an invisible face, until she reaches down to help me up. Not knowing what else to do, I accept it.

She huffs a humorless laugh. "Believe what you want." She shrugs, resignation in her tone. "Make me into whatever you need, but whoever did it—" she nods to my shoulder—"missed. If my aim is as good as you say, explain that."

I take a breath, wishing I could apologize and get her to admit it at the same time. I shouldn't have kissed her. I wasn't thinking, and now I've made an ass of myself. The feeling only intensifies as I realize, "You didn't miss."

Silence. Then she brushes past me out of the room.

21

JAKE'S GIRLS

STARE AT THE NUMBER ON MY PHONE'S SCREEN IN THE SILENCE OF my car. It's gotten oppressively colder since I took the key out three minutes ago. I swear I can see ice crystallizing on the windshield out of the corner of my eye already, and my breath fogs before me.

Dinner last night was, in fact, delicious, but I couldn't stop thinking about my dad. Mark and I could hear that Brandon and Ellie were yelling when they shut themselves in her room. I tried to ask Mark about it, but he was frozen, his eyes wide, lips parted. The two came out and tried to act normal, even with her hair a mess and the shell-shocked look on his face. We left shortly after. I haven't stopped wondering if Brandon knows something about my family that I still don't.

I clench my jaw. What the hell can he know that I can't? They may have their reasons for keeping me in the dark, but I don't care anymore. I will learn something about Dad. *Anything.*

Mark and Brandon are working, but Ellie agreed to catch a movie with me—a new action comedy that was surprisingly easy to talk her into once she convinced herself there's nothing to worry about. Still, she gave Mark a stern look that he returned with a sympathetic, "everything will be fine. Go enjoy yourself."

It pissed me off.

After Ellie and I went shoe shopping, I had the terrifying thought that maybe it's not Dad who's central to whatever trauma is going on with her. Maybe it's an abusive boyfriend back in DC. She's never talked about another guy, and I always assumed she didn't date. But what if that's another thing she just doesn't tell us? There was that mysterious *Jaythan* in her phone, after all.

I thought back to her reaction to my teasing her about Brandon, and it only made more sense. She wasn't just resistant; she was *scared*. Because of someone in her life who might hurt Brandon if she showed any interest? Has Dad refused to help her, and that's why she and Mark are so against him? Does he even know? Am I on the right track *at all*?

It's unjustified, but all these questions make me a little pissed with Ellie too.

I'm currently parked outside her building, but I have a few minutes before she's expecting me. So naturally, I'm staring at my dad's phone number as I have been for the past week and a half. I haven't been able to work up the nerve to go any further.

Until today. I'm going to do it. This time I will do it. *I will. I will. I will.*

I press the *call* button and have a mini heart attack—which is why I'm in the darkness of my car where no one can witness this pathetic display. Here goes nothing. I press the phone to my ear and watch my breath swirl in front of me. It's ringing. Every time it stops, my heart jumps into my throat. But it always rings again. Until it doesn't.

"*Hello?*" My father's voice, deep and rumbly, like it's been run over gravel. I imagined a gentler voice, something more akin to the way I remember Mom. She was friendly and soft. This man sounds the exact opposite. "*Hello?*" Is that a touch of annoyance?

This is the voice of the man who married my mom. Who later left her. Who then had no contact with any of us even when she died. Who may or may not be ignoring my sister's suffering. I tense. I hang up. I relax.

Well…progress.

⟩⟩⟩⟩⟩⟩

UPON ARRIVING AT THE THEATER, ELLIE INFORMS ME THAT SHE DOESN'T want popcorn. This is, of course, ridiculous, and I order us a large with extra butter while she's in the bathroom unable to fight me on it. They offer Parmesan cheese at the concession stand now—I used to smuggle it in—so I heap loads of that on top as well, mixing it around. She'll thank me for this later.

"Hey." The voice is slightly too high to belong to Ellie.

I turn, and startle only a little, though I knew it was her. "Chelsea." I don't know whether to be happy to see her or not. Some part of me is, but the other part wants her to leave before Ellie gets back. "What are you doing here?"

She notes my skittishness with a furrow in her brow and a smile. "Just out with some friends. What about you?"

I glance back toward the bathroom, relieved to see Ellie hasn't come out yet. "I'm just here with my sister."

Somehow, she doesn't question that. I mean, obviously I'm telling the truth, but I'm acting sketchy enough—yes, I acknowledge it, doesn't mean I can stop it—that I could easily be lying. It's possible she trusts me…but we haven't known each other long enough for that. Have we?

"Hey, I've missed you." She playfully hits my arm. I frown. We talk all the time. "Dinner. We're doing it, finally. When are you free?"

"Uh…yeah." I glance behind her again, and sure enough Ellie's on her way over now. "Tonight?"

She smiles. "Great." I ignore the nerves that spark to life at the notion. *It's just a date. You've done this before.*

"Great." I repeat, inching away from her. "I'll pick you up around six? Um…my sister is back, though, so I gotta go. But dinner tonight." I snap and point, backing away. She laughs at me, still not questioning my behavior.

Ellie reaches us and eyes Chelsea. Before she can say anything, though, I grab her arm and steer her toward our theater. Ellie twists, looking back. "Who was that?"

"No one. We're gonna miss the movie."

She guffaws at me. "We're a whole ten minutes early. Come on, Jakey." I hate that stupid nickname. "Oh!" She pokes me in the chest. "Was that the girl you were talking about the other day?" I don't answer, but that's enough for her. "It is! I want to meet her. Let's go back."

"No, that's not going to happen." I grab her around the waist and pick her up when she turns, physically hauling her down the hall to our theater.

"Wha—Jake, what are you doing?" She kicks and squirms halfheartedly. Popcorn is shaken from the container, and half my effort goes into protecting the rest. I know if she was really trying to escape, she'd be able to easily, especially with me preoccupied with the safety of the loot. She pushes her head back into my shoulder and groans. "Fine. Fine. Let me go." She stares me down—or *up* with her stature—when I do so. "Okay. I will let this go if you promise me something."

I enter this deal with only caution and fear.

"I get to meet her before Mark and Brandon." *Oh.* I open my mouth to agree to this reasonable proposition, but she holds up a finger. "Notice the *before*. That means *before*. Not at the same time. I get to meet her first and then they meet her."

"Okay…" My hands come together, popcorn tucked safely in my arm so my fingers can tap against each other one at a time. "That might be problematic."

"Why?"

"Well, you see, that would involve you and her meeting with only me to buffer. I'm not even sure anything is going to happen with her." And that's a big reason I don't want her meeting Ellie. She confessed to wanting the gossip, but I don't know how that will translate to social interactions outside our group. Mainly, with others we are maybe interested in bringing into the circle. Absolutely under no circumstances will I risk Ellie chasing Chelsea away before I get to see where this goes. And I can never have the two of them alone in a room with me. I'm not a dramatic person, so when I say I might die, I mean it.

Ellie's mouth gapes open. "So, you would let some random guy meet this woman you like before your own sister?" She shakes her head, eyes tiny slits of outrage. "I'm so annoyed that you would hypothetically do that."

I squint at her, tracking her logic but falling short. "Brandon's not random. And that's not what I said."

She rolls her eyes. "Whatever." Then she takes a handful of popcorn and throws it at me. I immediately scramble to catch it all.

"Hey, hey, hey! Precious cargo! Do not throw the cuisine!" She just laughs at me.

》》》》》》》》

"WHAT WAS THAT ABOUT AT THE THEATER?" CHELSEA SITS IN THE booth across from me, sipping her Coke. I brought her back to the little Mexican restaurant Ellie took us to. There isn't much indoor seating, and waiters and patrons are constantly bustling past our table, but the food was amazing.

Chelsea's red hair is half pulled back with a mound up top that defies gravity. The rest flows over her shoulder, blending with her shimmery purple dress that has a plunging neckline. She certainly looks better than me. In my defense, these are my best jeans, and the leather jacket is my favorite.

"What do you mean?"

She grins at me, perfect teeth sparkling. "You ran away pretty quickly." I cough into my fist. Here's the line of questioning I was waiting for. "Are you embarrassed by me?"

Okay, not what I was expecting.

She reads the confusion on my face and chuckles. "I trust you, Jake. And you told me you had a twin before. She looked exactly like you.

Relax." I mean, I wouldn't say *exactly*, but… "So, are you? Embarrassed?"

"No! No." I shake my head, reaching for her hand. My thumb rubs a circle on her smooth skin. "Not you. Just not thrilled about the idea of my sister meeting you. I love her and all, but she can be a lot. And I'm not sure what her relationship with another female would be like." Chelsea raises a brow, so I explain. "Whenever she's here, she only spends time with *us*: my brother, me, our roommate. I don't think she has any girl friends in DC either. She never talks about any." But I can't be sure of *that* either.

"Sounds lonely."

I try to keep the frown off my face. "Yeah, it does." I pull my hand back.

Chelsea laughs suddenly. The sound triggers a reaction in me like touching a live wire. "I like that you're nervous about her with me. I wish I had siblings."

My own laugh is humorless. I rub my brow. "Care to take one of mine?"

She tilts her head, her smile turning concerned, noting the tone of the joke. She's a perceptive one. "You don't mean that."

"How do you figure?"

She rolls her eyes, leaning back in her chair. "Oh, come on. You don't have to put on this act with me. I know your brother annoys you, but you can't convince me that if he ever needed you, you wouldn't drop everything for him."

I shake my head, something cold and bitter settling in my gut. "He doesn't need me."

"He might need you more than you think." Her lips pull into a weary frown as she assesses me. I take a long drink from my Sprite—regular Sprite, this time. Stupid sister got into my head.

When she remains silent, contemplative, I change the subject. "What was it like growing up without any siblings?"

Reluctantly, she takes the hint. "Well, it meant that my parents focused all their energy on me." She grins, and I blow out a sympathetic breath. Her eyes crinkle at the sides. I don't stop myself from reaching out and brushing my thumb there. "It wasn't all bad. My mom taught me a lot."

"Yeah? Like what?"

"I mean, there were the basics: cooking, cleaning. Being an only child meant no switching off chores with anyone or tricking them into doing them for me." She glares in mock disapproval. I knew telling her about that time I tricked Mark into doing the dishes for a solid month by convincing him that I was allergic to the soap would come back to bite me. "But she also taught me a lot about how to properly research. I basically aced all my classes because of it." She grins.

Of everyone in my life right now, Chelsea has shared the most with me. I've learned so much about her while simultaneously coming to the realization that I don't know my own sister. I don't have relationships like this, but it feels right with Chelsea. She's the one who convinced me to get in touch with my father. Even if I haven't succeeded yet, that's the support I need. She's here for me now when my own family refuses to be.

22

ELLIE'S MISTAKE

CALLED JOEY CROWN. HE'S ANOTHER OF MY FATHER'S ASSASSINS, NOT one I've ever been fond of. His reputation is one of the most ruthless around the compound, not because of his brutality like most, but because of his stone-cold silence. Crown helped me survive my second assignment. He warned me the woman was in witness protection, and then he took out those watching Sierra Donovan from the street, leaving me the simple task of pulling the trigger on her. We haven't stayed in contact, and he hasn't been pleasant in any of our few dealings since. I make a point to interact as little as possible with the assassins now.

Especially after Rowan…

I shake him from my thoughts.

An exception must be made because I needed Crown's help again.

"*Richards,*" he drawled when I got him on the phone just after that ill-fated dinner. "*To what do I owe this unexpected pleasure?*"

"I need a job," was all I told him.

A hearty chuckle. *"Why, pray tell, are you coming to me?"*

"The last one…" I stopped myself. "I just need one, alright?" I really didn't want to go to a fanatic like Crown—a man who somehow takes pride in this work just like my father—but I didn't have anyone else. I'd run through it all in my head. If I get another job and execute it perfectly, my father will forget this whole *Mark* business. He'll go back to leaving my brothers alone, and things can be normal again. I'm still a good assassin. I have to prove I'm still an *asset*.

I shouldn't have kissed Brandon. The anger just swept through me so violently, and I saw it as a way to prove my point. It was a solution that presented itself in a way that felt like staring into the sun. He said, *"You can't kiss who you tried to kill,"* and I *didn't* try to kill him, so kiss him I did. Because I'm an idiot. Because there was clearly no better way I could have handled that conversation. Because part of me has wanted to for a while.

The better solution would have been to let him alienate me. I didn't have to prove anything to him. I could have let him think he'd hurt me beyond repair and never spoken to him again, clearing up more than one of my current problems. But in the heat of the moment, I refused to take that as an option. I wasn't going to cut him out of my life, no matter how logical the move would be. Against all my better judgment, I like having him around.

The sooner I clear all this up, the better. I need to put an end to it.

"You want a trade?" Crown asked, and it was the scariest possible response.

My heart lodged somewhere in my throat. "No!" He was silent on the other end, but I could feel his suspicion radiating down the line.

"Just get me a job, Crown. Can you do that, or do I need to call someone better equipped to suit my needs?"

"No need to get testy, princess. You know the deal; I'll get you your job. You'll be back in your daddy's good graces and fit to inherit his kingdom in no time."

That was always the plan. I would take over the Enforcers when my father was finally ready to pass it down. I would be the one behind the desk, researching targets to hand out to assassins like Crown.

When I was a child, I meant to make him proud when I eventually took over. After Mom died, it turned vindictive. I wanted it just so I could run the operation into the ground. Now, I doubt my father would give it to me even if I *could* find my way back into his favor.

But Crown got me a job. For the promise of the bounty. I did my research. Just enough to tell me where she'll be.

Jake and Brandon are at work, and Mark is at their apartment. He should be safe there, secluded. I can't keep an eye on all three of them when they're spread out like this, so it's the perfect time to get this over with.

The target is a woman. From the tiny picture in the corner of her dossier, I gather that she's been successful in her field. She owns a real estate business and wears a pantsuit with black hair pulled back in a tight bun. I don't let myself analyze anything below the surface.

I set my rifle up in the house across from the one she's showing to a young couple. It's a nice neighborhood, white picket fences, gently frosted green lawns, picture-perfect houses. The setting of domestic bliss. Or pulse-pounding tragedy.

I kneel patiently in front of the window, watching the blue front door across the road. It's lucky Crown managed to snag an assignment in Oregon only an hour away from my brothers. The proximity to them should make me nervous, but seeing the crosshairs in my view makes me breathe easier than I have in weeks.

I catch movement behind the kitchen window. They must be wrapping up. I flick the safety off and settle my finger next to the trigger. Deep breath in. Deep breath out. My training kicks in and everything in my body goes still and silent. Deadly calm washes over me. The dusty smell of the home I'm squatting in fills my senses, cold metal bites my fingers.

The front door swings open. A happy couple steps out, smiling at each other and my target. She looks happy. I tell myself it's just the prospect of the sale that makes her so. I wait until she reaches her car and pulls out her keys.

My finger caresses the smooth of the trigger.

I take the shot.

And I miss.

The bullet hits her windshield, red spitting down the glass. I don't let myself panic yet. I fire again, and this time it hits her square in the chest. She's down in an instant, and the man rushes his wife back into the house, terrified.

I don't wait around for the pandemonium to come from the neighbors. I don't let myself question why her windshield *bled*. My hands shake as I pack my rifle and retreat out the back door.

This was supposed to solve my problems, not create new ones. I missed. I've never missed a shot. It only takes one bullet to do the job. Now I've both interfered with an assignment and botched one. This will be so much worse for my brothers.

I am so sorry, Mom. I've failed.

23

BRANDON'S FRIEND

I CATALOG EVERY SHOEBOX STACKED IN THIS PACKED ROOM FOR THE third time this week. I haven't been back at work long, but every day my boss assigns me to the back, still wary of letting me out front. On top of the shooting, the gossip sites have made me a popular case, especially in town. I can't blame him, though I've joked more than once that a celebrity appearance could be good for business.

I'm mostly undisturbed back here, my boss only coming back when he needs to bring another shoe up front. It leaves me a lot of time to think about all the things I said to Ellie.

Everything seemed to line up so nicely. I was so sure, but could I be wrong? If I am, then I owe her a huge apology. I'm just still not convinced that I am. And that parting shot… *If my aim is as good as you say, explain that.* She wanted me to say it. To admit it. *You didn't miss.* For her sake and mine.

I was starting to like her. A lot. How could she kill people for a living? How am I supposed to feel about that? What makes me even angrier is that I'm not even mad about what she possibly does for a living. The fact that she might kill people doesn't aggravate me as much as the fact that I *liked* her. Just my luck.

That's such a lie. I've had great luck up until now. I've led a very fortunate life. Until Ellie showed up.

And the worst part—the absolute worst part—the cherry on top—the one that takes the cake… I don't want to go back to how it was before I met her. I don't want her to disappear. Even if this turns out to be true, I don't want to lose her.

The kiss keeps replaying in my mind. Every time I close my eyes, I can feel her lips on mine all over again. I've wanted to kiss her since the first moment I saw her at the airport. I imagined she might feel a teensy bit of the same. But she only did it out of spite because of what I said to her. In hindsight, it felt more like she was telling me I was an absolute moron than anything else. And she'd be right.

I need to apologize.

As if summoned, my phone buzzes in my pocket. Her name lights up my screen like a beacon. I hesitate only a second before answering. "Hey?" It's been two days since her dinner, but I still phrase the greeting like a question. She's never called before, and I certainly didn't expect her to after the other night.

"*Something's wrong with Mark.*" Instantly, any lingering anger at her or myself disappears at the fear in her voice, shaking as she speaks. "*He just doubled over. It sounds like he's in pain.*"

"Okay," I say, keeping my own voice calm in an effort to soothe her.

"Can you tell me if he's hurt? Is there a wound?"

"*No, no, there's no injury anywhere.*"

"Is he saying anything, Ellie?"

"*No. Mark, what's wrong?*" A short pause. "*He just keeps shaking his head.*"

"What's he doing now?"

"*He's…*" Her voice still trembles, but she forces a breath down. "*He's bent over the toilet now. He threw up; it doesn't look like there's any blood.*"

"Okay, El, I need you to fill up a water bottle for him. He needs fluids." I hear the sink running on her end. "You've got to get him to the hospital, El. Can you do that?"

A deep breath, and her voice is steady now. "*Yeah. I can do that.*" No hint at all that she was ever terrified for her brother. Shutting off her emotions again, but this time it took her awhile.

"Good," I tell her. "I'll get Jake, and we'll meet you there." My boss will be more than happy to get me off his hands a few hours early anyway. "He's going to be fine. It's probably just a migraine; he gets those sometimes."

"*What?*" she snaps. "*Never mind. Thanks, Brandon.*"

"Of course," I mutter, but she's already hung up.

24

ELLIE'S REVELATIONS

BRANDON FINALLY RUSHES IN ON MY TWO-HUNDRED AND SIXTY-fourth pass through the waiting room. There aren't very many people in here, but the few that are cast me worried glances. I want to wipe the expressions right off their faces, but I can't stop pacing.

When Mark's attack happened, I didn't know what to do. I've never dealt with that issue before. I didn't think he had either. I saw his growing agitation, but it shouldn't have led to this. I wasn't even going to tell him about the assignment, but it's like I had no choice. It spilled out of my mouth when he asked where I'd been all day, like I had no control. I've completely lost all my control.

And I didn't know who else to call. Brandon's name jumped out at me when Mark keeled over, clutching his head. Despite that he figured out what I am. Despite that maybe he wouldn't help me because he hates me.

But he answered, and still, there's only a kind, gentle expression on his face when he reaches me. He's a damn good person. So much better than I deserve right now. "Jake wasn't at work, and he isn't answering his phone, so I left a voicemail. Have you heard anything?"

"No. He's been back there for fifteen minutes!"

"Okay, well." He puts a hand on my shoulder. "You did everything you were supposed to. He'll be okay."

"I know." But my breathing is becoming too harsh. *No!* Before Brandon came, I was working my emotions down, putting them in their neat little box. Yet the second his hand hits my shoulder, everything comes rocketing back up. He undoes all my hard work with a single touch. I know he only means to help, and that makes it even worse.

This is my fault; I upset Mark enough that he landed here. I don't deserve Brandon's comfort. I shouldn't *need* it. I should be able to control this. But I'm back to breathing too jaggedly. "I know he's going to be fine. I know that."

"Hey, come here." He pulls me to him, and his arms are a warm blanket. He's a muscular guy, but the embrace is so soft. It's like being hugged by a cloud. I didn't receive affection from my father growing up—not past the age of five when he knew he had me successfully separated from my mother. I learned to live without. My brothers were the first to hug me in eleven years except for Rowan. Not like this. I can't even pinpoint what's different now. I hate Brandon a little bit for it. And then I'm annoyed because that's not true, but I *wish* I could hate him just for a minute.

I force myself to take deep breaths to keep from crying. There's no way I'm going to shed a tear in front of someone I barely know. This is pathetic. I am pathetic. I caused *all* of this. And all because I can't handle the stress of my dad *not* doing anything. The pressure got to me, and I cracked. I didn't need the job. *Why did you take the job?* I've spent my life trying to protect Mark, and I'm failing miserably when he needs me the most.

"I'm sorry." I hate that those words are said into Brandon's shirt as I'm near hyperventilation. He starts rubbing my back in firm strokes. "This is stupid."

"It's not. It's not stupid, Ellie." He huffs a small laugh. "This isn't a fun place to be."

I sigh, turning my face out so I can breathe. "Last time, I had everything under control. I don't know what happened today. This wasn't supposed to happen."

Brandon's hands stiffen on my back, and I feel his entire body go rigid against me.

I freeze. Did that just come out of my mouth? I never think out loud. What is wrong with me? This can't keep happening. *What is wrong with you?*

His face is a mix of shock and fear. It's something else for me to focus on, at the very least. Unaware of any other option, I let the killing calm sweep in and meet his eyes. I slide out of his arms and back away until three paces separate us.

He continues to stare at me even as Mark walks up to us with a dark pair of sunglasses over his eyes. I'm the first to turn away, taking my brother's arm. "What happened? Are you okay?"

"Yeah," he replies casually like I haven't been worried sick out here. His face scrunches in pain even as he gives me a thumbs-up. "Migraine.

They gave me something that should clear it up in a couple hours." He shrugs. "Until then, dark and quiet."

"What happened?" Brandon asks.

"Just stress. I'm fine." He's talking so softly, he's nearly whispering.

A wave of sickness takes me. "Stress," I repeat. It *is* my fault, then.

He turns and wraps his arm around me. I hate his pity. "Stop, El." I avoid meeting his eyes—or his sunglasses—and look over his shoulder. "It's not your fault." A kiss on my forehead, and I almost feel better. At least enough that I'm able to shut myself down again.

I stand straighter and finally breathe normally. "We should go." I glance at Mark. "Go home with Brandon. I'll meet you there." I walk away from them both, not daring to look back.

I. Am. So. Stupid.

BRANDON AND I FORCE MARK TO STAY ON THE COUCH ALL DAY EVEN after he says he's feeling better. At one point Brandon tries to tie him down by burying him under all the blankets. That doesn't exactly work, but Mark stays down, sensing the tension. It's smoke in the air. Their typically cozy apartment is wrought with the unsettling sense of a bomb about to detonate.

Brandon hasn't spoken a word to me. He hasn't cast mean glares or petrified glances at me, either. He's just silent…processing. I give him his space. And when he goes to the store because Mark mentioned in passing wanting a Twix, I let him go alone.

I try calling Jake again. It goes to voicemail. I tell myself he left it on silent. He'll be home soon like every other night. But that sick twisting in my gut isn't just because of Mark.

"Ellie." Mark draws me out of my head. I blink once and turn to him, finding his brown eyes wide and pleading. "Why did you take another job?"

Because I'm an idiot. "It's my job, Mark. If I didn't take it, Cooper would come after me. I don't want anyone else coming out here." And just like that, we're back to lying to him.

Mark says nothing of the fact that I just referred to our father by his last name. "But you didn't say you got a job. You said you *took* a job. If you tell me it was assigned to you, I'll believe you. But please be honest with me; did you ask for it?"

I stay silent. He already knows. His mouth drops open, and before he can make his migraine worse, I cut in quickly, "Mark, it's my whole life. I can't just stop working. Besides, I blew off my last job. I had to make up for it."

"You mean, you've already gone through with it?"

I'm barely able to meet his eyes. "I'm sorry. You don't understand; I didn't have a choice."

"You always have a choice." He cringes. In pain? I tense, but he continues. "We can handle what happens to us. I don't care if it puts us in more danger—"

"*I do.*" It comes out harsher than I intend, but he snaps his mouth shut. I close my eyes and take a breath. Two. He has every right to be furious with me.

I say nothing more, and Mark just stares at me for a while. His big, dark puppy eyes begging me without words. I look away like the coward I've become.

"What's going on between you and Brandon?"

"Nothing," I answer automatically.

"You don't think I noticed you ignoring each other all afternoon? I heard you two yelling the other day. What's wrong? I thought you liked him."

"*Nothing's* wrong," I insist, looking toward the door.

"Something is definitely wrong." Mark is shaking his head. Then he stops, eyes widening. "Did you tell him about—"

My eyes thin to dangerous slits. "I didn't *tell* him anything."

"But—" Mark doesn't get to finish that thought because Brandon comes through the door. *Finally.*

I pop up to my feet. "I have to find Jake."

"He didn't come back yet?" Brandon's gaze sweeps the room.

I shake my head, take out my phone, and press *call* as soon as I'm in the hallway. He saves himself from a verbal beating by answering immediately. "Jaythan, find everything you can on Jake. He hasn't been answering his phone, and he's not home yet. I don't care how trivial it is, I want to know everything."

"*Hi, E.*"

I'm trying to be better about grinding my teeth—I'm developing lockjaw—but Jaythan makes it so difficult. "Get on it!"

"*Hey, I answered right away. That means I get nice E.*"

"Jaythan!"

"*I'm already on it. Go find your brother.*"

"Call me as soon as you find anything."

⟫⟫⟫⟫

FOUR HOURS LATER, I BURST THROUGH THE DOOR TO THEIR APART-
ment, dripping wet and brotherless. The torrential downpour did not
help improve my mood. I shake out my sopping hair on the carpet and
slam the door behind me.

It's one in the morning, but I know neither of them will be asleep.
And a quick survey of the room tells me Jake hasn't shown up here either.

"Did you find him?" Mark sits up straight, looking over the back
of the couch.

I glare at him with the force of all my pent-up rage from the last
month. "Yes, Mark," I snap. "He's right here. Can't you see him?"

"Okay." Brandon jumps up and steps between Mark and me, even
though there's already a couch separating us. A tiny sliver of shame
trickles through me that he would think I'd do anything, but I'm too
angry to fully focus on that. "What did his boss say?"

Talking to me again, I see. I'm tempted to yell at him too.

"He said he never showed up to work this morning, and he left
him a bunch of voicemails too. So, he's been missing at least seventeen
hours." I throw my keys hard against the wall, the ring of metal-on-
metal ending in a resounding clack as they chip the blue paint. I run
my hands through my hair, having the sudden urge to yank it all out
at the roots.

Brandon comes a little closer. "It's gonna be okay."

Light musical chimes from my back pocket save him from my
temper. About time. "Talk."

I hear Jaythan typing on the other end. *"He just disappeared. I can't
get his phone or his face on any traffic cameras. There's nothing on the tapes
outside his work. I even tried abandoned warehouses in the area. Nothing. He*

walks out of the apartment this morning and then nothing. That can really only mean one thing, E."

"No."

"*I'm sorry.*"

"Damn it, Jay," I snap, then rub my temples. "Are normal psychopaths taking holidays all of a sudden?" Every horror we've dealt with this *wonderful time of the year* has centered around just one organization. Just one man.

"What?" Brandon's eyebrows shoot up under his thick dark curls which have grown out to his brow line.

"*Yup.*" Jaythan's clicking stops.

"Great." I hang up and turn to Brandon and Mark. "I know where Jake is."

They both sigh in relief, shoulders sagging.

"Wrong." I massage both my temples. Lots of explanations are coming. "Definitely not good."

"Why?" Mark doesn't look concerned about any of this anymore. He, of all people, should know better.

I huff a breath, turning from him. "Brandon—"

Then my phone rings again. I don't even bother looking at the caller ID. "What?" I shout into the receiver.

"*Sorry.*" It's Jaythan again. "*There's something else. I found some other stuff you might want to know.*"

I pause and glance at each of the men whose attentions are wholly focused on me. "I need to take this." I make for Mark's room.

He reaches for my arm but doesn't grab me. "Ellie."

"Trust me, Mark." I back out of his range. "It's important." As soon as the door shuts behind me, my attention is all Jaythan's. "Go."

"*Okay, so I dug into both their lives like you told me to. And I found absolutely nothing.*"

"*That's* what you called to tell me?"

"*Patience.*"

"I've not got any of that left, Jaythan." Everything in me right now is wound so tight, the second I relax even a little, I'll make a hole in the roof.

"*You told me Mark was your new target, and that got me thinking, right? It just didn't seem right, you know?*"

My teeth are clenched. "Don't tell me what I already know."

He sighs. "*Fine. Anyway, it seems like the only reason Mark was targeted was to get you back on track. Set you straight like some sort of lesson. Point is, I couldn't find anything to criminalize either of them, but I did find stuff on the organization you work for.*"

"Enough preamble, Jaythan! Get to your point!" I feel kind of bad about it since he's taken all this time doing this for me, but not enough to apologize.

"*There's another organization called Govenin.*"

"Never heard of it."

"*Not many have. It's short for Governor Infinity. It was started by a bunch of college kids years back. Basically, their goal was to keep politicians they liked in office as long as possible and take out the ones they don't as quickly as possible.*"

"You mean voting."

"*Yeah, well, these guys took it a little further than that. They used a more violent method. To be fair, they started out with innocent protests. Then they got violent when people disagreed with them. The protests became riots.*"

Then they started threatening government officials. Here's the clincher. They disbanded four years ago."

I bite my lip to keep from snapping again. *Deep breaths, Ellie.* "Then why the hell am I hearing about them?"

"Think about it. Four years ago, you were seventeen. A year of successful missions under your belt."

I ask slowly, "What are you saying?"

"The Enforcers were gaining traction with you. They absorbed Govenin. Now they keep the whole government under their thumb while the government is also the one unwittingly paying for this service. Ironic. Govenin has officially graduated from threats to murder—government-funded ghosting, if you will."

"Basically then, the Enforcers absorbed the very sort of organization they claim to fight against?" Everything Cooper sold me about taking out oppressors, fighting for the little guys, *lies.* I shouldn't be surprised. I suspected it was mostly a lie after my very first assignment. But there was a small part of me that hoped maybe he wasn't all bad. I should have known the second he handed me the file on Mark. I kick Mark's bedframe, and a sharp pain shoots through my toe and up my calf. My teeth snap down on my tongue, and my rage boils over. "Violence is always the answer, is it?" He's silent. "You still don't know why Brandon was targeted?"

"I just found this stuff on Govenin. I can do more digging and probably find something soon."

"Don't bother." I look toward the door where Mark and Brandon are awaiting an explanation on the other side. "I can find out right now."

After hanging up it occurs to me that Brandon could just be a conspiracy theorist with his determination to blame the assassins. But I know him better than that by now. He knows something.

I march right up to him, not stopping until I'm barely a breath away and have to tip my head back to look him in the eye. He doesn't flinch. "I *am* an assassin, and I *did* shoot you." He blinks hard, lips parting slightly. "You know my secret, now tell me yours. You were targeted by the Enforcers, but you always seemed to know that. You know why they sent someone after you."

He refuses to cower even now, and a distant part of me buried somewhere beneath the rage is impressed. "You just admitted to shooting me. Why should I tell you?"

"I wasn't the assassin assigned to you, but I did shoot you, and not a second later another bullet landed at your feet."

My glare remains harsh even as I watch the realization sink in. "You…" He takes a half-step back, and a breath rushes out of him. "You were saving me?"

I tire of his shock and advance on him again. This time he backs up until he hits the wall. "Tell me why I had to."

"It's my brother-in-law," he says, putting his hands up. He wants to push me away but doesn't touch me. I don't move. "He works for the Enforcers."

25

JAKE'S FATHER

HAVE DUBBED THIS CHAIR NORMAN. NOW, I KNOW WHAT YOU'RE thinking. *Jake, what are you doing naming chairs after having just been kidnapped?* Well, I've been sitting here for several long-ass hours waiting for someone to tell me what the hell is going on. At a certain point, my fear turned to boredom and annoyance. That point was much faster than I would have imagined, but everyone runs out of panic, right? Maybe not. But I definitely did, and now I just want someone to come in and take me away from Norman's steady company.

The room is tiny. Made smaller by the many pillars of documents that quite literally rise from floor to ceiling. Only the glass door in front of me is unobstructed, but someone put up a partition on the other side to block my view.

I'm seated behind a desk that barely fits in the room and has two more reasonably sized stacks of files, neither of which is labeled. The files have names on the sides, not of businesses but people. Possibly employees? Unless I've completely misread the surroundings and mistaken a thematic dungeon for an actual office. Norman's no help here.

I'm bored to tears, and the jittery fear I felt when I was first grabbed has long passed, but I jump when the door creaks open, almost having forgotten it can actually do that. A large man enters, swallowing up most of the remaining space. He's probably somewhere in his fifties, and I'm not going to lie, he reminds me of Santa Claus. He's of the same build as the jolly fellow, and I estimate three chins. He technically has a beard, not a great one. And for some reason he's wearing shiny black boots which kind of makes my situation seem even more ridiculous. Some bell in the back of my mind rings with recognition—other than the Christmas sweaters, of course—but I can't figure out why.

"Hey, Santa, what am I doing here?" I don't know why my brain insists I be a smartass in the face of death, but I guess I'm okay with it before the end. Better than going out a coward. I think. Really, I'd prefer not to go out at all, but I'm thinking that's not up to me.

This morning, I woke up—the start to every boring story ever told. But here's how mine differs: after I mentally prepared for another dreary day of bussing tables, a bag came down over my head, offering variety. Next thing I knew, I was waking up *again* but this time in a golden bedroom. Two minutes later, a man large in a different way knocked at the door to bring me here. Muscle man stuck me in this office and promptly left without saying a single word.

And now we have this guy.

He tips his head, brow furrowed in surprise that I just said that. I mean, but what is he going to do? Kidnap me again? I suppose killing me is still an option, but I don't see this guy as the mastermind of my misfortune.

"I understand you must be scared." His voice is deeper than I expected. I bite my tongue to keep from begging to differ with the man who might murder me. "Let me explain." But the way he says *explain* sounds more like *splain*, and what happens next is entirely out of my control.

"*No, there is too much. Let me sum up.*" I close my eyes and slowly lower my head even with the brilliant, accented delivery.

"Princess Bride?" He pauses, and I look up into his disappointed frown. It makes me suddenly defensive. "Really?"

Chelsea would have loved it. Has she noticed I'm gone? I glare. "What's your problem? That movie's a classic!" I sigh. He still might murder me, and I think if I anger him, it will be more brutal. I'd really prefer a quick death. I hang my head again, swallow my pride. "Sorry."

"Well, Jake Spencer, you are here because your sister is not doing her job. You know her as *Ellie Cooper*."

My face scrunches. *What the hell is that supposed to mean?*

"I know her as *Emily Richards*." I recognize the name from the news, but it takes another minute to understand the implication. My eyes widen, and I bite back the laugh that threatens to bark out of me. Am I supposed to believe this? "You've heard of her, I see. One of our top Enforcers, and your father's pride and joy." Is that bitterness, I sense? "If I'm correct, you've been kept in the dark about your father and sister's occupation. Your father would like to change that now."

My sister is an assassin? If she's my father's "pride and joy" does that mean he's her boss? Or did he train her? Somehow these possibilities don't rattle me as much as the fact that my father is behind my being here with Norman. "Can I talk to him?"

"I'm afraid that's not possible."

I raise a brow. Not possible seems a bit extreme unless this man killed him. Perhaps he ate him. *Why am I like this?*

"He wanted me to relay to you what he's been doing for the past two decades."

"*He* sent you?" I'm growing bolder now—probably for the worse. I guess that remains to be seen. "If I'm to believe anything you've just told me, I'm going to need to hear it from him. Tell him that he can tell me everything, or no one will. I'm not interested in hearing anything from you."

Santa doesn't even appear angry. He nods, lower lip jutting out like he expected as much. "I will give him the message." And with that, Santa's taking my message to deliver to another. How full circle of him.

〽〽〽〽

IT'S NEAR MIDNIGHT ACCORDING TO CONDIGO, THE ANNOYING TICKING clock above the door, before I hear from my father. I guess he doesn't sleep. It's not like I needed any either after spending the whole day making friends—or enemies, in the clock's case—with inanimate objects. Santa comes back and leads me out of the tiny office, collectively dubbed *Stephen*.

Oddly enough, most of the building's walls are glass so there's very little privacy. I suppose that could be a good thing for certain businesses. Keeps people honest. But there are no windows to the outside world. *None.* I knew they had taken me underground, but being stuck in the office all day kept it far from my mind. And now, it isn't sitting well. *Welcome back, fear.*

There's a room at the end of a long hallway with a solid door and walls blocking it off. Typical, I suppose, that my father gets the only private office. He poured his life into the company, after all. Let's see what was so precious to him he couldn't leave it for family.

Santa leads me into the room, and it takes me a moment to spot the gray head of hair—a blatant reminder of how long it's been—bobbing up and down behind the computer. I come closer to the desk, but he doesn't look up. His glasses rest at the tip of his nose as he studies the sheet in front of him. His forehead has those permanent wrinkles, and it's hard to tell from his downcast gaze, but it looks as if he's got no smile lines. Not surprising of the guy who cut out his family.

I look down at what he's studying so carefully. It's an official looking paper that seems to hold a lot of information for just one sheet. There's a picture in the top right corner. *My* picture.

I chuckle. "You know, there's an easier way to get to know me."

Slowly, he looks up, blue eyes meeting mine, crinkling at the edges with amusement that doesn't spread over his thin lips. "Hello, Jake. You're upset." He waves a hand, and I assume Santa left with the click of the door.

"Good guess." I can't believe this is the first thing he says to me in almost two decades. *Father of the year, ladies and gentlemen.*

He sighs. "I know I wasn't in your life a whole lot."

"Try *at all* on for size." I'm very impressed at the level of calm with which I deliver that.

He taps one finger on the desk. "Do you want to know why or go back to your room?"

I blink at his use of the common parenting tactic. *A little late for that, Dad.* Nevertheless, I bite my tongue. Damn curiosity.

"Did Hartley tell you anything about this operation I'm running?"

I squint, assuming he's talking about Santa. "Who?" I only ask to be a pain in the ass. After all, I was deprived of the privilege of driving my father up a wall for sixteen years. It's the least of what he deserves.

"Hartley." Then he nods knowingly. "The man who looks like Santa Claus."

I can't help it; I smile. "So, you noticed that too?" At my father's amused nod, I wipe the grin from my face. "He said something about Ellie being that assassin on the news, Emily Richards. He also said the reason I'm here is because she's not doing her job."

"That's all true."

I throw my head back with another laugh. "That's what a son wants to hear from his estranged father. You should know," I say, placing my hands on my hips and feeling only a little bit like a scolding mother, "the amount of sense this makes is exactly zero."

He sighs but brushes past my comment. "I oversee the Enforcers. We target oppressive forces in the country and keep them in check." That's broad, and I can't figure out if he understands that can refer to much more than just criminals. "Your sister is one such Enforcer. One of the best, actually. I handpicked all her trainers, and of all my agents, she has trained the longest and hardest. A while back she interfered with an assignment in an effort to take the glory for herself. I was forced to get *her* back in line. She ignored that assignment. And so, here you are. Questions?"

Some, yeah. One would expect me to be angry, scared, horrified, *something* at this revelation. But I don't react at all. Maybe I'm going crazy, but for some reason this news doesn't really surprise me. She was always distant; she snapped at me when I asked about Dad. I knew she was hiding something big. And after the month we've had…

I *am* a little relieved that I seem to be wrong about the abusive boyfriend theory.

"Is that why Brandon was shot?"

"He was never her assignment."

Does that mean he was the assignment she got in the way of? But Dad said she wanted the glory, yet Brandon's still alive, and Ellie appears intent on keeping it that way. Perhaps Brandon never was their target. Or he's lying. I shift on my feet. "Was I ever?" He's silent. Of course not. Why would I be here if I was? "Was Mark?" His lips tighten into a thin line, and I have my answer. My expression hardens. "Why should I trust you?"

26

BRANDON'S WOUND

"Say that again." Ellie's eyes are green slits, her brows scrunched in confusion. Her clothes are soaked through from her search, and her hair—usually in a neat braid—falls tangled and wild around her shoulders. She's so close that I can smell the coconut and mint of her shampoo as if she just stepped out of the shower instead.

"My brother-in-law, Wyatt," I say slowly, not to condescend to her, but to calm the steady fire in her eyes. "He works for the Enforcers." He begged for my forgiveness. I made him explain his job to me. Every part of it. And I can't forgive him.

"Your brother-in-law works for the Enforcers," she repeats with a sneer. "Why didn't you tell me this?"

"You didn't tell me you were an assassin!"

She closes her eyes, shakes her head. "Fair enough." And then she finally takes a step away from me. The constriction in my chest eases, and I let myself breathe. "Walk me through it, Brandon. What does he do for them?"

"What was the call about?" I counter.

Ellie raises a brow. When I stay silent, she grits her teeth and blows out a breath through her nose. "It was Jaythan. He was telling me about an organization the Enforcers absorbed four years ago."

"Govenin," I supply. Her eyes widen slightly. "Wyatt worked for them."

"Who's Jaythan?" Mark asks.

Ellie turns, blinking. Her fingers tap an uneven rhythm against her hip. "He's…our cousin." She walks away a few paces. "I found him after our mother died. He's helped me with different things over the years. Including finding you."

Mark doesn't say anything for a long moment, eyes shifting over the floor like he doesn't know what to think. "We have a cousin?"

"We'll have time for that later." She runs her hands through her hair, leaving Mark looking as if he was the one who got shot. She turns back to me. "You said Wyatt works for them. Explain."

"He only told me about it a few months ago. He got in when he was in college but said they're corrupted at the core, and now they won't let him leave. He wants to start a family." I remember being thrilled when he told me this, but after that initial high wore off, I couldn't quite get myself past the anger of him working with them. He married my sister while in their employ. It still doesn't sit well with me. "He said he wanted to do something. I don't know if he sabotaged them. It sounded like he might try."

"Hang on." Ellie pulls her phone out, dials.

"*Just can't get enough of me, can you, E?*" a deep voice chuckles over the speaker.

"It was his brother-in-law. Wyatt…" She flicks her eyes to me.

"Hull. Wyatt Hull," I supply.

"*Got it! Searching. Hey there, Brandon.*" I assume this man must be Jaythan. I glance at Mark, but he just blinks at the phone.

"Did you find anything?" Ellie demands.

"*Hang on, this isn't as easy as I make it seem. The process takes t—oh, here we go.*" He pauses. "*Looks like he worked with Govenin before the merger and has been with them since. He wants to start a family, doesn't he?*" I frown. "*Yeah, his wife wants a boy, but Wyatt wants a girl first then a boy.*"

A strangled sound comes out of me. *Who is this guy?*

"Shut up, Jay," Ellie says, casting me an almost apologetic glance. "There's no way for you to know that. What did you actually find?"

"*He's just an analyst, but the place runs on secrecy. You hadn't even heard of it, so he kinda locked himself in the second he signed on—like all other personnel.*" He pauses after that, seeming to realize Ellie is one of those personnel. "*Looks like he's been trying to fight from the inside, though. He's been like a slow leak, giving the press some of the real details about the targets, tying them to the politicians benefiting from the organization. It's slow work because it's not like many people actually care how the sausage gets made, ya know?*"

"So, Brandon was…what? Retribution?" Ellie asks.

"*Brandon was meant to put Wyatt back in line. Looks like the organization realized a long time ago that the people they have working for them are valuable—employee appreciation, right? But that means they can't kill Wyatt, but they* can *go after someone he loves to steer him back on course.*"

"And that person was the son of the family he married into? Why not his wife?"

My head snaps up, hurt and anger spearing through my chest like twin daggers.

Jaythan pauses too. "*That's dark, E.*"

"Wyatt and I are close." She turns to me, and I fold like soggy cardboard. I sink onto the couch, facing away from her. "Or at least, we *were*. He was the brother I never had. We talked even more than my sister and me."

Mark sits beside me, placing a gentle hand on my shoulder, careful of the soreness. Ellie takes the couch next to ours. She's bent forward, elbows on her knees, phone held out before her. She watches me like she's holding back that comforting impulse most people have.

"*Yeah,*" Jaythan confirms. "*They needed someone that would affect him, but not completely destroy him. Little different than what they did to you, E.*"

"What they…" A jolt like a defibrillator to the chest snaps me forward. Ellie freezes, gaze briefly shooting to Mark, and any residual anger I had with her evaporates. "What did they do to you?"

"Nothing," she snaps.

But Jaythan is already explaining, "*They pulled the same stunt they did with Wyatt except they definitely meant to destroy her.*"

"That's enough, Jay," she says through gritted teeth.

I know she's about to hang up, so I launch past Mark and snatch the phone from her hand. "What did they do to her?" Ellie stands too and grabs for her phone, but I circle around to the back of the couch.

"*They sent her after Mark.*"

I flip around, my heart tripping then sprinting.

Ellie clutches the sides of her head like she's in pain and screams, "Damn it, Jay!"

Her father sent her after her brother?

"What?" Mark's voice breaks.

Ellie's hands briefly clench against her skull, then she drops them and ignores Mark, taking her phone back and hanging up. Fire ignites in her eyes as she glares at me. I don't usually care to prove myself to people. However, her challenge hits me differently. I stand taller and stare down at her. She opens her mouth to say something.

But doesn't get the chance. Her phone starts ringing again. She scowls and snaps, "*What?*"

Her face completely drains of color a second later. Eyes wide, she pulls the phone away from her ear. I raise my hand, possibly to rest on her shoulder, but I clench my fist and put it back down at my side. Her voice comes out in barely a breath. "It's Jake."

Mark surges then, leaping over the back of the couch to take the phone from her. He puts it on speaker. "Jake? It's Mark. Are you okay? Where are you?"

"*Is Ellie still there?*" Mark's breath catches at the sound of Jake's voice. He sounds okay. His voice is steady. Somehow that doesn't comfort any of us.

Ellie still looks pale, and she's only moved enough to keep an eye on her phone like she can see Jake through it. "I'm here." Her voice is so small. All I want is to go to her, wrap my arms around her, and tell her everything will be okay. I shake that thought out of my head.

A deep breath from the other end of the line, then calmly, "*How could you not tell me?*"

"I…" Her eyes meet mine then, and I blink in surprise. The tightening around her eyes and the firm set of her mouth make her appear almost ashamed. The urge to comfort her rages through me this time.

Jake continues, *"When were you planning on telling me you were an assassin?"*

She takes a breath, standing straight, chin high. "Never," she admits. "Jake, I can explain."

"Please do," he snaps.

She closes her eyes for a moment but doesn't hesitate. "Cooper started the Enforcers twenty years ago. It's what split up their marriage three years later. When he took me, I was integrated directly into the Enforcers. Every second of every day was spent training. When I was sixteen, I got my first assignment and became a full agent.

"Last month I saw an assignment pass over the desk of the CEO." She meets my eyes. "I contained the situation, so I left. That was Thanksgiving."

"You shot Brandon," Jake breathes.

"But it was only to protect him," Mark interrupts, his voice wobbling, and he brings the phone closer than strictly necessary for Jake to hear. "She only ever wanted to protect us, Jake."

"Shut up, Mark." Jake doesn't snap this time, exasperation and weariness weighing heavily on the words. *"So, you've been lying to us the entire time."*

She grinds her teeth. "I had to keep Cooper away from you. I came back to protect you from him."

"Protection," he repeats. *"That's all this is then?"*

She stays very still, expecting the other shoe to drop but not knowing where it will. "What do you want from me?"

"A sister!" Jake shouts. And Ellie flinches. *"Did you ever think to try*

just being my sister? I don't care to have you protect me. Whatever happened to being a normal family?"

Ellie's gaze darkens. "We haven't been a normal family since Dad left Mom to start an organization of assassins."

"Which no one bothered to tell me about! Did Brandon know? You two were pretty loud, shut away in your room the other day."

Her eyes flick up to mine with a resigned sigh. "He does now."

"Well, that's great. The person I never cared to befriend is somehow the only one who didn't keep this shit from me. Just the people closest to me."

"Jake, I'm so sorry." Mark squeezes his eyes shut, a tear slipping down his cheek. "I didn't think it would help if you knew. I was trying to protect you."

"By lying to me." Mark can only let out a shaky breath now. *"Just like she did."* A dark chuckle from Jake. *"Just like Mom did."*

Mark's eyes pop so wide, they could fall right out of his head, and it makes the deep pain swimming inside them all the more obvious. "Jake—"

"She never told us why she left Dad. Well, now I know." He's silent for a while, and no one on this end dares say a word. *"Maybe she was wrong,"* he finally murmurs. Ellie visibly jerks and goes rigid, but still, she says nothing. *"Maybe she was wrong to keep us in the dark. Maybe she was wrong to leave him. Maybe you were all wrong not to tell me. Here's a concept! Maybe I can come to my own conclusions about these things."*

"Jake," Ellie tries. "Cooper's not—"

"He's the only member of my family who bothered to tell me the truth. Maybe he deserves a chance for that."

"Jake," she barks.

"I don't know what I'm going to do." He pauses. *"But I'm definitely not going to let you tell me."* And with that, the line cuts out.

"Jake?" Mark brings the phone to his ear, his hands trembling. "Jake?" He shakes his head. I watch the moment his heart shatters. His eyes slowly creep up to meet Ellie's, chest heaving. "Dad really sent you to kill me?"

Ellie stares at him and simply takes her phone back. She doesn't have to say anything. She takes a breath. "There's more. We've come this far, might as well know everything, right?" She takes a step away from us, head bobbing to the side. "When we went to the Mexican restaurant, I was using you as bait. I tried to force Cooper to act because it was making me sick to wait." She pins her stare on me then. "The reason Mark had a migraine serious enough to land him in the hospital was because I freaked him out when I told him I took another job. I figured if I could do another job right, Cooper would forget about sending me after Mark. Then things could go back to how they were before. It didn't work out that way, though, did it?"

Neither Mark nor I say a word. I catch her wrist, and her eyes burn into mine, but I have no idea what to say. "Do…" I try to nail down a question as too many swarm in my head. "Do you remember them? Your targets?"

She softens, tears glistening in her eyes before she blinks them away. Ellie reaches behind her, and keeping her eyes on me, she pushes a small black book into my chest. "Every last one." Her voice is small again, but not weak. She pulls free and turns away from us. I don't stop her this time as she walks out the door.

27

JAKE'S DECISION

Because I've done all of this for you.

I don't give Ellie or Mark a chance to respond before I hang up. Let them stew in what I had to say. They lied to me. Ellie would have continued living in her lies for the rest of her life if I hadn't ripped the truth from her myself.

I chuckle—a dark, vicious thing—because I didn't even get my information from Ellie. She only told me her motivation, revealing nothing of what she's actually done besides the little tidbit of her having shot Brandon. *She shot Brandon. My sister.* I thought she was starting to like him. What does it even mean that she *shot him to save him*?

I hope Brandon's making her squirm. He's a nice guy, but even he has his limits. I feel a little bad for him too. It was obvious how he felt about her. Shot by the woman you're falling for.

Almost as bad as being betrayed by your entire family.

When I asked my father why I should trust him, he gave me an answer. *I've done all of this for you.* Whether or not it's the honest truth hardly matters. He believed what he was saying, meaning he gave me everything he knows to be true. And it's more than I can say for any other member of this dysfunctional family.

"You left us," I asked him, "*for* us?"

"I did not choose to leave my family," he explained. "If you recall, your mother kicked me out." I did not recall. I was four. "She didn't see things the way I did. She did not understand that the only way to stop a bully is to hit back harder."

"You still left. We never saw you."

"I wanted to bring you in on the ground floor like your sister, but your mother fought tooth and nail to keep you away from me."

I didn't know what to say to that. I couldn't hate Mom for holding onto us. Any good parent would do the same. But she kept us away from him for years. Never spoke about him or let us see him. Dad tried to see us, though. He *tried.*

When did everyone stop trusting me to make my own decisions? How long has my family treated me like the baby they clearly still think I am? Mark literally brought his friend into our home to try and change me. He and Ellie carried on the tradition of lying to me about the important things.

I dial Chelsea's number into the hotel phone, but she doesn't pick up. Likely, she doesn't recognize the number. I'd keep calling, but she'd probably just block me. Which is fine. I shouldn't be so dependent on her anyway. I functioned just fine before her.

I functioned just fine before all this shit was dropped in my lap.

I can make my own decisions.

It's about time someone acknowledged that.

28

BRANDON'S REACTION

MARK DIDN'T WANT TO KNOW WHAT WAS IN THE LITTLE NOTEBOOK at first, but it's been three days since she dropped the bomb, and it's all she left for us. Each page holds a different name, and beneath the names are random bits of information. For some in the beginning, it's their families; for each one after, their habits and haunts. Her targets. Logged away in a book, and I still can't decide whether it's nice that she keeps them all with her or sick.

We flip through page after page, reading each one. And then near the end she has Mark's name. The only thing under it is a very unfriendly curse word and a couple marks that look as if she stabbed the book with her pen. One mark is so deep it punched through more pages than were left and made a puncture wound on the leather back cover.

Mark's isn't the final name, though. She told us she took another job, and the name is spelled out in all caps on the last page: *ANITA WOLF*. And below, only two words. *Two shots.* Every page after that was ripped out.

The statement is obvious. No more jobs will be logged in this little black book.

I've been carrying it with me everywhere. It's a piece of her that I've been trying to come to terms with. She's a ruthless killer, but this book tells a different story. I've been trying to stitch the versions together.

I haven't forgiven Wyatt for marrying my sister when he still worked for the Enforcers, and it's been months since he told me. But he's only an analyst. Ellie is a killer. An assassin. The fundamental difference between them, though, isn't the amount of blood on their hands.

Ellie pushes people away; she even keeps her brothers at arm's length. She doesn't engage in personal relationships like Wyatt because she knows the consequences. She's unwilling to bring that danger to anyone else. Even now after she's betrayed the Enforcers, she attempted to seal her fate with her final words to us. And giving us the list of all seventy-four assignments she's had.

It didn't have the desired effect.

After a couple hours of torturing myself at the gym, I finally leave, sweat dripping down my back and making my shirt stick uncomfortably. I'll go home and shower, and then I'm not sure what will distract me next. I'd never tell my past self, but I wish my exams hadn't been last week because I could really use them now.

There's a flash of gold in the corner of my vision as I slip through the parking lot, but when I turn, nothing. I don't ask myself why that's a disappointment.

I slide into my dingy green truck. The gear shift sticks and there's a leak in the oil tank, but working off a part-time shoe-salesman's salary and going to medical school isn't going to get me anything better for a long time. I turn the key in the ignition, and the engine rumbles but doesn't start. I release the key and try again. And that's our winner.

Mark is burning mac and cheese when I come back to the apartment, the metallic odor accosting my nostrils before I even enter the apartment. Four boxes of noodles are open on the counter behind him, and he's still in his sweats from this morning and a two-day old band t-shirt. At least he brushed his hair.

I crinkle my nose against the assault. "You burn that?"

"I burned round one," he corrects, stirring what must be round two.

"You throw it out?"

"Nah." He gestures behind him with the spoon. "It's right there."

I'm starving enough to go for it even without the cheese packet. I grab a fork and heap a rubber glob down my gullet. It's disgusting. I inhale another mouthful. "How are you doing?"

"Not great," he blurts, glancing at me briefly before going back to his noodles.

I don't know why I keep asking. He's been depressed since Ellie left. It's made worse with Christmas approaching, a time he hasn't spent with any other family than Jake since their mom died. I think this year, he was hoping that would finally change. I want to help, but what can I do?

We were both targets of an entire group of assassins in the last month. Both lost Jake and Ellie. But those are his siblings. The only real family he has. He wants Ellie to come back, and I do too. It's so confusing.

"Have…have you thought any more about Jake?"

We've been trying to come up with ways to get him back, but every single one is either too fantastical and reliant on magic or…

He drops the new pot of mac and cheese on the counter in front of me. "Yes, I have," he snaps. "And you know where it's gotten me? Nowhere. Because do you know the only person who can help us? The one person who's not talking to us. It's freaking me out because I have *no idea* what Dad is capable of."

I swallow hard, and not just because of the nearly inedible mac and cheese I can't stop eating. "We don't have to talk about it." I feel terrible for hoping he takes the hint.

"No, you know what?" He aggressively scoops the edible mac and cheese into a bowl for himself. "Yes, we do. We have to talk about it at some point. She's my sister, and I love her! But how could she not tell me that my own father wants me dead? What about Jake? Is that her way of protecting us?"

There's a twinge in my shoulder. It's still sore, especially after my workout, but I've been steadily working it back to where it was before all this. I swear though, sometimes I can still feel the bullet ripping through skin and muscle. *She didn't even graze the bone.*

"Her version of protection is…different." It's the best word I can come up with for it. She does have a strange way of protecting people, but when I think back on all she's done, I realize it *has* worked. To a point. But I'm not dead right now, and neither is Mark. That's because of her.

He waves me off. "Yeah, but it's always been that way. I mean, she shot you in the arm to keep you from getting shot in the head."

Obviously, he sees the benefits too, but I can't easily push aside the reality. Protecting us or not… "She's an assassin. She kills people for a living." That's the hardest part. I know I shouldn't want anything to do with her. I know she's dangerous. But this just creates a rift between the impulsive organ in my chest and the overcritical one in my head.

Mark tenses. "Our dad pushed her into it when she was four."

I admire how he stands by his family; I really do. But she's not my family. I can't afford to blindly trust her again even while I fear keeping her out of my life will hurt me more than help. "So, you're just okay with it?"

"Of course not!" There's a pause, and he hangs his head. "I'm sorry."

I shrug, shaking my head. We both need to air our grievances. Mark especially, because I get the sense he's never been able to. He bottled it all up, and now it's exploding. Now there's a mess no one has any clue where to even start cleaning up, and it's terrifying.

"No, I'm not okay with it." He stirs around his noodles without actually eating any. "I only found out about all of this last month. I wanted her to quit, but she's so stubborn. I told her she could live here, but she turned me down. You know why? Because when she saw *your* name—" he jabs his cheesy fork in my direction—"come across her supervisor's desk, she rushed down here to make sure nothing happened to you. She stayed so she would know if any of our names showed up again, and guess what? *Mine did!* And it was only because she saved *you!*"

My phone rings at that exact moment. My dad. I want to be a good friend and be here for Mark through this. But I can't. Not with this. *Deep breath.* "I have to take this." I back away gingerly, but he nods in understanding, and I shut myself in my room, relieved that I don't have to come up with a response.

"Hey, Dad." I muster as much cheerfulness as I can for him even as my mind whirls. "What's going on?"

"*Hey, kid.*" He breathes out the words, the last deeper than the first. He sounds tired.

"Is something wrong?"

"*Not anymore. Don't worry.*" But as that phrase typically does, it makes me anxious. The butterflies are in that jittery pre-flight mode, and thoughts of Mark and Jake and Ellie slip from my mind. "*Mom's in the hospital.*"

The butterflies explode. "What!"

"*Everything's fine now.*" His words are quick like they're racing against my anxiety—news flash: they're losing. "*She had a fairly minor seizure this morning.*"

"*Fairly* minor?"

"*The doctor said she's doing great now. I can go in and see her in a few minutes, but I wanted to call first and let you know what was going on.*"

"She'll be fine?"

"*Yes. Good as new in no time. You know your mother.*"

I sigh deeply, telling myself to take that as the good news it is, but part of me still wants to throw up. Mom doesn't let much take her down. If she actually admits to being sick, it's because it's bad enough that she'll refuse to get out of bed. Otherwise, she won't say a word about it. This is a little different than just being sick, though. I rub my temples. "I'm coming up there."

"*You don't have to worry about us, Brandon. We're doing fine.*"

"I know, but I want to see you. I wanted to come up for Christmas anyway." It would also give me time away from the chaos I've found myself in this past month. A change of scenery could be exactly what I need.

"*I'd like that.*"

29

ELLIE'S SURVEILLANCE

I WAS TOO LATE. I WAS KIDDING MYSELF THINKING THINGS COULD GO back to the way they were. How was I supposed to know Cooper had already given up on me? It's not like years of being a consistent asshole could have clued me in.

He took Jake. He turned my brother against me. I took out Anita Wolf for nothing. All because I was too late when I even asked for the job. Cooper only ever kept my secret because I did everything he asked, but he was only waiting for the opportunity to cut all my personal ties. Now he's cut every string in one clean snip.

Following Brandon's little beat-up truck and Mark's small car and staking out rooftops across from their frequents is my full-time job now. There's no way to fix what I've done. All I can do is keep it from happening again. I don't need to be a part of their lives to protect them. I've got Jaythan on the lookout for any updates on Jake and keeping an eye on Cooper, but I can't do anything until I get information, so I'm stuck playing the waiting game. I was always great at that part of the job. Lately, though, it's what I'm worst at.

Mark and Brandon left the apartment at the same time this morning, and I'm only one person. I tailed my brother. The thing is, Mark got back a few hours ago. It's almost nine now, and Brandon's not home.

I lose patience at ten and get Jaythan on the phone.

"*E! My favorite person!*"

"I need you to locate Brandon's truck for me."

He sighs, but I can already hear him clacking at his keyboard as I give him the license plate. "*Okay. Yes! Here we go. He is at…*" He pauses. "*He's at the airport.*"

"What? Why?"

"*I don't know. Why don't you ask him?*"

I swallow the pain, willing it to stay the hell out of my voice. "I can't do that." I shouldn't feel this way about that fact. He wasn't a big part of my life before a month ago. He was just my brothers' roommate that I kept tabs on for *their* safety. He wasn't supposed to be any more than that because some part of me knew it would end this way. My time with my brothers was bound to run out. I'd foolishly hoped it would be later.

"*I thought you were friends.*"

"I can't."

"*Well, then, ask Mark.*"

I close my eyes. "Can't do that either."

"*Are you kidding me?*" His tone becomes strained, and I can feel his frustration through the phone. "*Well, you're going to have to ask one of the two because I'm not hacking into that man's phone or doing any more surveillance on him until you do."*

"Jaythan." But he hangs up. *He* hangs up on *me*. I'd kill him if he weren't on the other side of the country.

Jaythan ignores my next three calls, so I'm forced to confront my brother. I hesitate at the door, but I need to know where Brandon is. If something happened to him now, I could never live with myself. I finally land a knock on the gray door with a little too much force. Mark answers immediately, his eyes going wide.

"Why is Brandon at the airport?"

"Hi, Ellie." He sighs, trying to sound annoyed, but the look in his eyes is eager. I squirm. "He's with his parents in Washington."

"He's in Washington?!" I yell then blink, suck in a breath. To Mark's credit, he only jumps a little at my outburst. I ask more calmly, "He's in Washington?" and hate the way my voice wavers.

"His mom had a seizure."

My chest hollows, and I squeeze my eyes shut. Of course there was a good reason. Even just going to see his family for Christmas would have been a good enough reason. "I'm sorry. Is she okay?"

He smiles a bit. "Yeah, she's okay." Then he takes a tiny step back, concern lining the creases beside his eyes. "What?"

I'm fidgeting. My fingers twist around each other, squeezing tight and flicking apart. *Stop.* "I'm sorry I didn't tell you. I didn't want you to have to live with the fact that…" *our father is a madman who put me on your tail.* "I thought I was…" *protecting you.* Lately, the cause of all my problems is the way I choose to protect those I care about. It's no excuse. I clamp my mouth shut.

But Mark shakes his head. "I understand, and I appreciate what you tried to do even though I wasn't a fan of the method. Not really even sure what I would have done differently." A small laugh and a shrug. "I'm sorry we haven't talked."

"I…I am too." I pause. *Back to business. Go back, go back, go back.* "We should go up to him."

"What?"

"He's up there alone."

Mark frowns. "He's with his family." I stay quiet, and Mark nods. "You mean without you." I start to clarify, but he ushers me inside. "Just let me pack a few things." Surprise flickers through me when he doesn't argue with or yell at or hate me. All perfectly reasonable reactions.

Then I finally remember he has his own life. "Wait, you don't have to be at the hospital, do you?"

With a pleased grin, he tells me, "No. They gave me until after the New Year since Jake's…" The grin slips.

Right. Okay. Good. I nod. His smile now is tight, but his eyes are soft, and then he disappears into his room.

I wait for my brother in the living room. Jaythan only answers my call when I text him the situation with Brandon—proof that I talked to Mark. I don't give him time to speak first. "I will kill you for this."

"Now, wait a minute. You're on speaking terms with your brother again because of me."

"And?" The nerves and fidgeting die away as I let anger fill the cracks.

"A-and shouldn't that count for something?"

"Do you know me at all?"

He pauses. *"I'm an idiot."*

"You'd think you'd know that by now."

"*Are we cool?*"

"After I kill you, we are."

His voice gets high. "*Might I request my punishment be something less permanent?*"

"If you can tell me exactly where in Washington Brandon is, and if he's even still alive."

"*Okay, he's in a little town called Pe Ell.*" He's as ready with that information as Han Solo was with his gun. That in no way makes him Han Solo. I am the Han of this relationship; he's more like…C-3PO.

"Never heard of it."

"*Believe it or not, it's even smaller than the town their apartment's in. I'll send the exact address to your phone. And, for your information, he's alive and perfectly well. I just got off the phone with him. He said his mother is great too. It's like nothing ever happened.*"

"You called him?" My irritation with him can never take a rest.

"*Don't worry, I didn't tell him who I was.*" Not the problem.

"Who did you say you were?"

"*Well, I thought I'd call as one of Brandon's friends—I called their house phone. Can you believe they still have one?*" He doesn't wait for me to respond. This conversation is between him and himself. "*Insane, I know. But then he picked up, so I said I was a friend of his parents.*"

"He bought that?" I really hope he's not naive enough to fall for Jaythan's halfhearted attempts at stealth in human interactions. Computers are Jaythan's domain. Nothing more.

"*I don't think so,*" Jaythan admits. "*He might have remembered my voice from the other day, unfortunately, but he said his mother was doing great.*"

"He didn't believe you, knew you were with me, and he still told you about the state of his mother?" My stupid heart wants to believe that, but my mind tells me Jaythan's full of it.

"Well, not really, but I was trying to show you that talking to him isn't that difficult."

Deep breath. "Uh-huh."

"I may have made up the part about his mom, but he's alright enough to answer the phone."

"Great, thanks." I lower the phone from my ear just in time for Jaythan to screech through the speaker.

"Wait! You should know, there's been stirrings around here about you. There was even a special on the news that said Emily Richards has gone rogue and is now a threat to national security. You're famous."

Why would Cooper do that? It undermines the Enforcers' authority. All this could possibly do is stir the feeling in the public that the Enforcers can't control their assassins anymore. It leads to too many questions that I know my father doesn't want to answer, like if he's really fit to lead this organization if he loses control of one of his best assassins, or if the Enforcers are still the ones for the job. But I've lived with him too long to think he doesn't have an angle.

"Has he given away my location yet?" I try to keep my heart from racing.

"You think he knows it?"

"You think he doesn't?"

"He hasn't said anything to the public yet."

"He'll keep it as a last resort. No need to involve Mark." Right now, I think Mark's the only reason I'm still alive. If I know Cooper, it's more to get on Jake's good side than my father's sudden development of a heart.

"Didn't he send you to kill him?"

I pinch the bridge of my nose, breathe in. "An open mission."

"But he's fine with having Jake kidnapped?"

I push a breath out through pursed lips. "I forced him to do that."

"You don't believe that."

"No." *Yes.*

"When do you want your flight to leave?"

"We can't fly." *Not anymore.* "I'll drive us there."

"You should leave soon then, because chances are, your father has assassins inbound on your position. I don't know that you're supposed to come in alive."

"Thanks for that."

"Stay safe."

"I know."

➤➤➤

MARK AND I ARE ON THE ROAD WITHIN AN HOUR. MY BLACK CHARGER is one of the only luxuries I've dumped a ton of cash into. I had it spruced up so it could take a punch, even got bulletproof glass. I kept it in Oregon because I'm out here most of the time anyway, and I want to be able to drive it. In the back of my mind, though, I knew I would finally bring the fight to my brothers and need bulletproof glass around them.

Despite the midnight hour, Mark refuses to lay his seat back and sleep. He switches between talking obsessively and messing with the temperature controls, unable to choose between extreme heat and extreme cold.

Currently, the car is roasting the two of us while Mark prattles on about what happened just before Brandon left. "He invited me to come with him," he says, staring out the side window as the damp forests pass us by. "After everything that happened, he said a simple family Christmas would be like a breath of fresh air. Well, he said something like that. But I told him no. Not because I didn't want to, but his family's not my family. I was hoping you would come back to us. So, I stayed."

My stomach turns. He stayed at the risk of being alone on Christmas for me, and the only reason I came back was because I didn't know what was going on with Brandon. He deserves a much better sister than me. He deserves better than all of this. Mark should be living with his friend and his brother in a tiny apartment, eating easy prep meals and watching movies into the night, blowing off responsibilities for spontaneous adventures and all the other things guys their age do. Instead, I'm mucking up his life and yes, he's going on spontaneous adventures to satisfy his restless sister's invasive tendencies.

"I'm glad you came back, Ellie." He twists his hands in his lap. It's the third time he's said that since we left, and each time he seems more nervous admitting it. I know why. I haven't been able to respond to it, to concur, to argue, to anything. Because the truth is, I don't know if this is a "*yeah, same*" situation. I love him, and I love talking to him, but I know why I left. It's the only way they can stay safe. Haven't I proven over and over again that *I* am the danger to my brothers more than my father ever was?

Maybe my mother saw that too, and there was more than one reason she couldn't fight to get me back.

I shake my head. I *know* that's not true. I read every text she sent me. She couldn't fight for me on Cooper's terms, so she tried a new angle, unaware he beat her to it.

Cooper has never done anything impulsive in his life. Everything is a plot. Everything is designed. He didn't one day wake up and decide to be done with my bullshit and kidnap Jake instead. No, every time I defied him—in the big ways at the end and the small pokes and prods before that—he had another twin as a fallback. I forced him into it. I overplayed my hand. And my brothers are paying for it.

Mark goes silent again, back to fiddling with the temperature controls. The sweat dripping down my brow scurries into my hair when the air blasts my face. Mark turns the intensity down with a mumbled apology, but he keeps the cool air going. It's winter and forty degrees outside, but the inside of my car has toured every possible climate over the last three hours.

"Dad really wants me dead?"

I have to bite back a groan as my stomach twists again. How to answer that… "I honestly don't know." I can't imagine Cooper wanting his own son dead. But given what I learned about his entire business, I can't be sure where he'll draw the line anymore.

"Did you know about what he was doing?"

I know what he means. Did I know about the targets? Did I know they were leverage and never a threat? Did I know that means I was likely killing innocent civilians for *years*? I glare at the road ahead. "No."

"You thought you were protecting us."

"I *was*." I'm not willing to accept that I haven't been. Mark is alive. Brandon is alive. Jake is alive—for now. That counts for something.

Mark doesn't respond to that, and my jaw clenches. I glance in the rearview mirror and take the next exit. Mark's brows click together. He leans up to check the dash, but it displays no lights and over half a tank of gas. "What are you doing?"

I check the mirror again. "We're being followed."

He turns around so quickly his back cracks with the force. I grab his arm and jerk him back around. "Are you sure?"

It's hard to tell at night, but I've developed certain instincts over the years which are hard to ignore. The LED lights behind us have been giving me a bad feeling for almost an hour. Now he's followed us into this exit. "I'm sure."

Mark takes a shaky breath. "What do we do?"

"You? Get in the back, buckle up, stay down. I'll take care of it."

"What?" His hands tremble, and his jaw hangs open.

I give him a piece of my logic, hoping that helps. "If he starts shooting, it will be safer for you back there. Middle seat; in the event of a crash, it's best."

If the way his breath hitches is any indication, logic did not help. "What are you going to do?"

Frustration boils under my skin even as I try to reason with myself that Mark's never dealt with this before. Of course he's going to have questions. Still, I need him to do what I say. "Back, Mark. *Now.* Buckle up and stay down. He can't follow us to Brandon."

He nods and finally does as he's told. His transition is anything but smooth; he nearly kicks me in the face more than once. But finally, he flops into the back seat, buckles up, and puts his head down. I pull my pistol from the glove box, toss it into the passenger seat, and floor it. Unsurprisingly, our tail does the same. I jerk the wheel, taking the next turn sharply, and Mark yells at me for it. I ignore him, weave us through the backroads, and pull into an alley that some poor, terrified homeless man is unfortunate enough to be in. He scrambles and flees down the street.

"Stay inside." I leave Mark, gun in hand, and slip to the end of the alley. The sedan speeds around the corner. For a second, he's only on two wheels. Not good for the tread. *You should let him know he needs new tires.* I blow out the front two. The vehicle makes a horribly loud clang and scrape as it skids to a stop a few yards away.

I jog toward it. Blacked out windows. I'm not about to waste ammo trying to hit something I can't see. When I reach the car, he's ready for me. I spin out of the way of the bullet, but he shoves the door open, slamming it into my middle. My gun clatters to the asphalt, and I gasp as he slips out of the car. He grabs a fistful of my braid and yanks it back, exposing my throat to his blade—a gun isn't personal enough for killing someone you hate. And there is focused, searing hatred blazing in his eyes.

Tony Corval. One of the first and youngest assassins my father ever employed. He was there when I rose up into the position of assassin at only sixteen. It didn't bother him then. After all, a little girl could hardly steal all the best jobs. But then I humiliated him after my mother died when he tried to comfort me in a way I didn't want, and I did, in fact, steal all the best jobs. Since then, he's hated my guts. The feeling is mutual. And now, he's finally gotten the green light to kill me.

I bend backwards, bringing him down over me. He sees my play and spins me. But on my way around, I send an elbow into his abdomen, and his grip loosens just a bit. I whip a blade free from my sleeve and flick it down into the meat of his foot. He crumples to his knees with a shout and finally lets go of me. Corval lashes out with his own dagger, but I throw myself back, searching for my gun. Another blade in my free hand.

There. Just a few feet away beside the back wheel of the sedan. Corval catches my wrist before I can get ahold of the gun—*so close*. He squeezes tightly but a deep slice to his wrist opens those fingers right up.

Forgetting the gun for the moment, I grab the hand I sliced, holding it tight. He splits a hole through my shirt, attempting to gut me. I throw myself back but feel the sting across my abdomen. Blood seeps onto the dark fabric of my shirt. Shallow. I'll live. He's furious. I can't let go of my knife to grab my gun—clearly, that would be a death sentence. So, I fling out my leg and catch him in the jaw. The clack of his teeth is music to my ears. Blood leaks from between his lips, and fire rages in his eyes.

I still don't go for my gun as he must suspect because when I spin behind him and double fist his shirt until it's cutting off his air supply, he definitely isn't expecting it. I force Corval against the ground and step down hard on his wrist. The knife slips from his grip. He struggles to rip my hands from his shirt, only managing to rip the shirt itself. Not the neckline, though. The person who made this shirt deserves an award for how durable the neckline is.

"How did you find me?" He doesn't answer. I yank on the shirt. Not so much as a groan of discomfort. "Tell me!"

"Just like any other target." He wheezes with a grin, blood oozing from his mouth. "You should know, *Richards*." Flecks of dark blood spit out with my name.

I don't give myself time to savor it. "How many are coming?"

He laughs, the sound abruptly cutting off a second later as he continues to lose oxygen, his face growing steadily purple. "As many as he could spare." *Shit.* "I should have killed you while you were still living under our roof, you useless—" The rest of the insult falls away when I shock him by releasing my hold on his shirt. By the time he's sucked down enough air, my blade is already cutting slightly into his throat, producing a steady red stream down his neck.

"We've hated each other a long time now, haven't we, Corval?" I observe casually. "Cooper gave me the banquets and left you the scraps." I lean down and whisper close to his ear. "And while you burn in Hell, you'll know why."

I draw my knife against his throat. Hating being contained in his wretched body, blood erupts from the slash, drenching my hands and my shirt. I ignore the momentary nausea that the act unleashes in me, gather up my gun and Corval's, and run back to Mark…who's standing at the end of the alleyway, his face a ghostly white and also a little green.

"I told you to stay in the car," I growl, shoving him into the back seat again.

His eyes land on my abdomen. "Your shirt…you're bleeding."

"It's not serious."

He glances dazedly back at the street. "You're…just going to leave him?"

"There's no time for a funeral." I throw the car in reverse.

"No, but…"

I turn sharply and look him dead in the eye. His mouth slams shut at the steel in my gaze. "Do you want to get to Brandon before they do?"

His breath locks in his throat, but he gives me a curt nod. For a few moments, he's silent. Then, "Was he here to kill me?"

"No, Mark, they're not after you anymore." I race back onto the freeway and push my car well above ninety. "They're after me."

》》》》

I NEED TO SCOUT THE TOWN FIRST, SO I DROP MARK OFF IN FRONT OF Brandon's house. Brandon already invited Mark along, so I have no doubt he'll be welcomed inside even at eight in the morning with no logical explanation for how or why he's there. I'll be back in a few hours, but I can't bring my brother with me, and it would probably be best if Brandon had ample warning that I'm here.

I try not to let the possibility that he won't speak to me hurt too much. It would make perfect sense. I shot him. I'm the reason he's in danger right now. If I were him, I wouldn't want me anywhere near my family.

I won't leave, though. Does that make me a terrible person? He doesn't have to see me, but he's weaseled his way into my family, so I have to make sure he's alright and stays that way. It was so much easier when it was just Jake and Mark.

Jaythan was right: this town is tiny. No chain stores anywhere, and we had to drive a half hour from the interstate to get here. It's like the town came straight from an old Western. Mark even pointed out a small building with a giant red Texas star above the door. There's one main stretch lined with businesses, a school front and center, and everything else is houses.

I find a small shop to purchase some clean clothes, alcohol, and bandages. The cashier gives me a concerned and mildly terrified look when I—with crusted blood all over my skin and staining my current clothes—drop the supplies in front of her, but she doesn't dare comment. She rushes me through the line, and I wash away the gore in the little bathroom in the back, sterilize the wound, and bandage it up as best I can. Still feeling the ghost of everything on my skin, I scrape my face until it's raw and watch the pink water swirl into the drain.

I came out at Thanksgiving because Brandon was a target, and I was worried about how it would impact my brothers. Now, though, with him being hours away from either of them, what excuse do I have? I can lie and say it's still because he's close to my brothers, but I'm not even sure that applied back then. The Enforcers don't do collateral. It's sloppy. My brothers would have been fine. Devastated and shaken up, but they would have lived. Still, I came, and I shot my life to hell with a single bullet.

He was in the circle as soon as he moved into that apartment. I don't care because my brothers do. I care because I genuinely like the guy. I always have, even from that first, extremely awkward visit where we barely said three words to each other. It's not been *just my brothers* for two years now.

I sigh and splash cold water onto my face.

The worst part is that even if he cuts ties with my entire family, I know I'll still have the obsessive compulsion to protect him. From my family.

Thankfully, I find no evidence of any more assassins in this town. For now, everything is normal, safe. I circle back around to Brandon's parents' house and find myself standing outside the bright yellow door far too soon. The gray house is small, and there's a deck with white railing, bushes on either side of the steps leading up to it. And a giant ornamented wreath hanging on the door. It's too perfect, and the big, shiny globes reflect just how pathetic a picture I make standing on the *Merry Christmas* welcome mat thirty times over.

I'm not ready for this. My stomach wants to explode—I wish it would. Save me the trouble of this confrontation. There's no helping it.

I knock. It's too loud, and I jump. I want nothing more than to run in the opposite direction. Watch the house from some nearby rooftop. I hate that. *Don't answer. Don't answer. Don't answer.* I half convince myself to just turn and run when the door swings open on faintly creaking hinges.

Brandon doesn't look terrible, but he certainly isn't at his best. He's in a loose T-shirt and sweatpants. His hair is disheveled. There are bags under his eyes, though not super pronounced. I try to ignore the rush of relief that washes over me at seeing him again.

He doesn't say anything.

"I was just checking out the town," I explain to fill the silence. "I surveyed the perimeter to make sure no one… I wanted to make sure nothing was going to happen. I didn't find anything. It's possible nothing will happen at all, but I wanted to be certain. You can never be too careful." I sound insane, but I can't make myself stop. *He's not saying anything.* "I'm really sorry if this makes things awkward, but just because you never want to talk to me again doesn't mean I won't look out for you in my own twisted way. But I totally understand if you want me to go, and I will. I'm sorry about your mom, by the way. That…sucks."

He stares at me a moment longer, and when he finally moves, I flinch. But he pulls me close, wrapping his arms tight around me. I'm so shocked that I hold my breath, sure that breathing will remind him he's supposed to hate me. I ignore the sharp tearing sensation on my stomach. There's a good chance this isn't really happening. Have I completely lost my mind? Tentatively, I put my arms around him and lightly pat him on the back, a child being forced to hug a distant relative they have no memory of.

"Thank you," he whispers into my hair above my ear.

I'm able to breathe deeply now, but I can't find words. I nod.

He releases me, patting me on the shoulder. There's a broad smile on his face now, and it's so beautiful and genuine, I want to run again. "Just to clarify. I never wanted you to leave, and I definitely didn't want to never talk to you again." He pauses, face scrunching to the side, making sure he said what he meant there. The corner of my lip twitches, which he catches and breathes a laugh. Without hesitation he ushers me inside.

30

JAKE'S BETRAYAL

I HAVEN'T LEFT MY ROOM IN THREE DAYS WHEN THERE'S A KNOCK. IN my solitude, I'm half convinced I imagined it until the pounding comes again a few seconds later. I ignore it a few *more* seconds because I suspect it's Hartley back to take me to my father.

I still haven't figured out what I'm going to do about the whole situation. Three days is not *nearly* enough time to process that my father runs a corporation of assassins that includes my sister and also figure out what to do about it. And on top of it all I have to look at is gold—literally everything in this room is shiny including the bedspread. I'm not sure where my father found such a gaudy place, but you know what they say: "*All that glitters…*"

Point is, I don't have an answer for him.

As it happens, I don't need one because it's not a sickeningly overweight errand boy waiting on the other side.

"Chelsea." In a momentary loss for words, I can only stare. Red hair thrown up in a messy ponytail, black leggings hugging her legs and hips, loose white t-shirt underneath a long teal frock coat—*gorgeous.* "What are you doing here?"

She takes a breath that's surprisingly shaky. "Can we talk?"

Something about the way she can't meet my eyes makes me not want to let her into my room. "How did you know I was here?" I ask instead.

She looks around me into the room and back down the hall. "We really need to talk, Jake. Please?"

I nod and step aside. She seats herself delicately at the end of the bed, golden sheets crinkling beneath her. I remain by the door. This is too weird. "How did you know where to find me?"

"Okay." She rubs her palms on her pants like she's trying to get rid of the moisture. She's been nervous around me before, but never like this. Never like she genuinely fears what I might do. "But before I explain, I want you to know I really do like you. I hope this doesn't ruin what we have."

I blink, stare, take a deep breath. Chelsea watches me, placing her hands under her legs to keep from fidgeting. "Okay, this isn't really boding well for you, so why don't you just come out with it?" I don't feel bad about the harshness of my words. I should.

I should.

Her gaze drops to the floor, and even then, there's no guilt turning my stomach. No sympathy forcing my hands to comfort. "I actually… kind of…work for your father."

Why doesn't that surprise me?

"Not as an assassin." Her green eyes find mine again, wide, anxious. She laughs nervously. "I wasn't cut out for that." She waits for my response which only comes in the form of a raised brow. Do I owe her a healthy dialogue, or does she owe me the entire truth? Because both cannot be had. "I became a spy instead. My last assignment—"

My laugh is harsh and aggressive, cutting her off. "Let me guess. It was me."

"I was supposed to get you to agree to talk to him. That was it. I figured I could do that if I could get close enough to you, but you're so wary of letting people in."

"I wonder why," I deadpan, crossing my arms.

She only misses a beat. "But you never called, so he resorted to—"

"Kidnapping me. Right. I got that."

"I'm sorry, Jake." She does a great job of putting on a sorrowful act. Wide, innocent eyes glazing over with tears, full lips parted. She even fists her hands in the sheets like she's holding herself back, giving me space to think.

"I'm sure you are." I jerk my head behind me to the door. "Get out."

"Jake, please. I don't want to ruin what we have."

"What we have?" I sneer. "*What we have!*" She jumps at my tone, jolting back on the bed. Further away from me. Good. "What do we have, Chelsea? You asked *me* out, remember? You started this relation-ship. Half our conversations were you trying to get me to talk about my dad, henceforth known as *your boss*. So, what do we have? Tell me. What are you losing here? Because I know what I'm losing. I'm losing the person I started to trust over my own family. The person I felt safe with. The person I could turn to." I take a step closer, angling my head. "Do you know what my first thought was after I found out? *I want to talk to Chelsea because even if she doesn't have advice for how to handle this, she'll at least help me calm down.* But yeah, I'm sure you're losing out on a nice, temporary plaything. Certainly not the payday, though, right?"

All those late nights talking on the phone. The way she tucks her chin in when she laughs. Everything I've discovered about her. *Lies.*

She shakes her head, tears carving paths down her porcelain cheeks. "Everything I told you about myself, and how I feel about you—it's all true. It means so much to me. *You* mean so much to me. Doesn't that count for something?"

English major. I hold back the wicked laugh that comes at the thought. Just another ploy to get me to like her. I never knew why I chose business; maybe it was a subconscious attempt to be closer to my father. But it was never what I truly wanted. *She said she was an English major.* But that was just another in a line of calculated moves to mastermind my life.

I approach her slowly, and she stiffens until she sees the look on my face. I stroke her cheek gently with the tip of my index finger and bend close. She takes an anxious breath, her chest heaving when I stop a hairsbreadth from her pink lips, glistening from the tears she let slip free.

It *did* count. It meant more to me than anything has in a long time. She was the first person that I was willing to pursue a relationship with. I *did* trust her more than my own family in the end.

I watch the depths of her eyes where anxiety rips apart her spirit, but hope builds it back up double-time. She believes in us so much, in what we made together. But the thing is…

"No," I whisper against her lips. She's fallen for her own lies. "It doesn't."

Her lashes flutter, and her breath whooshes out like I just punched her in the stomach. I linger on her mouth until her eyes flick up to mine. Then I move away, and she fumbles for understanding and words. I'm patient.

"I'm so sorry, Jake." Her voice comes out shaky, pathetic. She stands on trembling legs and holds her hands out placatingly. "I hurt you, and I understand you need some time. Will you call me when you're ready?"

I open the door wide. "No."

She takes the hint and walks out with one last apology, but I slam the door before the word finishes leaving her mouth.

Lies, lies, and *more lies*. Is there no end? Everyone, it seems, is unwilling to trust me with anything vaguely resembling the truth. Everyone but…

So what if he orchestrates the movements of assassins? How else is change supposed to happen if it's not forced a little bit? People get too comfortable with the way things are and always have been, but maybe they shouldn't.

My father said he did everything for us. I'm inclined to give him the time of day to hear him out. If he's willing to speak with me, why shouldn't I let him?

31

BRANDON'S CONFESSION

OM'S INSIDE WAITING FOR US WITH A GRIN AND WHAT I'VE DUBBED *crazy eyes,* which happens when she gets so excited, you can see the whites all the way around her brown eyes. Ellie doesn't even balk at the generally frightening look. Her eyes stray to the rest of the room behind the woman.

Mom keeps a clean house. Or as clean as she can with a giant fluffy white dog that sheds year-round. She vacuumed and mopped as soon as she found out Ellie would be coming. Mark helped dust, chuckling as my mom bustled through the entire house which was spotless to begin with.

It's a vast difference from the blanket hoard that is our apartment. Here, Mom has one accent blanket draped over the corner of the large tan *L* couch—the rest are hidden in the ottoman. My dad usually moves it so he can sit in the corner, but Mom made him sit elsewhere, so it could look presentable. Her tree is decked out in ornaments my sister and I made as kids as well as store-bought ones to fill in the gaps. She's set up a tiny village on the mantle above the electric fireplace where four stockings hang—correction, six; I don't know where she got the other two so quickly.

Ellie tracks all of it back to my mother, taking in the sight of the woman. Mom's in her favorite sweatshirt—black, slightly baggy, and says *Love is a Four-Legged Word*. Birthday present from me a few years back, so it's stretched out and long, white dog hair has made its permanent mark, and there are poofs of flour on the cuffs. She's been baking all morning since she finished cleaning. She likes to do that when I'm around to bribe me into staying longer. And then when Mark showed up, she insisted on adding to her list of baked goods so he could try everything I ever told him about.

"You must be Ellie!" Mom pulls her in for a hug, and Ellie goes stiff. I grin. I should be furious. I shouldn't want her anywhere near my family. But watching her tentatively wrap her arms around my mother sends a flood of warmth through me.

Two days after her seizure, Mom is already acting like nothing happened. It was due to a drop in blood pressure after she missed a couple doses of her medication. Dad and I have policed her heavily to remember since then. She calls us overbearing but listens, knowing if she doesn't, I won't hesitate to force the medication down her throat like she has to for the dog.

"Brandon's told us so much about you."

My cheeks heat when Ellie raises a brow at me. She smiles brightly when Mom pulls back. "Nice to meet you, Mrs. Harwood. We won't stay long. I've got a hotel room so Mark and I won't be in your way."

"Nonsense." Mom waves her off. "Hotels are expensive. You'll stay with us; we've got plenty of space." She winks…for some reason.

Winston comes charging in as a flash of white, growling, the fur along his spine at attention. "It's alright, Winston," I say calmly but firmly and reach down to pat his back. His fur stays alert, and he leans just close enough to sniff Ellie's now outstretched hand. He's reduced to heavy panting and fluffy tail wagging in seconds.

Ellie kneels to give the large dog scratches behind the ears.

"Wow, he warmed up to you a lot faster than he did Mark." I throw a smirk over my shoulder at my friend, seated on the edge of the poufy purple loveseat in front of the window.

"Whatever," he grumbles, faking annoyance at the dog's betrayal.

"Harwood!" Mom turns back to my dad who's peering over from his spot on the couch. "Get over here and meet Brandon's friend."

He groans, hoisting himself up off the couch. "Ellie." He holds out a hand to her, and she stands and shakes it. Dad gives me a look, and I'm reminded of what he once taught me. *You can learn everything you need to know from the strength behind a handshake.* I smile. "I'm Brandon's father."

She offers a firm nod. "Great to meet you."

"Make yourself at home." Mom ushers Ellie toward the couch, but Mark stands then.

I put a hand on Mom's shoulder. "Actually, we need a few minutes to talk alone."

"Oh." She nods. Ellie is stiff again, and her smile vanishes. "Of course, of course. I'll get the cinnamon rolls finished."

My room is upstairs, and as soon as I swing the door open, I'm very aware of how it must look to Ellie. It's the exact same as it was when I was in high school. I tried out a plethora of sports in school but didn't stick with any, so I've just got participation trophies and medals all over. There's a piano keyboard in the corner that also never stuck, and two guitars. Besides that, I never made my bed this morning, so the blankets are thrown around, and my suitcase is open by the door. I kick it closed, hopefully before Ellie could see the mess inside and the underwear tragically on top.

The door snicks shut, and that's all it takes for Ellie to break the silence. "Can I just start with I'm sorry?" Mark and I share a look. "I really am. I didn't want things to get this bad. I thought I could prevent it, but it only made things worse. I'm so sorry."

Mark sighs. "We didn't bring you in here to force an apology out of you." His phrasing makes it seem obvious, but Ellie blinks. "We missed you." She blinks again. "Why did you leave?"

She steels her breathing, the tick in her jaw revealing that she definitely thinks this is a trap. "I…didn't think you'd want to see me after everything."

"Why not?" I ask. My heart breaks for her. She really thought we wanted nothing to do with her. To be fair, I tried hard to convince myself to want just that.

She sucks in a breath. "Did you guys…not understand what I said the other day?"

I shake my head and watch her eyes thin to irritated slits. Her jaw clenches tight. "What?" I ask. "About you saving my life? Or about how all you've done is try to keep your father and his assassins away from your brothers?"

"That's not true." She tips her head back and swallows, unwittingly drawing my gaze. "For the last month I've had my cousin digging through your life, looking for *anything* to tell me why you were a target. You've had no privacy with me. I had him track your phone just to know you were here."

I shake my head again slowly, taking a step toward her and repeating her own excuse back to her. "For protection. First, your brothers. Now, me too." Because it's true. Because I believe that's all she's wanted to do these past weeks. When things get messy, you don't blame the person trying to clean it up. This situation is unprecedented, but that doesn't mean she's handled it wrong. We all make mistakes. We all do crazy things for the people we love. "I can't blame you for that."

She huffs. "Why?"

I can't help the way my lips turn up at the edges. It's the strangest question, yet not unexpected. I take another step closer. If I reached out, I could touch her. She doesn't move a single muscle; it keeps me from closing the distance. "Ellie, we missed you. We wanted to talk to you about all this. Sure, I was angry at first. But then I came to terms with it…mostly. I wanted to be able to hash it all out *with* you, but you left so I couldn't talk to or yell at you at all."

"Well…yell at me now."

I never thought a day would come where I would find an assassin so adorable. I've seen the headlines of *Emily Richards* all over the news, the haunting stories of her victims. It was easy to hate her when she had no face. When she turned into the person standing before me, it became a lot harder. Impossible, actually. I shrug. "I don't really need to anymore."

"I don't understand." Ellie frowns.

I laugh. "I don't either." None of this makes sense, and I'm not about to attempt to rationalize the fact that I'm this close to the infamous assassin and not even a little bit scared for my life. There are more pressing matters to clear up. I swallow hard. "I'm sorry for what I said at your apartment, Ellie. I shouldn't have come at you like that. I was completely out of line."

She raises her brow. "You really weren't."

"I was. I was angry, and I shouldn't have taken it out on you."

She gives a one shoulder shrug. "In your defense, I did shoot you."

A relieved breath, and my toes scrunch into the fibers of the carpet. "I'm sorry," I say again for good measure. My parents didn't raise me to be uncivilized, and that night I was awful to her.

Rolling her eyes, she mumbles, "I hate it when you apologize." I almost laugh, but then she takes a half-step toward me. "I'm sorry too. For my part."

She's not talking about shooting me. The memory of that kiss hits me like a brick, and I tilt my head. "I'm only sorry it happened like that."

A smile splits her face into a grin that resembles the one I first saw at the airport and equated to being shot. It's the furthest thing from agonizing, though. At the risk of sounding cheesy in my own head, it's Christmas morning. Yep, that's bad. At least I don't say it out loud because this moment would be a lot less smooth.

I close the distance between us, lifting her chin. My hand slips around to the base of her neck, my thumb tracing the skin of her throat. Another blink, another breath, and she rises up on her toes. I'm light-headed the second her lips touch mine.

It's barely a whisper before someone clears their throat behind me. I freeze. Ellie freezes. *Mark.* I need to concentrate to get words back in my head…which is a hard thing to do with the scent of her coconut and mint shampoo filling my nostrils, infecting my brain functionality.

"Did you remember he was here?" I keep my whisper as low as it can possibly go, but it's so dead silent in my tiny room that Mark can still probably hear me. He doesn't mention it. I don't deserve him.

Ellie shakes her head once, eyes wide in shock and staring straight ahead at my chest. I should let her go, but I can't make my hands release. She doesn't try to pull away, though, either.

"Has this ever happened to you before?" *Please say no.*

Another shake.

Before I can ask her what we should do, I hear the rustle of Mark's jeans behind me. "Um." But he doesn't say anything else. The door squeaks open painfully slowly and thuds shut again.

For a second longer, we say nothing. Then, "Do you think he saw?" I don't know why I ask, but it seems better than the silence. She smiles, eyes going wide in surprise and delight, finally looking up at me, but now I think I might throw up. I take a large step away from her even though the damage is already done and run my hands through my hair. "He hates me."

"What?" Her brows wrinkle, and her smile turns into an amused frown. It's honestly adorable, and I mentally slap myself for the thought. *This is exactly the kind of thinking that he's going to scream at you for later.* "How do you figure *that*?" I do not appreciate the tone that conveys I'm overreacting because I am certain I am not.

"You're his sister," I point out unnecessarily. "This is a betrayal of our friendship. I broke the *code*."

"The code?" She holds up her hands and shakes her head instead of demanding an answer. "Never mind. If he's going to be mad at either of us, it'll be me."

I glare at her. "I don't like that much better."

"It's basically impossible to be mad at you anyway. You're his best friend."

"You're his sister."

"The assassin." She rolls her eyes. "And that brings us to why he'll be more upset with me."

I shake my head. "But I already accidentally told him I loved you. He was…" I catch myself a second too late. She raises her brows—a mirror to her brother's reaction the last time I said it—and I attempt an epic backpedal. "Not that…I love you. I don't. I mean, I like you a lot, but not like… Please stop me." I wipe the back of my hand across my slick forehead. "Sometimes I wish you *had* killed me."

She laughs but sobers quickly, her hand going to her stomach with a small groan. She looks down as her palm comes away red. I tense, but she just mutters, "Damn it."

"What happened?" I step closer. Her shirt is dark, but now I can see a slight shine where blood soaked through. Not a lot, but she's injured.

"Nothing." She waves me off. "We ran into trouble on our way here. I took care of it, but he got a lucky strike. I'm fine, I promise. It just needs a new bandage."

I step closer, reaching for the edge of her shirt. "Can I take a look?"

Slowly, she nods, and I gently peel her shirt up, revealing the blood-soaked bandage. I can't believe I didn't notice sooner, but her shirt is dark enough that it hides the blood well. Probably on purpose so she could hide it from my family. From everyone, I'd imagine.

I drop her shirt back into place and guide her with a light brush of my fingers on her elbow to my bed. "Here, lie down. I'll get the first-aid kit."

"You don't have to, Brandon. I can…" Her sentence trickles off when I meet her eyes earnestly.

"I want to take care of you," I tell her. She just stares back, frozen again. "Please."

Again, with slow movements, she lowers herself to lie flat atop my bed. Her gaze doesn't drop from mine, but I nod and turn my attention to her wound. I pull back the bandage to reveal the mess beneath. It's a long cut, maybe six inches across, below her belly button. It's not too deep. The edges are scabbing over, but the thickest part in the middle still wells. Someone tried to gut her.

I cast that thought away and grab the first-aid kit from the hall closet. Mom keeps one upstairs and downstairs, and she consulted me heavily when I started my schooling in what to stock them with. I also grab a small bowl and fill it with warm, soapy water.

When I return, Ellie hasn't moved. I can feel her eyes on me, but I keep my focus on the wound. How to fix it. Luckily, she's right; it's not a big deal. She just irritated it, and the blood wasn't allowed to clot properly.

I soak a paper towel in the water, wring it out, and wipe away the blood. It disappears easily which means she must have cleaned it up and bandaged it not too long ago. By the time I'm finished, the blood has stopped flowing so much. I take some of the gauze and dab the center of the cut. Ellie sucks in a breath.

"Sorry," I pull my hand back. "Did that hurt?"

"No."

My eyes flick up. She's still studying me as I dress her injury. It's a weird dynamic between us now, but I stop my mind from thinking further on that. Injury. Help her, first. Drama, later.

I nod and put pressure on the cut until the bleeding officially stops, then grab the jar of petroleum jelly. "This might be a little cold," I warn. She makes a small gasp when my fingers meet her skin as I spread the jelly across her lower stomach. But then it's finished, and the wound is again covered. The air feels too charged after the moment we just shared.

It was barely anything. I wish I could take it back. I wish I could kiss her again.

I give her a small smile when I finish and offer my hand. "Now, I should recommend you lie down for a while and rest, but I have a feeling you won't be doing that."

She takes my hand with a grin. "You'd be correct." The grin softens. "Thank you."

I know she doesn't just mean about the first aid. My lips pull tight, and all I can do is nod.

〉〉〉〉〉〉〉

MY MOM SNATCHES ELLIE UP AND TAKES HER INTO THE KITCHEN, BUT it's not before Mark notes his sister wearing one of my shirts. He shoots me a look. I pat my stomach as I take a seat on the couch with my dad. Mark understands and looks back at Ellie who has disappeared, so he turns back to me, lifting his brows in question. I shake my head once and hold out my hand. He visibly relaxes against the couch.

He and my dad have been watching the cooking channel all morning. For the next hour, I join them. They intersperse the silence with commentary on the quality of the competitors' work or their attitudes. The two men on this couch fancy themselves chefs.

Winston proves more interesting to me, sprawled on his back in front of the brick fireplace. His airborne legs slowly fall to the side in his sleep. About halfway down, he flips to his feet. Poor dude startled himself from what looked like a deep sleep.

And then the doorbell rings, slicing into the calm morning like a grenade. Ellie appears, leaning against the column near the kitchen, emanating nonchalance like a pro. I glance down at her stomach, making sure there's no shine off the shirt before I open the front door and blink a couple times to make sure the image doesn't disappear. "Mare?"

"Dish soap!" My sister comes in and wraps me in a hug, straining to lift me—she can't. "I missed you, little buddy." I'm taller and have more than a handful of pounds on her, but okay.

"Is that my baby?" Mom screeches. Ellie just barely presses herself into the column in time to avoid my mother barreling out of the kitchen. She reaches Marianna in only a few strides, squeezing her hard enough to make her eyes bug out. I step back to give them space. "I didn't know you were coming!"

I haven't seen my sister in a little over a year. Last Christmas she got stuck at work and couldn't come home, so it was the Thanksgiving before that when we last spoke face-to-face. She's called me a handful of times since then, but it's always shockingly inadequate compared to seeing her in person.

"We wanted to surprise you!" Mare grins.

"Harwood! Get over here and hug your child." But when Mom turns, he's right behind her.

"Right here, Kennedy." He grins, taking my sister from her. My parents have called each other by their last names forever. It started when they were dating, and they've used it in lieu of *honey* or *sweetheart* since. It's both a victory and a defeat.

Wyatt stumbles in with the bags and a smile then. I pause, a queasy feeling rooting around inside of me. I hate it. "Wyatt." I back up a step under the pretense of moving out of his way too, but I back right into Ellie, who apparently moved on cat-feet as soon as Wyatt showed up. She takes my shoulder to steady me, and I move beside her. "Sorry."

She ignores me, keeping her eyes on Wyatt. I lean down so my mom can't hear me and whisper into her ear, "I don't think he's any threat."

El blinks a few times, looks at me, back at Wyatt, and finally nods. I don't think she believes me. I just wish I did.

32

ELLIE'S PROBLEM

IT SEEMS BRANDON WAS RIGHT. WYATT HASN'T TRIED ANYTHING since he arrived yesterday. Both Brandon and Jaythan said the man wants out of my father's grip *for* his family, but there's no telling what a desperate man will do, so I keep my guard up.

This morning Brandon's parents took us to the Christmas Eve service at their church. I know Brandon and Mark go to church regularly, but I've never attended a service. I tried to get out of it this morning to scout the town again, make sure no one came in the dark of the night, but every single person in the house insisted. I still would have blown it off if not for the large puppy dog eyes I got not only from Mark but Brandon too.

I got to talk to Wyatt before we left. I was up early, and he came down in his nice suit and Christmas tie so he wouldn't be in the rest of the family's way as they got ready. We didn't talk about much, and I wasn't able to draw meaning from anything he said beyond a general love for his family. Before I could steer the conversation to more lucrative grounds, Marianna came down, shortly followed by Brandon.

From them, I learned that when Brandon was a baby, an older gentleman thought his name was *Don*, and Marianna, being nine, was reminded of the dish soap brand, hence the nickname. That was the most interesting thing I learned about this family all morning—granted, it was positively delightful.

Even during the service, I watched Wyatt for signs of distraction—checking his phone, bouncing his knee, rapid blinking, a faraway look—but he was completely locked in. He sang the Christmas songs, he smiled at his family, he listened to the pastor. He was a picture-perfect Christian family man, and on the way home he even had things to add to the discussion about the sermon.

I didn't expect him to be a distant husband or a cold man, but he's worked for the Enforcers for years. This makes as much sense as me having a secret life where I raise chickens.

Mrs. Harwood laid out a giant spread of food on her counter for us to partake of what we will when we will. Apparently, in their household there are no meals on Christmas Eve, just endless snacking, and they'll watch Christmas movies and play games until it's finally time to go to sleep.

I haven't celebrated Christmas since I was five. Cooper didn't prioritize celebrating any holiday. I was usually busy anyway, and he had the Enforcers to deal with. And since I reconnected with my brothers… They tried to bring me in on all their traditions, but I knew where those traditions originated. Christmas was too hard to be a part of without Mom, so I found excuses to avoid it.

Rowan always gave me a gift, though. Every birthday and Christmas. It came to an abrupt halt after I turned sixteen, as did my sense of joy in celebrating any holiday. They became mere backdrops of tragedy.

The decorations all over this house are meant to be festive and happy making, but I can't shake the feeling that it's just another backdrop.

Everyone is sitting at the dining table midway through the day. We're playing a card game called Nertz which is apparently very popular in Brandon's family. They explained it like group solitaire which sounded casual, relaxed. It's not. This game brings out a savage side in them all. Mark, seated across from me, jumps right into the bloodshed, but I keep calm. Observant. And I win a few rounds to Brandon's surprisingly competitive irritation. I shoot him a grin each time I claim a victory. He laughs.

We're in the middle of a round very much not going my way when my attention snags on the sliding glass door behind Mark.

No one notices when I stop playing the game.

Sometimes if you listen hard enough, nature will tell you the things that would otherwise remain hidden. This time it's the steady rattle of the winter breeze against the glass, the smooth snow covering the yard. It's too quiet.

Before I can think, I launch across the table, scattering the cards, and flipping behind Mark just in time for a fully armored man to burst through the sliding door. Glass shatters in his wake, shards slicing into my back. Not deep. Wyatt, having been seated beside Mark, gets sliced up too. He launches for Marianna.

Freezing winter air blasts into the warm house. The man makes no move to use his gun, only starts shouting orders to the family behind me. "Everybody move!"

Another man kicks through the front door. One takes out the skylight. I shove Mark out of his chair and usher him into the living room where these men want us to gather. Mr. Harwood keeps his wife close, and Wyatt has both Marianna and Brandon moving toward the living room too.

One of the soldiers grabs Marianna's arm, and Wyatt attempts to punch him. But the soldier is trained. Wyatt isn't. He catches the flimsy punch and lands one in Wyatt's stomach. Marianna screams. Wyatt goes down on one knee, gasping.

The twinkling tree is crushed by the next wave of intruders. *Just another backdrop.*

Winston plows through the commotion, getting a firm bite on the arm of the first man to grab for Mrs. Harwood. The man cries out and tries to kick the dog loose, but Brandon throws a punch, bloodying the man's nose. Another man gets his arms fully around the valiant dog and holds him down as the rest wrangle everyone up.

Distantly, I hear Mr. Harwood shouting threats at the men who dare attack his family. He might even be putting up a fight, but it's all white noise in my ears. My gaze locks with Brandon's as two men grip my arms and a third locks my hands behind my back. He watches me allow it, and his chest hollows—but two more men file in through the door, and there's nothing I can do. I don't even know what these people want.

Within minutes the rest of Brandon's family are brought to their knees, and we're lined up awaiting our slaughter. *Just another backdrop.*

Brandon leans close to me, but I keep my head down. He whispers, "What is this?"

I only shake my head. This is my father's move. I thought he would stop at taking Jake, but again, I was wrong. Cooper doesn't do anything small.

"Do something," he begs.

I lift my eyes to his then. The plea in his voice makes it clear he doesn't care what method I use, as long as his family survives. I don't have to prod to know he understands exactly what he's asking for. Already the anger has settled in my gut like a living thing. A beast chomping at the bit to be unleashed. But that white noise plays above it, wondering when it will ever stop. When will it be enough?

Brandon's dark brown eyes are wide, terrified. "Please."

"I don't know if I can," I breathe. Even at my best, six hostiles mixed with as many hostages would be a terrible gamble. If any member of his family died even because I tried to save them, Brandon would never forgive me. He would never forgive himself. He understands the monster he means to unleash in me, but he doesn't understand the consequences he'll be forced to live with for it.

One more man comes through the door, strolling in like he owns the place. Of course Hartley came to collect me for my father. He's always been good at playing errand boy. "Well, well, well. Four targets in one place. Good news, though, only two of you matter to us anymore."

He grins, looking down the row. He nods to his men who grab me and Wyatt and drag us forward. Marianna squeaks in terror. Mr. Harwood wraps his arm around her, glaring at the man holding a gun in his face for the unauthorized movement. Winston struggles beneath the soldier, growling for all he's worth. A family of fighters. They don't deserve this.

"Hartley?" Mark's voice pipes up behind me. I don't dare turn to him, but I wish I could shut him up.

Of course Mark recognizes Hartley. He used to babysit us. The man practically worshiped my father and was so obsessed that he did whatever my dad needed. Mom hated that, but it wasn't like he was going to do anything to us. He was much too preoccupied trying to impress my father and show him what a great job he'd done. He had hoped, I'm sure, that that would look like him in a suit with the answer to their business problems, but instead it looked like him preventing me from burning the kitchen down and Jake screaming in his face until Hartley lost it. Mark was his favorite.

Hartley turns to Mark and every muscle I have tenses. I force my emotions deep down, staring straight at Hartley. There was no chance of him hurting us back then. That doesn't mean he won't do it now.

"Hello again, Mark." Hartley smirks at my brother. Mrs. Harwood and Marianna are blubbering beside Brandon, but they keep it as quiet as possible, terrified to bring any attention on themselves. *Good.* "You're looking well. How's school going?"

"It's good." Mark sounds too surprised to stop the answer from slipping out.

Hartley nods, and his attention shifts back to me. My shoulders relax.

He *tsks*, making a big show of shaking his head in disapproval. Winston barks and keeps barking, viciously. Hartley groans. "Would someone please take care of that dog?"

One of the men produces a syringe and sticks the dog with it. Mrs. Harwood screams, and her arm flies into my line of vision only to be yanked back by Brandon. I watch it all with practiced, mild disinterest. The dog, fighting with every last bit of strength, slowly slumps to the ground in a slumbering heap.

Mrs. Harwood sobs, and I hear Brandon whisper, "He's not dead."

"Please." Everyone's attention goes to Wyatt as he speaks up. "Let them go."

"Begging." Hartley shakes his head. "I expected as much. I must say I'm disappointed. I was hoping to at least get a fight out of Emily."

"Emily?" Wyatt asks. When Hartley looks down at me, Wyatt shakes his head and snaps, "That's not possible. You have the wrong girl. She's just my brother's friend." I study him, admiring his outburst and appreciating the support, but at this point he should be able to put it together.

Hartley smirks at Wyatt. Then he turns the expression on me. "Of course they don't know. It would be better for them if they didn't, right?" I don't give him anything. He already said he wants a fight out of me, and I've made it my life's mission to deprive this man of everything he's ever wanted. It hasn't been hard, considering number one on that list was my father's admiration. The tension in the room is taut as a bowstring, and reacting to his jabs would be the shot to my foot. "I could tell them for you."

I'm perfectly calm, but Wyatt is more anxious by the second. "She's not Emily. She's my brother's friend. His sister." He gestures with his hand toward Mark, and I want to hit him for it. Instead, my attention snaps to him. I can see in that moment as he meets my fiery gaze, and his face drains completely of color. He knows the truth. His breath rushes out, but he turns back to Hartley, silver lining his eyes. "Please, I don't know who you are, but my family is innocent." I smirk, knowing it annoys Hartley not to be known and feared in the company like Cooper is. "Just let them go."

Hartley gives him an appraising look. Wyatt's shoulders tense as he realizes this is a losing battle, but credit to him, he holds Hartley's gaze. "Care to enlighten him, Mark?"

"Don't," I growl, now casting an unyielding glare at Hartley, my mask slipping. Hartley shifts on his feet but doesn't let his gaze leave Mark's. The bastard knows my hands are literally tied, but he also knows I'm a threat even now. It's why his strategy will be to turn the entire room against me.

"He works for my father," Mark mutters.

"*With*," Hartley corrects with a hiss. "Your father and I began this business together. It's as much mine as it is his."

In the years since I have become my father's greatest achievement, Hartley's obsessive admiration has taken a turn toward jealousy. Not enough room for both me and Hartley in my father's good graces. Now, however, I've cast myself aside. He should be thriving. Only he's not. Sent here to bring me back, so I can pay for my crimes. It's not an honor. It's another chore.

The wicked grin slices across my face. "Keep telling yourself that." I know this is the reaction he wants, but I need his attention off Mark. Besides, pushing his buttons makes the white noise dim just enough to feel that monster deep inside. Just enough for me to want to let it off its leash at last.

"And what about you?" If he had knees, he would crouch down in front of me. Instead, he stands, looking down at me in a very awkward manner but forcing me to look up, undoubtedly stoking his ego. He can have the high ground; in a fight you get low.

"They don't seem to know you at all. Your brother does." He looks up at Mark and smiles. I clench my jaw tight. "He didn't take that too well, did he? I'd like to know how the rest of them take it." Now his attention turns to Brandon and his family. "You all seem like lovely people. Do you know what kind of person you've invited into your home?"

Logic tells me I should wait and find out his endgame. There will be an opening. But rage tells me I've starved the monster long enough.

As if he can hear my thoughts, "Oh, and in case you get any ideas." Hartley looks pointedly to the door where a final man appears. This one, the polar opposite of Hartley. In his late thirties, all muscle. He's got the scruff of a working man, and the face of one who would snap a person's spine with just his pointer finger and thumb for interrupting him. The thick white scar across the side of his suntanned face only adds to the effect.

Rowan, my old mentor. He stares down at me with the same blank expression that's on my own face. Rowan's the one who taught me that. He was more of a father to me than my actual father—not one I wouldn't betray too, however. Especially after *he* betrayed *me*. And that's all it takes for the white noise to come back. *Just another backdrop.*

Now that his insurance is here, Hartley's shoulders relax, and the smile comes easily once more. "Do you want to be the one to break the news to the family?"

Rowan doesn't even acknowledge Hartley. He remains stiff, eyes only for me. I can't stop staring at him either. It's been years since I saw him. He's always been hard and unyielding, but he had a soft side too. He watched my first victim's news spot with me and worried when I ran out of the room to hurl. He was my father when my real one refused to be. Now, with the firm set of his jaw, perfectly squared shoulders, and hand rested on the gun at his side, he looks harsher. Like something killed that softness. I'm tempted to pity him.

"Alright, I'll tell them." Hartley makes the barest movement, inching away from Rowan, the smartest thing he's done all afternoon. "Ever heard of the Enforcers?" His gaze drifts over the Harwoods. When he turns back to me, he's put on a slimy grin. "Ever wanted to meet one?"

The room goes deathly silent.

"You haven't even heard the best part." Hartley waddles past me to Brandon. "Well, aside from the fact that she's the one who shot your son."

Mrs. Harwood makes a strangled sound, choking back a sob.

"No," Brandon says quickly. "She saved me."

Hartley *tsks* again. "She may have had the heart for that then with her partner in crime." A nod to Wyatt. I jolt but still say nothing. "But has she told you of her most recent work? She stole files off my computer earlier this month." He moves back over to me, stroking my hair. Revulsion surges through me, and I whip my head away from him, but it only makes him smile. "Been going down my list, crossing them off." He pauses to bend down close to my face. "Future targets."

My stomach drops as he punctuates each word. So that's his angle. Emily Richards went rogue but as a means to take more jobs for herself. My father has painted me as a vigilante. Someone who got too carried away with her work, wanted a little more glory for herself. I did get files off Hartley's computer, just not *those* files. I could laugh. Hartley doesn't even keep a master file of every target. Once they're printed, they're erased from the computer. Leave no trace. But still, I say nothing.

"Ellie," Brandon shifts toward me. One of Hartley's goons grabs his shoulder. He winces. "Please."

33

ELLIE'S SKILLS

"**P**LEASE."

Seven men, including Hartley. Six to worry about. Rowan's the only Enforcer. The rest are brute squad meant more for numbers than skill.

Rowan kneels in front of me now, cupping my face almost delicately. He has a syringe in hand. Another tranquilizer. I grew up with him, but he backed off when I made it clear I never wanted to see him again. Now he's back, possibly near the end of my life. How poetic.

He tilts my head to the side, exposing my neck to his needle, and meets my eyes. Something flashes across his—something like atonement. And I picked the lock on these handcuffs seconds after they put them on.

Screw caution. The monster's slipped its leash.

I grab his wrist and slam my elbow into his ribs. My hand slides from his wrist to pull the syringe free and stab it into his neck. He goes down with a groan, clutching the puncture mark, but his hand drops uselessly beside him. Not dead. I quickly slip the gun from his holster into my hands.

I jump toward Hollin—the soldier closest to Wyatt, and one I've seen around the Enforcers many times over the years—and slam my fist into his face, but he turns, and I only clip his cheek. Some of the other brutes have gotten wise to my actions and one raises his gun. I shoot him between the eyes. Hollin is on me before I can take out the next, and his own fist slams into my jaw. My teeth clack against each other, but I swallow the pain. He grabs my sleeve, but I spin out of my sweater, following through with the movement and wrapping it around his neck. He flicks his wrist and cuts right through it with the knife he just pulled. *Damn it, I liked that sweater.*

His gun is in his free hand now too, but he manages a gash to my wrist with the knife. I notice another one of the brutes taking aim over his shoulder and grab a fistful of Hollin's shirt and pull him close just as the man pulls the trigger. It goes straight through Hollin's side, grazing mine before slamming into the wall. My hip burns, and the old wound on my stomach pulls tight, but those are distant pains.

Hollin brings up his gun underneath my chin, and I have just enough time to throw my head back before he shoots. He grunts and shoves me back, but now I aim a round at his chest. He's ready for that, slamming his fist into my wrist and knocking off the shot. I flip the gun up barely in time to avoid shooting Brandon's dad; it hits a lamp behind him instead. Mrs. Harwood screams from where her husband is wisely keeping her head covered.

Hollin slashes out with his knife again, and I grab his wrist, twist, and flip him onto his back. He hits the ground with a thud, and the air whooshes from his lungs.

I slam my foot down on his other wrist, forcing him to drop the gun, and kick it away. Then for the moment, I turn away from him. All three of the other brutes have their guns pointed at me. I lunge for the closest one, and his shot goes past me. I throw him between me and the other two. Peering around my human shield, I shoot the other two cleanly, and they land in heaps on the floor behind Brandon and Mark who are looking green. My shield falls victim to me a heartbeat later.

It's just Hollin left. And I've only got one more bullet. Rowan never fills the magazine. He trusts himself never to need them all, and if an enemy gets ahold of the weapon, they might misjudge the number of bullets. I don't. Hollin's got Wyatt on his feet, providing him defense. I find Marianna huddled with her mother and father not too far away and nearly sigh in relief. Lucky Hollin wasn't smart enough to take her. Wyatt's eyes are wide, pinned on me.

Hollin's knife is against Wyatt's throat. He presses hard enough to draw a thin trickle of blood. He doesn't realize that while that would intimidate anyone else, it only serves to stir the bloodlust inside of me.

I ignore the cries from the family around us. My hair sticks to the sweat on my neck, forming a thick noose.

Hollin sneers. "You won't risk killing this one. You're too sentimental. The Enforcers have one basic rule. No attachments. You used to pride yourself on how much better you were, and now look at you. They'll all die. Because of you."

Wyatt meets my eyes. "It's okay," he whispers, thinking only of his family. It's okay to shoot. It's okay to kill him. It's okay.

No, it's not.

It happens in the span of four seconds.

I drop my eyes behind Hollin, widen them. "Back, dog!"

Hollin turns just enough.

I pull the trigger.

Wyatt jerks to the side, blood now splattered across his face and shoulder.

It weeps from the hole in Hollin's temple too before he topples over into a heap with the rest.

And I drop the empty gun.

I turn slowly toward Hartley, who has the good sense to squirm again. I step close. My voice drops low, a physical manifestation of the effort it takes not to peel the flesh from his body until he begs me to take his life. "Know that the only reason I don't kill you now is so that you can see that familiar disappointment on my father's face when you return to him emptyhanded." He reaches out, probably to put his hands up in surrender, but I grip his fingers and angle the flat of my blade against his wrist. I don't look down as I twist the blade slightly. A thin line of blood blotches his white skin. "Your move, Hartley." He pales as I slip the edge along his wrist before letting go of him. It will heal quickly. He clutches it like it's fatal. "Come back to this house." A dare. He knows better than to respond.

Once the rat scurries away, it takes no time at all for the adrenaline to dissipate and for me to remember where I am, who just witnessed everything. The winter chill blasting through the demolished house freezes me to my core.

I take a few seconds to agonize over the state of things. The windows and skylight are shattered, I shot one of the lamps, blood is everywhere, I'm covered in it. Not to mention the bodies strewn all over the living room. The tree crushed, the garland sagging, the tiny village smashed to pieces.

Backdrop. Backdrop. Backdrop.

There's shifting behind me, but when I turn, everyone freezes. Mr. Harwood clings to his daughter's shoulders as she kneels beside her husband who's slumped on the ground, holding his ear. Brandon is at Wyatt's side. Mrs. Harwood is with her still unconscious dog, confirming for herself that he's still alive. Mark stands in the middle of it all, breathing heavily. But they all stop to watch me.

"I'm so sorry," I say dumbly. *What are you supposed to say when you almost get your friend's entire family killed?* "For all of this. I'll pay for repairs and cleanup. I have a safehouse a few towns over. You'll be safe there." Technically, it's Rowan's safehouse. He brought me once during training. Since he's my hostage now, he shouldn't mind if I put it to use. I start to back away. "I'm sorry."

"Ellie." The surprising part is that it's not Mark who says my name in that calm, empathetic thrum. It's not even Brandon. Wyatt pushes himself to his feet and walks up to me. I don't know what to do, so I hold my ground.

He wraps his arms around me, squeezing tightly. I tense before I realize it's a hug. I can't make myself move as he envelops me entirely into his soft warmth. He only holds me tighter. "Thank you," he says a bit too loudly. "You saved my family. I'll never forget that."

I close my eyes and let myself have this for just a moment. Gratitude hits different than a paycheck. But as soon as he backs away, my mask is on again. Things need to get done, and they won't get there through sentiment.

Wyatt's whole demeanor shifts as he faces his family. "I'm so sorry," he says to them. "This wasn't Ellie's fault; it was mine. If I had made better decisions years ago, this never would have happened."

Something about his words reminds me of what Hartley said just before I set myself loose. *Partner in crime*, he'd called Wyatt. *My* partner in crime. Like he thought I was working with Wyatt. Like he thought I knew Wyatt even existed in this setting before a week ago.

Wyatt shifts away from me a hair, sensing the turn of my thoughts. "What did he mean?" I keep my voice flat, but my suspicion increases when he understands what I'm talking about.

His shoulders hunch inward, and he raises his hands in a placating gesture. "Okay, but could you first put down the knife?"

I lift a brow but open my hand. *Thud.* The growing fire coursing through my veins assures me he's made a wise request. No one moves.

He waves his hand toward Rowan, still unconscious with the dog. "Rowan came to me a few years ago. He said he needed an analyst to make…people real. He never told me why." A gulp. "He started bringing me names that I was supposed to authenticate. I made sure they had passports and licenses and histories. Same faces, different names. Different *lives*."

My brain stalls. I can't be interpreting this right. It takes me too long to form words. "They're still alive." My targets. I struggle to swallow. "All of them?"

"The first few were real, but after that…" He nods. "They're spread all over the place. I can show you the files if you—"

"How." The killing calm settles over me.

He shuts his mouth abruptly. "Rowan found a supplier. He never told me who, but your bullets are fake."

I wait. Everyone is still so quiet. Slowly, I pull my gun from where one soldier stashed it in his waistband.

I take a deep breath.

Then aim it at Wyatt's chest.

He goes utterly still, hands out before him. Each heartbeat echoes like a gong. Even Marianna, trembling at her husband's feet, doesn't dare make a sound.

"Your handgun's bullets—" Wyatt sucks down a shaky inhale— "are real."

"I know." I flick the safety off.

"Are you going to kill me?"

"Still deciding."

The confession doesn't make him cower. He sets his jaw, puts his hands down, and stands tall. "I won't apologize."

He won't apologize for saving those people.

He won't apologize for interfering with my *life*.

He won't apologize for putting my brothers in *danger* with his heroics.

He won't apologize…

I grit my teeth. Brandon's parents hover by their daughter, ready to drag her away from her husband and get her out. Mark breathes heavily in the corner. And in my peripheral, I see Brandon, focused on me. I don't dare meet his eyes.

I raise my chin, click the safety back on, and lower the gun. Keeping my gaze on Wyatt, I say, "Neither will I."

Then I walk out the front door.

34

BRANDON'S OBSERVATIONS

I STARE AFTER ELLIE, ANXIETY AND ADRENALINE UNWILLING TO leave the pit in my stomach. My mom and sister are still in tears, Dad's taking a closer look at Wyatt's ear, and Mark hastily offers his help, casting terrified glances at my family. I don't blame him. It's doubtful they'll warm back up to Ellie soon, but she did just save our lives, so they're not going to do anything drastic. I know I should help them, maybe clean up some of the glass or something, but my attention is dragged back to Ellie.

I grab my coat on the way out and spot her on the top step of the porch, hands clasped between her knees. She must be freezing, but she doesn't show it. She doesn't protest when I push her hair away from the back of her neck to assess the cuts. They're shallow, no glass is stuck in her skin, and none penetrated the back of her shirt. They will be a nuisance as they heal, but nothing more. Carefully, I wrap the coat around her shoulders and silently drop down next to her. I can't pretend to know what she's feeling. So, I offer her the comfort she needs. Or at least what she'll accept.

There's a bright red gash on her wrist, and when I lightly tap her elbow, she offers up her arm to me. It's not bad enough to need stitches, and it doesn't appear to be bothering her too much. It just needs to be cleaned and wrapped. I push aside the jacket and glance at her hip where there's another splotch of her blood. She sits up a little straighter to allow me a closer look. I lift her ruined shirt just enough to prod the edges of the wound. I do so gently, but she still sucks in a breath.

"Sorry," I mutter. It's just a burn. Get a bandage over that too, and she'll be good as new. "How's your…"

Without needing me to finish the question, she straightens and lifts her shirt. The bandage is soaked through with blood, but so is her shirt. It's possible it's not hers. She knows my thoughts and pulls aside the bandage so I can check the actual cut. It's messy, blood drying around it. I glance up, and she nods. Gently, I run the tip of my finger along the seam. It's closed up nicely, and somehow, she didn't rip it back open.

She shivers. "That tickles."

I smile a bit and pull back my hand. She replaces the bandage and lowers her shirt. When I meet her eyes, she's already watching me. Studying me. A purple splotch mars the corner of her jaw. I turn my focus onto it and cup her face, gently running my thumb along the bruise. She barely reacts, just keeps staring at me.

"Why?" she finally whispers. My eyes find her calculating green ones, and she clears her throat. "Why do you do all this?"

My thumb brushes the underside of her jaw now. "You protect the people you care about. So do I. Just a little differently."

Ellie takes a deep breath, and my hand slips down her neck. "Why me?" My heart cracks, and I think she sees it because her eyes shutter, and she looks surprised she said anything.

But I make it clearer for her. "Because I care about you."

Another breath and more studying. "I've had people care about me." She doesn't say any more, but I get the sense it's not the pleasant statement it sounds like. I don't push her, though. I can't begin to piece together what it must have been like to grow up how she did. She needs time. I don't have a problem giving it to her.

She turns her head. My hand falls away. It's not a dismissal because she says, "I don't even know why I'm upset." She's shifting the conversation on purpose and won't look at me now. Her eyes scan our little snow-covered lawn and the narrow street beyond. A cold breeze drifts by, and she shudders deeper into my coat. My skin prickles against it too, but I ignore it.

"It's been my whole life, Brandon." It's the first time her use of my name breaks my heart. "Training for it, doing it. I hated it, but you know why I did it?" I do, but I know she's frustrated and needs to talk through it. "Cooper was always ruthless. He never cared about me. Not really. And I knew nothing else would stop him from using Mark or Jake, so I stayed. I hoped that my cooperation would keep him from turning his attention on them." She laughs humorlessly, looking down at her lap. "The worst part is that it probably would have worked. If not for Wyatt."

"Do you hate him for it?" I ask without judgment. Of course, killing should never be taken lightly, and I for one am glad to know Wyatt was working to save each of her targets. But she did it to keep her own family safe. Her father put her in a horrible situation, and she did the only thing she could. Wyatt undid that work without her knowledge, but that's not how it looked when her father found out.

She shakes her head, but not in answer. "I don't know."

»»»»»»

ELLIE TRIED TO GET MARK AND I TO STAY AT HER SAFEHOUSE WITH MY family, who also wanted us to stay. Needless to say, we did not. The house is spacious enough that my family will be comfortable there for now.

My mother nearly threw a fit when I insisted on staying with Ellie. The only way I could pacify her was to agree to calling every single day and answering whatever text she sends within two minutes. Otherwise, she's calling the police. I looked to Ellie, unsure whether she would want the police potentially tangled up in this mess, but she merely gave me the same expectant look my mother did without any hint of sarcasm. I think that more than anything else helped my mom feel comfortable with the assassin. Especially after Wyatt and I explained the circumstances leading up to me being shot last month. I'm more than happy to avoid the fallout between her and Wyatt.

I wrapped Ellie's wrist, bandaged her side, and cleaned and re-bandaged the old cut on her stomach despite her protests that she was fine. She patiently allowed me to work, though.

She refused to bring the giant assassin to the safehouse with my family, so we tied him to a chair that's been nailed into the concrete in the middle of the basement away from anything he can get his hands on to free himself. While we waited for him to wake up, the three of us straightened up the house as best we could—threw away the lamp Ellie shot, swept up the glass, and took every cleaning spray we could think of to the blood strewn everywhere. Cardboard covers the busted windows, and the door merely rests against the frame. Most of Mom's Christmas decorations had to be scrapped, and to my disappointment, only a handful of the ornaments Mare and I made as kids survived.

I've caught myself grinding my teeth a few times since it all happened. If the Enforcers can help it, no one will know what happened here. Not even the neighbors who started coming back a few hours ago. I don't even know how everyone was evacuated without us knowing.

Rowan's entire Captain America body sags with exhaustion when he finally does wake up. My eye is drawn to the vicious scar that runs across his face from ear to chin. What sort of person do you have to be to earn that?

A text from my mom confirmed Winston woke up twenty minutes ago, to which I responded with a *thank goodness* mere seconds later.

Ellie sits in the chair across from our prisoner, elbows propped on her knees. "You're obsolete to our current mission." The giant assassin only blinks once, unbothered. "But we could use your help for the other if you're willing."

All three of our attentions snap to her.

Rowan blinks again, slowly this time, showing the mildest of surprise. "Why?" I must admit it's a good question. What is she thinking?

"Because we're going to take out the entire organization. Isn't that why you were having Wyatt forge a bunch of fake identities and swapping my bullets?"

We never discussed that. *What is she doing?*

"Ruthlessness runs in the tap there." The giant assassin's jaw ticks. "You'll need a hell of a lot more help to pull that off."

She tilts her head. "I'd say two doctors, a tech-wizard, and two assassins make a pretty good team."

"Two med students, you mean. And one assassin." He has a good point.

She ignores him. "You've been MIA three months now, am I right? No assignments. No trace. What happened?"

"I left."

"You knew Cooper a long time. You guys were friends, and you just left?"

He frowns, and I swear something like pain crosses his features, but it's just for a blink. "We were never friends."

Ellie wrinkles her nose. "Why would you come back then? You could have stayed away. But you came back to taunt me. Why?"

Rowan glares. Then there's almost thirty minutes of complete silence. I know this because every few minutes when I glance at Mark, he checks his watch and signals how much time has passed. Rowan and Ellie never look away from each other. It's so much eye contact that I manage to convince myself they're having a telepathic conversation. That is, until Rowan finally speaks.

"What almost happened to you, happened to me." His words come out slowly like he's trudging through molasses.

Ellie shakes her head. "What's that supposed to mean?"

Rowan's hands tighten to fists on the arms of the chair, and I tense. "A few years ago, my kid was born." Ellie's eyes shutter almost imperceptibly. "It forced me to rethink everything. You read lots of stories about heroes and villains to kids. I didn't want to be the villain for him, so I dug deeper into my targets to be certain. But I found their connections to powerful people. Most of them were innocent. Even before the merger. Their only crime was being connected or a nuisance to someone powerful."

I focus on Rowan, even as I feel Mark's gaze turn on me.

"So, I started hiding them. Making them disappear. It was going great until Wyatt Hull ratted me out."

"Wait." Ellie holds out a hand to stop him. "I thought you were working together on this."

"We were. But then he must have gotten cold feet because he told them everything. Assassins were sent to hunt down every last person I helped hide. And then I was ordered to kill my wife."

"Did you?" Mark blurts. They both glance at him, and he tucks himself into the wall. "Sorry."

"They told me if I didn't, they'd take my son and throw him into the Enforcers," he says directly to Ellie. "I couldn't let that happen."

Ellie's quiet a moment, and I realize she's forcing down her emotions again. That's sympathy tightening her shoulders. She swallows thickly. "If you were worth this much trouble, why didn't they just send someone to kill you?" Her tone is flat, but I know what she must be thinking. Wyatt told her the targets were still alive, but Rowan's saying they're dead. Who are we supposed to believe?

"Now that'd make me a martyr, wouldn't it?" Rowan smiles, but there's no joy in it. "It's much easier to discredit a man who's got no dignity left. I didn't come here for you." Cold determination in that dark tone of voice. "I came for Wyatt Hull."

I stiffen, terror seizing me at the aggression toward my brother-in-law. Wyatt is the man my sister loves, and despite my anger with him, I won't hesitate to defend him.

Ellie takes care of it. "Ah." She leans back, at last showing emotion, even if it is only mild amusement. "You mean the other man trying to get out of this job? That's why you utilized him, right? Did you know Brandon was almost killed for Wyatt's dissension?" Rowan's black eyes flash to me.

I try not to squirm.

"He wants to start his own family, a real life. Want to know my guess?" She leans closer and drops her voice. "Someone found out what the two of you were doing and found a way to drive in a wedge. They let you believe Wyatt turned on you, and then they broke you. If I hadn't stepped in to save Brandon, Wyatt would have been dealt with too and likely left to assume *you* betrayed *him*." Her smile falters then, and she stops talking.

I withhold the sigh of relief that Wyatt did not hand me over to the Enforcers on a silver platter. Her theory makes perfect sense. Everything's fine. I mean…in comparison, I guess. Hopefully Rowan can believe it too and wipe that vengeful glare off his face.

Ellie lets that information settle over him. He stares at her, and that apparently is what she wants out of him. "Help us take them down."

Rowan shakes his head. "I can't leave my son without a father after I took his mother away."

"But you could leave him in a world with the Enforcers." A challenge.

"It's not the best of options, but I can't leave my kid."

"They made you kill your wife." She stands, kicking the chair away. "You came back for a reason, Rowan. It wasn't revenge on Wyatt. We're doing this with or without you. With you, we might actually stand a chance. You don't want our blood on your hands too, do you?"

I blink at the harshness of her words. That must be the worst argument for our cause that I wasn't even told about. They stare at each other for a while. I'm not sure how long this is supposed to go on…but then Rowan says so quietly I almost miss it, "You trust me to help?"

He looks desperate for the answer, and I wonder what happened between them. Outside of the news, I hadn't heard of Rowan before today, but it's clear he and Ellie share a past. And it left him ruined.

She just shrugs. "Whatever loyalties you reserved for Cooper were shattered when he threatened your son." She pauses. "Why would you have Hull take my targets? How did they even survive?"

"I switched out your bullets whenever you left town. Jaythan created them." Her eyes widen, then narrow to slits, and I have a feeling her cousin will be getting an earful later. "He made them look and feel just like normal bullets. I don't know the technicalities of the design, but they contain a serum that slows the heartrate enough that any medical instruments won't be able to pick up a heartbeat. He also fills them with fake blood to make the deaths seem authentic, and since the Enforcers never take the time to examine the bodies, it flew under the radar. Local authorities took the bodies, and all I had to do was intercept them on the way to the morgue."

"Why?" Her question is quiet, and I blink at her. How can she not see it?

The strain in his eyes is back, and this time he isn't fast enough to cover it up. "Just because you stopped caring what happens to me, doesn't mean I stopped caring what happens to you."

I've had people care about me.

There's another long silence. When he grins, it doesn't quite reach his eyes. But Ellie returns it. Then they're laughing. Ellie starts untying him.

"What are you doing?" They both look at Mark again, and he doesn't seem to enjoy that one bit.

"He's going to help us." Ellie frowns at him like this is obvious.

He lifts a brow at me, I shrug, then he squints at his sister. "That's what you got from what just happened?"

Rowan tilts his head but doesn't say anything.

The second he's freed, Ellie hums, shakes her head, and heads for the stairs. Apparently, she trusts him with us now.

"Where are you going?" Mark rushes after her but stops short at the bottom of the staircase.

She chuckles heartily when she reaches the narrow opening, and it echoes off the walls. "I had a thought."

"Which is?" I ask.

She pulls her phone from her back pocket, and holds it up over her shoulder, not looking back as she climbs. "I'm going to give *Bosom* a call."

I frown, not sure whether she's serious or joking. I don't know if there's any such thing as logic in my life anymore. Easier just to go with it.

35

ELLIE'S SECOND

THE FOUR OF US LOAD INTO ROWAN'S PRIVATE JET CHRISTMAS morning. He used to fly me to my training all over the world in this thing. He advised that I don't practice while in the air, so I had free time to do what I wanted like read or watch a movie or just sit without worry of interruptions. There's a tiny kitchen near the front where I'd make myself eggs, so many eggs—it was the one thing I could make without burning until I finally learned to cook after moving into my own apartment.

This time he's not taking me to train until I drop, and I'm not making eggs. He's flying us to DC where we'll meet Jaythan, who will let us in on the plan he's been cooking up. Unfortunately, once we land, there will be quite a bit of driving to do since Rowan can't land anywhere but an airport in this thing. I'm not upset about the extra travel time. It gives Mark and Brandon plenty of time to back out.

I try to prepare them for what they're about to take part in, that they could be killed. I see fear in their expressions, but there is also excitement and determination. They refuse to turn back. It makes me queasy enough that I leave to check the status of our flight progress and fill Rowan in on my phone call before we left.

I'm on my way to fill Mark and Brandon in on it too when I hear Mark. "So…about the kiss…"

I stop outside the door at the little coffee station and start to turn away, not wanting to hear this or interrupt or be dragged into it, but then Brandon speaks.

"I'm so sorry about that, Mark. I should have talked to you first. I feel terrible."

"No, I'm not mad about it." Mark lets out a small laugh. "You can both make your own decisions." He pauses. "I'm just worried."

"I would never hurt her," Brandon says quietly, and I feel my lips tug up in the corners.

"I'm not worried about *you* hurting *her*." Butterflies turn leaden in my stomach. My gaze drops to the floor. I saw it coming, and I understand it, but it still hurts coming from my brother.

Brandon takes a moment before responding. When he does, his voice is low. "I don't think you have to worry too much about that. We haven't had a chance to talk yet." I close my eyes, lean my head on the wall separating us. I'd bang my head against it if it wouldn't give me away. *I should leave.*

"She's never had a relationship," Mark tells him. "Not like this. She spends her time absorbed in…I guess, this kind of thing. I'm wondering if whatever happened with Rowan is why she's so wary of letting anyone close. I think she's scared. She would say she doesn't want to hurt you. But deep down, I think she doesn't want you to hurt her. I know you won't, of course, but she won't want to trust that."

Part of me is angry at Mark's assessment, but I know he's right. It twists my gut to hear it put into words. Of course I'm scared. Taking a good look at the relationships in my life, what reason do I have to be hopeful? My father stopped caring a long time ago, but it was Rowan who felt like the worst betrayal. Jake has been kidnapped, and I'm taking Mark and Brandon into a situation I may not be able to bring them back from.

"What are you saying?" Brandon asks, something sad in his tone. Too much like pity. I grind my teeth.

"I don't want either of you to get hurt, and I'm not sure she'll let you in even if she wants to. If she continues to push…" Mark doesn't have to finish the sentence. He's worried I'll hurt Brandon if I continue to push him away, and I can't blame him.

I can still be angry that they're trying to psychoanalyze me and solve problems they suspect I might create in the future. I come around the door and lean against it. "You know, for guesswork, you're remarkably accurate." No use pretending otherwise. My brother has me pegged. I try to laugh, but it doesn't sound right. I raise my brow. "You guys sit around talking about me a lot?"

"Well…" Mark glances at Brandon, then back at me. "A lot more lately. You're kind of the most interesting aspect of our lives at the moment."

"Ah." I nod. "That would make sense if you were talking about what I did back at the house and not hypothesizing why I push away relationships." Guilt writes itself on Brandon's face, but it's Mark whose eyes I meet. "What are you doing?"

He stands and faces me, back straight and chin up. His cheeks color, but he doesn't cower. "I'm sorry, Ellie. I know you're adults, but I'm still your big brother and his best friend. I'll end up shoving my nose into lots more of your business, I'm sure. You're capable of so much, but you've never been good at handling your emotions."

"Because I'm scared?"

"Well, aren't you?"

I throw my hands up. "You're not? I know you're still new to all of this, but given everything that's happened to us, you've got a good enough idea. Cooper's ruthless. He doesn't care about anything but the success of his Enforcers. If it's a choice between family and the Enforcers, we both know which he'll choose. And yes, that *terrifies* me." I swallow the bubble in my throat.

His wide, green eyes shift between mine. My eyes. Mom's eyes. Maybe I could have known her enough to recognize the similarities if Cooper had cared even a fraction. But for those first few years when I cried myself to sleep, calling out for my mom, no one was there. I loved my dad and wanted to stay with him, but that didn't mean I didn't *need* my mom. He didn't care.

"What did he do to you, Ellie?" Mark breathes.

"Besides order me to kill you?" I hope that will shut him down, but he stands firm, looking down at me.

He says quietly, "I want you to trust me." I open my mouth, but he shakes his head. "No, you don't. Love and trust are not the same. You love us, but you've never trusted us."

I want to scream at him, tell him he's wrong, ask him what he thinks my bringing them out to DC means. But I don't because again I know he's right. I don't trust them. I don't trust them to be able to protect themselves against what I hide. I don't trust them not to try and help me.

I don't trust myself to keep this up most of all. Protecting them. From the Enforcers. From Cooper. *For* Mom. It's too much, and I don't know how much longer I can do it.

It might be a relief to let them in, but it's more possibly a mistake. I roll the dice.

My eyes shift from Mark to Brandon who grips the arms of the chair he's buckled himself into, and I realize the flush on his face isn't entirely from embarrassment. Weeks ago, when he picked me up from the airport, he told me he hated flying. Apparently, it's more fear than hate. I'm sure trusting them with my secrets certainly won't help him relax, but this is what they asked for.

"I almost died," I blurt. Brandon goes rigid, and Mark stumbles back a step. "My second assignment I got after challenging Hartley in front of the other Enforcers. I would have died if one of them hadn't wanted to spoil Hartley's punishment. The target was in witness protection. She had guards all over her. Crown told me and said he would take care of the guards if I just took the shot. But there was someone else in the building I was using as a stakeout. Threw a knife in my leg." I pat the spot on my thigh that still bears the long, ugly scar. "I finished the job, but I would have bled out if Crown hadn't come looking for me after.

"He bandaged me up, brought me back to base, and afterwards we hardly spoke. We're not close. He only wanted to foil Hartley. I limped to Dad's office for my payment, and he gave it to me. He didn't ask how

I was doing or even look up from his work. He didn't care. He would have let me die because if I did, I clearly wasn't fit to be one of his killers. But I survived; I proved myself. His attention can only mean you've done something wrong. Even when it comes to his own daughter."

That day was the worst of my life. Not only being stabbed in the leg and nearly bleeding out, but it was the day I learned of my mother's death. That was the day I gave Rowan the scar across his cheek.

Brandon is gripping the arms of the recliner so hard now that the leather squeaks, but his eyes have gone distant. He doesn't move. Mark is before me, arms hanging useless at his sides. They wear twin expressions of horror, but this is what they asked for. And it only gets worse.

I glare at Mark. "Is that what you wanted?"

"Ellie, we love you. We would never hurt you like that." Somewhere deep down, I know that. Reality has a funny way of being less than we desire but more than we can accept. I blink away the tears as he continues. "Can you try to trust us?"

I glance between the two of them. Brandon's gaze has returned and landed on me with so much sympathy, but there's more than that. He's angry for me. Mark has the look of pain that I've always avoided by not sharing these things.

Before, the best way I found to protect them was to keep my secrets. But after the first one found the light, I'm learning I can't keep the others locked up. And just maybe the more I harbor, the more pain will be had.

I meet Mark's eyes and take a deep breath. "I can try."

36

BRANDON'S USE

Ellie drives us out into the middle of nowhere, which I didn't know you could do in Washington DC. But I guess, technically, this is just outside DC. Still strange. There hasn't been a house sighting for miles, only trees. Everywhere I look, all trees. Until we dip onto a low road. The *No Trespassing* and *Violators Will Be Shot* and *Beware of Dogs* signs set up on either side of the tiny road do not lend any comfort to the situation.

Ellie pulls up to an iron gate and rolls down her window to enter a code on the keypad which looks oddly new compared to the fence with vines overtaking the rusted hinges. But the keypad is definitely high-tech. This guy has clear priorities.

"*Welcome, E.*" The electronic male voice startles me in the dark gloom of the woods, but Ellie just rolls her eyes. The gates swing open, allowing us passage to her cousin's home, which looks like it's been through an apocalypse. The dull yellow paint is chipped and peeling like a banana in sections. The roof is warped, and the corners look rotted. It looks like a bulldoze fix situation.

As if the guy needed a backup, he has a Jayco brand camping trailer sitting out front, but the letters *C* and *O* have been scraped off. I grin despite the growing suspicion of my impending doom.

This is all very new to me, so I've found that a good way to cope is to find something to laugh about. It keeps up the façade that this is somehow not real.

The wooden steps up to Jaythan's house creak, and I regret it as soon as we step onto the porch. A recording of Shrek shrieking, "*What are you doing in my swamp?*" sends my heart into an arrhythmia. It seems appropriate, honestly. Mark jumps out of his skin too, but Ellie and Rowan proceed uninhibited. El glances back at us with a smirk.

The door swings open on squeaky hinges to furious growling, and a lumberjack fills the space. Scruffy beard, disheveled brown hair, burly, muscled build. Red, plaid button-up and tan cargo pants. It's like this guy studied for the part of "creepy, loner woodsman." He wears a huge grin, very out of place, and the dogs quiet in an instant. "You must be Mark and Brandon!"

Mark offers a tentative hand for him to shake, but Jaythan knocks it aside, going in for a hug. "Put that away, cousin. We're family!"

Mark laughs, casting a nervous glance at me, but I don't know what to do in this situation. I'm fairly certain I've met all my cousins. I don't think my family can surprise me with a new middle-aged hermit one like this.

I look around the house that's sparse enough to be believably abandoned. A small table sits in the entry with a blue vase on it—no flowers, just the vase. And there's a rug smashed up against the wall. I peer around the corner, but I can't see anything. "Where are your dogs?"

Jaythan tilts his head. "I don't have dogs."

I squint, but Ellie explains. "He has an alarm with a recording of snarling dogs. To scare people away."

Jaythan turns a pointed glare on her. "Not as effective as I was promised."

She just grins and flips him off. Even though twelve seconds ago I accepted the inevitability that they were going to rip out my throat, I'm still disappointed in the lack of dogs.

Jaythan throws out a hand for me to shake. "It's great to finally meet you. I've kind of been in your life a lot lately." He leans forward conspiratorially. "E was worried about you." He aims a wink behind us at her, and my heart jumps.

At first, I was disturbed to find out that some random person had been combing through every detail of my life. But after my family was attacked and saved by the girl who authorized all the snooping, it didn't seem like a huge invasion anymore. Now that I've met the man personally, I don't know what to think, but I'm leaning toward *it's fine.* Everything worked out, right?

Jaythan's face scrunches. "Seeing you in person is a bit weird."

"Seeing *you* in person is weird." Ellie glares at Jaythan. "Enough with the pleasantries. We have work to do."

Jaythan finally releases my hand. "Do I have to apologize for her? You guys know her pretty well." Then he does a double take at what's behind me, and I tense. But he's just grinning at Rowan who entered silently and stands sentry-like by the door. "Rowan! It's great to see you again—" He cuts off abruptly, glancing at Ellie out of the corner of his eye. "Wait, does she know?"

"I know." She watches Jaythan for a moment, contemplating something. "Thank you."

Jaythan sways, his brows shooting up into his hairline. The lightness of the mood dips to deep sincerity. "Of course, E," he says so quietly. He lets the silence sit, but when she turns and leaves the room, he completely forgets it and flashes his grin at Mark and me again.

I smile, squint. "Sorry, it's a little weird meeting you too. Ellie was telling us about you, and she made it sound like…" I realize my mistake too late and search for a word that won't offend him.

He nods, apparently knowing what I'm about to say. "Like I'm insane?"

I shrug awkwardly, trying to hide my cringe. But there's no anger in the wrinkles beside his eyes.

"She might be right, but I am still perfectly capable of being a civil host. Drinks?"

"Jaythan!" Ellie's voice booms, making the three of us jump. Rowan just strolls into the next room after her.

Jaythan rolls his eyes, and I marvel at their ability to flip on a dime. "She's so impatient." He begins walking backwards. "My offer stands."

"Offer for what?" Ellie is typing on one of Jaythan's many computers.

"What are you doing?" His laid-back attitude disappears instantaneously as he rushes toward her, a shrill factor to his voice.

She doesn't move for him. "What are you offering?"

"What are you doing to my computer?" He pulls at his hair, making it stick up all over.

Her brows wrinkle. "I'm using it for its intended purpose. Research." Jaythan slides her away and gets to work on it himself. She lets the desk chair roll to a natural stop and aims her question at us. "What's he offering?"

"Drinks." She looks at me, her head tilting to the side. An innocent gesture, blank. No sign of the conversation from the plane staying with her either. But Jaythan perks up and turns to her.

"But not for you." His accusatory finger is very close to her face, which he realizes at the delicate arch of her brow. He snatches it back to his keyboard.

She glares. "But I'm thirsty."

Jaythan's eyes widen. He sucks in a breath and says tightly, "You should have thought of that before you messed with my computer."

Ellie rolls her eyes. It's such a strangely normal exchange. If I didn't know he was a middle-aged hermit that encounters no secret he can't fish out and she an assassin, it might *feel* normal. "If you would have come in here right away, I wouldn't have had to." Jaythan continues typing furiously, not even pausing to glare at her. "Oh, please, I didn't break anything. Relax, Jay."

"*You* relax," he snaps, then pauses. Slowly, he turns toward Ellie's crossed arms. He's much older than her, but it's clear she holds the power in this relationship. "I didn't mean that. I was angry. Can I offer you something to drink?"

She nods once. "I don't need anything."

Jaythan scoffs. "You can never make anything easy. You suck." He keeps her in his peripheral. "I'm not taking that one back."

"Tell us how we get to Cooper, and I'll let you get away with it."

The calm arrogance slips over him like a veil. He smirks at Ellie then at Mark and me. "Well, then, hold onto your butts—"

He barely gets the words out before Ellie cuts him off. "No. Stop it." She shakes her head, exasperated. "Absolutely not."

"What's your problem?"

"When you get like this, your explanations take three times as long."

His brows shoot up to hide underneath his dusty hair, and he stands up straight. "Well." He surveys us all as if he's preparing a lecture. "Allow me to go back to where it all began. A long time ago—"

"Jaythan." A note of real anger enters her voice now, and Jaythan sobers immediately. I feel bad for him for a second, but it's also admirable. From just a few minutes with them, it's clear that their relationship is made up of them giving each other a hard time. But as soon as that note crept into Ellie's voice, Jaythan stopped without a second thought. Like an underlining code to their conversations.

Without thinking, I move to stand next to her and squeeze her shoulder. She's so tense; even when she glances at me, the movement is stiff. But she takes a deep breath before exchanging the desk chair for a seat at the little round table in the middle of the room. I take the seat next to her, and Mark goes to her other side. Rowan remains a sentry on the back wall.

Jaythan takes a moment to gather some papers and his laptop, and he plops it all down. The table creaks under the pressure. "Okay, so I gathered the blueprints for all the buildings surrounding the headquarters." He spreads them out over the table. Six in total.

Mark pulls one to himself. "Why?"

"I was looking for a secret entrance to the headquarters. It wouldn't show up on a blueprint of their building, but something may be on the surrounding ones."

"Any luck?" I ask him.

He sighs. "No."

"That's because there is no secret entrance." Ellie doesn't look up from the print she has in front of her, examining it like she can make it give up its secrets.

"It's not safe to have just one exit," Jaythan argues. "What if there's a fire? What if the entrance is blocked, and they're trapped?"

Ellie's eyes flick up to him. "Then they burn." There's not a hint of sarcasm in her words. I shift uneasily, but she continues. "Corporation of assassins. Underground. Cooper's a proud man. Burn all evidence. The captain will go down with his ship."

Mark told me before that Ellie used to live in the headquarters, like a lot of the assassins. Until she finally moved to her own apartment, she had to grow up under the knowledge that her own father would watch her burn to keep his secrets. Part of me can't believe that someone could be so cruel, but this is the man who turned a little girl into a notorious killer and then sent her after her own family. I'm nearly overwhelmed with the desire to pull her close and never let go. *She deserves better than this.*

Mark frowns. "Why would he do that?"

She musters sympathy as she meets her brother's eyes. "It's the one thing he's proud of." I know she doesn't say it to hurt him, though from his wince, it hurts more than either of them would have liked. She holds his gaze, and her point is made. She's given up on their father. His abduction of her twin was the last straw.

I restrain the urge to tuck her into my side.

Jaythan blows out a breath that breaks the tension. "Well, I'm gonna keep looking. If the Eiffel Tower can hide an entire apartment without thousands of tourists being all over it, the super-secret Enforcers Corporation can hide a doorway." Ellie just shrugs and throws the blueprints on top of the stack. "Anyway, before we get into any sort of planning, I need to know what I'm working with here. I already know E is pretty much useless in this type of thing." She scoffs silently, but Jaythan moves on, pointing to Rowan. "You, obviously, are another assassin. Brandon and Mark. I know you're studying to be doctors, but do you have any skills besides the healing?" He wiggles his fingers in a twinkly fashion as if to suggest healing is done by magic. He may not be entirely wrong. I'm not going to lie; I'm starting to like this guy. "Something that could, say, help us break into the Enforcers and break someone else out? Anything would be helpful."

Honestly, I don't know why I'm here. Of course I want to help get Jake back, but what can I do? I can't fight, and I'm terrible with computers. I decide to throw something out there since Mark is silent too. "My dad taught me to shoot when I was eleven."

From the look Ellie gives me—blank, unreadable—I wouldn't be surprised if she laughed at me for it. It's not much use to be relatively able to shoot in a rescue mission where we'll probably face much more intense weaponry and individuals trained to use them *very* efficiently. Especially since I haven't shot anything in at least two years. But she turns to Jaythan. "I can work with that."

I frown even as pride swells in me at the possibility of being useful— I still might disappoint her. "What?"

She pulls a gun from somewhere on her person and sets it on the table. "Did he teach you to shoot something like this?" I nod, but she reads the hesitance in the motion. "I'll help you refresh that memory of yours and become more precise." She turns back to Jaythan. "What's your plan, exactly?"

"Two teams. One will be the data retrieval team and the other will be the distraction."

A nervous flutter in my stomach. "So, would that make me part of the distraction team then?"

Ellie doesn't wait a beat before turning on me. "Absolutely not. The training will be a precaution only. I'll teach you to defend yourself in the time we have. But Rowan is going with you. You shouldn't need to use any of it." There's a hint of desperation in her eyes that she wipes away a second later.

Jaythan smuffs. "You've been here all of ten minutes, heard, like, a tenth of my plan, and you're already hijacking it."

"Did you have something better for Rowan or Brandon to be doing?"

He purses his lips and ignores the question. "Okay, so our data retrieval squad will be Rowan and Brandon." He waves a hand at us as if to shoo us away. "Confer amongst yourselves for a team name."

"And me." Mark sits up straighter in his chair, something like fear in his voice, but it's steel in his eyes. "I'd like to help."

"No." This, too, from Ellie, and Mark deflates. She's silent for a moment, possibly hoping he'll understand her refusal without having to say it. But when he says nothing, she explains quietly, "He's already got Jake."

The unspoken question hangs in the air among us in the ensuing silence. What would their father do if he had all three of his children?

Jaythan clears his throat, not looking up from his computer. I don't think he's doing anything with it; it's just a safer place to look than out at everyone. "That's fine. I could use Mark here anyway. The files we're gonna be able to get aren't actually real files. The organization recognized the risk of electronic ones, so everything's on paper."

"But aren't there fail-safes that can protect them?" I ask, and Jaythan finally glances up at me and tilts his head to the side. "I mean, there are technological means of security for that reason, right?"

"Fail-safes aren't there to prevent things. It's not like a shield. It's more like a backup. Take elevators, for instance. They've got those emergency brakes in place in case the elevator decides to drop, but they're not going to stop it from happening. The fail-safes can be unreliable. I hate to say it, but technology can be unreliable." He pets his computer as if in apology. "The Enforcers keep everything on paper in big, hefty file cabinets. Very old-school. Impossible to steal without getting onsite."

"Then what am I going to do?" Mark asks.

"You'll sift through the maps."

Mark frowns at the blueprints on the table.

"Not those ones. The organization's files are all paper, but it can be hard to find anything that way, so they keep electronic maps of what they have and where to find it. Brandon and Rowan will get those maps. You will have to locate the financial records for E to then grab so we can see if they're holding Jake offsite. A record of food being sent somewhere must exist. I'm pretty sure they're feeding him." He chuckles to himself, but it becomes strangled when no one else laughs and Ellie glares.

"Wait, this is all just to find where they're keeping him, not to actually get him back?" Mark lets an edge of anger creep into his words. It's unsettling to see him like this. He's usually so calm.

"Well, your father isn't stupid enough to keep him in that facility with him. That would be too obvious."

"Or just obvious enough." I jump when Rowan finally speaks. It's like he was simply an extension of the wall for a bit there.

Ellie shakes her head, though. "Jake won't be there. Surrounded by assassins isn't the ideal situation for someone they very well might hate simply because he's another spawn of the boss. Plus, you and I know how to reach him there. Cooper's got somewhere else to stash him."

"Then how are we getting the maps?"

Jaythan points at me in emphasis. "Great question. You'll need to take over the security office. You'll be Ellie's eyes as she goes in as the distraction. One of you, at least. The other will need to find an exposed wire to attach this beaut to." He produces a small object that looks like a tiny beetle. "I'll be able to download what I need as long as this is connected directly to the system. I call it '*Hippopotomonstrosesquippedaliophobia.*'"

Momentary confusion, but then I recognize the word. "Isn't that the word that means *fear of long words?*"

Ellie blinks. "That seems counterproductive."

"Why would you name it that?"

"The irony." His grin overtakes his face. "This little device will wreak so much havoc if we use it properly. And it looks like a little bug that can just be squished. I would not recommend this, however, as I have countermeasures in place." He pauses, and I realize everything he does, down to having that word memorized, is for dramatic effect. He is the human equivalent of a cape billowing in the wind. "He'll blow up."

As one, we all scoot our chairs away from the table. Jaythan cackles.

"So, we go in, they plant that, be my eyes, and I pick up the files Mark locates?" Ellie's recap makes it sound easy.

"Basically." Jaythan shrugs. Then to me he says, "I can teach you about the security systems. As you can imagine, they're quite advanced for that business. They're touchscreen so you can watch in real time or skip back to a previous timestamp nice and easy. But then if you don't know what you're doing, it could be easy to get stuck somewhere without knowing the way out." I suck in a breath and nod. Jaythan smiles again. "And then you can go to Ellie to learn how to use your arm as a shield."

She arches one slender brow, directed at Jaythan. But she speaks to me, arms crossing over her chest. "You use the outside of your arm to protect the major arteries on the inside."

Jaythan's laugh is quick, and gone just as fast when Ellie doesn't crack a smile. "Oh, are you serious? You're serious." Then to me. "She's serious. Um…good luck."

I don't know what it is in that moment that makes me do it, but I chuckle. It rumbles through my whole body, becoming a full laugh. This could all go so spectacularly wrong.

37

JAKE'S QUESTIONS

"Have you thought about what I said?" For once my father's gaze isn't boring holes into the scattered papers. He sits with his hands folded on top of his desk, back straight, like it's an interview. He doesn't wear glasses, but I'm sure if he did, they'd be perched at the tip of his nose.

For four days, I've done nothing but think. I went mostly undisturbed until this morning when Hartley came with an invitation to come back to meet with my father. Something made me believe it really was an invitation rather than a command.

"I did, and I really don't know what to do about any of it."

He nods. "That's perfectly reasonable." I feel a spike of anger that's become a comfort in my life as the only normal thing left. I don't need him telling me that this feeling is alright. He tore our family apart for this job. Of course it's *reasonable* that I'm not entirely comfortable with it all. It's hard to tamp down, but I manage it and plaster a bland look on my face. "Well, if you're still confused, you may ask me whatever you like."

"I'm not confused. I think I understand the concept of my father and sister killing people for money."

"Now, son." He holds up his hand. "I run the organization, but I am not out in the field like your sister. My job remains mainly behind this desk. It's a standard business setup like you're learning about in school."

"Oh." I chuckle humorlessly. "My mistake. You just tell her who to kill, and she actually kills them. I do have a question, though. Do you have a selection process, or do you just tell her to kill anyone you don't like?"

His trademark reaction—a sigh. "I do heavy research into every target. My spies—one of which you know, of course—" my jaw clenches—"report any threats to me, and then I do some more research of my own before handing them off to one of my Enforcers. You need to understand, we only target people who are viciously lording power over another. The true threats to an otherwise stable society."

Well, there's no accusing this man of fighting for a cause he doesn't believe in. "Ah." I shrug. "So, Ellie's been fully briefed on every single target she's been assigned, yes?" He doesn't respond right away. "I mean, why do all that research and not prep your staff?" To put it in *standard business* terms.

"Each of my Enforcers, including your sister, is on a need-to-know basis. Frankly, they do not need to know the reason. They must simply follow orders. The research is to cover us legally."

I purse my lips. "Essentially, you gave her no reason to kill Mark. You just expected her to do it."

"Ah. I suppose I should have seen that coming. Did Ms. Benson tell you?"

If this were a cartoon, my head would be splattered all over these walls. It still hurts to think about Chelsea. "No, your little *spy* didn't tell me. I figured it out!"

He tilts his head, chin down in that pacifying way that never actually works, and looks me dead in the eye. "No, I never expected Emily to go through with that. It was merely motivation."

"And how many more of the assignments you've given out have been mere motivation?"

He turns to the papers on his desk and creates a neat pile. "Aren't you curious about what I've been working on since you arrived?"

Now it's finally my turn to sigh. "I assume you're wanting to tell me, so why don't you without all the preamble."

"I've put together a file for you of several of our targets. It has the research I did before handing them off." He slides the papers into a thick yellow folder and hands it across the desk to me. "Take it. Look it over."

I take the stack because what else am I supposed to do? Flipping through the names doesn't reveal Mark's. Maybe Dad didn't include him because as he's saying, Mark wasn't a *real* target. "One more question." I almost don't want to ask it, but it's been in the back of my mind for days. "Brandon Harwood. Do you know anything?"

"Ah yes, that friend of yours. As I told you before, he was never Emily's assignment, though she learned of it and put a stop to it. I did do some research into his case, of course. It seems that one of those Enforcer copies made an attempt on him."

I take a breath, tuck the file under my arm, and leave. I'm tempted to believe him. No matter how insane he sounds, he's been forthright about everything else.

38

BRANDON'S TRAINING

ABOUT TEN MINUTES PAST JAYTHAN'S HOUSE IS A GIANT, SNOW-coated clearing with a helicopter sitting in the middle. Jaythan's, Ellie explains as she parks us along the outskirts. Ignoring it seems impossible, even though that's what she tells me to do. Her cousin who lives out in the middle of nowhere owns his own helicopter. Logic.

The field is huge and open like a stadium with the frosted forest for an audience. We won't disturb anyone out here as we train. I breathe in deeply, the fresh, chilly air purifying my lungs.

For only a second, I believe Ellie may be taking me here to murder me. Not because she hates me—I don't think she does—but as some way of protecting me. My mom had a dog like that once. She used to have a bunch of chickens in a coop in the backyard, and the dog herded them around. He had to be broken of creating collateral damage if he wasn't obeyed. He killed one trying to pull it back through the fence once. Sad.

Funny in hindsight. My sister called it *saving them to death*.

I'm fairly certain that's not what Ellie's about to do to me.

She takes a large duffle bag from the trunk and throws it down in front of me, pulling a small handgun from it and holding it up. "Kimber .45; not a hard kick, and the bullets will stop a man easily. Hollow point. Always hollow point." She makes a fist with the knuckle of her pointer finger sticking out. "It's the difference between this…" She hits me in the chest with the knuckle—not too hard, but still, it'll leave a tiny bruise. "And this." She opens her palm and hits me again with the same force, but this one makes me stumble back half a step. "The magazine holds seven plus one in the chamber. This is the same model I gave you. Did you bring it?"

"Yeah." I pull the case from the back seat. I checked a bag at the airport and paid extra when I flew to my parents' so I could have it with me. I wasn't going to leave it behind after everything I'd just learned, even though I wasn't sure what I would do if someone actually attacked me without Ellie being there. But the gun was with me, for what it's worth.

"You'll want to keep track of how many bullets you use. Most of the security guards carry these, so you might be able to reload with their supply if necessary. But you can't *count* on getting any more bullets, so you need to conserve."

My dad took me out a few times a year for target practice when I was younger. After I went off to college, I didn't have time for it anymore. We still shoot sometimes when I go home, but a target is very different from a human. I chose a career in saving people for a reason.

On the way up, Ellie tried to help me get my mind right. She keeps telling me I don't have to shoot someone who isn't trying to kill me.

Obviously, I know that, but she added that if someone *is* trying to kill me, I need to take the shot. I don't want to kill anyone. I don't even want to injure them, but it's better than killing. But according to Ellie, shooting to injure risks missing completely. Which I also know. Someone with her skill can afford a shot like that, but my shots are supposed to be deadly with the hope of at least injuring, which—much to her dismay—is easier for me to swallow. Then she showed me breathing techniques to calm my nerves in the last few minutes before we got here. With the jittery energy that's been flowing through my veins since I got in the car, it seemed a wise place to start.

She pins a bright yellow target that has a tiny red dot in the middle to a nearby tree and positions me far away so that it looks about the size of my phone. "Keep both eyes open when you shoot. Stance." I get into the shooting stance she showed me yesterday: body slightly angled in front of the target, arms bent in front of me, gun at eye level. Something more natural, improved for accuracy. She nods her approval, and I fire a couple rounds. Then she has me step closer. I shoot some more. Closer. Shoot. Closer. Shoot. Then I'm only a few feet away from the target.

"Don't pay attention to the shots you've already fired. Focus on the tiny spot you're aiming for. Aim small, miss small."

I fire until the magazine is empty. We go through three for this exercise. Each time I reload, she times me; I started at fifteen seconds, but by the third I find a groove and get it down to eleven. She thinks I can do better, though, so we're working on that some more later.

She takes the target off the tree and sits on the ground, patting a spot in the fluffy snow beside her which I take, rubbing warmth back into my hands. Her coconut and mint scent washes over me, and I force myself to focus. My shots are all over the place but all within the circumference of the target, none in the surrounding white. Four landed in the center.

Ellie points to three different holes. All wide of the bullseye. "These were your first ones." I blink, amazed that she remembers the exact holes—then again, she might be messing with me. "They wouldn't exactly kill a person, but they'd stop him enough to get away." My stomach knots, but she pays no attention to my discomfort, pointing to three more holes. "These were your next shots." She points to the lowest of the set. "If this were a five-and-a-half-foot man, he would be having a very bad day." She laughs. I pity the imaginary man as she goes through the rest of my shots. The ones that hit the center, unsurprisingly, came from the closest two positions.

She walks me through a few disarming strategies next, some a little more complicated than others. When I catch onto the simpler ones quickly, she decides to show me a few more to use against various holds my opponent might be using.

"Point the gun at me." She performs the move she's about to teach me. In the mess of our arms, she gets the gun, turns me around, and shoves me forward.

I stumble a few steps, then turn back, and she hands me the gun again. I rub my nose which she tapped very lightly in that maneuver. She snickers a little. I roll my eyes even as I smile.

"Alright," she says. I point the gun at her again. "First, take your opponent's wrist." She grabs mine firmly in her cupped palm, keeping her fingers open. "Like this. Not too hard, but don't let him out of it. You won't be holding on for long if you do it right. Crouch to the side so the gun's not pointed directly at you. Next…" She brings her fist into the crook of my arm. "Take your free hand and slam it here with as much power as you can." She applies light pressure, and I slowly bend my arm to her will. As I do, her hand on my wrist crawls up, and the heel of her palm finds the butt of the gun. "See what I did?" I blink too fast. *Deep breaths.* "Don't hold your opponent's hand, either. That constricts their reflex to cover their nose. Slam the gun into their face." She taps it against my nose. "Grab the grip really tight because until you can get the gun to your hip, that's all you have to hold onto." She brings the gun down to her hip; while she adjusts her grip on it, she grabs my wrist again, twists me around like it's a dance but lets go when I'm facing away from her. Her hand presses into my shoulder and her elbow into my back. "Shove hard. Back the hell up. Shoot." She waves the gun around. "Now you."

After beating that maneuver to death, she announces, "You need to get used to pointing a gun at someone."

I try not to let her see the stiffening in my shoulders because I know what she's about to have me do. I'm reminded of the Nerf gun. Dad taught me *never* to point the weapon at someone I don't fully intend to shoot. It'll be a hard habit to break, but considering my dad now definitely knows my situation, I think he would consent to this violation of the rules.

Ellie doesn't take the gun from me when I hand it to her. Instead, she takes a step back. "I want you to point it at me." When I hesitate, she pulls the magazine from her pocket. "It's not loaded. You can't hurt me. All I want you to do is point it at me."

I take a deep breath. It's pointing an empty gun. Like she said, I can't hurt her. Even so, I check the chamber first, just in case. We've been using it for practice, but of course she noticed I haven't been pointing it directly at her. No bullet. Satisfied, I bring the gun up and aim it at her chest, watching the steady rising and falling.

She nods. "Now pull the trigger."

I drop my arms. "Wait, what?"

"Aim the gun and pull the trigger. It's completely empty. You checked it yourself."

"I'm not—"

"Brandon."

I glare at her, take another deep breath—then another—raise the gun, and aim it at her chest again. The weapon is heavy in my hands, taunting me. I try to focus on the sight and aiming, but my target is Ellie, so that doesn't work very well. I pause to suck in another breath, and then slowly squeeze the trigger. My entire body flinches when I feel the click. I release my breath and double over, resting my hands on my knees and dropping the gun on the snow—delicately.

Ellie comes over and crouches before me. "You were looking into my eyes." I do so again, the green irises demanding excellence, but also offering sympathy. "You can't do that. It'll just freak you out." *Because my targets will all be human.* "I'm sorry, Brandon."

I shake my head and stand back up. I understand the meaning of it well enough.

"Can I ask you to do one more thing before we move on?" I don't answer. "Do you trust me?"

An involuntary groan bursts out of me. I don't like where this is going. "Against all reason."

She smiles, and it makes her look so harmless and gentle. Her hair is in its usual braid, draped over her right shoulder. She's wearing a gray beanie and winter coat. Her gaze is compassionate. It's become too easy to forget she's an assassin. She won't hurt me, and she won't let me hurt her. I know I can trust her, but the reasonable part of me still doesn't want to.

Ellie bends down to pick up the weapon, taking the magazine from her pocket, and to my horror, loading it in the gun. She cocks it and peers up at me through her lashes. "I'm not going to have you pull the trigger this time."

I shake my head, failing to find words. How can she look so cute and innocent right now, but be so terrifying at the same time? She can't possibly think I would do this. It's incredibly dangerous, not to mention stupid.

"I just want you to point it at me." She holds it out to me.

"No." I back away from her, staring at the gun in my hands.

"Brandon."

"No!"

"Brandon." Her voice is softer this time. "That gun can't hurt me unless you pull the trigger. If something happens, and you need to shoot someone, but you can't even point the gun at them, you'll be dead. You need to get used to the weight in your hands as you do it. This is just worst-case scenario practice."

"You're not the worst-case scenario."

"You better hope I'm the worst case you encounter."

"Ellie." It comes out as more of a growl.

"Brandon."

"You can't change my mind just by saying my name over and over!"

"Do I need to tell you that this could save your life? Do I need to tell you that this could save any *one* of our lives? What if it's not just this? What if some other person finds some bizarre reason to have you killed? Your brother-in-law is where this all started. What if they go after your sister?"

Rage boils in the pit of my stomach at the mention of my sister in this context. I glare at Ellie. "Woah."

She widens her eyes, shaking her head slowly. "Make it personal, Brandon, because it's always personal. I've learned enough about you to know that if killing someone meant saving your family—" she snaps her fingers—"you would do it in a heartbeat. It's why you asked me to intervene back in Washington even though it meant your family witnessing. If you want to protect your family, protect yourself."

I want to scream at her. Instead, I throw her question back at her. "Do *you* trust *me?*"

She smirks. "You're studying to be a doctor, right?"

I glare again. "Not funny."

"Sorry." She sighs, and when she meets my eyes, there's sincerity in hers. "Yes, I trust you."

I scowl and scrape my palm over my beanie, half wanting to rip it off and tear out my hair. "This is crazy."

"You'll thank me for it later."

"No, I won't."

"Well." She shrugs. "I'll only make you do this once."

I clench my jaw so hard it might just break. I finally let out a frustrated groan which she takes as agreement, backing up and standing tall. She throws her shoulders back, looks me straight in the eyes…and waits.

I tear my eyes from her and down to the gun. I hate the sight of it. This gun is loaded. Ellie wants me to point it at her. That goes against every instinct I have. I can't do it.

"All I want you to do is point the gun at me and put your finger on the trigger."

"*What?*" My gaze whips back up to her calm face. "Ellie—" It's too much of a whine. *She's insane.*

"You're not pulling the trigger this time." As if that helps. "Just resting your finger on it."

"Ellie," I rasp, unable to do much more. *I need water.* "I'm not doing that."

"Yes, you are. Point it at me, put your finger on the trigger, hold it there for a few seconds, and *do not* squeeze." She stands tall, a performer about to walk the tightrope. Her terrible, beautiful green eyes bore straight into mine, straight through to my soul. "I trust you." And just like that, the words I thought I wanted to hear are like poison to my ears.

The wind freezes the burning tip of my nose, and a thought occurs to me. If she's going to make me do something that makes me squirm, then I might as well return the favor. I've been looking for an opportunity to talk with her anyway. "Alright, can I at least ask you something first?"

She shifts on her feet, unbelievably already uncomfortable. I squint, but she finally answers, "Yeah."

"What is this?" I gesture between us. "We haven't talked about what happened at my parents' house. The kiss, I mean—*sort of* kiss. And I… kind of want to know where we're at. It's felt almost like you've been avoiding me lately. I understand if that's what you want, but I'd like to know for certain."

"Avoiding?" She casts a wide look around the clearing. "We're completely alone in the middle of the woods." She smirks, and I can't help but return it. I wish she wasn't as good at deflecting.

"Come on, you know what I mean. Where are we?"

I can almost see her bite her tongue like she's holding back another sarcastic answer. She blows out her breath. "Um—" Her eyes drop to her feet, where she's kicking at the snow. "I…have no idea." When she looks at me again, she grimaces. It's so much like she's in physical pain over this line of questioning. "Do we have to do this now?"

I shrug. "I'd like to know who I'm pointing a loaded gun at."

She laughs, her eyes leaving mine instantly. "Fair enough." It's a few seconds before she speaks again. "I've never done this before. I mean, this hasn't happened to me before. I'm not really the relationship type. At least, I didn't think I was." I remember her saying something along those lines when we almost kissed in the elevator. She told me she's more suited to being friends. It had sucked to hear, but I understood. Now, I understand that even better, but she seems to be saying something different.

"What do you mean?"

She exhales. "I don't know exactly. You deserve better than this."

I roll my eyes. "Let's assume, just for the moment, that's not true. What would you do then? What do you want?"

"I…" She looses a harsh laugh. "This is ridiculous. It doesn't matter what I want."

I keep my face stern, determined to get an answer. Something I have witnessed her doing many times. "Humor me."

She watches me for long moments. I hold her gaze the whole time, and she's the first to drop it. "If…" She growls, shakes her head, makes furious eye contact. "I want *you*, okay?" My brows shoot up, but now she's focusing hard on her feet. "But things are so complicated and dangerous right now, and I don't want to make you my guinea pig while I figure all of this out." Deep breath. "You deserve better."

"Can you maybe let me be the judge of that?"

She blinks, stunned. Her chin lifts. "I can't promise anything."

I shake my head. "You don't have to."

Her smile is small, and inevitably she glances away. When she turns back, she half rolls her eyes at me. "Would you just point the gun at me now?"

A thousand butterflies took flight in my stomach at her confession. *I want you, okay?* They all die at the reminder of the gun.

"I was hoping you forgot," I grumble. It's only a few seconds. She's not going to let me bail. I suppose it's only fair since I made her talk about feelings. I straighten my back.

"Don't look into my eyes." She's much more comfortable slipping back into teaching mode. "Focus on where you're aiming."

It becomes too personal to look into your target's eyes. I know that's what she means even though she doesn't say it. If I watch, I'll see the pain or fear and won't shoot. I try not to think too much except to make sure I don't actually shoot her. Because that's just what you want to happen the second you get the woman you're falling for to admit she wants you too: shoot her dead.

I take several deep breaths before raising the gun. Its tremendous weight threatens to drop my hands to the ground. The sight climbs her body slowly, shakily. I take another deep breath to steady it.

Her chest rises and falls easily, not so much as a hitch. I try to mimic her. In deeply. Out slowly. I move my index finger to the trigger and feel its terrible smoothness. In a low whisper, I start to count. She said only a few seconds. "One…two…three."

My arms fall limp at my sides, and my knees buckle. I breathe heavily on all fours like an animal. *There is a reason I chose a profession that saves lives.* How anyone made a teenager actually pull the trigger is beyond me.

Ellie stays back this time, silent, like she knows I need some space. After letting me breathe for a while, she kneels in front of me.

"Do you hate me?" The command in her voice is completely gone now, replaced with…caution?

I should. I shake my head. "No." The grass in front of me is squashed, the snow having been pushed aside under my boots. "I don't hate you." I mean it. I don't hate her. I want to, but it's just not possible for me.

"Well, that's sweet. But…" She takes the gun and turns it on its side. "You might when I tell you I turned the safety on."

I huff a laugh and roll onto my back. "So, you don't trust me." Despite that statement, I smile. The stress of moments ago completely evaporates, leaving behind something like hysteria.

She lies down next to me. "I don't make a habit of trusting people. Especially with a loaded gun pointed at me. Mostly because whenever someone points one at me, they're going to pull the trigger. You're the first person to not want to do that."

"How do you know?" I ask, tone heavy on the sarcasm.

"Oh, Brandon." She pats me on the shoulder, snow crunching under her at the movement. "You couldn't hit me if you tried."

"But I could try."

She shakes her head slowly. "You nearly collapsed after pointing the empty gun at me."

I snort.

"It's not easy for me to trust," she continues, and I turn my head to look at her. She's already watching me, and the words keep coming. "I even have problems trusting my brothers. It's hard when I know how vile my line of work is. How fragile any relationship I have is." She pauses. "But I trust *you*, Brandon."

I prop myself up on my elbow, taking her freezing cheek in my hand. She doesn't try to avoid my eyes or divert attention from what she said. Her words settle between us, and I grin.

"Aw," I say, running my thumb along her bottom lip. "Thanks."

She bursts out with a laugh, and her hand comes up to shove me, but I lower my lips to hers softly, brushing against them once. Twice. Letting her know, letting her *feel* that I trust her too. And not only to protect me during this mission or any other time in our lives. I trust her with everything.

I break away to kiss a line along her cheek. I peck her temple, then decide it's not enough and plant a firmer kiss there, breathing her in.

It's a beautiful thing when she not only reveals that she wants to be with me, but also that she trusts me as much as I trust her at the exact moment I realize I'm no longer falling, but fallen.

39

BRANDON'S DOOM

Jaythan's house is empty when we get back four hours later. As soon as Ellie shuts the door behind us, I spin toward her. She blinks, eyes widening. "I want to teach you something now," I tell her.

She squints, peering at me from the corner of her eye. "You already got information out of me."

"Yeah," I agree. "And you made me point a gun at you. Twice."

"Yes, and I think that's enough interaction for today." She pats my chest with a smirk teasing her lips as she passes in front of me. "There's only so much time I can spend in your presence."

"Are you calling me high maintenance?"

She shrugs, whirling to face me and backing away. "You might not realize it about yourself, but you're pretty needy. Let's face it, I've saved your ass twice, hauled you along with me all the way out here, and then spent a whole day with you. And you still want more. It's like you can't get enough of me, and I don't blame you. I'm a delight, after all—"

El doesn't get to finish that thought because just as she turns again, I grab her hand and spin her back to me. She gasps, her hand lands on my shoulder, and my arm wraps around her waist. "You *are* a delight." I know she meant it as a joke, but I hold her gaze as I confirm it.

She hasn't shared everything with me yet, but she's told me enough that I know it's not a phrase she hears often enough. As long as I'm around, she will know I genuinely enjoy every second we have together, no matter what we're doing.

Her mouth falls open like she wants to respond, but no words come. I lean down and give her a quick kiss. It reboots her system because she whispers, "What are you going to teach me?"

A grin spreads across my face. "I'm guessing you never went to prom."

Her brow furrows. "Didn't quite make it, no."

"I didn't go either."

She frowns. "Why not?"

I shrug. "Not really my scene. This may surprise you, but I'm a bit of a workaholic."

She gasps again, this time as if she's in a courtroom drama. "No. You?"

"I know. It's a real blow to my reputation on the street, but…" I look down at her. "I secretly always wanted to go. So, will you go to prom with me?"

She tilts her head. "Are you proposing we raid some high school's prom or something?"

"Of course not." I pull out my phone, put on an instrumental version of "O Come, O Come, Emmanuel"—nice and slow for our purposes—

and rest my phone on the little table with Jaythan's flowerless vase. "You only need two people for a prom: yourself and your date."

She swallows, staring straight at my chest rather than meeting my eyes. "I can't dance."

I smile and lean in, speaking softly against her ear. "That's what I'm going to teach you. It's simple; all you have to do is let me lead."

With one hand holding hers and the other resting at the small of her back, I start to sway us along with the slow rhythm. She's a little hesitant at first, but eventually follows my lead. Her fingers play with the little hairs on the back of my neck, and her head rests on my shoulder after a while.

The next song has a quicker tempo, but we stay with our slow and steady swaying.

"You're not what I expected," she says after a while.

"Is that good or bad?"

She rolls her forehead into my chest. "I feel like it's good...but I'm worried it's bad."

"I really like you, Ellie. I..." I stop myself before I admit it. She's having a hard enough time believing I want to spend time with her, I can't spring anything more on her. Not yet.

She looks up, noticing the pause. I bend close to press a kiss to the sensitive spot behind her ear, and she shivers against me. I don't move away as I speak. "I wasn't able to show you a traditional Christmas, and this isn't exactly prom, but merry Christmas, Ellie. And happy prom night."

She breathes out a throaty laugh. "I'm so sorry I ruined your Christmas," she whispers.

I pull her in tighter against me and rest my chin on top of her head. "Did you know it's not actually possible to ruin Christmas?"

Ellie sighs. "No, you should have been with your family, opening presents, baking cookies, doing whatever the hell people do on Christmas."

"Were you paying attention at all to the service the other day?"

There's a pause. "I'll admit, I was a little distracted trying to pin down Wyatt."

I nod. "Let me recap for you. None of that's really Christmas. We picked a day in December to celebrate the birth of Jesus. Now, this is going to sound cheesy. Just bear with me. He was born so that He could die, and we wouldn't have to. Because He loves us."

She snuggles closer. "I like it when you're cheesy."

"Good, because it's going to get worse." She laughs, and I drink the sound in. "Most Christmas carols will tell you it's not about the presents or the decorations or the food, but what they don't tell you is that it's not about being with family either. Not really. We get together because nobody likes to celebrate good news alone. And to us, this is the *best* news. So no, you didn't ruin Christmas, because that's impossible." I let my words linger between us for a few moments before adding, "You just ruined the holiday part."

She balks and smacks me on the shoulder. I pull her back in, though, and bury my nose in her hair, swaying through the end of the song and into the next.

»»»»»»

I CRACK MY EYES OPEN WHEN SOMEONE TAPS MY SHOULDER, AND JUMP when I see Mark hovering over the back of the couch. Something weighs down my right arm, and then I remember.

I lost track of how long we danced, but eventually Ellie and I got tired. Jaythan had scrounged up a couch from the stockpile of furniture in his garage when we arrived yesterday, and I slumped onto that. Ellie flopped down next to me, and eventually we fell asleep. She's tucked into my side, breathing evenly.

"Hey." My voice is groggy, free arm stretching out. "How was the store?"

"Fine," Mark whispers, careful not to wake his sister. "I think Jaythan was once kicked out of Walmart, but he won't tell me anything more than that. How was training?"

"Great." My eyes are closed again, and a chill sweeps over me. "Hey, can you pass me that blanket over there?" I gesture in the vague direction of where I think I saw a blanket earlier.

I can hear the smirk in his words. "Ellie not keeping you warm enough?"

I glance down at her. Her golden hair spills out of her braid and across my shoulder, her face tucked into my chest. "No." I hold out my hand. "I'm cold."

Mark laughs silently but drapes the blanket over us. He helps me adjust it, but it's not covering my shoulders which are still catching that cold wind like sponges. I pull the blanket up under my chin, and it buries Ellie. I don't think she'll mind.

There's a moment of rest where I start to drift off again, but someone claps their hands together loudly. My heart jumps clear into my throat.

"Alright, I have news." Jaythan. I force my eyes open and fight to keep them that way. He walks up to the back of the couch and looks down. "Where's E?"

Mark falls onto one of the mattresses randomly in the room as well. "She's under the blanket."

Jaythan frowns at him, looks down at me. I slide my arm out from under the blanket and point to the breathing life form next to me. Jaythan tilts his head and unearths her head. She turns her face away, groaning into my shoulder.

Jaythan thumps the couch. "Actually, Rowan should be here too. Where is he?"

Ellie makes incoherent noises that sound suspiciously like "*shut up.*"

"I think he went back to his place," Mark says. Ellie nods her confirmation, no doubt hoping that will end the conversation. When's the last time she had a nap?

"Okay, well listen up." Jaythan will not be deterred. He pushes Ellie's shoulder, but she doesn't respond. He continues anyway. "I found an opening…tomorrow."

That makes her shoot up, alert now and flipping around to face Jaythan. My heart starts pounding, and I'm fully awake too, not just because I was nearly flipped off the couch. We can't do this tomorrow. From the dark glare she throws Jaythan's way, she agrees. She challenges slowly, "Come again?"

"Hartley is taking the new recruits overseas for training, which means they're going to have some of the guards with them too. So, there will be slightly fewer people there tomorrow."

"Hartley is hardly a concern we have to work around." Ellie talks slowly, menacingly, but somehow, he doesn't back down.

"That doesn't mean it's not better if he's gone."

"We're not ready for that. I just started training Brandon *today.*

We've been making these plans for *two* days. There's no way we're ready for this."

He glances at each of us. "Do you guys want to get Jake back?"

She inhales sharply, and Jaythan looks like he's about to spend the rest of his breath on apologies. She's up over the back of the couch and in his face in a second. He trips backwards. "I'd like to get him back in one piece, and rushing things won't help us do that."

"Look, you know it would be best to go tomorrow. Your dad will be preoccupied, making sure Hartley and the assassins get off the ground okay. He won't be busy doling out assignments, which means no assassins. There will only be guards at least for tomorrow."

"And you don't think my father would be expecting us? Maybe this is a trap. It's possible Hartley's not leaving at all."

I hadn't thought of that. I share a skeptical look with Mark. He's just as unnerved by this as I am, but neither of us seems capable of putting forth an opinion on the matter. Ellie is handling this, and I trust her to do what's best for us. If that means moving tomorrow… I'll trust her.

"Would you rather wait to get Jake back?" There's no regret this time as he says it, and I realize he wants Jake back as badly as we do. He may not know Jake well, but he's still family. He has every reason to want this mission to be a success. It settles a few of my nerves.

Ellie stares at him a long while. No one moves, waiting for her response. I silently hope it's not another situation like the too long stare-off with Rowan. Jaythan puts up a valiant fight, however.

Finally, she turns to Mark and me. "Do you feel ready for this?"

Mark still says nothing, but I shake my head. "No, but…will we ever?"

Her jaw ticks.

"If this is how we get him back," Mark pipes up, voice unsteady, "then we go tomorrow."

"You mean that?" Her brow lifts, fists clenching at her sides.

Mark nods. I nod. Ellie watches us. Then she grabs her coat and heads for the door.

I shoot to my feet. "Where are you going?"

She glances back, tired. "If it's happening tomorrow, Rowan needs to know. And we need to get some things worked out before then. I'll be back in a few hours." With that, she takes her keys and strides out of the house.

We all wait as if she's going to come back in, proclaiming this was all some elaborate prank, and she's really a college student doing this for extra credit. When she doesn't, I turn to Jaythan. "Tomorrow, then?"

Jaythan nods solemnly, lips in a thin line. "Afraid so. I suggest you do what you need to do before then, mend any broken relationships, make your peace with death because this could all end very badly."

"Why would you say that?" But Jaythan's already in the next room with his computers. I turn to Mark instead and try to stop the sense of our impending doom from crushing down on me. "Why does he have to be like that?"

Mark shakes his head, shrugs, but says nothing. His breathing is coming out all shaky. Locating his brother tomorrow is a great thing, but possibly dying tomorrow is less great. I miss when my biggest problems were just med school.

40

ELLIE'S THOUGHTS

TURN THE PLAN OVER AND OVER IN MY HEAD ON MY WAY TO ROW-
an's. The route down from Jaythan's is long and winding, but I've
driven it a hundred times. I know that before this cliff there will be a
sharp right turn and a curve back left. I know that the road gets narrow
up ahead and also very icy in the winter. What I don't know is if this
is a good idea.

We got here yesterday, and we're moving tomorrow. I saw the fear on
Brandon's and Mark's faces. I don't like pushing Brandon this way, but
we both knew I wouldn't have enough time to fully train him. He will
never be as prepared for this as he should be. Rowan will be with him
the whole time. If Brandon dies, I will kill Rowan for it. The thought
makes me nauseous.

I told Brandon that I wanted him, and I do. I wasn't lying, but this
could all be over tomorrow. I don't know what I could have wanted from

a relationship. Spending time with him has been fantastic. We were training, but it was deeper than that. I've never trained anyone before. It was more intimate than I thought, spending so much time with a person. Sharing the details of how I do what I do.

I should have been more prepared for that. Rowan trained me, and he was the person I was closest to for most of my childhood even when I still believed my father loved me. I spent so much time with him; he *was* my family.

I can't picture Brandon and I as a couple, getting dressed up and going on dates. I like him a lot, but that's not me. I don't think it ever will be. He said I didn't need to promise him anything, but what am I supposed to do with that? I don't want him to feel trapped in a relationship he's not happy with, and I am notoriously stubborn. I'm not known for trying new things. A relationship is enough of a jump, and I might not be able to make myself take another for a long time. Or perhaps I'm wrong, and I'll be great at this.

It won't be a problem if something goes wrong tomorrow.

We won't even find Jake for another few days. We'll have to sift through the records to find the trail, and we run the risk of Cooper moving him first. This is a fool's errand.

Rowan knows it as well as I do. But we'll do it because if there's even the slightest chance at getting my brother back, I'm going to take it.

Jake sounded willing to immerse himself in Cooper's lies when he called last week. He's fed up with us demanding his trust, which I now realize I never gave him in return. Mark and I smothered him. Every time he brought up our father, we shut him down. He *tried* to talk to me on multiple occasions. I should have read the signs. Maybe I even should have told him.

Cooper abducted him, but what if Jake's not angry about it? Based on his phone call, Jake has traded us for him. Cooper lies; he knows how to tell people what they want to hear. And I was never open enough to warn Jake about that. He's primed to fall right into the trap. Because I can't trust people.

This very mission is a testament to that. I grew up in the Enforcers. My father and Hartley were always around. Now I'm preparing to break in and kill anyone that gets in my way. I've traded my whole life for the last few weeks. My career for my freedom. My father for…my family.

This is a better cause than I've ever had, and I will fight for it with my last breath. It terrifies me.

Rowan lives on a quiet street, neighbors not close enough to be invasive. Most of the houses are decked in colored lights along their fences and rooftops. They illuminate the dreary evening. Rowan's house only has a blow-up reindeer on the porch with one antler; the other lies deflated on the side of Rudolph's head.

I knock on his door. There's a three-paned window at the top where I can see the carpeted stairs and a stuffed dog lying on one. Such a cozy setting for someone who trained me extensively in methods of death. The sound of tiny feet precedes the door groaning open.

A little boy stands there and frowns at me. "Who are you?" He's wearing elastic waisted jeans, white socks, and a Darth Vader sweatshirt. I try to smile as guilt swirls in my stomach.

"What did I tell you about answering the door?" There's a hint of fear in Rowan's voice I've never heard before as he swoops in and picks up the boy hastily, but he pauses when he sees me. Releases a breath.

I take an involuntary step back. I've never met Rowan's son. He's only three, so he wasn't around when Rowan and I were still close. It's unsettling to see him now, right before everything can go so wrong. Rowan is helping me protect the ones I love, but this is who he loves. This boy is his world.

"Sorry, Daddy." The kid's voice is so little and squeaky. I want to run far away from here and never look back.

Rowan strokes the kid's hair, so pale compared to Rowan's dark blond that's almost brown. I wonder if he got that from his mother. "It's okay, kid." He sets him back on his feet. "Go on and play now." When the boy runs off, Rowan motions me inside.

It's a completely different version of him than I've ever experienced. The odor of steamed vegetables wafts toward me as soon as I step inside. Colorful toys are strewn all over the carpet—action figures, stuffed animals, picture books. An orange plastic cup half-filled with milk and a plate with scattered peas and carrots sits on the counter.

He leads me away from the kitchen into the living room where his boy is playing with an action figure on the floor before the long burgundy couch. He makes the toy jump high into the air and flip end over end in slow motion. Then I catch sight of the princess doll. She's sitting by the couch behind another action figure that the flipping one lands in front of. The boy talks in a deep voice, wiggling the new figure. I quickly catch on to the fact that the flipper is attempting to rescue the princess. The banter between the two figures continues, but one of the kid's hands goes to the princess now who stands and kicks the villain from behind. She quickly rushes away while the hero finishes him off.

I can't pull my eyes away from the domestic scene taking place. In Rowan's house. With his child. He looks just like him.

Rowan sits, also watching his son. "Did you come to tell me when we're moving?"

I swallow thickly. "Tomorrow."

He nods, eyes still on the oblivious child. The boy stands, having wrapped up the one game, and is now flying a car through the air. I stop breathing when he comes up to me and drives the little car up and down my leg, making *vroom* noises. I keep myself very still.

"Richard," Rowan calls. My head shoots up, a million memories of him barking orders at me or simply getting my attention flashing through my mind. *Push-ups, Richards. Happy Birthday, Richards. Good luck, Richards.* But the boy turns too. Rowan holds his hand out to him and orders softly, "Give her some space."

Richard runs and hops into his dad's lap. "Who is she, Daddy?" He continues flying the car around and starts driving it over Rowan's chest.

Rowan looks up at me. "She's my friend." Richard drives the car higher until it's on his dad's face, and Rowan grabs it. "Hey, go upstairs and play, okay? Daddy needs to talk to her. I'll be up to put you to bed in a bit."

"Can I have a cookie?" the kid blurts.

"You didn't finish your dinner." Rowan's stern dad-look hits me right in the chest. I remember being on the receiving end of some of those.

"Please?" Richard adds at least three syllables to the word. "I promise I'll finish my food tomorrow."

Rowan huffs once. "I'll tell you what, if you bring a cookie for my friend here, you can have one too. *Only* one, and you *will* finish your dinner tomorrow."

"Yay!" Richard jumps off him, yells, "Thanks, Dad!" and races into the kitchen.

A few moments later, he's back, grabbing my sleeve and holding up a chocolate chip cookie for me. "Here you go."

I take it and barely manage a choked *"Thank you,"* before he charges up the stairs.

I fish around for something to say, but all I can think is, "He's cute."

Rowan smiles, ever the proud father, but then it turns sorrowful. "I never forgave myself for what happened. I should have told you about your mother. I just didn't want to hurt you." Cooper told Rowan the day my mother died. It was an extra two days before Dad told *me.* He waited until after I'd completed my mission. That fateful second assignment. "I had no idea how to tell you, so I told myself it was better if it came from him.

"When you found your cousin, I was so glad you had someone since it couldn't be me anymore. I remembered you telling me once that he was good with computers, so I tracked him down too. That's when we started switching out your ammo and relocating your targets. I thought if I couldn't speak with you to apologize, it was another way to atone. Cooper got to them anyway." His brown eyes bore into mine when he says, "I'm so sorry."

I nod. And keep nodding. I thought all along that they were dead. I'm not sure I ever let myself process when Wyatt told me they were alive. But that's no longer the case. They really are all dead, but they had a second chance for a while. Rowan gave that to them.

And he was right. The news about my mother should have come from my father, but only if I didn't have the father I do. He told me eventually, but in doing so, broke me in every conceivable way. I always believed Rowan would never hurt me like Cooper had so often, but the news would have been better coming from him. It would have been better to have known when it happened, rather than postponing the update because of a job. Would have been better if the voice telling me was sympathetic.

But that was years ago. So much has happened in that time. Rowan got married. He had a kid. I reconnected with my brothers. I met Brandon. And it took our worlds crumbling to bring us back to each other.

I suck in a breath, but I can't stop the tears now. They stream down my cheeks. Rowan pushes to his feet and steps close just in time for me to collapse into his arms. He wraps me up tight, holding me while I sob. I can't make myself stop. The sorrow deep inside me refuses to let up now that the walls have come crashing down.

He was my only family for so long. Cutting him out was the hardest thing I ever had to do.

I try to control myself, but my breathing becomes choppy. "I missed you so much."

His arms tighten, and he sways back and forth, planting a kiss atop my head. "I missed you too, Ellie."

It's the first time he's used my real name, and it undoes me all over. I curl further into his chest, and he urges us over to the couch where he lets me dehydrate myself into his shirt as much as I need.

Finally, I pull myself together. It's exhausting realizing people care. Realizing some always did even when I thought otherwise. I tricked myself into believing there was no one because it was better than straining for it and coming up short as I had with the person who was supposed to love me most in the world. But Rowan isn't Cooper. Neither are my brothers. And neither is Brandon.

I hastily swipe the tears away and clear my throat. "We need to make sure we have all the supplies for tomorrow."

Rowan dips his chin. "Right." He pulls out a sheet of paper so he can make a list, just like he taught me all those years ago. "Jaythan will supply the tech. That leaves us with weapons and the disguise."

I nod and take a bite of the cookie still in my hand. I pause, glancing down at it. "Did you make these?"

"Rich and I made a batch yesterday."

I shake my head. "Damn, Rowan." His brow lifts. "You know, since we're blowing the whole assassin thing to hell, you could try your hand at *baker*."

He chuckles. "I'll keep that in mind."

41

BRANDON'S ROLE

Rowan, Ellie, and I walk up to the Enforcers headquarters. It's like the start to a bad joke. I've heard that said about a lot of things, but I think my situation takes the cake. Two assassins and a med student are going to attempt the rescue of a mutual friend from professional killers—there's another bad one. I hope more than anything that there's no punchline.

The headquarters is honestly not what I expected. It's a small building that looks more like a home for a family of four than the main setting of a psychotic businessman with unlimited access to assassins. The exterior is covered in chipped green paint, and the windows look like they've only ever been cleaned with soiled rags that are leaving behind streaks. The flowers out front give out a confusingly pleasant aroma. Roses have no place at a crime scene.

Ellie goes in ahead of us to draw her father's attention and to latch one of Jaythan's devices to a security camera. It should loop him into the feed, so he can erase Rowan and me. But only in the house. The headquarters are a whole other beast.

Which is why Rowan and Ellie found a spare security guard uniform for me. I don't know how, and I don't want to know. I like to think Ellie has them lying around for times like this. She just showed up with it last night after seeing Rowan. The sleeves are a little short on my arms, and tugging on them becomes a natural outlet for my anxiety.

They made me slick back my hair to further disguise my features too. Ellie actually cringed when I walked out of the bathroom. I'm not a fan of it either; it feels weird, and my forehead feels too exposed. But her disgust is an amusing distraction.

"*You're up*," Jaythan's voice says in my ear after about six minutes. I swallow hard.

Rowan and I make our approach. I thought getting in might prove to be the hard part, but it's not. Rowan still has a key—yep, a regular house key. I was disappointed too. And a little relieved. Inside the house looks just as you'd expect from the outside. A regular dining room, living room, and kitchen. A thief would be hard-pressed to know something else lurked beneath.

"So, you trained Ellie?"

Rowan glances back at me, brows furrowed. I assume he's not much for chatting, like Ellie. Are all assassins like that?

In the hallway past the living room, he opens a closet door, and there's an elevator inside. Suddenly, I feel like I'm in *Mission: Impossible*. I convince myself that Rowan's about to slide a panel aside, revealing a hand-eye scanner that will lock the place down if he doesn't scan within five seconds. He doesn't, though. He presses a button like in a normal elevator.

That's disappointing too. Bad dude that he is, I put a lot more hope into Ellie's dad being a cool businessman than I thought.

"Yes." His response makes me jump. He was so silent; I thought he'd just continue to ignore me.

"How was she?"

He smiles to himself. "Temperamental. And stubborn. But a quick study." His smile disappears. "Sometimes I wonder if I did the right thing."

I take a breath. Befriending an assassin wasn't something I ever thought I'd do. Might as well add consoling one to my list too. "I mean, if you look at it this way: you gave her what she needed to be where she is now. She'd never be able to get Jake back if it weren't for you."

A grunt is his only reply. I'd need to know a few more assassins to prove my hypothesis, but I'd rather not. I'll just retain the theory. Assassins don't like talking. Especially about feelings. Fair enough. I suppose with a job like theirs, making friends wouldn't be quite as high a priority. Nor would spilling all their emotional secrets.

I can't stop myself from asking, though, "What happened between you two?" I wonder for a moment if it's too personal a question and tack on, "If you don't mind me asking."

He surprises me when he sighs, eyelids drooping. "Her mother died, and I didn't tell her. I told myself it would be better for her to hear it from her father, but I knew I was just hoping I could keep her from finding out."

"How did *you* know?" I frown.

He shakes his head. "Cooper told me. I still don't know why. Must have been another of his mind games." His voice drops to just above a whisper. "He plays a lot of those on her." Then to himself with a simmering rage and gritted teeth, "Treats her like a damn lab rat."

My chest hollows, and I fall silent. How did she live like that? Then a warmth trickles in, and I wonder if Rowan is a big part of the reason she survived it.

The elevator drifts down, down, down until the doors finally open. There's a tall guard on the other side. I was hoping we'd have more time. He's guarding what looks like just a long, gray hallway. No doors before the junction at the end. Or maybe he's guarding the exit from anyone inside. That sets my stomach squirming.

The guard spots Rowan and shifts back to take him in. This guy is around the same size in both height and weight, but the giant assassin next to me doesn't seem concerned. I try to wipe the fear from my own expression, putting on an air of haughty indifference I've seen Ellie don many times.

"Rowan." The guard blinks. "I thought you were captured."

"I was." Rowan lashes out, quick and precise, striking a nerve at the man's neck that knocks him out cold. Before he can thump to the ground, Rowan catches him and nods to the man's feet. I blink. "Help me carry him to the supply closet."

I take a moment to remind myself that breathing involves both sucking in and blowing out. Once I get that down, I tell myself one foot goes in front of the other to walk, and then I grab the man's legs and heave them up with a grunt. He's much heavier than I anticipated even with Rowan helping. That could be the heavy-duty vest, weapons, and ammo strapped to him. People in movies make this look too easy. Maybe I'd do better to stop comparing my actual situation to the movies. We all know Hollywood is full of it.

"Where's the supply closet?" I ask, my voice strained. *Should I be lifting weights more at the gym?*

"Just a couple corridors down."

"A couple, like how many?"

Rowan doesn't answer that one.

There's no comfortable way to carry a man by the legs, so I'm forced into an awkward shuffle/waddle until we find a closet that's *not* actually an elevator. Turns out, when Rowan says "*a couple*" he really does mean "*two*". We set the unconscious guard on a mop bucket, Rowan ties him up, and I neatly shut the door like there's not a man stuffed inside.

"Security's this way." He walks away from me, immediately moving on. I throw up my hands. This is exactly what Ellie does, following up something crazy by acting like nothing happened. No wonder.

We move down each hallway at a quick light-footed run that Ellie was careful to teach me this morning. Rowan slows before each turn, peering around the corner to make sure the coast is clear. This place is a maze, and it's not very logically laid out—I mean, one of the hallways had that random supply closet. Four turns in, we come to another oddly placed room with a sliver of a window on the door. I choke on a gasp when I see the two security guards on duty inside.

Rowan nods to me and mouths, "*Wait.*" He slips inside. Smashes sound, people grunt, and thunks are had.

"Okay." He steps back out. We drag those two men into the same closet and tie them all into a cluster together. I'm surprised when we successfully fit three grown men into a janitorial closet—not only by the size of the inserted goods to the shoebox-like closet, but also in that time no others came snooping around here to catch us in the act. I mean, we were efficient and all, but Ellie's father seems to think very highly of himself not to have tighter security—even in a maze. Rowan touches his earpiece. "Surveillance room is secure."

"*Copy*," comes Ellie's response. "*I'm making my way to Cooper's office. How are you hanging in?*"

Jaythan's voice crackles over the line. "*Pretty good, thanks for asking.*"

"*Not you.*"

I know she isn't talking about Rowan. "I'm fine." Stupidly, despite the gray cloud of life-threatening danger looming over this day, warmth gathers in my chest at her concern.

"*Okay. How does it look outside the office?*"

It takes me a few seconds to find the correct camera, but Rowan helps, and I pull it up to the larger screen. "Empty. You were right. No guards."

"*Why wouldn't he post guards?*" Mark asks.

Ellie grunts, and there's a sound like metal warping. "*He doesn't trust them.*" There's something that makes me claustrophobic, knowing she's in the vents.

"*Are there some inside with him, though?*" Mark's voice is a bit shaky.

"That's a risk we'll have to take," Rowan says. "He doesn't have cameras in his office, so we can't even be sure he'll be there."

"*He will.*" Ellie sounds confident.

"How's it looking on the outside?" Rowan asks.

"*Nothing suspicious out here,*" Jaythan reports. "*Everyone is going about their normal business. It's like we're not even here.*"

"Alright, guys," Ellie whispers now. *"I'm at his office. Am I still clear?"*

"Yes." I desperately hope I'm right.

"Going in and going dark."

"I'll start the data transfer." Rowan pulls out the bug, plugging it into the computer. He types furiously at the keys, and my eyes zip between all the cameras, looking for trouble. The six people I've spotted in that hallway have simply walked past the janitor's closet, and honestly it makes me wonder if there even is a janitor here or if that closet is just to complete the look. Do evil corporations have janitors? Every time somebody walks through *this* hallway, my heart jumps into my throat. But they all walk past the surveillance room door too.

Until one doesn't. I barely have time to yell at Rowan before a man walks through the door.

"Wait!" I immediately scream at the giant assassin as soon as I see the intruder's face. The assassin freezes. So does Jackson, Mrs. Bishop's grandson. He's a guard at a nameless company. *This* company. No wonder Ellie was so weird in his presence. Did she recognize him?

I don't know why I stopped Rowan from dealing with him. Jackson has every right to kill me right now. It's his job. But he doesn't move. He just keeps staring at me, trying to make sense of me in this context.

I know if he does attack me, I won't make a move to hurt him. If somehow I survived, I'd never be able to look Mrs. Bishop in the eye again.

Someone else is coming down the hall behind Jackson, and he peeks back out the door. "Everything's fine here," he says with a relieved and mildly irritated huff, like he's been put out. "False alarm. Come on." Then he's gone, leading the other man far away from the surveillance room.

After my heart stops pounding in my ears, Rowan asks, "Are you alright?"

"I think so?" I answer honestly.

"Good because we've got a problem."

"What?" I almost don't want him to answer. It seems scarier than not knowing.

"It's not enough. Security doesn't have access to the maps. I can download the camera data and blueprints. But no maps. We need Hartley's or Cooper's computer."

"Why didn't we see that coming?"

"We did. We just hoped we were wrong."

"Ellie's never wrong," I joke.

"Never tell her that." He surprises me with a laugh. It's a deep, rich rumble. I'm reminded in this moment that he has a son. It's easier to picture him as a father like this. I smile. "I'm going to Hartley's office."

I stop smiling. "Wait! Maybe Ellie could get it from Cooper's computer." I really don't want him to leave me. Ellie dragged me out of bed before the sun was up to go over the drills she taught me yesterday one last time, but I have no desire to learn if I'm capable of putting them to use. Plus, Jaythan gave a copy of his bug to both Ellie and Rowan as backups—"*You can never be too careful,*" he said.

Rowan touches his earpiece again. "Ellie. Ellie, do you read? We need the data from Cooper's computer. Can you get it?" She doesn't reply. "Ellie, do you copy?" When she still doesn't respond, Rowan brings his hand down and shakes his head. "We can't wait for her. I'm going now. Keep watching the cameras. Don't move." Then with a quick glance at them to make sure he's clear, he slips out the door.

42

ELLIE'S REASONING

SLAM THE GRATE OUT, LANDING IN A CROUCH ON COOPER'S DESK. A quick survey of the too organized office tells me he's not in here. But that doesn't make any sense. No. He's always in his office. He's here somewhere. He must be.

I wiggle the mouse to wake up his computer. The screen lights up, and it's unlocked—likely means there's nothing here, but I pull the flash drive from my pocket and start transferring as much as I can anyway. While it's working, I take a better look around the office. He's here somewhere, and I *will* find him. I know Cooper saw me in the decoy house, and now he's found some secret hiding place.

For a long time, I suspected he actually lived up in that house, but I've never been able to confirm or deny it. As a kid, I tried to get him to let me move up there because I was afraid of being underground. I never got used to it as I got older, but he didn't let me go. Not until I left on my own.

There are no pictures in his office. No items of personal value. File cabinets line the walls interspersed by a few safes. I start shifting things around. Cracking the locks on each of them is something I don't have time for, but I can see if he's got anything nailed down. Hidden in the crevices.

Nothing stands out until I encounter one safe that doesn't budge when I ram myself into it. It's flush with the wall and only moves half an inch. I pull a knife from my boot, slide it behind, and the blade catches on something halfway in.

I check the flash drive. It's only about twenty-five percent through stealing whatever may or may not be there.

The lock on the safe is an electronic keypad. Six-digit code. I consider asking Jaythan for suggestions, but how could he know? How could *I* know?

Statistically, people use their birthday. I can't imagine Cooper would be so simple. I'm right. A little red light flashes along the top; two remain unlit. Three tries then, with one spent. He's not the sentimental type. Even the walls in his office aren't painted—they're just white, psych ward white. Despite that, he had three children with my mother. He must have loved her at some point.

But her birthday doesn't work either. I have one try left.

On a whim, I try my own birthday. Out of every family member, he only took me. And to my surprising disappointment…it works. The door clicks open.

Behind the magic door there's…guns. But my father didn't raise a quitter, which is why I find the secret compartment behind them. Another door, secured with a key. Slamming the butt end of one of his rifles into the slim handle breaks it easily enough. The door swings wide, and there I stumble into Cooper.

He jumps back, his chair hitting the wall, and reaches for something beneath the desk. A gun? I slide over the desk purely on instinct and kick his hand aside, pulling my own gun and slamming it across his face. That'll give him a nice bruise. Then I compose myself and aim it steadily at his head with the knife he failed to draw from his suit pocket before I did poised over his heart.

"Hello, Father," I croon.

He grins at me. "It's nice to see you again, Emily."

There's a secret entrance after all. My father has been hiding his true workstation. His studio apartment, from the look of it. It's a tiny space, but it's big enough to fit a desk and a small mattress covered in haphazardly flung sheets. I guess that finally settles whether he uses the upstairs house. He has a decoy office. This is a whole new depth to his insanity.

This office is significantly less organized than the other one. As he's the only one with access to it, it seems he keeps things looser—bachelor pad style, if you will.

I don't take the time to determine what's on his desk further than to note that I don't know any of the names on the papers, but if I had to guess, these would be the files that really mattered to the company. There's plenty of information Cooper could give up before it hurt the Enforcers. *This* is what hurts him. He must have killed everyone that knows about this place because I've never even heard a whisper of it. I'll bet even Hartley's been kept in the dark.

But now *I* know.

"I hear tell you've been seeing a lot of Jake lately. Where is he?"

"He's resting now," Cooper responds cheekily. "You don't want to disturb him."

"He's my brother. Of course I do. Where can I do that?" He just keeps grinning. "Why are you doing this?"

He nods to a small couch on the other side of his desk. "Take a seat, Emily."

I pause. "I don't think I should."

"You don't trust me?"

"You're surprised?"

He shakes his head, disappointment writing itself on his drooping eyelids and frowning mouth. "Look here." He reaches for his keyboard and stops, glancing at the weaponry I still have trained on him. "Do you mind?"

I blink, shift away, change my mind and go back, then change my mind again and step away from him. He nods, typing something into his computer. An image of an outrageously golden room pops up—gold curtains, gold sheets, gold midday sun streaming in. The only imperfection in the photo is the bed that isn't made. Much like the one in Cooper's office, its sheets are bunched at the foot. A second later I realize this isn't a photo but a video. Jake comes into the picture from a small room that must be the bathroom. I blink again and realize I should be breathing.

My brother. Rugged blond curls, lightly suntanned skin, lean form. He looks great. His hair is wet, and he's in a pair of boxers—thank goodness—having just gotten out of the shower. There are no bruises or cuts or abnormalities to be seen on his person. He throws on some sweats and sits down on the bed, grabbing the remote. When he finds a channel he likes, he leans back, takes a file from the stack on the nightstand, and starts reading. He's a strange one, but it's undeniably Jake.

"It's a live feed." Cooper watches me, but I can't take my eyes off my brother. *This is sick.* "As you can see, he's perfectly fine. He gets all the room service he wants. He's happy."

"So, you abducted him for sport, then?"

"To conduct a test."

"On what?" I spit, making sure Jake doesn't spontaneously disappear.

"You." Now I turn to my father. His brow is raised in challenge.

I wipe the surprise off my face. "What could you possibly be testing by abducting your own son?"

"You think too small, Emily. That's always been your problem. When Brandon Harwood was our target, you went straight to Oregon to save him. You panicked when I sent you after Mark and watched over those three boys like a hawk for weeks. Now, here you are making it a bigger deal that I have taken my own son into my home."

Jake must be in some hotel room because Cooper said *"room service."* A crushing weight presses in on my skull. There are almost a hundred and fifty hotels in DC alone. He could be anywhere. I need Jaythan to look at all the hotels in the area *now* if we stand a chance of finding Jake, but I can't risk getting this task to him while Cooper is within earshot.

"You abducted him." My voice is too quiet.

He huffs with a sympathetic head tilt, mimicking someone with actual compassion, though I know he has none. "Do you want to know why?"

"*Ellie,*" comes Rowan's voice in my ear. My name still sounds strange from my old instructor. I ignore it. "*Ellie, do you read?*"

"I—"

"You thought it was because of you." How can Cooper still make me feel ashamed? He should be the one feeling this shame. He stole his son away from his life, and I'm the one squirming?

"*We need the data from Cooper's computer. Can you get it?*" Rowan's deep voice is calm, but I know he's about to leave Brandon alone to find what he needs. "*Ellie, do you copy?*" I can't do anything.

My father sighs and shakes his head. "It didn't occur to you that your little stunt in Oregon got me thinking?"

I take a deep breath. There's a lot coming at me, but I don't trust him enough to go around the desk and take a seat. I force myself to hold my ground. "You…what?" I want to scream at the lump forming in my throat. *He's not worth it!*

"You were doing so well for so long, Emily." His eyes darken. "Deceptively well, as it seems. But even so, you always had that affection for your brothers. And that held you back."

That helps me swallow past the lump, and I scoff, waving my gun at him. "You never let our family get in *your* way."

"Correct." He doesn't regret this at all. His gaze is flat as he says it, and slowly it turns hard. "Except for you."

I step back, hitting the desk and making it screech noisily against the cement floor. I'm not sure whether to be touched or offended by that. It's the closest my father has ever come to saying he loves me, but he doesn't make it sound like a good thing. "Are you saying you want Jake to replace me?"

"No." He chuckles. "Jake is going to replace *me*. It was supposed to be you. I was going to hand everything to you." As if this is supposed to be flattering. I knew this, and my plan from the moment I turned sixteen was to run it into the ground. "For the longest time you had me thinking you were the perfect candidate, but then all this happened. You just don't have what it takes. Mark certainly doesn't. Jake, though… He's studying business. He has high marks in all his classes despite his childish lifestyle. He knows the game. Assuming he grows up, he can run this organization when I'm gone."

My eyebrows climb my forehead. "You think he will? Up 'til now, he didn't even know what you did."

"Didn't he?"

I pause.

"Jake reached out to me a while back. I didn't hide from him what we do."

Does he know that Jake called me? Could he be telling the truth? History says it's probably manipulation, but what if Jake did know about Cooper and all his prodding was to get me to admit to it? How long has Jake known? I force my ragged breath to slow. *Make him explain.* "He was with you in all this?"

"Not at first. But of course, when everyone else in his life failed him, he eventually saw things my way. He understands what it takes to pull out from under the thumb of tyranny. He understands what it takes to survive."

I blink hard. "This isn't surviving. You kill whoever you want. Whoever goes against your agenda for that week. Who are you to judge who's oppressive when you sit here on your throne ordering the deaths of countless people? In fighting as you've been, you became the very thing you claimed to hate, don't you get that? You aren't the solution, you're the *problem.*"

"That's what your mother used to say." His eyes grow distant, almost wistful, but then they cut into me once more. "Did you ever read her texts?"

I choke. Breathing is no longer an option. My hands shake. I read her texts. I read every single one of them, looking for an answer I will never get. *Why would such a sweet and wonderful person ever marry Cooper?*

My father continues, not waiting for my response, preferring to let the question fester in my mind. "Mark was always more like her, but I had hoped that you would turn out to be like me. You were so strong. Always following orders. Never questioning them." He shakes his head again. "Until things got too personal. You failed my test, Emily. Your loyalties shift when things get personal. I can't have that in this organization."

I freeze. "Are you firing me right now?"

"I could never let go of such an asset."

My jaw drops. This was the approval I so desperately sought from him. This is what I wanted all along. Recognition that I'm valuable. To the Enforcers. To *him*. A lump rises in my throat. "First, I'm a liability, and now I'm essential? What the hell do you want?"

"I want you to do your job, Emily. And I want you to do it right this time. No more Wyatt or Rowan or cousin to interfere." He leans back in his chair, and it lets out a menacing squeak.

My voice comes out too softly as I say, "I had no idea they were doing any of that."

He hums. "Shall they be your next assignments, then?"

Dread drops my stomach to the floor. "No," I breathe out.

Another hum. He turns away. "Of course, if you pull anything like that again, I will be forced to take the extreme measures you claim are so corrupt." I have no air. "I already have more than enough cause to take such action, but your skills can still be useful to me. Don't make me hurt them, Emily. I believe one of your little friends is already in the building, is he not?"

Cold silence settles inside of me. I raise my gun. My hand doesn't shake as I aim between his eyes. "Move. Now."

"You're not going to shoot me, Emily."

He's right. As much as I hate him, he's still my father. I can't kill him. I stab the beautiful chestnut of his desk, freeing one hand to pull the taser from under it because yes, I did notice he doesn't have a real gun under here.

"That's not my name, Cooper." I shoot. He collapses into a convulsing heap on the ground.

Stepping over him, I pile up as many of the documents on the desk as I can carry. A quick search of the drawers produces flash drives. They could have nothing on them, or they could have something. Either way, it wouldn't hurt to take them. I stuff all of this into the bag I smartly folded into my pocket beforehand and sling it onto my back.

I stun Cooper again on my way out to ensure he won't be getting up any time soon. Back in the decoy office, I retrieve the flash drive that thankfully had time to complete the download and stow it in the zippered pocket of my pants for safekeeping.

Then I pause. There's a number written on a sticky note in the corner of the desk. I stare at it. It's a business number with an extension attached to it. Curiosity overtakes me, and I pull out my phone and dial.

"*Hello?*" I'm so startled to hear Jake's voice on the other end that I forget to respond. "*Hello?*" he repeats a bit impatiently this time.

"Jake, it's Ellie. Where are you?"

"*How did you get this number?*"

"Why are you working with Cooper?"

"*Cooper?*" he spits. "*When did he stop being* Dad?"

My heart stops. "Are you serious?"

"*Lose this number,* Emily." The line cuts out as my heart shatters. I go numb. Cooper was telling the truth for once.

I scramble out of the office, desperate to find Brandon. If Jake is working with Cooper, our plan is shot. We can't rescue someone who doesn't want to be rescued, and I can't risk Brandon being here anymore. Jake made his choice, and I've made mine.

Brandon's still in the security room, watching the monitors. He launches out of his seat, crashing into the keyboard when I open the door. He reaches for his gun, then immediately releases a deep breath, clasping a hand over his heart. "Oh, it's you." Another breath. "Did you find him?"

I grab his arm. "Jake's working with him." Brandon's face falls. "We have to leave."

"What?" I pull him out the door, not allowing him the luxury of shock. "What do you mean he's working with him? Your father?"

"Jake is being groomed to take over the Enforcers. He's being kept in a hotel with room service and everything. He's *working* with Cooper, Brandon."

Two guards round the corner. They take aim with their rifles, but I shoot one between the eyes. The other is already too close. I shove Brandon behind me, and a shot whizzes right past us. I aim the pistol again, but the guard grabs my wrist hard, forcing me to drop it. I pop a blade free and slice into his bicep. His grip releases, but in a flash his gun is aimed at my head.

A shot behind me, and the guard slumps to the ground. I flip around to see who fired it. Brandon stands there, gun raised. His breathing becomes very heavy, eyes wide.

I set aside my own shock, take his arm, and steer him down the hall. "Don't dwell on it." I make a mental note to thank him later for saving me.

We turn a corner, and a loud bang precedes a terrible searing pain under my ribcage. I clutch my side and hit the wall behind me. Brandon might be yelling as he pulls me back around the corner, but another bullet hits my leg. I crash to the floor with a cry, and a ringing screeches in my ears. Brandon drags me the rest of the way, propping me against the wall, so he can assess the damage.

There's no fixing this in time to escape. Even if he were to bandage me up, I can't get him out of here. I can't save him. I couldn't save Jake, and now Brandon will die because I tried. *I'm so sorry, Mom. I couldn't do it. I couldn't protect them.*

I blink past the tears in my eyes and tap my earpiece. "Rowan," I rasp. "Rowan, get down here." It's too hard to breathe. "Just…around the corner from security. *Now!*"

I don't hear his response. There's a lot of shrieking in my ear, so I rip the earpiece out. Then it's just the ringing. My vision swims, the lights become fire on my eyes, and I'm suddenly too dizzy to hold myself up. When I slide, Brandon catches me, muttering something—or maybe he's yelling. It's like listening through water. Everything hurts. "You'll be okay…stay with me…you'll be okay."

I put my trembling hand over the gun in his. "You have…to kill him."

I can just make out the shake of his head. Separating his words from the ringing is nearly impossible. "No…be fine…fix…"

I grab his hand and force myself to focus on his face. He meets my eyes with his watery dark ones. Is that the pounding of footsteps down the hall or is it my heartbeat? There's still someone out there.

"You have to. Or you'll die."

His mouth doesn't move for a moment. "We're not going to die." *We.* If all the blood seeping out of my body has any say in the matter… Nevertheless, Brandon starts firing down the hall.

His family will never forgive me. I brought their son to this point. I'm the one who's going to get him killed. He's here because of me. He's being forced to kill a man because of me. It's my fault. It's my fault. *It's my fault.*

I grip his shirt, losing my mind completely. *He needs to focus.* But he turns back to me instantly, eyes wide and brightening by the second. *I need to tell him.* "I'm so sorry." I can't hold my head up anymore, and I don't hear if he responds. The ringing becomes unbearably loud as everything turns white.

43

MARK'S DESTRUCTION

IT TAKES TOO LONG FOR JAYTHAN AND ME TO MAKE THE DRIVE TO the hospital. I'm shaking from head to toe, and Jaythan's hands are white-knuckled on the wheel. He starts clenching and unclenching them the closer we get, and I make myself focus on that rather than what's waiting for us.

Brandon is in the waiting room, and he shoots to his feet as soon as we enter. It only takes one glance at his clothes for my heart to constrict and drain all the blood from my face. *No, no, no, no, no.*

I choke. "Is this all hers?" I ask of the blood drenching his shirt and pants.

He nods, barely able to speak himself.

"Is she…is she going to be okay?"

He swallows hard. "I don't know." He looks down at himself. "She lost so much blood."

Jaythan grips his shoulder, forcing Brandon to look at him. "What happened?"

"Okay." The word shakes, and Brandon forces a few breaths down. "Okay. She came to get me from security, and we ran into two guards." My breath catches, but he shakes his head. "She took one out…easily, and I shot the other." He speeds right past that point. "She was dragging me away from that, but there was someone around the corner that she didn't see. He got a shot off under her ribs…and her leg." My pounding heart nearly stops. No, no, *no*.

Jaythan asks, "Where's Rowan?"

"He…" Brandon looks around the room. I struggle to draw in my next breath. "I don't know."

Jaythan just shakes his head. "Okay, well, what happened? Where's Jake?"

"He's working for him. Jake is working for Cooper."

A weird sound comes out of me that would best be described as a gasp interrupted by an already choked sob. I should have taken his questions about our father more seriously. He didn't know; I thought I could keep it that way. I should have seen this coming.

I race to the front desk and slam my hands down. "I need to see Ellie Cooper." That will have to change. She cannot share a name with that monster. Not after what he's done. Jake and I took Mom's name after the divorce, Spencer. *Ellie Spencer.*

The nurse's face crumples too completely. "Are you her brother?"

I open my mouth, but nothing comes out.

"He is," Brandon answers for me. "Why? Did something happen?"

My heart does an ugly stuttering thing where it skips at least two beats.

"We had her stable, but there was an accident."

"Wh—" I can't get the question out past the bile rising in my throat. Brandon's hand tightens to the point of bruising on my arm. I hadn't even realized he was touching me.

"I'm so sorry. I was just about to call you. Her injuries were worse than we thought. She deteriorated too quickly. We did everything we could."

I don't hear if she says anything else. It doesn't matter if she does. My sister is dead. "She's…" My mind goes entirely blank.

"Let me see her." Brandon's voice is calm and steady.

"I'm sorry," the nurse says, her image swimming before me. "I can't do that."

"Why not?" Brandon grinds out through his teeth. He pulls at his bloodstained shirt. Again. "Let me see her. I need to *see* her."

I don't know why Jaythan grabs Brandon's arm then. "I think we should sit down," my cousin mutters. Then his eye catches something behind the nurse. "Rowan."

I flip around to see the assassin stalking toward us. He's here. He loves Ellie. He wouldn't let anything happen to her. "Rowan!" I call to him, but there's a bubble in my throat that's strangling me. "Is it true?" Please say no. *Please say no!*

A terrible expression takes over the assassin's face, and my knees give out. Jaythan releases Brandon to catch me before I eat the vinyl. The rasp of Rowan's voice is poison. "Let them back. They're family."

The nurse glances at Brandon and Jaythan. "If they're not—"

Rowan cuts her off and breathes, "Let them back." But I don't think I can do it. The ground turns to water, a river rushing out from under my feet.

Understanding this, Jaythan keeps a firm grip on my arm and guides me down the hallway. The fluorescent lights burn into my skin and breathing becomes harder with every step.

But then we make it to the room.

And we step inside.

And Ellie is lying on the white sheets. She's covered in another sheet from the chest down, but her arms lie atop it. Pale. The glow of her tan has vanished from her skin, and her chest doesn't move as it's supposed to.

I vomit four feet away from my sister.

My legs come back to me, and I stumble to her side, launching for her wrist. My fingers search her entire forearm. *I can't find it.* "I can't find it!" I sob.

The sounds in the room become muffled and oppressive all at once. The buzzing of the fluorescent lights sizzling in my ears. The too white walls blinding me. And I think someone is screaming.

I think *I* am screaming.

I don't think I'll ever be able to stop.

44

BRANDON'S ARGUMENT

 standing at the counter staring at half a glass of water. Poetic.

It's been three days, and the pain hasn't eased. It's like a person that's determined to make the joke land way past when you realized it wasn't funny in the first place. Like when you realize you've lost the fight, and you're trying to tap out, but your opponent is determined to beat you into the ground.

My stomach rumbles, killing the illusion. I haven't been able to eat. None of us have. The only complaining has been from our stomachs.

I circle to the other side of the counter. "I'm leaving. Day after tomorrow." It was the soonest I could get a flight that I could actually afford during the holidays. He doesn't look up. "Back home. I think you should come with me."

He releases a breath but offers a slow nod.

"Wait!" The two of us turn toward the living room-turned-computer room. Jaythan stumbles in. "Wait. You can't leave."

"Are you going to stop us?" I'm ready to fight him on this. The sooner I can get my life back to normal, the better. Aggression simmers under my skin, begging for a release.

Jaythan holds out his hands. "Of course not. I know you guys are hurting. You don't think I am too? We all loved her." He gives us a meaningful look, and I shift. Some of the fight evaporates. "But she died fighting for what she believed in. She believed the Enforcers could be taken down. We can still do it."

"Can we?" I glare, stepping forward. Too close to him, but he's the one who backs up. "She died trying to protect what she loved. She died trying to save a brother who betrayed her."

"You don't know that. You don't know what he's been through."

"You're *defending* him?" I'm shouting now. I can't make myself stop.

Jaythan's eyes shift briefly to Mark, and I realize I'm being a terrible friend for slamming his brother. But I've had it.

"Do I need to?" Jaythan asks.

"He's the reason we're in this mess in the first place! If he just told us what was going on, she would still be alive!"

"You don't know that."

"Of course I do! Why are we here? Jake was taken. Why was he taken? He reached out to the maniac they call a father. Why did he reach out? Jake couldn't leave well enough alone!"

"That's not true, and you know it." Jaythan's voice booms off the walls, matching my fury now. I stumble back only a step. "Think, Brandon! You didn't know any more about Cooper than Jake did. Now listen, you're close with your family. Your mother. Your father. Jake lost his mother. He never knew his father. Are you telling me you can't sympathize with his desire to know the man?"

A tiny trickle of shame seeps into my conscience, but I ignore it. "My father isn't running a politically charged murder frenzy."

"You seem to be forgetting that Ellie literally worked for this man for years, knowing full well who he was and actively participating."

My vision goes red. "Don't you dare start blaming her!"

"Why? Because she's dead?" I'm ready to break my hand on his face, and he knows it. He grabs my arm. "Am I to understand that if Jake were the one we were mourning, suddenly he'd be free of this blame? We can't blame Jake when we don't have his story. I'm sorry we lost Ellie. I hate it, but blaming everyone won't solve anything. We can fix this. We can take out the Enforcers."

I scoff. "Right. Two med students, an ex-assassin, and a hacker. We're basically the Avengers."

I should never have come here. What was I thinking? That I could help her when I've had absolutely no training in this type of situation? Jake may have been why we came, but Ellie would still be alive if it weren't for me. She was so preoccupied with getting me out alive that she barely paid attention to her own wellbeing.

If you want to protect your family, protect yourself. She told me that. I knew it was a sound argument, but she never took it to heart. Her version of protection never involved protecting herself. That's where everything went wrong.

She let herself be used by their father for years so he wouldn't turn his gaze on her brothers. She cut off communication with us after she told us everything about herself even though it was clear she was desperate not to lose us. Even though she still followed us to make sure we were okay. I know she would have continued like that for years if Jaythan hadn't cut her off from his supply of information. She kept herself always in the line of fire so that no one else would get hurt.

But now she's gone. And we're all hurting for it.

There's a buzz on the counter, and we both turn. Mark is pale, tear tracks streaking his cheeks. Jaw clenched, knuckles white. His phone continues to buzz beside him, and he just stares at it. He takes a deep breath and finally turns it over. "It's Jake," he whispers.

Jaythan turns to me with a raised brow. "And a business major?"

45

JAKE'S REGRET

Numbness. I have no idea what's happening, and I have no idea how to figure it out. What I do know is numbness. And only that as I sit at the edge of my bed, pounding my phone against my head.

They were here. In DC. For me. To rescue me. And where was I? Feeling all high and mighty with my father ready to hand over his business to me. My father. I wanted to know him so bad. I wanted to know him so bad that he went and did this.

He did this.

No.

I reached out to him. I got to know him. He may have abducted me so he could offer me his entire business, but I stayed. I didn't let Mark or Ellie or even Brandon know that I was okay. I didn't tell them anything at all. They had no idea I ever reached out to my father. *Why didn't I let her know I was okay?*

I can't get down a full breath.

I hung up on her. I must have talked to her precious seconds before she died. That's how she got the number. She was at the headquarters. I told her to lose the number.

I need to talk to him.

I'm back in Cooper's office three nights later. It's the first time in days I've been able to drag myself anywhere besides the bathroom. He never stops working. He doesn't look up at me. *He never stops.* I rip the papers off his desk, throwing them on the ground and cluttering this stupidly clean office just a little bit. He sighs and finally acknowledges me with partially raised brows. A nasty purple bruise envelopes one eye.

"Is it true?" I snap, drowning that numbness in wrath.

Another heavy sigh. "Sit down, Jake." He somehow still manages to look down his nose at me from his lower position. The high ground is everything in a fight. I don't sit.

"Is she dead?"

He blinks slowly. "Yes, Jake. She's gone."

The words are thousands of tiny shards of glass piercing my heart. I force myself not to collapse. "For trying to rescue me? She thought I was in trouble, and you killed her." My voice rises with each word, and I'm worried the second my anger dissipates, I will fall and keep falling.

My father doesn't even flinch. "I did not kill her."

Even when I slam my hands down on his desk, nothing. Not so much as a startled blink. Just another sigh, and if I could reach down his throat and tear out every last one he had, I would in a heartbeat. *Which Ellie no longer has, thanks to him.*

My voice becomes deadly quiet. "She died because one of the men under your employ shot her on your grounds. Don't tell me you didn't kill her. You did *nothing* to stop it. You did nothing to help. She's dead… because of *you*."

He takes a deep breath. "Do you know why she was here?"

"She was here to get me back—but given your tone, you believe there was something more. So, enlighten me."

He laughs, shaking his head. I clench my fists hard, nails digging bloody half-moons into my palms. He turns his computer screen to me with a video pulled up. It's of his office. Empty, but then a grate slams onto his desk, and Ellie comes next. She glances around the office, confused. Cooper isn't there. But then she's at the computer, plugging a drive in and downloading a bunch of things. She looks around the office some more and then spots the note on the desk.

I watch her pull out her phone and dial the number.

Shock hits her, then relief, hearing my voice on the other end.

It turns to confusion and then terror as she realizes what I've done.

And then she's gone.

I shove it aside in my mind and clench my jaw. "What did she take?" I assume that's why it was so important for him to show this to me.

"You see, Jake, she was here to get you, yes. But she had another agenda." He pauses, and I hold my tongue. Let him have his dramatic effect. It changes nothing. "She was trying to take out the very foundation of this organization."

"And why would she do that?" She's not stupid or impulsive. Every one of her moves is calculated. I hate to compare her to this monster, but she is just as thorough as I've discovered Cooper is. If she suddenly turned on the organization she's been working with since she was four, she had a reason. And I'm not sure my father can talk his way out of it.

"She feels as if our methods are an intrusion on people's rights."

"Are they?" I snap. Another sigh. I suck down a deep breath to keep from ripping him to shreds.

"Almost a month ago, I gave Emily an assignment."

"*Ellie*."

"Her target was Mark."

I freeze. I deduced this already, but it hurts to have my father's blatant confirmation without a note of guilt. He could be reporting on the weather.

Cooper shakes his head. "She was never meant to go through with it, of course. It was merely an experiment. I needed to know what she would do under the circumstances. I needed to know if I should give up on her and start pursuing someone else for the job. All her actions pointed to the fact that she was incapable of handling this position. I believe you have what she lacked."

It hits me like a freight train. *What she lacked.* The single-minded focus to plow ahead no matter who it hurts along the way. Even family. Ruthlessness. And he thinks *I* have it? *You've done nothing but prove it to him over the past two weeks.*

I'm going to be sick.

"Do you ever regret it?" I ask after careful consideration. "Leaving Mom? Us?" I know the answer will hurt no matter which it is, but I can't go on without knowing.

He doesn't ask for clarification. He doesn't answer either. "How did you find my phone number?"

I consider ignoring him. Turning around and walking out the door right now. But I don't. My curiosity gets the better of me. "Ellie's phone."

He nods. He already knew that, I'm sure. "I gave that phone to her. Her first."

"Why does that matter?"

"I gave it to her only after your mother died." It takes me a while to understand the gravity of its meaning. "Another test. But this one for me. I needed to be fully dedicated to my work and the success of this company in order to succeed. I could not let her be compromised, same as any other Enforcer. I did what had to be done to ensure my future and that of this corporation. And so also yours. Everything I do is for the Enforcers, so we can continue the fight so many can't. I will never regret that."

She didn't see Mom's texts until…

Hundreds, maybe thousands of texts over the years from our mother, telling Ellie she loved her, that she always would.

I leave without another word, shaken to my core. My brain has stalled. I can't think. I'm not sure if my heart has stopped or if I just stopped feeling it.

Chelsea finds me in the hallway. "Jake." I shove past her, a fuse about to reach its end, but she follows. "Jake, I think we need to talk."

I'm done talking. I jerk to a halt, flip around, and slam her into the wall. Tears burn my eyes, but I blink them back and seethe, "What did you know about my sister's death sentence?"

"I swear I didn't know anything," she gasps, eyes wide, but not terrified. Sympathetic. Because she's not scared of what I might do to her. Because she's trained to break holds like this. "Please. I'm so sorry, Jake."

I can't believe I ever once trusted a word coming past her lips. I shove away from her and don't look back.

Once again, at the hotel, I do the one thing that might actually help. I kneel beside my bed and talk to the only one powerful enough to do something…if He even cares to listen to me anymore. Mark trusts Him and has tried to get me to for years. He's all I have left.

After, I'm left with only one thought: I need to talk to my family.

>>>>>>

THIS IS THE MONSTER YOU'VE ALIGNED YOURSELF WITH.

I was surprised when he agreed to see me, but I'm not surprised when I arrive at the warehouse in which he insisted on holding this meeting. It's just like in all the movies: dark, dingy, like a murder definitely took place here. My father didn't think to employ any security measures for me. He was fairly confident I wasn't going to be found, and no one besides Hartley and Chelsea know I'm in DC. I'll bet he thought Mark and Brandon would leave after… I'm monumentally grateful they didn't.

Mark texted me the day Ellie died. *Your father did this.* I had hoped that would mean a warm welcome. That he was reaching out because he did still think I was worth saving. I don't know why I ever thought that.

I chose my side.

And now I'll pay for it.

Mark looks awful. His hair sticks out every which way. His eyes are bloodshot with terribly defined bags under them. He's hunched forward as if he's forgotten how to stand up straight. It's like he's not stopped sobbing since her death. However, despite his obvious despair, he holds my eyes with a glare.

Brandon is in near the same condition, though he stands straight, angled toward my brother. The gun in his right hand trembles slightly, but his grip on it is firm. His glare is harder than Mark's. I was never close with Brandon. I actually hated him just a little, but the feeling was never mutual. Seeing something like hate radiate off him now twists my gut.

I drop my gaze to the cement beneath my feet. It would be a blatant lie to think I was the only one who loved her.

When I muster enough courage to face them again, their expressions haven't changed—again, I don't know why I expected them to. I open my mouth to speak. To apologize. To beg. I don't know. I step forward.

"That's close enough." Brandon's voice rumbles off the walls of the warehouse, deep, rough.

I stop a good six feet away and hold up my hands. "I'm so sorry." Even though Brandon doesn't have the gun pointed at me, I know with almost complete certainty he will kill me without hesitation if I make one wrong move. It's respect that I feel for him now. That and the desire for him to pull the trigger. It's no more than I deserve. "I didn't know." My voice fades to a whisper.

"No, you didn't." The way Mark spits the words makes me forget my caution and my sympathy. *I'm hurting too!* Or did he forget I'm part of this family?

"And whose fault is that, Mark? Whose fault is it that I never knew about any of this?"

"I told you exactly how monstrous that man was!"

"No! You told me *that* he was monstrous. What did you expect? I knew nothing of my father! I barely even knew my sister!"

"Don't you dare blame me!" Angry tears slide down his cheeks. "You're the one that left without a trace. We thought you were in trouble. But then we get here and find out you've been working with Dad this whole time—"

"And I regret that!" I cut him off, throwing my arms wide. "I should have told you that I was talking to him. I should have told you that I was alright when he brought me here. But I never would have reached out to him in the first place if you had told me what he was from the beginning. If you would have just told me—"

"Yeah, what if I *had* told you?" Now he steps forward. "What if I had told you our father commands a bunch of assassins and that our sister was one of them? Sometimes it's better not to know these things."

"You had no right to keep that from me. You don't get to decide what I can know about my family." I try to talk myself out of it just for a second before I burst. "You know what Dad did? I took Ellie's phone a few weeks back to pull Dad's number from it. She only had two text chains: you and Mom. Mom sent her text after text telling El that she loved her. She sent her our Christmas picture every year. No responses from Ellie." Mark already looks destroyed. "And I just found out Dad only gave her that phone after Mom was already gone. She never responded because she never got the chance. She never knew Mom reached out until it was too late."

I watch this hit my brother like a ton of bricks. He doubles over, moaning. Brandon grips his shoulder, and I see tears in his eyes as well, utter heartbreak on his face. His grip on the gun tightens.

I take a breath and manage to calm myself down. "And you tried to do the same thing."

Mark looks me in the eye, tears in his and absolutely no hint of anger anymore. "I—I didn't think of it like that." He comes closer to me again, and I involuntarily take a step back, eyeing the gun in Brandon's hand. Mark freezes, face slackening. "I'm sorry, Jake. I just wanted to protect you from him. That's what big brothers do."

I manage a small laugh. "Protection seems to be this family's biggest problem." A treacherous tear slips down my cheek. I swallow the others.

Then, as if he can't contain himself any longer, my brother throws his arms tight around me. I'm too stunned to respond with more than a pat on his back. Brandon remains a healthy distance away, gun still in hand, but he watches Mark with something like pity. I can't say I feel much different when it concerns my brother. He's lost too many people. He's been so devastated that he'll hold together what last shreds of his family he can find in whatever way he can. Even if it destroys him in the process. Even if that shred is just me.

46

MARK'S BROTHER

THE RELIEF OF HAVING JAKE BACK IS ALMOST TOO MUCH IN CONJUNC-tion with the overwhelming grief. We're all back at Jaythan's house, and our cousin was thrilled to meet Jake. It was almost like nothing had happened. I don't believe my brother has any malicious intent. Not anymore. I know he told me about Ellie's phone to hurt me, but he also made a good point. Staying in the dark hasn't worked out for any of us.

I can hardly look at him. Not only because of my shame, but I never noticed before how much he and Ellie resemble each other. It's hard to miss now. They have the same nose, lips, even their small ears are the same. And the differences cut just as deeply. Jake's blond hair is a shade darker than Ellie's. Ellie was all toned muscle, whereas Jake has broader shoulders. He's also much taller than her, and his eyes are the blue of our father's, hers the green of Mom's. I can't look at him without seeing her, and it's like having my heart ripped out of my chest over and over again.

The five of us convene around Jaythan's tiny dining room table. Rowan takes to standing, arms crossed, practically displaying the arsenal on his person. And Brandon's gun is resting in his lap. It's as if they're waiting for Jake to betray us.

Watching my brother now, though, with his eyes downcast, hands wringing each other dry, and breath almost forced…he looks terrible. And all I want is to be a brother to him, comfort him, talk with him. I hate the mistrust that still roils around my stomach. We were so close when we had Mom, but since then it's been so hard. Too hard.

Jaythan has one of his laptops in front of him where he's uploaded all the information from the flash drives Ellie stole, and the physical files she retrieved sit next to him. A blank Word document is open on the screen.

"Alright." Jake shakes his head, blinks heavily and surveys us. He slips on a mask just like Ellie used to. All business. "What do we know about the Enforcers?"

Jaythan immediately types out a title on the document: *What We Know.*

Brandon sighs, dropping his head into his hands.

"Rowan." The scary assassin turns on me; it's like a gong. I can hear the resonance of the boom when his neck swivels. It's the most intimidating thing I've ever seen, and I regret everything that has led to this moment. Ellie loved him. *He* loved *her.* That makes him family, but my voice still starts out a bit strangled. "You know the most about them, I think. I mean, you're the only one of us who's worked there," I choke out.

His permanent glare rests on me, but when he finally turns away, I release the breath I'd been holding. You know that feeling when you're being stared at, and it feels like a crime to breathe under the scrutiny? "It only works with secrecy."

"What do you mean?" Now the glare turns on Brandon, but he doesn't even blink at the attention. He meets it head-on. "Everybody already knows about the Enforcers. They have a TV special every time they kill someone."

"They employ fearmongering to exert control. It keeps people from looking deeper. We need to expose the truths they don't want out. They won't survive if people know. I left because of the truth. Richards left because of it."

"Ellie." All four of us say it, and it practically rings off the walls. I try not to hold it against Rowan. He's known her as *Emily Richards* all her life. But that person never really existed.

Rowan's glare softens. "Ellie," he corrects with a nod. "The point is, it could implode if people know who their targets really are. Is the intel she got any help?"

Jaythan blows out a breath. "The flash drive she put everything on was shot—" My breath hitches. He clears his throat. "Unusable. Most of the others didn't have anything on them. Some had a few of the target's beginning files, but nothing incriminating."

"So that whole mission was for nothing?" Brandon clenches his hand, and I jump out of my skin when he slams it down on the table. "She… It was for *nothing*?"

Jaythan holds out a hand to him. "No, no it wasn't. I downloaded the security system and gave myself access while you were in there."

Brandon frowns. "The bug you had us plant?"

"Well, actually, I may or may not have stuck another little device to the inside of your jacket before you went. It was just a prototype. But I've been tampering with it, and I think I have it perfect now." I frown.

It was a prototype only four days ago, and somehow, he's already worked out the kinks?

"Another bug?"

"Better. Hang on." He shoots to his feet, suddenly excited, and darts into the other room, leaving the rest of us to share uncertain glances. "Yiss!" precedes Jaythan's glide back into the room and his chair which he nearly tips over. Jake's arms shoot out to help him, but Jaythan catches himself. "Here it is." The thing in his hand looks a lot more like a birthmark than any sort of device. "Small. Super concealable. And super effective. Here, look."

He turns the computer screen to us which now shows the security footage of Rowan and Brandon entering the building. Another one shows a later timestamp with Brandon and Ellie running through the halls. Jaythan slams the computer shut before the video goes any further. We all know what happens next.

Brandon shakes his head. "So, it downloaded it off the computers?"

Some of Jaythan's enthusiasm has left him now. "Well, no, not exactly. It's connected to my computers here. What happened was it linked based on your proximity to any device. I set it to automatically feed the information to mine here, and my computers automatically back up everything they're fed."

"So…it downloaded it off the computers."

Jaythan sighs dramatically and mutters, "Yes, fine." His bottom lip tucks behind his front teeth as he says in a mocking voice, "It downloaded it off the computers."

"You said you improved it?" Rowan asks beside me.

"Yes!" Jaythan extends his arm, pointing to the man with gusto. "Well, this was the one on Brandon's security guard jacket." He holds the two devices next to each other. "As you can see, this one is bulkier than the updated model here." Barely. If he hadn't pointed it out, I honestly wouldn't have noticed. "Therefore, my good fellow, it'll be easier to conceal."

"Brandon was already able to smuggle it in, and even he didn't know it was there." I point it out more to have an opinion than to be contrary. Sometimes I like to feel like I'm helping. Besides, that can't be the only improvement.

Jaythan nods. "Fair enough. I also extended the range. Only by about an inch in diameter, but it'll help, trust me. Any little bit, right?"

"So, is that it?" Jake asks when Jaythan pauses. "You made it smaller and extended the range?"

"No. One more thing. I figured out how to put a camera inside."

My eyebrows clack together, and I lean forward to inspect the freckle. "What? In that thing?"

He drops the older device on the table and clicks at his computer. When he turns it back, there's an image of my face. I look down at the device still in his hand, back up at the screen. The image copies me milliseconds later. I sit back, unsettled and intrigued. "How?"

He looks at me, all seriousness. "I never leave this house." He says it as a joke, but some of his energy leaks out of him again.

I do him the favor of not mentioning it and purse my lips with an impressed nod.

"What are we going to do with it?" Brandon rests his elbows on the table, surveying us all. "We can't exactly walk back in there."

"*We* can't," Rowan says in a deep rumble. He nods to Jake. "But *he* can." I tense up.

Jake blinks at him. "Yeah, Cooper still thinks I might be taking the business." I note the use of our father's last name and lack of "*Dad.*" Should I be concerned at the hopefulness that I feel with it? "I…yelled at him a bit, but nothing some groveling can't fix. I could go in, and I can probably even get him to give me more files." He pulls something from the satchel hanging off his chair and plops it on the table. "He already gave me this as a sort of preliminary, but if he wants me to take over, I'll need more."

"Yes." Jaythan points again. "That's good because this device will work on a lot as long as I have time to crack the security, but I doubt I'll have that luxury with Cooper's computer. But if *you* could get it unlocked for me—his or Hartley's—I'll be able to download from there whatever files you open. But you *have* to open them. I can't just take the whole computer with me. My precious isn't that advanced yet." He leans back, looking around at all of us. "But don't worry." He grins. "I'm working on it."

47

JAKE'S PERFORMANCE

MY FATHER SAYS NOTHING TO ME AS I USHER IN THE NEW YEAR BY walking into his office. But he does look up this time, and a bruise still covers half his face. I'd ask, but I doubt he'd tell me the truth. The room is still compulsively neat after losing his daughter. I clench my jaw, wishing I could scream at him again. He should be in shambles right now, not moving on as if her death was no more important than misplaced keys.

Our measly little gang of revolutionaries decided to act as early as possible. There's no reason to strategize when I'm just lying to my father to get him to give me access to a bunch of top-secret files anyway. Should be a piece of cake.

Cooper raises a brow, and I swallow my pride—nearly choke on it. "I'm…sorry…about my outburst the other day." I look down, bringing my hand to my face, hoping that hides the fact that I'm swallowing my own vomit. "I was upset because…" My throat closes up. *Nope. No because.* "I want to talk to you about taking over the business. I think you have a solid foundation here, and I would love to get in on it." I pause, meeting his ice blue eyes, pouring as much desperation into my own as I can muster. "I want to work with you, Dad. If the offer still stands." I shake my head as if refocusing myself. "Um, I looked over the files that you gave me, but they were incomplete. Would you be willing to let me see them in full? So, I could get a better view of the business and what we're working with?"

He smiles. A real smile. That's an odd look, going against all the frown lines. His eyes soften at the edges. "Of course, son." I release my breath. That was easy. "However, there is something I need you to do for me first." Of course, it was *too* easy. "Loyalty is the key to the operation. I need to know that you hold no reservations."

He's going to make you kill Mark. "What do you need me to do?" I add an impressive amount of eagerness to my voice. If I don't die here, I'm becoming an actor.

"You're going to find the next target, and hand it out in two days."

I pause only for a second and hide it easily with a tilt of my head. "You want me to find the target and then assign it? Don't you have a process I should learn?"

He leans back, folding his hands on his chest. "The woman is Sarah Michaels. Find someone close to her, someone she cares about. She's been causing problems, and I need her to understand where her place is."

Beneath you. I bite my tongue hard to keep from saying it. "You want me to find someone who will teach her a lesson? Why not just go after her? If she's a problem—"

"Because she's still useful."

And a person's right to live is exclusively tied to how *useful* they are. How many other people have had to deal with this? How am I supposed to cope with having a genocidal father? That's not supposed to happen. This man is the worst.

I bounce one brow and nod. "Yeah, okay." I deserve an award. "I can do that. See you in two days." I put two fingers to my forehead and salute. The door smacks shut behind me.

>>>>>>>

"WHAT AM I SUPPOSED TO DO?" I'M PACING WHAT WAS MEANT TO BE the dining room in Jaythan's house but is rather an empty space with a couple metal folding chairs and a small sofa.

Mark's sitting on a chair, elbows resting on his knees, head in his hands, not saying anything. He looks better now. Not great, but he showered this morning. And I get the impression he slept a little better last night. The bags under his eyes have softened, and he breathes easier. I can't imagine there will be a lot of that for me in the near and possibly distant future.

Jaythan is lounging on the sofa, typing out something on his laptop, so nothing new there. Brandon and Rowan lean on opposite walls, both with their arms crossed. They even wear matching glares.

I never remember Brandon being remotely…intense before. He would have been a lot more interesting, for sure. But he's a good guy. I have to keep reminding myself that he's not just the guy my brother wanted to rub off on me—if he ever really was. He's the guy that fell in love with my sister and did everything he could to protect her while I was causing her nothing but pain.

The late afternoon sunlight filters in through the blinds, casting striped shadows on the ground that are starting to make me nauseous as I watch them. "Obviously, I can't give him a target." Their silence makes my pacing come to an exasperated halt. I glance up. "Right?"

"I think you do, actually." The last person I expected to hear that from. Brandon's tone is so matter of fact I want to hit him. The wrinkles on my forehead must spell out *Excuse me?* because he continues. "We need those files, Jake. We need the evidence."

"You're telling me I should find some random person and send an assassin after them so we can gather *evidence*."

He rolls his eyes. *Definitely more interesting now.* Oddly, despite the annoyance at his words, the desire to punch him vanishes. "Not a random person." He nods across the room to Rowan. "He can help with that. Make sure no one gets killed."

"Interfere with an assassination?" Rowan pushes off the wall and stuffs his hands into his pockets. "Easier said than done."

Brandon shrugs. "Ellie managed it."

Every head in the room swivels back and forth between the giant assassin and the med student, and I have to fight the smirk that threatens to creep across my face—it dies just as quickly, making that emptiness inside much more visible.

But I'm surprised to see that this gamble has worked. Rowan grinds his teeth, staring hard at Brandon, who challenges him right back. Rowan turns his glare on me, and I straighten. "I can do it."

"Okay." I slowly break eye contact. "So, how are we supposed to find someone who won't make Cooper suspicious? We can't just pick a name. He wants a dossier."

"Did he *say* he wants one?" Mark is staring up at me now. His pointer fingers are tented against his chin. "Did Dad specifically tell you to put together a dossier on the target?"

"Well…no, actually. He said I'd be looking for someone close to Sarah Michaels and handing it out in two days." Jaythan's keys clack loudly as he ducks his head behind his screen and begins his research.

"Okay, so we don't really have to worry about that then." Mark rubs his chin and faces the others. "I saw the file Ellie had on Brandon. It didn't have any more than physical appearance and some recent sightings that could help locate and execute."

"Did it make me sound good?" Brandon asks with a hint of humor.

Mark shrugs. "It wasn't as flattering as it could've been." Brandon mock-frowns, and something loosens in Mark's shoulders. How did I ever hate this guy when he has such a calming effect on my high-strung brother? "Anyway, this will be over before Dad can dig too far into the target if he even cares to. Kill people to keep others in line is his whole thing." An apologetic glance at Brandon. "It doesn't matter whether or not they're innocent."

My face scrunches up in disgust. "That's sick."

His eyes hold no pity or despair, just exhaustion. "That's Dad." I can tell he's trying to squash his own hope. He doesn't trust it anymore. I feel awful about it. This is one problem we can't just pretend away, and I'm pretty sure an apology won't be enough to fix it.

I give him a determined nod. As sure as I can make it. "Okay." I turn to Jaythan. "What have you got?"

"Let's see…" His eyes jump over the screen, taking it all in. "Sarah Michaels lives in Oregon. Huh, close to where you all live."

I frown, glance at the guys. They're both wearing the same confused expression, but then Brandon blinks.

Jaythan continues, oblivious. "She's a reporter for—"

"*Bosom*," Brandon interrupts. All the muscles in my face slacken.

"Actually, it's *Buzz 'Em*," Jaythan points out.

I shake my head. I thought her name sounded familiar. "That's the reporter that cornered you at the airport."

"What does…Cooper have against her?" Mark asks. The strain is back in his shoulders, but I give him a little smile.

"Well, um…" Jaythan does some more clicking. "Her last big article was about…wow. It was about the Enforcers, but it's definitely not something they wanted getting out. Apparently, they broke into a family's home on Christmas Eve. They were after a couple targets, but instead of just sending an assassin, they sent an army. Seven men—"

"Does it say who the family was?" I ask. They've never done something like that before, have they?

Jaythan shakes his head. "No, Michaels just said they wanted to stay anonymous for fear of retaliation."

Brandon mutters a curse; when I look over at him, his face is white as a sheet. "That was my family."

"What?" I blurt. "Are you sure?"

"Yes, I'm sure. We were there." And his gesture between himself and Mark makes my heart stop altogether.

"*What?*"

"Is that what Ellie meant when she said you'd run into a complication? *This*—" Jaythan waves his hand frantically at the computer—"was a *complication?*"

Brandon closes his eyes and shakes his head. "After she got Rowan to agree to help us, she said she was going to call *Bosom*." Then for Rowan and Jaythan's sake, he adds, "To get Sarah Michaels to back off of me at the airport, El made fun of the name of the site, calling it *Bosom*. She must have fed her the story."

Jaythan's shaking his head now, too, scrolling through something. "Well, it caused quite an uproar. Lots of the comments are sympathy for the family, but there are whole chains dedicated to speculations whether this is the first time the Enforcers have done something like this. In a handful of days, this article has made some very vocal enemies for the Enforcers."

"And Cooper wants to put Michaels back in her place because of it." After her attack at the airport, I didn't expect to admire the woman, but…she must have known the risks of an article like this. Ellie must have told her.

"*Buzz 'Em* is a huge gossip site for those theories that turn up about the Enforcers' targets," Jaythan says. "They spread the rumor that the shooter of Brandon was in love with him and couldn't fulfill the mission. There's lots of articles here about shootings, both Enforcers' and not."

The room is silent for a while. When Ellie set her mind to destroying the Enforcers, she hit the ground running. I would like to revisit the fact that my brother, and presumably my twin sister, were involved in this attack. Did Ellie fight them off? Did anyone get hurt? Is Brandon's family safe *now*? How does Rowan fit into all of this?

There will be time for all of that later, though. "We still have to do this."

"Don't really have a choice." Jaythan claps his hands and rubs them together. "So, what are we looking for? Relative? Friend? Male? Female? Blond? Brunette? Redhead, maybe?"

I quirk a brow. "Why don't you try eHarmony? I'm sure they've got what you're looking for." Jaythan frowns. I cross my arms. "This isn't something to take so lightly. This is someone we might get killed."

"Yeah, but it's not like anything'll happen to them. Rowan will be there."

"Yeah, but Rowan can still f—" I swallow the rest of that sentence and choke. I cast a tentative glance at Rowan, but he doesn't appear to care. "But if something *does* happen…"

"We have to prepare for the worst-case scenario," Brandon agrees. I silently thank him. "If, God forbid, Rowan failed, we can't send a working parent to the grave. We have to be logical about this."

"No real criminals either," I interject before they can get the idea. "Let the cops handle them. I'm not sending *anyone* to their grave." *Not again.*

Mark looks up at me, but there's nothing discernible on his face.

"Okay, okay." Jaythan stares hard at the corner of the room, nodding. "Good, so that gives us a morally gray target that society won't miss under the worst-case scenario. Great!"

"Actually," Brandon says, the ghost of a grin tugging at his lips, "I think I have an idea."

»»»»»

I BRING MY FATHER A HALF-COUSIN OF SARAH MICHAELS WHO'S REALLY more of a best friend and confidant. And doesn't actually exist. Brandon called up his brother-in-law, and between Wyatt, Rowan, and Jaythan, they were able to create a person out of thin air in two days. Apparently, Rowan had been having Wyatt do it for years to save Ellie's targets before

Cooper found out and killed them all anyway. Now I have a file with just enough information for an assassin to get to the fictional woman with a little extra for Cooper, just in case. But when I hold it out for him, he doesn't take it.

He looks up from behind his desk and merely nods. "Good. You'll be giving this assignment to Cai Jacobson. Create a brief dossier of your target; you can use Hartley's office today. Jacobson will be here in an hour." He goes back to his own files, and I simply turn and walk out the door.

Alrighty then.

As I walk to Hartley's office, I quickly realize I have no idea where it is. This place is a maze, and I've only walked the path between their offices once. Luckily, my father's best defense against dishonesty is glass walls, so I creepily snoop into each of the rooms, looking for the right one. At least there are names on the doors.

I finally come to the right one and sigh. It was foolish of me to think that my father giving me Hartley's office for the day meant Hartley wouldn't be in it.

I push the door open, and Hartley startles a little. "The boss said I could use this office."

Hartley scrunches his face in what I suppose to be anger. "He's not the boss," he mumbles. "I mean, yes, he's *a* boss, but not over me. We started this organization together." Mark told me Hartley gets testy when he's not given as much credit as Cooper. It'll be a fun button to push.

"Yeah, I don't care. Get up."

"*You* definitely aren't my boss."

"Fascinating. I'm supposed to hand out an assignment in an hour, and I need the desk. Are you going to move, or do I need to go take my father's desk instead?"

He glares at me, trying to determine whether I'm bluffing or not. I raise my chin, but I know there's no way he's going to test me. He caves. "You have one hour."

"Fantastic. Hey, thanks for keeping the seat warm." I wink at him as he stomps out and lazily swing the door shut behind him. I turn to the room. "Hello again, Stephen. Did you miss me?"

48

BRANDON'S CALMING

JAKE DOESN'T HAVE AN EARPIECE, BUT HE DOES HAVE A CAMERA. THE bug planted on him is hidden in a spot that should go unnoticed on his black jacket. The feed is coming in on Jaythan's computer, but so far all it's shown is Jake driving down there. Jaythan also has the security feeds pulled up. We can't hear what's going on, and there's no way to communicate, but we can see.

I've been trying to come back around to trusting Jake, and I really think I've made a lot of progress. It's taken a while, but I understand why he did what he did. I grew up in a very fortunate family. My friends, though…they're dealing with an insane amount of…well, insanity.

I never knew why Jake didn't like me, but just before he left today while Mark was helping Jaythan set the computers up, he pulled me into one of the empty rooms down the hall.

"It was petty," he told me, barely meeting my eyes. His sister did that whenever she got emotional, glancing at me but not really focusing. It broke my heart all over again to see it mirrored in her twin.

"I thought Mark only invited you to live with us so you might rub off on me. Fix me," Jake continued. "Granted, I still think that was part of it." He laughed. "But I've been kind of a mess since Mom died. Anyway, I held it against you, and I shouldn't have, so I wanted to say that I'm sorry."

I was too surprised to respond and spent a few seconds blinking until he started talking again. "I'd like it if we could start over. You seem like a great guy, and…" His gaze dropped to his feet then, shoulders bunching up to his ears. It immediately set my heart pounding, but he met my eyes. "I appreciate what you did for my sister. I messed up, and I'll always regret it. But you stayed by her. You stayed by both of them." He nodded toward the open door where his brother could be heard taking orders from Jaythan. "Thank you."

I still haven't recovered from that interaction.

Mark has been running circles around Jaythan, helping him with anything and everything. He jumped all over the opportunity to get the charger for Jaythan's phone, and he just finished getting Jaythan a Coke and continues to ask for something more to do.

Jaythan finally grabs Mark's arm and steers him onto the couch. "You need to relax. Your dad won't suspect him. He's a natural. We're just waiting now." Sure enough, Jake is walking through the halls of the headquarters now.

"I know." Mark tries to stand, but Jaythan pushes him back down. "No, I know. Are you sure you don't need anything? I could dust your computers for you."

Jaythan points at him. "You will *not* touch my computers." He waves me over. "Brandon!" Then he mouths, "*Calm him down.*"

I nod, seating myself next to Mark. "Hey, you know he'll be okay, right?"

"There's no way for you to know that." I squint. He hangs his head. "I'm sorry. I just… How can you be so sure?"

"He's not going to get caught. He's a smart guy."

Mark leans forward, rubbing his hands over his face. "So was Ellie."

And just like that, my confidence in this operation hurtles itself out the window. We sit quietly for a while, until finally Jaythan shouts from the other room. And based on the look we share, neither Mark nor I know if that's a good thing. Jaythan is smiling when we get there, though.

"He did it!" Jaythan claps, making us jump. "Jake got access to the computer, and my device is working splendidly. We're getting everything." There's a ding. "Oh! Rowan! Jake's got the name of the Enforcer!"

Rowan comes in with a huge gun.

"Cai Jacobson."

The assassin nods and turns out the door without a word.

"So, he's okay?" Mark wrings his hands. I grip his shoulder.

"Or else someone took the device off of Jake and is now needlessly opening a bunch of files, and this person also happens to look just like Jake." I shake my head quickly behind Mark, and it takes too long for Jaythan to acknowledge the signal. "I mean, yes, he's totally fine. I don't know why I was just sarcastic there."

Mark nods absently. "What now?"

"More waiting."

Nods all around, and silence settles over the room. I shift on my feet a bit and then notice that Mark's breathing is becoming too ragged again. I pull out the first thing that comes to my brain. "Did you name your computers?" I ask Jaythan.

The man's brows wrinkle, and his eyes slowly land on me. "What makes you think I have?"

"I don't know. You seem really attached to them. I just thought—"

He laughs. "I'm just messing with you. Of course I named them. This one here—" he pats the monitor in front of him with the footage from Jake's jacket bug—"is Eomer."

Mark frowns. "Like from *Lord of the Rings*?"

Jaythan tilts his head to the side. "I always thought he was an underappreciated character." He nods to the computer with the security camera footage. "That's Central Intelligence there. He's my main man. Head honcho. The laptop is Philly."

"Why?" I ask.

He shrugs. "I thought it was a funny name. You know, manlier than *Phillis*. Goofier than *Phil*."

But before Mark or I can figure out how to respond to that, the front door crashes open. Multiple sets of heavy footsteps sound down the hallway, and in seconds, the first man enters the room.

49

JAKE'S ASSIGNMENT

A MAN PROBABLY FIVE OR SO YEARS OLDER THAN ME FILLS THE doorway of the tiny office. He's tall and lean, looking more like a runner than the bodybuilder assassin I was expecting. Even the way he walks is more like gliding. Matching his hair, he wears all black.

I assume this is Cai Jacobson, but I decide to take a page from Cooper's book and wait for him to speak first. It doesn't take him long.

"Cai Jacobson. You were expecting me." His voice is smooth, like silk. I hate how graceful his whole demeanor is.

My own becomes stark in response. "Indeed." I pull the dossier and hold it out for him. He doesn't take it. I wave it around. "Your assignment." I try to convince myself this man is not scum. He—like Ellie—might have a very good reason for enduring this job.

"Actually, I received new orders."

I quirk a brow, keeping the file raised between us. "Unfortunately for you, my orders remain the same."

He shrugs. "Afraid that's not true." And he's rounding the desk before I can blink and yanking me to my feet by the collar. *Never mind, he's scum, for sure.* I shove him, but he hardly moves.

I've always hated that saying, *You learn something new every day.* It's so much to learn, and it's not always fun. Today's lesson certainly isn't: it's a terrible idea to even pretend to go into business with assassins.

"What is this?" I hiss. "Do you know who I am?"

"I know who you are, Jake Spencer." He punches me in the face. I should have known. When has that line ever worked? Blood spits from my nose, but I don't think it's broken. Hurts like hell, though. "*Unfortunately for you,*" he mocks. "That's why I'm here."

Then I start to panic. If my father found out what I'm doing here, what's happening to the others? Are they safe? They must be. Jaythan lives out in the middle of nowhere. They can't find him. Unless someone followed us. Followed *me.*

Jaythan's watching everything on his computers. I don't know what he can do, but at least he'll know I need help. Not sure how he can get it to me. Nine-one-one? That would be a hard one to explain. Something, though. Anything. *Please, let him be watching.*

Cai reaches for something at his belt. A gun. I grab the heavy file tray at the edge of Hartley's desk and whip it at Cai's face. Papers fly everywhere, and he puts a hand up to block the tray. I yank his gun from his hip into my own hands, but it's too easy for him to knock it across the room. Still swatting papers from his face, I use the moment to look for another gun. Hartley must have one somewhere.

Unable to find it, I stomp down hard on Cai's foot as the papers finally flutter to the ground. He shoves me, simultaneously hooking his leg behind mine and yanking. I fall onto my back. Cai goes for the pleasure of slitting my throat with the knife at his thigh. He kneels over me, and that's when I see it.

Hartley's gun is strapped underneath his desk. I can't get to it.

"I could get you more money!"

Cai stops, albeit with a vicious grin and the knife poised over my throat.

"I read up on you," I say, heart pounding. "You've been here since the beginning, haven't you?" He doesn't respond. "You must be pretty good. From what it looked like, my father doesn't keep many of you around. How much do you get paid each assignment?" He doesn't tell me that either, but he doesn't need to. I saw the records. "Way less than Emily. And now that she's…gone? He's kept you at a steady rate for a long time. And he takes out a hefty fee for himself, right? Did you know the fee is too steep?"

"I don't care," Cai says. "It's still good money." He presses the tip closer, but I force myself to stay calm. Deep breaths.

I open my palms to him. "You could be making more." He blinks. "Especially for killing me. Did Cooper tell you I'm his son? How much will he give you for this? The same as every other assignment? I'm the only living descendant he can hand this company over to. If he wants me dead so bad, you could make double. Triple, even."

A slow blink. "You think you can trick me into letting you live?"

"Well, I mean, you can't negotiate if I'm dead."

He shakes his head. "I'm not as greedy as your sister was."

He shifts the blade, and I have just enough room to slide slightly to the right and grab the gun. I flip it around and shoot too quickly. The bullet only grazes his bicep, but it distracts him enough that I can pull the knife from his hand. Lacking in grace, I lash out with it.

Blood seeps from the slice in his cheek, and he curses. I shove him off me and shoot to my feet, keeping the gun aimed at his kneeling form as I launch out of the small room and slam the door behind me. With the lock on the inside, it does me little good.

I turn and sprint down the monotonous hallways and slam right into Chelsea. She presses a cloth to my face, and I don't have time to react before the black sweeps in.

50

BRANDON'S EXAM

WE ALL FREEZE. I HAVE LESS THAN A SECOND TO REMEMBER MY gun is in the waistband of my jeans before the man is moving toward us. I pull it free and take aim, but he reaches me before I can shoot. He grips my wrist hard, trying to force me to drop my weapon. But Ellie managed to teach me a lot in the little time we had, and finding ways to not lose your weapon was one of them.

I crouch low to the ground before opening my hand and letting the gun fall. Right into my other hand. I pull the trigger, and the man drops with a cry, blood spitting from the hole in his leg.

Now, others have joined the party. Four others. And their guns are ready and aimed in my direction.

"Get down, get down, *get down!*" I shout, rushing for the only barrier in the room: the couch. Let this be a lesson that lots of furniture is not overkill, it's just good sense. I launch myself over the back to safety just as the bullets start flying and find Jaythan and Mark already there.

"What do we do?" Mark whimpers, casting an anxious glance at the camera feed that still shows Jake seated before a computer in the headquarters.

There's a whirring sounding from the corner of the room, and that's when I notice the smoke. *Fire? Smoke bombs? Gas?* At my panicked look, Jaythan says, "Fog machine." He shrugs. "Thought it couldn't hurt."

Maybe…

But my brain is in panic mode. *They found us out. We failed.* And now we're all going to die. Who knows what Cooper has in store for Jake? There has to be a way to warn him. A way to get out of this.

Think, think, *think*.

Thud.

Then silence.

The bullets stop all at once, but the creak of the floorboards tells me the men haven't left. Are they waiting for us to come out? Why wait when the couch is already pretty much in shreds?

Snick, ftht…thud.

Someone else is out there.

The wide eyes among the three of us say we're all thinking the same thing. *Rowan.* I flatten myself on the ground and army-crawl to peek around the end of the couch.

The men are no longer looking toward us. Their attention is on the door, something lurking beyond it. The fog is thickest in the hallway, leaking more and more into this room, but it makes seeing past the entrance nearly impossible. Two men lie unmoving, collapsed on the threshold. One is the man I shot in the leg, though now he bears the mark that killed him on the side of his head. Like he'd been dragging himself away, only to run into the new player on the field.

A third man steps bravely into the hallway. Smoke swirls, and the man freezes. I can't see what he's looking at, but then his neck twists with a terrible crack. He slumps to the ground, revealing the distorted shadow of a cloaked figure much too small to be Rowan. They wear a large hood and stand in the doorway as the remaining two men take aim.

Am I supposed to think that because this person is taking out the people who are trying to kill us, they're doing us a favor? Or should I assume this is an assassin here to steal glory for themselves?

One would be easier to fight than three. Even so, the newcomer is clearly skilled.

The cloaked figure takes one step forward; the two men, one step back. The men fire simultaneously, but the cloaked figure is already moving, slicing toward the man on their left. They take him out at the knees. A knife gleams in their gloved hand before it's buried in the man's chest. Blood glistens on the blade when the figure yanks it free, and then they flick it toward the second man. The gun flies from his clipped hand. The figure launches.

The newcomer's back is to me now, and I take my chance. If this person is here to take the glory and end us all themself, I'll at least put up a fight. I tighten my grip on my gun, stand up, and creep forward.

The second man lands a blow to the cloaked figure's stomach…just before the figure strikes a nerve in his neck that knocks him out cold.

Their hood has fallen back but they're facing away from me, and I barely have a second to register the flash of gold before I grab their neck and slam them against the wall. I groan internally. *If they are here to save us, I'm not going to be responsible for their death.*

"Who are you?" I demand, pressing my gun to the back of their head. "What do you want?"

A raspy laugh. "Gotta give myself credit." I freeze. "I taught you damn well."

51

JAKE'S TRAPPED

SOMETHING BURNS MY NOSE HAIRS, AND I JERK BACK, EYES FLARING open. I'm no longer in the hallway. *Damn it.* I was knocked out, and now my arms are tied behind my back in…Cooper's office. The guard next to me tucks the smelling salts away in his trousers. Chelsea leans against the door, watching me closely. Realization hits.

She must have been following me. She certainly was before DC; it was foolish to think she stopped. I should have been more cautious. My jacket is gone, and with it the camera that would let Jaythan know where I am. I really hope someone is listening when I send up a prayer. It's all I've got.

I refrain from sending Chelsea a vicious glare. That can't do anything to help me even though I'm petty enough to think I might feel better after. Instead, I focus on Cooper, who's completely composed behind his infernal desk—for once, bare. The mahogany wood is presented proudly, as he sits there looking very un-proud.

"Jake." He rises slowly, and I realize this is the first time I've seen him stand. He's tall. And somehow that's my only thought. Mark and Ellie are of average height, if not a little below, and I only grew a little more. But Cooper is tall. He grins down at me. "I'm impressed you evaded Jacobson, though he has been slowing down recently. I thought I was throwing him a bone, but here you are."

"What is this?" A satisfying amount of spittle rockets out with my words.

"Some parents might find it adorable when their child thinks they can outsmart them. I find it tiresome. This is now child number two?" He feigns thoughtfulness, then smiles with all his teeth. I nearly scoff at the drama. I always blamed Mark's dramatics on Mom. *Mom, if you can hear me, I'm so sorry. Clearly, you married the drama.* "And you already know what happened to the first."

A surge of anger and horror coats my vision in red, and I lunge for him. My movements are clunky with the handcuffs, and the desk between us slows me down considerably. I get nowhere near him before a guard drags me back, shoving me into the chair once more. His fingers dig into my shoulder, hard, holding me there. Cooper doesn't even blink. "You sick bastard!" I snap.

His chuckle says I'm a naive child. "I'm running a business, Jake. It's nothing personal."

My laugh says *you're an asshole*. "Of course not, *Father*."

His smile remains intact as he lifts my jacket from the corner of the desk and pats the sleeves, the pockets, the hood. When he gets to the shoulder, he finds what he's looking for and drops Jaythan's device on the ground, crushing it beneath the heel of his boot.

My laugh is truly amused this time as I stare down at the broken bits of our plan. "How mad are you going to be if I tell you that did nothing?"

It happens so fast, I almost can't process what I see. Without preamble—smoke, sparks, tick, *nothing*—the tiny, crushed bug *explodes*. A larger boom than I would have imagined—*props to Jaythan*. It's enough to make Cooper jump back to avoid losing a toe, and unfortunately no, he does not lose a toe.

He glances past me, irritated now, and I'll take that win any day. "ETA?"

Chelsea's once sweet voice rings bitter behind me. "They should arrive at headquarters in approximately six minutes."

His lips pull apart in something more like a snarl than a smile. "Your girlfriend has been very helpful." He pauses as if he expects another outburst. I remain calmer than I thought possible. "Soon, all of this trouble will be behind us." He re-seats himself. "Since you refuse to get out of my way, I will give you the chance to make this right. Tell me what you gave them."

I wrinkle my brow, tilt my head, the picture of innocent confusion when he and I both know I'm full of shit. "Who?"

The Cooper Sigh™. "If you do not tell me, then I will simply ask them when they arrive. You can be sure my methods will be decidedly less than civil."

I think back to the time when those men tried to steal Brandon's wallet, and Ellie calmly yelled at them. Then when that didn't work, like she was swatting at a fly, she flipped one onto his back, knocking the breath from his lungs with barely a thought. She was always able to stay so cool and collected. I should learn from her. Unfortunately, I am not her.

I thrash against the guard crushing my arm in a bruising grip to no avail. "Would you believe me if I told you I didn't tell them anything?" I seethe.

"No."

I grind my teeth. "Doesn't matter. You're done for anyway. If not us, then someone else will come after this madhouse you've built. Your business is *weak*. It depends too heavily on secrecy, and secrets have this annoying habit of never staying hidden. Everything comes out in the end. You're screwed."

He hums. "Haunting. If you have nothing to give me, then you will simply need to be removed." He nods at the guard. "Give him his late twin's old bedroom for the night. We'll see if he has a change of heart once he realizes what destruction he's brought on his only surviving family."

Pure white rage ignites in my very core, and I rip free of the guard's restraining hands at last, launching over the desk. Cooper crashes to the ground beneath me. Restricted from throwing a punch, I roll onto my side and kick as hard as I can wherever I can reach until the guard drags me up and yanks me out of the room.

52

BRANDON'S REPAIRS

I stop breathing.

And she turns around.

Her hair, for once, is not in a braid. It hangs loose, a few snowflakes caught in the cascading golden wave over her shoulder. Her chest heaves as she leans heavily against the wall, but I'm surprised she's able to stand at all. I'm surprised she's *here* at all. It's the manifestation of my most consuming dream of late—and possibly my worst nightmare if this turns out to be another dream.

"Hey again, Brandon." Ellie grins.

I'm pretty sure the footsteps I hear behind me are Mark and Jaythan, but I can't pull my eyes away from her. She's here. Are they seeing this too? I don't want to glance at them to check. What if she disappears? I blink heavily; certain it's a trick of the fog.

Her green eyes drift to either side of me. She sees them, at least. She releases a breath and cringes, hand going to her side. "Okay, I understand this is a lot to process right now, but I'll have to explain later. We need to get out of here. More are coming." We don't move. She groans in frustration. "I'm sorry about this, I really am, but you've got to move. *Now.*"

Jaythan steps into my peripheral vision. "Ellie?"

Her breath stutters, and it's definitely not from nerves or emotion of any sort. She clutches her side harder, and that's when I'm finally able to move again. I take her arm and drape it around my neck, pulling her weight off her bad side entirely. The side I vividly remember bleeding out onto my clothes. She's solid in my arms.

Ellie meets my eyes, and I swear the whole world stops. That expression used to be cheesy and meaningless to me. But it's the only explanation for this feeling. The room becomes a vacuum for sound, and we both hold our breaths.

"Sorry," I whisper, eyeing her neck.

"What have I told you about apologizing?" Her lips curve into a grin. "That was good. Great form." When she speaks, I can feel the exhale of the words on my cheek. Of all the things that have just happened, this is what makes everything the most believable. Her breath is warm, not the cold whisper of death.

She breaks eye contact first.

Mark is barely breathing. His expression has gone blank as he watches her.

"I'm sorry." She's desperate now. That much is clear from the way she stresses the words and shifts toward him just a little, wincing as she comes to a stop. "Please, I'll explain, but we have to go now."

Jaythan starts nodding. "Okay, Brandon, you…just keep holding her. Mark, help me pack up Eomer and grab Philly over there." Mark does so without a moment's more hesitation.

We're in the SUV Ellie came in less than ten minutes later, Jaythan's hardware packed safely in the back. She drove herself here, something I would lecture her about if I weren't still in shock. I asked Mark if he wanted to sit in the back with Ellie and take a look at her injuries, but he went straight for the front seat. So, I'm with her, checking the stitching which got very close to popping and caused her to bleed through her shirt. I manage to exercise the breathing technique she taught me to keep my fingers from shaking as I change the bandages around her waist. Jaythan had the good sense to bring a first-aid kit—and his is impressively thorough.

She presses an icepack to her leg while I clean the wound on her abdomen and replace her ruined bandages. Doing this in the car is not easy, and she winces at the strain but doesn't complain. I endeavor to bandage her quickly.

My fingers brush over her bare skin. Warm. I don't know when I'm going to start believing this is real, and no one else is bringing it up. So, I talk first.

"How is this possible?"

She takes a few breaths. "I needed Cooper to believe I was dead. It was the worst-case scenario. While I was in the hospital, they got me stable. Rowan gave me an injection that slowed my pulse way down. The same way he and Jay faked the deaths of my targets. Cooper clearly didn't care whether or not I died. Jake was working for him, or at least thinking about it. He needed to see what kind of person Cooper really is."

"So, you faked your death just so Jake would see how terrible our dad is?" Mark doesn't turn his gaze away from the road, but his tone is furious.

"Of course not—ah." She flinches, grabbing my wrist.

"Sorry." I finish covering the wound, a relieved breath rushing out of me when the bandage stays white, and I check her smaller injuries. The burn on her hip has all but vanished, as has the bruise on her jaw.

"No," she continues as I commit a laser focus on inspecting the cut I patched up for her at my house. "That was one reason, but I also needed to make sure Cooper thought I was gone. It's a lot easier to watch someone when they don't know to look for you."

"When were you planning on telling us?" Mark's head turns slightly this time, but he still won't look directly at her.

She stiffens, turning defensive. "As soon as your lives depended on it. I couldn't risk it any other way." She meets my eyes, reads the warning there, and lets out a breath. "I'm sorry, Mark."

"You failed to trust us again, Ellie." His eyes meet hers now, and I'm actually relieved. Even though they're fighting. It's undoubtedly better than that blank middle space. "It destroyed us. I, honestly, thought I might die from the pain. Jaythan only convinced us to continue because it was what you believed in and fought for. Jake is back in the hands of our father, and we're still running from him. Nothing has changed because you died, Ellie."

"Jake's back, though, isn't he?" she argues. I nod to her, satisfied with my inspection, and she tugs her shirt back down, settling more comfortably into her seat with a groan. "He doesn't work for Cooper anymore. He's not considering it. And the only reason I know you were found is because Cooper wasn't looking for me. I heard it from his own mouth. As far as he's concerned, I'm dead. So, he's focused his efforts elsewhere, gotten careless. This had nothing to do with me trusting you, and everything to do with destroying Cooper. We've been over the fact that I would do anything to protect you guys. I'm sorry that it took precedence over me sincerely learning to trust you more, but it did. You need to survive for anything else to happen here."

"How were we found?" I ask, attempting to break the tension. Or at least loosen it a bit.

"Cooper has known about Jaythan for years, but he's never been able to find him. A few days ago, one of his spies tracked Jake here and immediately reported her findings, but Cooper decided to wait until you guys made your move. When Jake came back with the assignment, he sent Enforcers right to you."

"How did you manage to get all this intel?" Jaythan looks back at her through the rearview mirror.

She sighs, closing her eyes, deep exhaustion written on her deflating body. Has she rested at all? "I may or may not have been stealing from you."

"*What?*"

Her eyes crack open. "I have a stash of your old gadgets at my apartment in case they ever became necessary. Last week, they did."

Jaythan nods. "All right. New Year's resolution: I'm going to start keeping an inventory."

I blink. In all that's happened, I forgot about the holidays. We didn't even get a proper Christmas.

I glance out the window at the still falling snow that blankets the trees and piles along the edges of the road. This year's holidays were memorable, but next year, we're going to have to do better.

"I *am* sorry that I put you all through that," Ellie says quietly.

A huff of a breath from Mark, and he looks her in the eye. "Was it always part of the plan?"

Silence stretches in the car until it's thin as a hair. Ellie blows out a careful breath. "You don't really want to know that answer."

Mark's lips thin. A slight bob of his chin. "If you could go back…" He pauses. "Would you do it again?"

"Yes."

I'm surprised to see the ghost of a smile brush Mark's lips, and I find that the same comfort settles inside of me. He reaches out, and she takes his hand, squeezing it. I wish this calm could last.

We're not twenty minutes from Jaythan's house when a black sedan swerves into our lane, cutting us off. Jaythan slams on the brakes to avoid a collision, and Ellie is jerked forward against the seatbelt. She whimpers, clutching her side tight again, and punches the door.

A stab of anxiety spikes through me. "Are you okay?" There's no blood, but that doesn't mean there won't be in a minute.

"I'm fine," she gasps. She stares down the sedan and the people filing out of it, no longer concerned with her injuries in the slightest. She nearly rips the handle off the door as she stumbles out of the car. "Stay inside."

I don't even give a thought to listening to her. I fly out with a muttered, "You're hurt," and I'm at her side in a second with Mark and Jaythan.

The men coming for us don't waste time. They approach at a steady pace, unholstering their weapons. Ellie speaks under her breath quickly before they reach us. "Five guards. One Enforcer." She nods to the meanest, beefiest looking man. "Take out the others. Don't engage him."

The Enforcer jerks his chin to her. "Glad to see you survived."

"I couldn't miss this party."

He grins.

Mark and Jaythan rush the men closest, and I pull Ellie behind me. I know there's no way to keep her out of the fighting, but she needs time to heal. If a few extra seconds is all I get her, I'll take what I can. Her hand goes to my waist, and I'm momentarily confused and relieved that she doesn't fight to get in front of me. Until I remember what I have at my hip.

She pulls my gun from my waistband. "I'm taking this." Then she's in front of me. Immediately, she shoots one man between the eyes.

I heave a sigh. "Fine but be careful."

She smiles as she pulls the trigger again. It hits the shoulder of the man Mark is tangled with. He stumbles, and Mark gets the upper hand. With no training of any kind to draw from, he needed the advantage badly. I run over and pull Mark out of the way, and Ellie gets the shot off. I turn, and another guard comes at me. He throws a punch that grazes my jaw somewhat less than gently, but I keep my feet and kick him hard in the knee, giving Ellie another clean shot.

The Enforcer has squeezed past the grappling and makes it to Ellie now. Mark rams his knee into the ribcage of the last guard, and I'm slamming my elbow down hard on his neck when Mark spots the Enforcer too. He turns wide eyes on me. "Help her!"

Here's where it would have been helpful for her to have given me all her training. Or at least more than a day and a half's worth. I can't shoot the guy and risk hitting Ellie—besides that, she has my gun.

Just our luck, Ellie shoots the Enforcer twice in the chest, and it does nothing. Barely even slows him down. Kevlar vest. She shifts to block his attack, but I see the wince. Unfortunately, so does he. He punches her right in the stomach. She goes down hard.

I bulldoze the Enforcer, and the momentum rolls us away from Ellie. He's up faster than me and kicks me in the shoulder which is still annoyingly sore when I use it too much—this time not having the decency to be the exception. I grab his leg with the next kick, but then I'm not sure what to do with it. I pull, but only come away with his boot. Well…it's something. I leap to my feet and swing the boot at his face, and…I actually hit him. I think surprise more than anything got me that hit. I won't be so lucky again.

I need a real weapon. My gun lies at Ellie's feet. She rolls and spots me, tears spilling over her cheeks. Red blooms on her shirt. I glance at the gun. She won't be able to shoot him for me in her condition. This is up to me.

The Enforcer grabs my arm, but Ellie kicks the weapon toward me with a wince. It stops just out of reach. The Enforcer spots it. He has it in his hands before I can blink and turns it on me.

Ellie screams.

I grab his wrist, duck right as he fires, chop my hand into the crook of his arm, sending the barrel of the gun smashing into his nose—not hard enough—but his grip still loosens. I grab the gun, turn it around, shove him away.

I don't think.

I fire.

The Enforcer's head snaps back, and he falls, arms still outstretched to grab me.

I'm too shocked to move for a second. Breathing heavily, I try to tear my eyes from the sight of the growing puddle of blood. The coppery odor sears my nostrils, overwhelming the crisp winter air. *So much blood.*

A sharp breath, and I'm able to force my gaze elsewhere. Ellie lowers her forehead to the ground. Mark and Jaythan have gotten the other guard down and breathe heavily through the adrenaline.

I give myself one more second to panic before running to Ellie's side. I kneel, propping her up with an arm. That copper mixes with the coconut and mint scent of her in a horrifying resemblance of the last time I saw her. My breathing turns horribly ragged, and I can't catch my breath.

Her warm palm cups my cheek. "Are you okay?" she asks before I can, tears streaking down her face.

"*Me?*" I blink too fast. Her bandages are still intact, but...*blood.* The sight knocks the breath from my lungs, but she's still alive. I slowly convince myself as I watch the rise and fall of her chest that she just needs new stitches. "I'm fine. Are *you* okay?"

She nods and gives me a thumbs up. "So good."

I take another shaky breath, but she doesn't give me the chance to question her further. Her hand moves from my cheek to the back of my head, and she pulls me down until her lips are sealed to mine. It shocks me more than the fact that I just killed again.

But in no time, all that filters out of my head, and I find myself kissing her back. All the stress simply melts away at the contact, like she knows I don't believe her when she says she's fine. Like she knows her being here is barely enough to convince me she's real. I don't know who deepens the kiss as I fight back the oppressive sense that this could all be an elaborate dream. *She's okay.*

The kiss becomes too much. *Not enough?* We pull apart, and what I accidentally told both her and Mark was one hundred percent accurate, and I can't hold it back any longer. We barely knew each other before two months ago. I wanted to wait until she was in a place where she was ready to hear it, but she just came back from the dead. We have no time to waste. "I love you."

Her smile threatens to end me right there. Her fingers grip tighter in my hair. "I love you too," she whispers—pained. I make to bring her to the car, so I can stitch her back up, but she brings her mouth to mine again.

I'm incapable of keeping a ridiculous smile from spreading across my face as I take her up in my arms. Only then do I remember that Mark and Jaythan are still here. And they saw the whole thing. Mark is smirking at me, and Jaythan is giving me two thumbs up. Ellie laughs as my cheeks go bright red, and I duck away, setting her gently in the car. She cringes from the strain of laughter on her injuries. I smirk. She rolls her eyes.

Instantly, I know three things to be true: I will always love her, she will be the death of me, and that is undoubtedly how I want to go.

53

JAKE'S EX

FORCE MYSELF TO BREATHE AND THINK THROUGH AN ESCAPE PLAN. I'll need to get free of the guard again, which will prove a challenge because he won't be letting me go so easily now. But if I can do that, I'll have to run. I won't be a match to him hand to hand, and I can't stick around long enough to try to get myself a weapon. Not that I'd be much more effective with one.

Cooper can stall the elevator, I'm sure, so I'll have to use the stairwell, but that means I might run into any number of assassins or guards. Climbing up the elevator shaft might be the best option if I wasn't absolutely terrified of being crushed to death. I might die in any number of ways on the stairs, but I won't be crushed.

The elevator dings with each floor my guard and I pass on the way down. It would have been wise to try to break away before there were more stairs to take, but there wasn't time. It's also highly unlikely that I'll escape this. Even if I do, Cooper's got Enforcers on Mark right now. I can't protect him. It's my fault we came to this point. First Ellie, now Mark.

I'm led down a dim, cement hallway, bathed in soft orange light. It really upholds the dungeon aesthetic, and I'm struck with the knowledge that Ellie lived here probably from when she was four until she turned sixteen. I don't think I could have remained sane.

We walk so long, my legs start feeling it, before there are rushed footsteps. The guard turns calmly. No need to panic in a building full of assassins he works with. *I* panic, though.

Chelsea rushes up to us, slightly breathless. She stops short of touching the guard's shoulder. "You're needed back upstairs." He glances at me, and Chelsea shakes her head, reaching for my arm. "I'll take him. Go."

The guard rushes off, leaving me alone with her. As soon as we can no longer hear his footsteps, Chelsea flips me around and removes the cuffs. She tosses them aside, a mangled paper clip sticking out of the lock.

"Look." She holds up her hand before I can say anything. "For what it's worth, I regret the part I played in all of this."

"Not worth much." I say it before I can really think about what she just did. It looks like she's saving me, but I'm not sure I can trust that. She did just turn my brother over to Cooper.

"Okay, well, I tied up the security guards and mimicked the effects of a hack, so that should buy us some time to get out of here."

"That's worth a little more." I don't trust her at all, but I need out. She will either manage that or get me locked away where I was headed in the first place. *You need to find Mark.* I run with her back down the long hallway. It would have been nice if she could have rescued me closer to the elevator.

The numbers above the metal doors tick up every few seconds, shooting the guard far away from us but pretty much exactly where we need to go. Then something occurs to me. "How did you get down here so fast?"

"Elevator shaft."

I can't help it. I grin. She sees it before I can cover it up and smiles. It's stupid that I missed that, isn't it? The stairs are currently, favorably empty. We fly up them, but when my big feet trip me, trying to go too quickly, I switch to two at a time. Several flights up, we have to slow down to catch our breath. It's a good thing too, because otherwise we might have missed the footsteps coming down toward us. We flip around and head back to the supply closet a level down, crushing ourselves inside and waiting for the steps to pass.

We breathe heavily, mentally preparing ourselves for more running upstairs. But once we've caught our breath, we're stuck standing too close together in a small supply closet. Our eyes meet in a much-too-electric moment between a terrible person and someone he can't trust. We stare at each other, drowning in the tension.

I *missed* her, but I think I still might hate her.

"Why are you doing this?" I whisper.

"I knew from the moment I met you that things weren't right," she admits. "But it wasn't until Ellie died that I finally made myself do something about it. Cooper was onto you as soon as you came groveling back to him. He had me follow you again."

"You told him where Mark was," I snap, keeping my voice as low as I can while the anger rushes through me. "You gave him up. Where are they now?"

"I had no choice," she defends. "If I held off or tried to give a fake location, then nothing else would have worked. But Mark is safe, Jake." Her wide, amber eyes bore into mine. "The op is mine, so all communication from the team goes through me before getting to Cooper. She reached them in time; they made it to a safe location."

"*She? Who's she?*"

Chelsea shakes her head. "We need to keep moving. They're gone."

She launches out of the closet, and I stay close on her heels.

Back to running. A much better alternative. Neither of us says anything more, and somehow, we make it to the top of the stairs without seeing anyone else.

It's when we leave the stairwell that Cai materializes. And he is not happy, blood drying on the side of his face, rage tightening his features and turning him red. I'm a little surprised when steam doesn't spit out of his ears.

He goes for my collar and throws me into the wall. Air rushes out of my lungs. He's prepared to beat me into a bloody pulp—until Chelsea draws his attention.

Her fighting style strikes me as much more stealth than Ellie's flash. Chelsea keeps behind Cai and lands her strikes to the sides of his head and his spine. She has a knife now and manages a cut to his sleeve. The top of his shoulder.

I finally catch my breath and attempt to kick out his legs. It does nothing. Except turn his attention back to me. He steps down on my sternum, and I wheeze. Chelsea jumps onto his back, flinging her arms around his neck. But he's stronger and faster.

He twists, and his foot presses down harder on my ribs until I'm sure they'll crack. I desperately pry at his boot, shoving, pushing, anything to move it, but he doesn't budge. He spears an elbow into Chelsea's stomach. Her grip slips, the knife clattering to the floor, and he has a hand around her throat. I do the only thing I can think of to save us. I flail. My legs kick the air furiously, and my hands grab at his jeans over his knee—the only part of him I can reach.

It's pointless against someone with more training than all the ninjas put together. But he judges me long enough for a body to fall from a grate in the ceiling. The newcomer uses a force unheard of to yank Cai away from me, and Chelsea collapses when Cai's grip on her breaks. She clutches her throat and forces gulps of air back into her lungs. I crawl to her side, doing a quick scan for injuries. *Nothing.* The marks around her throat will undoubtedly bruise, though. I turn back to the fight happening right next to us.

A wonderful breath of relief rushes out of me as I see that Rowan has come to our rescue. The fight between the two Enforcers is quite the sight to behold. I wish I understood everything that was happening in the lightening quick movements of their limbs. But finally, Rowan does something that flips Cai onto his back and then stomps down on his face, slamming the assassin's skull into the ground and knocking him unconscious.

He turns, dark hair flipped over his head, and glances down at the two of us, pitiful and breathless on the floor.

"About time," I grumble, dragging myself to my feet. I extend a hand to help Chelsea up. She offers me a small smile.

Rowan raises a brow. "Apologies. I was leaving Cooper a surprise." He holds up a small remote with a big red switch. I don't need to be an assassin to know what that is.

My jaw drops. "You planted a bomb?"

He grins wickedly, and I'd run away from him if he weren't my salvation. God gave this man a *child*. "We should get out of here."

On the one hand, blowing up the Enforcers is a necessity. As my dear father would say: change doesn't happen unless you force it. On the other hand, there are dozens of people here that have families. Sure, they're doing terrible things, but they deserve a chance to learn from the explosion of their place of business. I can extend mercy to the same sick monsters that wrecked my sister's life and then killed her for wanting out. Maybe some of them want out too.

Before I can change my mind, I start screaming, "Bomb!" The other two join the call, and the place becomes a rush to the elevator. Though, not as many as I would have expected. Rowan shoves us into the tiny compartment with four other terrified individuals, but they'll have another chance at life after this.

"Chelsea and I already got most of the people out," Rowan explains under his breath when I ask.

"So, that's what you were doing rather than saving me."

Rowan shakes his head, an actual smile tugging on his lips. "You're just like her."

A twinge of pain hits me at that, and I look away from him. But not before I catch the quick glance between him and Chelsea.

The doors *ding* open, and it's a sprint out of the house while the elevator goes to retrieve more people. The three of us find a place to hide across the street until the trickle of people evacuating the building dies out. Then the discreet little green house goes up in flames.

54

COOPER'S DEMON

THE HACK WAS A FAKE. I SEND JACOBSON BACK TO FIX THE MESS HE created. I had my suspicions that Chelsea was no longer loyal to me, though I'll admit, I didn't believe her foolish or brave enough to act on it. Now she's alone with my son.

I finish firing the security guards who were on duty and saunter back to my office. Sometimes I think I can take a vacation and relax as so many people have told me to do—none of whom work for me anymore—but then someone screws up like this. If I weren't here to put out all these fires, this organization would have gone up a long time ago.

The alarms start blaring. I sigh. "What now?"

I don't need to wait long for someone to wisely decide to fill their superior in to why his eardrums are being blown out. "There's a bomb," Rogers reports. "We need to evacuate, sir." He knows better than to grab for me.

I nod. "I'll be right there." He waits a moment, uncertain, but a bomb scare will make any man fend for himself.

Instead of going for the elevator, I head back to my office and ignore the files there. None of them are worth saving. The safe in the corner is where I can get what I need to keep us afloat until we can move into a new location. We'll be required to lie low for a bit with all the bad press coming out, but that shouldn't hurt us too much. Give the people a chance to breathe, and there will be more work for us when we crop back up. I push open the false back.

And there's already someone inside.

The top of her head is all I see until she swivels around in my chair, leaning all the way back and chewing the end my pen. She grins at me when I cringe. I hate when she does that. Her mother used to chew the ends of her pens. Emily did it constantly when I first brought her here before I broke her of the habit. I almost gave up on this whole endeavor and sent her back to her mother for it. She had a lot of those little nods toward her mother, and once she learned they aggravated me, she only ever used them as a weapon.

I'm not surprised she found a way to survive. She's my daughter, after all. When her time comes, it will not be so easy. I *am* surprised, however, to see her here. No one knew this office existed before her, and even less than absolutely no one knows about the tunnel. I made sure of it.

"Ah, yes." She flips the pen between her fingers, propping her snow-, dirt-, and blood-covered boots up on my beautiful chestnut desk. "I suppose you want to know how I got in here." The pen stops, and she stares directly into my eyes. "Again." I don't deign to react to her jab. She nods to the door. "You may want to close that, because something I also happen to know is that you reinforced this room to withstand a bang."

"How could you possibly have known about this?" But I can't help the tiny glimmer of pride. I taught her well. *Too well.*

"You see, in the time you thought your precious princess had died," she says, steepling her fingers, "I had the time to seek out the help of a seer." She leans forward, dropping her voice low. "He told me things he never could have known. He told me that I would find you in your reinforced hobbit hole. He had no idea what that meant, but it's okay because I knew. But then I had to figure out how I would get in without you knowing, and what do you know?" She spreads her arms wide. "The seer had an idea for that too."

"Stop." I sigh, shaking my head. Her mother liked to make up stories too. "None of that happened. This is utterly ridiculous."

She nods. "Ah well, I was hoping you would buy that story so I wouldn't have to tell you the truth. Jake and I have telepathic powers. So, what happened was that he read the secret office entrance in your mind, and then sent it to me through our twin mind connection."

"No."

She smiles, but there's a rage simmering in her burning green eyes. *My* rage. "You're no fun. And because of that, I'm not going to tell you whether either of those scenarios are true."

"Why are you here?"

"Not happy to see your little girl again? That hurts." She tents the fingers of one hand over her heart. Always so theatrical. She and her twin. "Not as much as when you had me shot, but it still hurts." I don't respond to her anymore. The more I speak, the more sarcastic she gets.

That's one part of her personality that *is* my fault. "We're taking apart your little group of murder buddies. There's a bomb in your midst, so rest assured, that threat is real. Should detonate any second now." She waves delicately. "Goodbye headquarters."

As if she planned it, there's a terrible boom and the ground shakes. I stumble only a little.

Emily goes back to flipping the pen back and forth over her fingers. "Here's the bottom line. I'm not going to kill you."

I raise a brow. I can truthfully say I was not expecting that.

She laughs. "Surprised? Alas." Shaking her head, basking in this moment, she points that infernal pen in my direction. "*You* are going to pay for your crimes properly. You will be tried in a proper court and will serve out your life sentence in a proper cell. You will be properly fed slop and properly meet your end behind bars without anyone to care. Perhaps you can even get Hartley as a cellmate! Assuming he's not been lost to the flames." She grins. "Doesn't that seem a nice change of pace?"

I wrinkle my nose but settle comfortably again on my feet. "You don't want to kill me where I stand?" Emily stares at me, her face perfectly blank, expertly sealing her secrets behind a mask. "After everything you feel I've done to you? I did think I had you killed, Emily. Which reminds me, is there someone I should fire for that?"

"No need. Brandon took care of that for you." Her grin widens unnaturally far at the furrow of my brow. *Wicked little girl.* "You remember Brandon. You tried to have *him* killed too."

"I remember well." A medical student. Not a killer.

"Good to know old age hasn't robbed you of *everything*."

I quell my growing unease. "Why would you do this?"

"See, there's a teensy little difference between us, Father. I can only assume it's because I share the blood of both you and an actual human being."

I hide my smirk. Her mother left because she thought I was too invested in my work. Perhaps she was right, as most nights I sleep in my office. She hated what I was getting into, and she didn't even know the half of it. If she had, I have no doubt she would have tried to give me over to the authorities. She couldn't see the full picture.

We used to be happy together. In the beginning we had an easy way around each other. In the beginning, I kept too much to myself. As time went on, however, I began to realize that real change does not come about by keeping your thoughts to yourself. So, I shared them with her. I hoped she would join me. Perhaps help me with the business end, as she used to have a knack for logistics that I never did. It's why I was forced to pull in Hartley instead.

"I have this little thing called self-control," Emily continues. "It's that thing that keeps you from doing stupid things when those stupid things will hurt you or someone you love. I guess, though…" She pauses and surveys me with an infuriatingly pitying gaze. "You don't have anyone you love. This is awkward."

I do not know what stirs within me now. My daughter, whom I thought dead, sits inexplicably at my desk, having just blown up the organization I have built up since before she was born. She has finally gained the upper hand.

She pulls a gun from her hip and points it at me, waving it briefly toward the second exit which blends into the corner of the room. "Well, I suppose we should be going. We're expected."

55

ELLIE'S RETIREMENT

As soon as we emerge from the tunnel, I stab Cooper in the neck with the tranquilizer. He drops without a thought of trying to escape. I climb through the hole in the wall of the drugstore, wincing with each movement. Brandon gave me drugs to help with the pain— not enough; I had to remain lucid for this.

It really wasn't difficult to figure out where Cooper's secret tunnel let out. Especially after I got the blueprints for all the surrounding buildings. Can't do a whole lot when you're recovering from two bullet wounds, but it's the perfect time to learn all your father's secrets.

The most convenient outlet for the tunnel would be where the man can get his medication and groceries. And the only other building in the vicinity with as much shady architecture as the Enforcers was the drugstore. I put two and two together, what can I say?

Rowan is exactly where he said he'd be, in the old diner across the street. It's been vacant for years now, which worked out perfectly. He spots me coming and nods. My heart constricts with the need to get to my brother. I keep a hand firm on my waist to slow its desire to tear, already feeling the blood oozing down my leg, and quicken my pace.

But Jake comes into view then. No limps, no cuts. There's dried blood under his nose, and his cheek is bruised, but he's okay. I halt, take a breath. Sharp pain accompanies it. Brandon won't be happy about this.

Then Jake sees me too. He freezes, blinking heavily. Rowan whispers something to him, and then my brother bolts. The amount of pain that courses through my body at the impact of Jake colliding with me makes me groan, but I ignore it. I hold my brother tightly, trying to pour all my apologies into the gesture.

He mumbles the words *"You're alive,"* into my hair again and again and again as he trembles against me. His hands don't stop moving, scraping over my shoulders, gripping my hair, squeezing tight. I bunch the back of his shirt in my fists.

"I'm so sorry, Jake."

He shakes his head, voice muffled in the back of my hair. "No, no, no. *I'm* sorry. I should have—"

I cut him off with a laugh. "Let's just call it even, okay?"

He laughs too, rubbing his hand firmly up and down my back. He takes a few deep breaths, then mutters, "Tell me again you can't die of a broken heart."

I bite my lip and wait another minute before pointing out, "Well, you didn't die, so I'm still technically right."

He balks at that and releases me. The searing pain catches up, nearly blinding me, and I bend double with a gasp. Leg, side. Yep, everything's spilling freely again. Getting shot's a bitch. I owe Brandon a thousand apologies.

"What did you do?" Jake grips my arm and inspects the damage. There's so much damage. Blood leaks through my shirt, dark blooms seeping through my black pants and making them glisten in the late afternoon sunlight.

"It's fine. I just popped the stitches again. Brandon can sew me back up."

"Wha…*again*? You tore these stitches once already?"

"Yeah, an hour ago, but it's fine." The meaning of those words is lost by the strangled way they come out.

"Ellie, I swear," he says through gritted teeth as he slings my arm around his neck. "You are *terrible* at letting yourself heal."

"That is not true," I argue. He gently lifts me into his arms, but I still suck in a sharp breath and pause a moment to let the pain pass. "I am perfectly capable of healing at the same pace as everyone else." Rowan saunters past us to collect Cooper, and Chelsea appears in the doorway of the diner. She nods once. I offer one back.

"Please." Jake guffaws. "I'm going to slam my ankle in a car door just to prove I can heal faster than you."

»»»»»

COOPER IS CUFFED TO A CHAIR IN THE MIDDLE OF MY LIVING ROOM. I brought everyone to my apartment after Jaythan's house was compromised. Brandon stitched me up as soon as we got back and lectured me the whole time about the importance of resting so my wounds can heal, Jake nodding behind him in total agreement. It seemed to calm

Brandon down, so I let him talk. Now he sits on the couch behind me with my brothers.

I'm sitting on the coffee table in front of Cooper. Some people look peaceful as they sleep; Cooper has a permanent scowl on his face that makes him look like he's plotting everyone's demise while unconscious.

After so many years of being ordered around by this man, told to kill, and possibly be killed, he is entirely at my mercy. I should feel triumphant, but all I feel is grief. I wish things could have been different. I wish we could have been a normal family and had normal Christmases together every year. I wish we could have been sitting around a fireplace drinking lukewarm, watered-down hot chocolate because none of us are actually good in the kitchen. I wish we didn't have to ring in the new year by sending him to prison.

Jake shoves the smelling salts under Cooper's nose—the one thing he requested he be allowed to do—jerking our father awake before taking his seat back on the couch. Cooper tugs at the restraints and squints, suffering a terrible headache. I give him one of those grins he loves so much and rise to my feet with a groan.

He surveys us all congregated around him.

"I believe you know everybody." He's gagged, so I don't wait for a reply. I limp around the coffee table to where Chelsea is standing. "But I would like to show you just who aided in your downfall." I grab her shoulder, hoping it looks more like camaraderie than stabilization. "This is our spy. None of us actually knew she hated you until you killed me. Well…tried to kill me, so thanks for that. She was a great help, letting me know exactly when you sent your goon squad to kill my family and just how many I'd be up against. Think I'll keep her."

I move on to Rowan. "And over here we have our Hulk." I wink at Cooper. "Yeah, you know him. Threatening his son? It was very difficult to convince him not to kill you, so if you're smart, you won't speak because I don't have a leash on that one. And my cousin, the guy with all the fun gadgets. Jaythan's pretty creative, right? You should have hired him." I chuckle. "Our lovely journalist couldn't be here today, but Sarah Michaels has been instrumental since she hounded Brandon at the airport. That's the danger of employing a gossip column to steer the narrative. Gossip is gossip. And the Enforcers are juicy.

"Now, the father of the group, trying to keep the rest of us out of trouble. That'd be your son, Mark. You should be proud." I get to Brandon and wrap an arm around his shoulders and plant a kiss on his cheek just to throw Cooper off—that's the *only* reason! I ignore the protest of the stitches—something Brandon will be able to yell at me for later. "We've already been over the fact that you remember Brandon. I taught him to fight. And because I'm a proud teacher, I must tell you: he's the reason I survived when you had me shot, and why we all survived your little goon squad a couple hours ago.

"Finally," I say as I plop myself down on the arm of the couch next to Jake, trying to disguise my heavy breathing, "my better half. The one you traded me for and also ditched. He's our compromised agent turned inside man. And of course…" I flick my hair, which Brandon braided after he finished patching me up, behind my shoulder. "Every group needs their genius, charismatic one."

I slide onto the coffee table in front of him again, biting down hard on a whimper, and rip the duct tape from his mouth. "Any questions?"

Cooper blinks. "You're not charismatic."

"Right." I cringe. "I guess I get that from you."

He actually laughs. "So, it took all of you to bring about my end?"

"Yeah," I deadpan. "Two assassins, a middle-aged hobbit, a spy, a journalist, and three students." I look him up and down. "What a truly unstoppable force *you* turned out to be." I stand straight again, ignoring the pain and forcing him to look up at me. "You stole my mother from me. You sent me to kill my brother. You abducted my twin." In that moment, I can't convince myself to do anything else. I haul off and punch him in the face. My side protests, but he's out cold.

I've heard forgiveness is a thing everyone deserves. Maybe someday I'll find it in myself to forgive this man. This man who stole every piece of my life. He's lucky I was able to piece together something better.

Brandon comes up and wraps his arms around my waist, pulling me back to rest against him. "Feel better?" Yes, my leg instantly stops aching at the relief. But I know that's not what he's asking about.

Warmth spreads through my chest. "As soon as he's behind bars." I turn my head up and crook a finger at Brandon. He grins and leans down to kiss me. He's careful not to hold me too tightly. Just enough to keep me upright. Just enough to keep me close. Good, because he's a part of my family now until the day he dies. Which, if I have anything to say about it—and so far, I have—will be a long time from now.

I pull back, remembering. "I'm deeply sorry about shooting you, by the way. This really sucks."

He laughs, a deep, full one that I feel rumble against my back, and kisses me again.

56

JAKE'S EPILOGUE
ONE YEAR LATER

Brandon's parents are saints. We sit around the fireplace in the aftermath of a chaotic Christmas morning. Unwrapped gifts and paper litter the whole of the living room floor, nothing left under the sparkling tree. The Harwoods invited all of us to spend Christmas with them this year against all reason.

Mr. Harwood sits in a lounge chair, and Mrs. Harwood is on the floor next to him scratching the tummy of their new puppy—a German shepherd she's named Soldier—a gift from Brandon, Marianna, and Mr. Harwood. Their big white dog, Winston, is not too sure about the little friend yet.

Wyatt and Marianna share the loveseat, Marianna with a hand resting on her swelled stomach. Ellie leans back against the couch between Brandon's knees while he braids and unbraids her hair—I believe he's on round four. Mark sits next to him deep in conversation with Jaythan who has forgotten how couches work and sits on the back of it. Rowan leans against the wall, watching his son play with the cars that Santa—Mrs. Harwood—brought him.

I'm on the ground with Chelsea. It was hard to stay mad at her when Ellie had already forgiven her in light of everything Chelsea did for us in the end. Apparently, she figured out what Rowan had done, that Ellie was still alive, and offered her help. El did exactly what she told Cooper she'd do and kept her.

So eventually, Chelsea and I were able to work things out ourselves. We're just friends. I've been busy with school—I switched from a business major to English, not quite sure what I want to do with it yet, but it's certainly more fun than business ever was. And she found work as a private investigator. She's been a really good friend, and I'm very lucky she's decided to stick around.

I turn at the sound of Mark's laughter.

Since we put our father behind bars, Mark and I have had a lot less tension in our relationship. We fight occasionally, but our arguments are much less damaging than they used to be. I've stopped jabbing him for trying to control my life—perhaps if I had listened to him in the first place, we could have avoided a lot of pain. And he's stopped doing the things I used to find overbearing…or he's continued doing all of them, but I let him for the most part. I still can't believe he ever forgave me. Even before I betrayed them, I was a horrible brother to him. But I plan to spend every last second of my life making up for that.

I smile to myself.

Then Marianna says from the couch, "Wyatt and I actually have another gift." They share an intimate smile. "Well, kind of a request." She glances over all of us, but her gaze finds her mother's as she says, "We found out our baby is a girl."

Mrs. Harwood squeals, climbing to her feet to embrace her child. The puppy yips and runs between and around her feet in the excitement; Winston watches him closely, then jumps up onto the couch and squishes himself between the two women. Brandon and Mr. Harwood make their way over to the couple too while the rest of us share our congratulations from afar.

"That's fantastic!" Brandon claps Wyatt on the shoulder. "Have you started thinking about names yet?"

"Actually, yes." Wyatt's eyes land on Ellie whose hair is coming loose from half a braid where Brandon left it. She sits up straight when Wyatt kneels in front of her. "I cannot thank you enough for what you did to protect my family." He takes her hands, and she chokes on a small gasp, staying very still. "Marianna and I can't think of a better way to show you what that meant to us. We'd like to name our daughter *Ellie*, with your permission."

Ellie simply stares into his sincere eyes, her own wide in shock, and she's still utterly motionless. The entire room seems to be holding its breath. But then Ellie breathes once more, a puff of a laugh, and she nods. The room is again thrust into laughter and clapping and hugging and maybe some crying from Mrs. Harwood and Marianna. Wyatt holds Ellie tight, shaking a little, and I'm honestly surprised when she returns the gesture just as passionately.

El is still not big on physical contact, but she's made herself okay with it—only with certain people, of course. Brandon, Mark, and I were able to break her in pretty well for that while we were getting over her death-not-death. And she's allowed Brandon's family to hug her as well, gently patting them on the back until they decide to let go. Now, though, Ellie wraps her arms fully around Wyatt, handing out one of her rare, real hugs.

Pride wells up inside me, and my only thought is *this is my sister.* When Wyatt finally releases her, Mark is there to envelop her again. I'm down there with them to throw my arm around her too. "You're a namesake!" I squeeze her shoulder. "You have two whole people named after you." None of us missed the fact that Rowan named his son *Richard* after Ellie's alias.

She laughs, still unable to speak. I plant a kiss on the top of her head.

※※※※

A FEW HOURS LATER, AFTER WE'VE DEVOURED THE HUGE TURKEY MRS. Harwood prepared for dinner at three in the afternoon, Brandon stands next to me. Most everyone else migrated back into the living room to talk until the food comas set in, but I stayed in the kitchen to help Mrs. Harwood clean up. She's rejoined her family now. I remain by the doorway, observing.

"You don't have to keep punishing yourself, you know." Brandon smiles at me, and the expression holds real love in it. He's become like a brother to me this last year. Once I stopped being petty, it was really easy to like the guy. Not only did he stand by my family when I didn't, but he never held my mistakes against me—not even jokingly. I fully expected him to hate me. I wouldn't have blamed any of them if they had. But none of them did. There's not a glimmer of distrust anymore when Brandon looks at me. Not a glimmer of the man who brought a gun to our meeting and looked ready and willing to use it.

I huff a laugh. "How did you know that's what I was doing?"

"You have the same expression Ellie sometimes does."

We both look to my twin then. She's sitting with Rowan now, playing with his son who's laughing in her lap. She puts on a comically exaggerated expression of surprise as the boy crashes two cars into each other and then mimes them going up in the air in slow motion, flipping end over end.

"You know," Brandon says, not taking his eyes off her, "everyone here was instrumental in taking down the Enforcers." He glances at me now, but I can't make myself meet his eyes. Instead, I watch the boy wildly throw his cars in the air and giggle as Ellie catches them easily. "We could never have done it without you, Jake."

Every file that I got from Cooper was used in his trial. The police and the FBI tried to gather up the assassins too, but the organization used a lot of aliases and no images, making it impossible to find them. Any proof of their identities that might have existed lost in the explosion. Rowan used his real first name, but in the news, it was *only* his first name that identified him. Once he tagged his last name onto it, he fit right back in with the masses.

I smile toward my sister, in this instance alone glad for how Cooper ran things. He'll be locked away for the rest of his life because of what we did. Everyone keeps reminding me what a big deal that is. In moments like this, with everyone alive and happy, laughing together, I believe it. But then I also think how easily I could have been the one to destroy all this. How close I came.

"You deserve to be at peace. You deserve to forgive yourself." Now he makes a nod toward Chelsea, who's talking with Mr. Harwood. He's been fascinated with her stories as a spy and investigator. He's one of those crime show enthusiasts.

As if she senses me looking at her, she meets my eyes. And smiles.

"You deserve *her*." When I blink at him, Brandon nudges my shoulder with a laugh. "Come on, I see how you look at her. You like her. More than a friend. A lot." He leans in to mutter slyly, "A friend can tell."

I blink again and return his smile. Honestly, what did this world do to deserve him? "What about you?" I nudge my chin in Ellie's direction.

The two of them are practically inseparable. I have never known Ellie to be a physically affectionate person—like I said, that's changing just a little. But with Brandon, it's effortless. They're almost always holding hands or sitting close to each other. He's constantly giving her those hugs from behind that I would have assumed she'd hate. But every time, she relaxes into him, and he keeps his arms around her as long as she lets him. Even when they fight, it's romantic because they won't leave until they've reached a settlement. It never takes long. It's like their own perfect little romance bubble. The med student and the assassin.

For several months after everything happened, Brandon was waking up most nights, screaming. He never told me what the nightmares were about, but he had killed three people and the love of his life had died—however briefly. It wasn't hard to figure out. Sometimes he was fine after Mark was able to convince him we were all okay. Sometimes it took hearing Ellie's voice over the phone. Sometimes it took her being there with him. There were many mornings that I woke up and found them together in the living room because he had called her over. And being him, he wasn't going to sequester in his room alone with her. She liked to complain about him never letting her get a good night's sleep, but she always came when he needed her. And, as I liked to point out, more often than not she was fast asleep on our *terrible* couch when I found them those mornings.

Color crawls up Brandon's neck and touches his copper cheeks, and he looks down at his shoes, fiddling with something in his pocket. He doesn't answer me, but I already know.

"You should do it tonight," I tell him, and he looks up at me, eyes wide. "After everyone goes to bed. Just the two of you." Before he can ask how I know, I lean in and whisper, "A friend can tell."

He laughs and nervously glances at Ellie. "You don't think it's too soon? Maybe she wants to explore other options before settling. She told me herself she's never dated before."

I arch one brow. "Are you serious?" He doesn't understand; I roll my eyes. "She loves you, Brandon. Ellie never dated before because she had no desire to. She never found anyone worth her time. Not until she met you. She's not one to give her heart freely, but when she does, she gives it completely. It belongs to you, Brandon."

A glance at his shoes. But when his eyes come up again, there's resolution in them. "Tell you what. I'll do it tonight if you take a chance with Chelsea."

I grin and hold out my hand to shake his. "Deal."

He leaves to sit with his fiancée-to-be, and I remain by the doorway. No longer to punish myself, but to plot my course of action.

That night after everyone has gone off to bed, I knock on the door to Chelsea's room. She's sharing it with Ellie, but I know for a fact that Ellie is downstairs with Brandon right now, meaning Chelsea is alone. I bounce on my heels and shake out my hands, unable to keep myself still.

She answers the door in a pair of fuzzy penguin pajama pants and a blue T-shirt that match the sets Mrs. Harwood got for all the girls. Mrs. Harwood's set is purple with bears, Marianna's is orange with chicks, and Ellie's is green with moose. I smile to see Chelsea wearing hers. I never would have pegged her for the matching clothes type.

"Hey! Couldn't get enough of me downstairs?" she teases.

I laugh abruptly, my nerves all over the place. What *happened* to the game I had when we first met? Emotional vulnerability is not my strong suit. "Um, I kind of wanted to talk to you, actually."

"Okay." Her brows furrow, but her smile remains intact. *That's good.* "Do you want to sit?" She gestures for me to come in, but I stay where I am.

"No, no, I'm good standing."

She laughs at that. "Okay." And when I don't continue, "What is it?"

I nod. "Okay, um, listen, I really like you a lot. Getting to be your friend for this past year has been the greatest gift. I know I was terrible to you before, and I'm grateful every day that you were able to forgive me for it. But, I think…I want more. If you want to," I add quickly. "I don't want to ruin our friendship at all. I would totally understand if… but, I mean, if you'd be willing…" *Damn, is Brandon contagious?*

"Stop hurting yourself, Jake." She grins, raising an eyebrow. "Are you asking me out?"

"Yes?"

She moves closer, her citrus scent washing over me, and stands up on her tiptoes to press a feather-light kiss to my lips. "I would love to."

The intense excitement that surges through me at her response leaves only the word *thanks* in my brain. I make myself kiss her again, instead. No need to say anything that way.

I step away, grinning from ear to ear. "Okay," I breathe. "Well, goodnight."

She nods, a smile matching my own on her face.

I wander back into the room I'm sharing with Mark, Brandon, and Jaythan. Mark sits on the cot, looking at something on his phone. He looks up when I enter and squints at my unshakable grin. "What's up with you?"

"Got myself a hot date."

He chuckles. "*Finally!* We were wondering when you'd ask her out."

"We?" I flop down on the mattress next to his, courtesy of Jaythan's stash that he brought so everyone would have a place to sleep while we're here. Mrs. Harwood did them all up with sheets and thick comforters before we even got here. *Saint.*

"Yeah." He nods, gestures to Jaythan. "Us, Brandon, Ellie." A shrug. "Chelsea."

I balk. "*Chelsea?*"

"What? We talk."

I roll my eyes and nod to his phone. "Who are you texting?"

"No one," he says, then holds it out for me to see. "Mrs. Harwood sent the pictures."

Carefully, like it's a fragile infant, I take the phone. Mrs. Harwood had a whole photoshoot before we ate. She got a picture with everyone, then split us up into strategic groups: all the Harwoods; Mare and Wyatt; Rowan, his kid, and Ellie; Brandon and Ellie; me, my siblings, and Jaythan.

But the one that catches my attention and holds it is the picture of just Ellie, Mark, and me. Ellie is standing in the middle with Mark and I kissing either cheek, the Christmas tree glittering in the background. Her eyes are squeezed shut, and there's a huge smile on her face. I swallow hard before I can embarrass myself, but then Mark's phone buzzes with a text.

"Sorry." He takes it back. "Keith is trying to get the guys together after Christmas." Some friends Mark has been spending more and more time with. He decided to do a fifth-year anatomy fellowship to be a more competitive applicant for residencies or something, so he's been helping teach and has actually connected with some of the other students. My face might just split with the amount of smiling I'm doing.

Jaythan doesn't look up from his cot in the corner where he's lying back with his computer on his chest. "Y'all should go sledding. I did once and decapitated a snowman. It was a really cool snowman, too. Looked like a statue. Broadsided it. Head came clean off."

Before I can respond to that, there's a squeal from downstairs. Ellie actually *squeals*, and yep, my heart is definitely cracking under the pressure.

Slight concern enters Mark's eyes, but then he seems to gather that the squeal was a good thing. In answer to his silent question, all I say is, "We have a new brother."

Mark's face lights up, and it's not two seconds later that we both shout, "I call best man!"

ACKNOWLEDGEMENTS

This book is almost ten years in the making! I wrote the very first draft of Assassin's Bane when I was a junior in high school back in 2016. I have told many people how it started, but in case you haven't heard, I had to write a 10,000-word novel for both my freshman and junior years. Needless to say, I wrote more than that. The first draft clocked in around 80k, and now here we are 115k later, and it's finally PUBLISHED!!

My very first thank you goes to the One who gave me this gift of writing in the first place. Even when I forgot to include this journey in my prayers, He was right there hovering over my shoulder and breathing down my neck in a way only the God of the universe can. Jokes aside, though, my greatest hope for this book is that it honors Him.

Next, I absolutely could not have done this without my wonderful, supportive, and insane family! Dad, thank you for brainstorming with me and for reading multiple drafts of this book and finding out I had no idea how to use a comma. Mom, thank you for also reading so many drafts and for being the first person to gush over this story and the characters—you are my original fangirl. And Daphne *shakes head* even though you have not read this book in its entirety yet, you still deserve the credit for answering my questions every time I stabbed or maimed or shot someone (in the book, I SWEAR!). Also, Brandon and Mark would be sorry excuses for med-students if you weren't around to tell me what it's actually like.

Thank you to my friends who have also been so supportive throughout this journey. Tisha and Jessica, thank you for entertaining my constant updates and requests that you read the latest draft to make it make sense. It wouldn't make sense without you, and for that, I bestow unto you this imaginary crown of gratitude.

As I write this, I realize this book has gone through many a editor. My English teacher who gave me the assignment in the first place and helped me flesh it out a bit in its beginning, grotesque stages, Mrs. Lynn. Gambi! As my grandma, I know you have to like my stuff, but the feedback I got from you was invaluable. Kylie Lynne, the first editor I ever paid to take a look at my work. And to the final editor I hired to bring this thing home, Genevieve Lerner. Thank you all so much for your help!

Thank you to all the people who were involved in making the movie RED. You don't know it, but those vibes settled in my brain and leaked their way onto these pages, so thanks.

And finally, thank you to every reader who has taken a chance on me and picked this book up! I appreciate all of you and sincerely hope you enjoyed the story! And I hope you know that no matter what you're going through, there is someone out there who loves you as wholly and unconditionally as Mark loves Ellie.

That ended sappier than I intended, but I am so grateful to all of you!

Until next time…

ABOUT THE AUTHOR

JAMIE SCHULTZ HAS LIVED IN OREGON ALL HER LIFE, CURRENTLY under the same roof as four dogs, three cats, two ferrets, two birds, and a lizard. She opened a small photography business upon graduating Liberty University with a bachelor's in English and Writing.

Jamie knew she wanted to be an author when she was a freshman in high school after an assignment to write a ten-thousand-word novel. She wrote fifty-thousand and never stopped.

Jamie has always lived by the ocean but still prefers the river. She is what many would call a Disney Adult who has never watched a Pixar movie with dry eyes. And if she could have dinner with anyone, living or dead, it would be the incomparable J.R.R. Tolkien.

Jamieschultzauthor.com | @jamieschultzauthor

www.ingramcontent.com/pod-product-compliance
Lightning Source LLC
Chambersburg PA
CBHW010652100726
47901CB00012B/2516